PENGUIN BOOKS

BLISS

Jill Tweedie, columnist on the *Guardian* for fourteen years, is
the author of two non-fiction books, *In the Name of Love* and
It's Only Me, as well as two fictional books, *Letters from a
Fainthearted Feminist* and *More from Martha*, which is now a
comedy series for BBC television. *Bliss* is her first novel. She
is married with three children and lives in North London.

BLISS
Jill Tweedie

Penguin Books

Penguin Books Ltd, Harmondsworth, Middlesex, England
Viking Penguin Inc., 40 West 23rd Street, New York, New York 10010, U.S.A.
Penguin Books Australia Ltd, Ringwood, Victoria, Australia
Penguin Books Canada Ltd, 2801 John Street, Markham, Ontario, Canada L3R 1B4
Penguin Books (N.Z.) Ltd, 182–190 Wairau Road, Auckland 10, New Zealand

First published by William Heinemann Ltd 1984
Published in Penguin Books 1985

Made and printed in Great Britain by
Richard Clay (The Chaucer Press) Ltd,
Bungay, Suffolk
Filmset in 10/12pt Monophoto Palatino by
Northumberland Press Ltd, Gateshead,
Tyne and Wear

To the World Wildlife Fund
for its work in preserving the
diversity of living things on our planet

[Acknowledgements]

Many thanks to Hugh Synge of the International Union for Conservation of Nature based at Kew for his invaluable help and kindness. I am also grateful to Tim Radford of the *Guardian* for pointing me in the right direction, to Gordon Warren of Aravco and to David Godwin for his unflagging enthusiasm and support.

'Adieu, farewell earth's bliss
This world uncertain is ...'

THOMAS NASHE

Road there is none, but only the river's passage through the impenetrable reaches of this Toro y Plata domaine, wherein flora and fauna of a most exquisite and rare beauty flourish in unimaginable abundance. I do not remember ever having felt a deeper delight or a more profound curiosity as to the nature of species that are, for the greater part, unknown to the most learned of my countrymen. The indios here live in the utmost harmony with their surroundings and are the sole inheritors of the forest's secrets, their knowledge of herbal lore has benefited many European travellers. A. W. Dunkley, my companion on this journey, was rid of a troublesome ulcer by a Venturan Indian woman who used leaves in her ministrations and an oil which she heated to anoint the sore and immediately benumbed it. The Indians also use the bark of a tree to alleviate the ague of malaria, marvellously easing the victim's distress, and it is said that the women know many herbal remedies with which to curb fertility and cure even virulent cancers. I myself suffered for some weeks from the insects that burrow under the skin and might be so suffering to this day were it not for a poultice laid upon the affected parts by an ancient tribeswoman, which gave out a most malodorous stench but succeeded in its purpose and brought my considerable agonies to a swift end.

The natives also derive their sustenance from the forest, consuming all manner of roots and berries and hunting the many creatures therein with admirable skill. I frequently observed the men call beasts to them by emitting an awesome variety of sounds calculated either to imitate the beast itself or its favoured prey. One Indian whom I accompanied on several hunts was wont to make holes in the toenails of tapirs and whistle through them, whereupon a tapir would invariably appear.

The same man attracted the great cats, the jaguar and the ocelot, by grunting into a hollow gourd or by imitating to perfection the shrill scream of genus Dasyprocta. This last feat was accomplished by dint of stretching hide over the hollow end of a bamboo stem and perforating the hide. A strong hair was then threaded through the perforation and this, extending along the tube, was tugged. The resulting noise brought a jaguar to his gun within five minutes.

These native Venturans are a primitive people and believe in a host of fearsome monsters, ghouls and forest ghosts of which the most interesting is curupira, a dwarfish boy-like spirit whose feet are set backwards upon black fibrous limbs. Curupira, we were told, rides in darkness through the forest on the back of the leading peccary, in a band of peccaries and, calling the hunter by name, lures him into the furthermost depths until he has lost all bearings, whereupon curupira steals his soul and abandons him to eternal damnation. Sure it is that the Indian is very much afraid of this chimera who is the forest's guardian and reeks vengeance upon too-greedy hunters and other intruders who lack proper restraint and despoil his domaine. Dunkley, wishing to hire an Indian as guide on an expedition to collect specimens, could not prevail over the man's terror of curupira, though he offered gold.

From *An Amazon Journey*, N. E. Caton-Peters,
The Botanist

[1]

Inside, it looked as if a jungle demon had gone berserk in the heat and rushed at the banks of greenery with a machete, slashing and ripping around him until every vine was lopped from its moorings and all the leaves hung in ribbons. He seemed still to be capering somewhere off-stage hooting at the mayhem, pissing himself with laughter – the air was loud with cackles and the sound of water. Under a fringe of dripping vegetation a parrot glared out of a yellow eye, edging irritably one way and the other along a branch, its long tail-feathers tipping back and forth. It stretched its neck out, revealing crusted sores between the sparse blue ruffs, the hooked wedge of beak opened, froze for a second and then shut with a snap.

Clare jumped back, cursing.

'The Señorita is hurt?' A man appeared at her elbow bowing deferentially, his hair slicked green in the green haze. 'Naughty Pepe, he does not like it here.'

'My sentiments entirely,' Clare said, rubbing her arm.

'He come from the Amazon last month only. He is sick for his home, eh Pepe?' The bird gave them both a look of loathing and dug itself fiercely in the ribs. Clare averted her eyes.

'Table for two, Lord Chedleigh,' she said. For God's sake, how long was Freddie going to take, parking his battered little heap?

'Of course, Señorita. This way please.'

She followed the waiter from the crazy greenhouse lobby into a blizzard of spinning lights that threw silver spangles over the crowds at the corner bar, at the tables and on the packed dance floor. Giant silver masks leered from the walls and coloured balloons floated across the ceiling. Clare wedged herself under a microdot of a table and as the band began again to deafen its audience Freddie loomed in the blue smoke, his black tie adrift, his lips buckled in a grin.

'One drink,' she said, lifting a finger at him. 'It's disgustingly late as usual and my eyes are coming to the boil. Some gruesome fowl tried to eat me out there.'

'Who can blame it?' Freddie propped his chin precariously on his hands and mooned at her. 'I could eat you myself.'

'Shut up, Freddie.' She jerked her shoulders nervously. It was long past midnight and the careful veneer of charm and artifice she put on in male company was beginning to crack. She wanted badly to kick off her shoes, ease the confining belt of her dress, wipe the hard spikes of mascara from her lashes and simply *be*, as you could alone or with other women. It had to be a man who'd written the story of Cinderella and, predictably, he'd got it wrong. He'd made the fairy godmother the one to insist on a curfew, but Clare knew better. It was Cinderella herself who eyed the clock and shot off happily as it struck. Midnight was quite long enough to dance with a prince or any other man; after that, a woman yearned to slip into comfortable rags and sit by the fire with mice running around, not footmen. Maybe Cinders had a good yak with the ugly sisters; the three of them probably got on very well. Men always liked to think that women were at loggerheads. It suited them.

Freddie gave a solemn burp. 'I know that bird,' he said.

'You would.'

'Perez told me, the chap who owns the place. It's called a Hyacinth Macaw. He paid a grand for it, under the counter.'

'Psittacosis,' Clare grumbled.

'Come again?'

'A disease of parrots. If humans get it, their psittas fall off.' Clare swivelled round and regarded the crowded room with contempt. 'God, what a dump,' she said. 'Freddie, what is this ghastly place?'

'This,' said Freddie, 'is the Club Rio Grande. Olé.' He clicked his fingers feebly.

'Never heard of it. What's wrong with Annabel's?'

'Not a thing,' he said vaguely.

'You owe them. True?'

'Preposterous. I merely fancied a bit of the old cha-cha-cha for a change. Dance?' He rotated a hand in the air.

'You joke.'

Their drinks appeared, straws emerging from a forest of leaves and bits of fruit. Clare took one sip and pushed hers away. She was feeling distinctly under the weather and her queasiness was not improved by that collection of bin lids they called a band. Freddie rocked back on the tiny gilt chair and she saw his eyes widen.

'Hey,' he called to someone over her shoulder and flung up both hands in expansive greeting. He teetered dangerously.

'Freddie,' Clare said through closed teeth.

A black-clad arm stretched across her, steadying Freddie's chair. 'Hullo there,' said Freddie, unperturbed. 'Thought I recognized you, Raul. Long time no see.' He lurched at the arm, which was hastily withdrawn. 'Clare,' he said, 'meet el king of the gauchos, all the way from sunny Ventura. Raul, this is the Lady bloody Clare.'

Reluctantly, Clare tipped her chin towards her shoulder and turned quickly back. She had no intention, especially at this late hour, of getting embroiled with one of Freddie's boring foreigners. For reasons she had never bothered to fathom, he seemed to know half the uncrowned heads of the world and in Clare's considered opinion, most of them were the pits.

'I want to go,' she said, glowering. Freddie was still on his feet but his grin was wonky and his eyes looked raw and mushy. The way things were going, he would soon be beyond driving her home to Flood Street in anything approximating safety and she knew all too well that neither of them could raise the price of a cab between them in cold hard cash. Besides, even if he could crawl behind the steering wheel, was the drive worth the inevitable mauling at the other end? She had known Freddie on and off all her life but since she had slept with him four weeks ago, he had been glued to her side. Possibly the only way, she thought sourly, that he kept himself upright.

'Please. You would like to dance?'

The foreigner was in front of her now, leaning towards her, moving Freddie expertly aside. It occurred to her suddenly that he might have a car and she arranged her lips in the smallest possible smile.

'Yes,' she said.

As they pushed their way to the dance floor, he spoke. His English was fluent enough, with a faint American drawl. 'Perhaps you have not heard of Ventura?'

Clare neatly swallowed a yawn. 'Of course,' she said. 'Saw her at the Ebor meeting. A flying filly over six furlongs, from the Mumtaz Mahal line.' That should fix him, car or no car. Few things irritated Clare more than being told things she had no wish to know and she was an old hand at fending them off.

The foreigner gave a grunt that sounded like laughter and she turned to look up at him with faint surprise. Straight black eyebrows, narrow close-set eyes, a long almost blue-grey face that showed no trace of humour. He looked, Clare thought, like a stone crusader carved on a tomb but if he resembled a corpse, at least he wasn't drunk, whereas Freddie – now sprawled on his chair as if God had dropped him from a great height – was possibly both. The man moved closer to her, she sighed and surrendered her hand to his and they danced crushed together on the tiny floor.

'Do you know that you are a very beautiful woman?' he said, bending to her ear.

'Yes, I do,' Clare said and noted with satisfaction the slight break in the smoothness of his step. He said no more after that and they danced through three more numbers and when they returned to the table, Freddie had vanished. To be sick, Clare supposed. This was the time of night he usually reserved for a bout of puking, locked in a variety of loos with other would-be users jigging up and down and banging on the door. Last week, he had slept all night in one of the Cathcarts' baths, leaving her to pacify old Lady Cathcart and bed down with a Cathcart daughter in an ice-cube of a room.

This evening, however, she was not to be stranded. After some minutes of polite shouting over the crunch of maracas, the Raul person took her home in a black Rolls with a flag drooping at its prow. In the rich leather-smelling darkness of its interior she prepared herself for some form of onslaught but none came. His hands, with their netting of black hairs, remained on the wheel and he looked straight ahead, not talking at all over the soft purr of the engine. She could smell him, though, pungent, expensive and alien. When they came to a halt at the door of Flood Street he asked her, still staring ahead, if she would dine with him the following night and Clare, woozy with tiredness and relief, graciously accepted.

Waking the next morning to the usual headache, the kind that made her yearn to drill a hole in her skull and let the steam burst out, she immediately recalled her acceptance and moaned aloud. Of all the things she didn't want to do that evening, what she didn't want to do most was to see that man again. Worse even than being a foreigner he was a stranger and Clare did not mix with strangers – they might be all very well in their place but out of it they were bound to alarm you, like spiders in the bath. Everyone she knew, she had always known or known about through being at school with their sister or taking dancing classes with their brother or having an uncle who was their

[17]

mother's second cousin. One did not wish to know people one did not know because if they were worth knowing, one would know them already. Naturally, this credo had its longueurs but you had to take the smooth with the smooth and, besides, what on earth would one talk to strangers about, since they didn't know anybody? Really, it was too bad. The last thing she needed was to become even mildly involved with a gaunt effigy from heaven alone knew where. It was all Freddie's fault, why couldn't he drink himself senseless in Shropshire, where he belonged, instead of reeling about London running up bills in unspeakable night clubs and forcing her into the arms of his outlandish blue-jowled friends?

As it was, Ma had never really forgiven her for mucking up on the Charles thing. Meanly, her mother blamed what she called Clare's 'reputation', choosing to ignore the obvious fact that however prissily her daughter behaved, the Queen would still have a word in her little boy's ear because the La Fontaines were of the Old Religion. Clare herself had relished stepping out on the princely arm — everywhere you went you were in the limelight without having to do or say anything remotely inter-esting, indeed it was far better if you didn't. Such a rest. Charles didn't get drunk, either, unlike so many other men she knew who seemed to think it the height of wit to pass out. All Wales required was that his female companion laughed a lot at his wireless jokes and that was easy. On those occasions, Clare called to mind a glorious emerald necklace that the Queen often wore and imagined it gleaming upon her own neck. This never failed to put an extremely cheerful smile upon her lips and she was quite as vexed as Ma when the calls from the Palace abruptly ceased after an incident at a May Ball, in which she was caught by some creep of a photographer stripped to her Marks and Sparks undies doing a wobbly can-can.

Miraculously, her name hadn't appeared in the papers, though H.M. naturally had her informers.

Ma had refused to speak to her for a week after that, but, against all common sense, retained her hopes that the calls would begin again if Clare would only behave herself.

'The La Fontaines,' she said doggedly and often, 'come of older and better stock than the Royals and a La Fontaine woman would make an ideal consort for any royal male. We have, after all, given generations of loyal and shamefully underpaid service to the Crown . . .' (Ma herself had been a Lady-in-Waiting to the Queen Mum and Pa was one of the princess's godfathers.)

'We haven't any money, Ma,' Clare would argue when she could be bothered, 'and besides we are Catholic.'

'Money,' Ma replied, wrinkling her nose in fine disgust, 'is irrelevant and our religion is neither here nor there. God, Clare, moves in mysterious ways His wonders to perform.'

However, God's wonders concerning the La Fontaines had not included renewed invitations from the Palace and if Ma had not yet entirely relinquished her Royal ambitions, Clare had. Better to marry money with far fewer strings attached and have some fun. Love was ridiculous, of course. She had never felt the slightest stirrings of that untidy emotion, for which she was heartily thankful. 'Love is for the Lower Orders,' Freddie said frequently, sticking his tongue against her clenched teeth. 'Sex is the thing.' Personally, Clare was of the opinion that the Lower Orders could have sex, too. Her own first experience of it had come at a time of high spiritual arousal and had been deeply detumescing. Much to her mother's alarm, Clare's preparations for First Communion had gone well beyond the bounds of moderation and good taste. The child had begun to chatter obsessively of nunneries and unlike normal girls who played little marriage games, doodling their Christian names in combination with the surnames of fancied boys, Lady La Fontaine found bits of paper everywhere about her daughter's rooms on which were written, in Clare's sprawling capitals, 'Sister Bernadette Clare', 'Sister Maria Theresa Clare' and other nicknames for a Bride of Christ.

'Can't have that,' said the Earl, told of his wife's discoveries. 'The girl's got to marry. What sort of a chap is this Father Garvey?'

'Thin. Hungry-looking. Burning with faith, I'm afraid,' answered Lady La Fontaine, sighing.

'Better have a word.'

The Countess could not quite bring herself to do this, it was hard to find words that conveyed the message without impugning her own undoubted piety. As it happened, her anxieties were misplaced, since it was not the Faith with which Father Garvey was burning. While her mother dithered, Clare continued to fall upon her knees in Church, in her bedroom and in odd corners of Tucolston's gardens, urging God to lay His hands upon her and make her His own as soon as possible – she ardently desired to vanish for ever behind the walls of some Closed Order to the greater glory of her Lord and her own blissful annihilation.

Instead, she had felt the hand of Father Garvey descend as she knelt before him one afternoon and, pressing upon the back of her neck, slowly move her face towards the coarse wool of his cassock. Unprotesting – who was she to say what was required of a supplicant? – she murmured on and fell silent only when the cassock's folds around her nose grew strangely alive and jumpy, like a rabbit in a trap, and then became damp, with a smell of the sea, while Father Garvey's hands clutched at her hair, stroking away. Afterwards he had turned from her and walked swiftly down the empty aisle to the dim recesses of the altar where he prostrated himself by the candles that popped and fluttered.

The same thing had occurred four times again, though she had tried to avoid it, retreating on her knees from the advancing wool but invariably trapped by a priestly hand. By the time the Cardinal himself stood before her holding the silver chalice, the mingled smells of wool and candlewax and incense combined with her nervous awareness of the dark congregation at her back proved too much entirely. As the water lay lightly upon her extended tongue, as the deep voice above her intoned 'Body of Christ', her nostrils flared with feeling and in a last-ditch effort to avoid being sick in public, she fainted. After that, Clare had carefully suppressed the various emotions that seemed to her to have caused this humiliation and turned her attention to more worldly things, much to her parents' relief.

Her headache banged away. Ma and Pa were in the country so Clare lay most of the day in bed, with Nellie clucking in and out bearing cups of camomile tea and telling her she would ruin her skin and her liver and her life if she would stay up night after night with the lord knows who. 'Lord Freddie is who,' Clare muttered once but Nellie, who had known Freddie – as she was fond of saying – with cradle marks on his back, was not re-assured. In her view the entire male sex, young and old, known and unknown, was intent on debauching her chick, which at least made a change from Clare's mother, who thought the other way round. Sipping Nellie's amber brew, groaning occasionally, Clare tried to work out how to cancel the coming dinner but it was clearly hopeless. She couldn't remember the man's first name, never mind anything else, and all she had to hand was his card wedged in her purse, which said Embassy of Ventura, Belgrave Square. Momentarily, she considered ringing them up and putting out a message on the Tannoy. 'Lady Clare regrets she's unable to dine today, pom pom.' As daylight faded, she resigned herself to the inevitable, took three aspirin and pan-sticked her face into some semblance of life.

The Rolls arrived promptly at eight.

It was at dinner, after he had ordered from a menu as large as *The Times*, that Clare first understood she was not dining with an Embassy employee out in a borrowed Rolls. Don Raul de Toro y Plata, for it seemed that was his name, owned Ventura outright and Ventura was somewhere up above the Mato Grosso, a tiny country or an enormous ranch, depending on the way you looked at it, hemmed in by Colombia, Peru and a stretch of the Amazon River. The de Toro family had owned it since the sixteenth century when some Spanish explorer had stumbled upon it, realized it had been overlooked by its neighbours, gave it his name and handed it over on his deathbed to a fellow robber baron of Madrid, Domingo de Toro y Plata. In the nineteenth century, as Simon Bolivar began stoking up grievances against absentee Spanish landlords and threatening unilateral declarations of independence, the family dispatched a spare younger son to lay bodily claim to their heritage and de Toros had been there ever since, kings of all they surveyed. What they surveyed sounded quite dreadful, as far as Clare could read between Raul's florid lines. Four thousand square miles of jungle with assorted Indians tunnelling about in it, a few mangy villages, one half-baked town, a broken-down theatre where Oscar Wilde had once recited his poems for reasons best known to himself, a post office for posting letters no one knew how to write, a railway line that took people nowhere and brought them back again and a statue of the Virgin of Ventura that cured infertility, which nobody had. In short, the place was a Ruritanian joke.

It was not a joke to this Raul, of course. He sat bolt upright opposite her in a nimbus of flossy silks and shiny gold and polished hair, dealing out Ventura's assets like a man with a winning poker hand. As the minutes dragged past, Clare felt her face stiffen with the effort of listening and her mouth began to twitch at the corners with strain. What perverse fate had trapped her here with a middle-aged stranger who was turning before her eyes into a boastful boy emptying the contents of his pocket for her inspection? Look, Miss, a conker, look, three chipped marbles and a dud firework, a rusty knife, a broken lighter and hey, look at *this*, a dead rat.

'In the main square of Nombre Dios, there is a statue of my father,' Raul said.

The dead rat.

Involuntarily Clare shivered and goose-pimples ran right up her arms. Something about the way this man's voice drummed ruthlessly on made her itch all over. If he went on much longer with that salesman's patter she might just have to open her mouth and scream very loudly until the head waiter had her removed. The soup was jellied consommé and trembled in sympathy. She considered launching the bowl across the table into Raul's lap. Then he could say, 'Waiter, there's a soup in my fly.' Except of course he wouldn't, being foreign.

'My family has only the purest Spanish blood in our veins,' Raul said, tapping a perfectly manicured nail against his plate for emphasis.

'Really?' said Clare, wondering what the purest Spanish blood would look like if she pierced him with a fork and released a few drops.

'Many families in South America are of mixed blood, they are half-castes, mestizos . . .'

'Bless you,' said Clare but it had no effect. He was unstoppable.

'. . . we have never married mestizos. There is no Negro or Indian blood in the de Toros, none.' Raul sat back in his chair for a moment, his eyes fixed on Clare.

'Congratulations,' she said. Waves of his eau de cologne wafted across to her and snuffed out what little appetite she had managed to retain. The steak came and Clare stabbed it viciously. Pink globules oozed from its brown surface and stained the white plate. Blood everywhere. She could be dining with Dracula.

'My grandfather, Vincente, built the Palace in Nombre Dios. It is in the style of the Grand Trianon at Versailles and they say

[23]

it is one of the most beautiful palaces in South America. Do you know the Grand Trianon, Lady Clare?'

'No,' she said, sulking. Why was he telling her all this? What did he want? He stared at her as if she were a fruit machine. Perhaps he thought if he fed her the right number of Venturan assets she'd suddenly rattle and her eyes would come up lemons.

'... and so, when my father died,' Raul said – he had hardly eaten anything – '... I became the Head of State. In my country I am called El Jefe, The Chief.' He looked sternly into the middle distance, as if he had just been crowned.

Was it believable? Hail to the Chief. Oh God. Clare bit at the wafer from her raspberry sorbet and thought wildly of smuggling a message out. Help, I am a prisoner in a vampire movie. Suppose Jonty Spencer or Piers Cathcart or, worse, Piers's sister catty Kathy Cathcart, suppose all of them were to troop in now as they might do any minute and pull long faces at her across the room, snapping their fingers and hissing olé and caramba. My dears, she could hear them whisper, you should have seen her. Our little Clare at the trough with a Latin lover. The dreaded Don Juan in person, awash with gold. Tie-pin, cufflinks, chains, bracelet, even a gold toothie-peg. A diamond on his hairy little pinkie, I promise. Built like an adobe shit-house, sweeties, and ponging the place up with eau de wog. Dire.

Raul, oblivious to Clare's inner voices, talked on and on, edging his chair ever closer to hers, relentless and dedicated. He took her hand and held it gently.

'I shall call you La Dorada, the golden lady.' His voice dropped. 'In Ventura they sometimes call me El Dorado, the golden man.' He looked at her meaningfully. 'Your eyes, my Dorada, are as blue as the mantle on the Virgin of Ventura and your teeth are whiter than a string of pearls.'

'I should hope so,' said Clare, who had a low opinion of pearls and, for that matter, of virgins, but this and other tart remarks she essayed in increasing discomfort did nothing to stem the tidal wave of compliments that now threatened to drown her. To her horror Raul, waving a handful of pound notes, then summoned over a group of violinists who played their instruments an inch from her ear and embarrassed her almost to tears.

'I admire so much your English literature. Do you like poetry, my Dorada?'

'No,' said Clare. His Dorada. His? An edge of panic made her swallow hard. This was ridiculous, it couldn't go on. It could not.

'I like poetry very much. For me, the most wonderful poem in the English language is Eef. Do you know Eef, Lady Clare? Or may I call you now, Clare?'

'No,' Clare said tightly.

'I like it very much. How does it go? Eef you can keep your head when all about you are losing theirs ...'

'They probably know something you don't. Old English joke,' said Clare.

'Eef you can talk with crowds and keep your virtue ...'

He knew it all and recited it all, verse by boring verse, his eyes never leaving Clare, his hands spread out on the tablecloth as if he feared a sudden breeze would wrest it from its place. Clare put icy knuckles to her cheeks. Shortly she would lose her head while all about her were keeping theirs. The smile she had somehow kept going throughout most of the meal wobbled and vanished and for the first time a pale image of it appeared on Raul's thin lips. He seemed, as he droned out his Kipling clichés, almost happy. A lock of dark hair detached itself from the smooth wing across his brow and fell over one eye. Taking it carefully between thumb and index finger he replaced it, his eyes still fixed on her. The diamond ring winked. He ended his recitation and smiled.

In spite of herself, Clare felt a twist of pity for this bejewelled, stiff, too-handsome man. He was ludicrous but he was also pathetic, somehow hang-dog, desperate to impress her. He might even be trying to hypnotize her, his eyes stared so. The balloon of his ego floated in front of her, an inflated membrane she could reach out and puncture with one nick of a long pink nail. Why didn't she, then? She took a deep breath and felt her heart working hard, there didn't seem to be enough oxygen around for two. Reluctantly she saw that he yearned for her approval, that he was spreading in front of her every card he had to force her attention and her admiration. He looked like a man familiar with force, used to having his own way but frustrated now and bewildered. There was a crude power in him compressed just below the glossy surface. Like an olympic diving board, she thought, perfect in its place but ridiculous here in this London restaurant filled with idle London chatter and the screech of violins. Here he was disarmed, reduced, almost a figure of fun. Almost but not quite.

She was worn out, damp under the arms with mixed emotions. Beneath the table her high heels were off and her feet flat on the ground, easing the cramp in her legs. He jarred her so, his purblind masculinity and his voracious hunger for her praise drained every last bit of energy. She struggled for control, for distance, for some sense of proportion – after all, she would eventually make it back to her cool bed and Nellie's reassuring presence. But she was tired now, so tired that her head drooped and, stupidly, tears welled up under her lids. Raul noted the change in her. He took both of her hands in his and kissed them with passion. He spread out her fingers on the table, palm upward, and held her wrist while he reached into his pocket. Then, with his own hand, he closed her fingers over the sharp edges of little stones.

'Emeralds,' he said and smiled as if it hurt him. 'Raw emeralds from Ventura for my golden lady.'

Clare had the stones valued by Prichetts, Ma's jewellers in Bond Street. She emptied them on to the black velvet square spread on the counter by Mr Agnew, the man with whom Ma always dealt.

'May one ask where these stones were obtained, milady?' Mr Agnew made a practice of keeping his conversation as removed from the personal as possible, out of respect for his customers.

'Ventura,' said Clare, 'I suppose.'

Mr Agnew's eyebrows rose. 'That would seem to be a trifle unlikely in the circumstances, Lady Clare, if your ladyship will pardon one's doubts.'

'Why?' asked Clare. Go on, say it man, I've been conned.

'Because, as Your Ladyship is possibly aware, it is strictly forbidden by Venturan law to export emeralds from the country. Only the ruling family are in a position to . . .'

Clare smiled with great sweetness. 'They were given to me by Señor Raul de Toro y Plata who is, at the moment, here in . . .'

Mr Agnew raised a palm. 'Of course,' he said, 'of course Please forgive.' Then he folded the four corners of the velvet square over the stones, gave Clare a little bow and retired behind a mirrored door.

Half an hour later, Clare hailed a taxi home to Flood Street. She thought that with very little effort she could have flown. Men had given her presents before, silver bits and pieces, a swizzler stick, a cigarette case, once a gold pen, all of which she had promptly lost in various underlit discos but this was rather different. Rather more than rather different, really. To put it bluntly, she had never been in possession of so much loot in her life – Pa kept her on a tight string and she was normally hard put to it to find change for a cigarette machine if she did not have a male escort handy. By the time she arrived at Flood Street she was still euphoric enough not to care a damn for the cabby's four-letter comment on his tipless state but she had begun to realize that in this case, even for the highly desirable Lady Clare, there might be no such thing as a free lunch. Either she had to give back the stones, which she had no intention of doing, or she had to see the dreadful man again. Momentarily, she thought of emigrating but that was patently absurd. The whole thing was absurd, particularly the cause of her dilemma, Mr Raul de Fiddled y Dee. She sighed, though not too deeply. Plainly she was trapped but only for the time being. She would find a way out quite soon.

In that, as in many other and later assessments she made of Raul, she was as wrong as anyone could be. That afternoon a Constance Spry van unloaded twelve dozen white lilies upon a disapproving Nellie — 'where's the corpse?' she grumbled, trudging in and out with her arms full — and that evening Raul was on the doorstep himself, tall and austere, his eau de cologne mingling uneasily with the heavy scent of the flowers that filled the small house. Clare, breathing in to prepare herself for his welcome, breathed out quickly and felt nausea stir. Then she thought of her emeralds and felt better. A few meals, a few dances, a couple of theatres and, she supposed, a poke or four was not too high a price to pay if she could keep him out of the way of her friends and after that he'd be back running Ruritania and she could bestow her custom on some grateful bank manager in an area unfrequented by her parents. Clare was perfectly aware that she was entering upon a form of prostitution but she was not much given to guilt or moral judgements, especially on herself; that was one of the perks of being a Catholic. You could always confess and be given absolution and what were a few Hail Marys compared to becoming a woman of independent means? A vision of Father Garvey's latticed features appeared in her mind's eye and she smiled beatifically. Raul, ushered in by Nellie at that moment, saw before him a wondrously serene Madonna and, with reverence, kissed her hand.

Two of Clare's suppositions failed to materialize. Over the next five weeks, Raul fed her, danced her and took her to the theatre. He did not, however, make the slightest move to get her to bed and Clare did not have to keep him away from her friends.

He kept them away, a very long way away. As Clare flagged, which she did quite soon, wilting under the heat of his fixed and hawkish eye, she telephoned Freddie and asked him round, telling Raul she was tired and needed an early night. Seeing Freddie, sulky, rumpled and none too steady on his pins, she nearly wept with relief at his ordinariness and embraced him most tenderly, only averting her face a little from the familiar petrol-and-whisky Freddie smell. He, considerably heartened by his reception, immediately launched into one of his execrable jokes.

'There was this chap, d'you see, wanted to become a woman. So he canters off to have the operation. The doctor says look, old boy, this is going to be awfully painful. We'll have to have it off, you know. Go ahead, says the chappie, gritting the old choppers, and bob's your uncle. Then the doctor says there's just one other thing we'll have to do before you're a real woman and this is really spectacularly painful. I'm game, says the chappie. So they took his brains out. Ha! Good, that.'

Clare laughed hysterically and hugged him again. 'God, Freddie, you're too awful,' she said into his lapel. He was awful. He was also familiar, safe, entirely predictable and well within her control.

'Jolly good,' said Freddie. 'Dust yourself down, my poppet, and let's totter off.' He weaved to the door gripping Clare's arm, chucked Nellie under the chin to her great disgust, and the two of them departed, Clare still giggling, in a roar of noise and fumes.

On their return at two o'clock in the morning, there was a black Rolls Royce parked outside the house. Freddie, heavy-eyed, lolled affectionately on Clare's shoulder attempting to pull his lips together for a kiss. She pushed him off abruptly. 'Don't,' she hissed.

'Wha?' His head rolled back again to its perch on her right clavicle.

'It's him,' whispered Clare. 'Raul. You know.' She had spent much of the evening moaning to him about Raul but Freddie was not a good listener, tending to say Yah a lot and taking little in. He took only a little in, now. Peeved, he rolled the window down and called belligerently into the night.

'Hey, is that you, Raul? Clare doesn't want you hangin' about, d'you hear? Piss off. Pisso offo.'

A dark figure unfolded itself from the Rolls and walked towards Freddie. Clare froze. Freddie said 'Olé' in a rather quieter voice and rolled the window up. There was a sharp crack and the window clouded over, shattered and opaque.

'Good Lord,' said Freddie, 'I've gone blind.' He was covered in splintered glass.

'I'll get out,' Clare said, scrabbling at the door, frantically pulling at its handle. Yanking her skirt out of Freddie's grasp, hissing at him 'let go, let *go*', she almost fell through the open door into Raul's arms. He steadied her carefully and with a firm hand on her elbow led her across the pavement and up the Flood Street steps. As she fumbled for her key, her hands shaking, light flooded from the house. Nellie stood within the pillars in her candlewick dressing-gown, holding a poker. Behind them, Freddie's indignant shouts died away.

'What in the world is going on?' Nellie said, peering out. She saw Freddie's car and her eyes travelled back to Raul, standing protectively beside Clare. 'Didn't I tell you, Missie? That one's nothing but trouble. Come in, for heaven's sake.' She plucked at Clare's sleeve. There was a roar from below, Freddie's car pulled away and screeched into the darkness. 'Good riddance,' Nellie shouted after him, waving the poker. 'Don't bother to come back.' Then she turned to Raul, pulling the lapels of her gown modestly together. 'Thank you, sir, thank you. I'll look after her now. Come in, chick, you're cold as ice. Goodnight, sir.'

Raul smiled and nodded. 'Goodnight,' he said. 'Señora, Señorita, buenos noches.'

*

Freddie didn't come back. Nor did the few other men friends whom Clare encountered and sneaked out with here and there in the following weeks. Inevitably, they came up against Raul and melted away in the heat of his glare, either because they wanted no trouble or because they assumed Clare was his proper possession, flirting where she ought not, a cheating woman. Also they sensed, as Clare by now knew well, that Raul would abide by no rules known to them to keep her. Only the company of her female friends gave her an acceptable excuse to avoid his presence. I'm in purdah, thought Clare on such occasions, like any Arab woman. Masked, veiled, confined to the harem. That, in itself, was no penance, indeed it was pleasurably familiar, the boarding school left a mere two years ago all over again, with its easy warmth and bustle, its relaxed companionship, its gossip and giggles and challenges uncomplicated by males, that mysterious sex still on a distant horizon, interesting but essentially comic. Not yet divisive. Not yet necessary. Not yet the only proof of attraction and status and success in the outside world.

Louise Lawson, Clare's best school friend, dark and sour as an olive, sprawled over Clare's unmade bed on one of her Raul-free evenings, watching Clare's face upside down in a basin. 'How's the gorgeous gaucho?' she finally said after recounting the week's events at Lady Margaret Hall.

'Bloody,' said Clare. She gave her hair a final squeeze, wrapped a towel round her head and stood up, turbanned.

The old tremors assaulted Louise. Clare looked like some ancient Egyptian goddess bleached of all colour by a desert sun. Snappily, she said, 'I wish I could do my hair at home. If I didn't spend a fortune at the hairdresser's I'd look a ruin.'

On the bed beside her, Clare said, 'What am I to do about him?' Water dripped from beneath the towel and ran down her cheeks. 'Louise, he won't let me alone.'

Louise thought of a tall muscled History lecturer who let her alone and said, 'Don't be so wet. Here.' She pulled off the towel and began to rub hard at Clare's head. Clare gave herself contentedly up to this vigorous mothering, letting her head roll in Louise's ungentle hands. The white hair crackled and rose in a radiant halo. Louise stopped, panting. 'What's wrong with him, for heaven's sake? He's rich, isn't he? Sexy as hell. Mad about you. That's enough to be going on with.'

Clare knuckled her eyes and looked at her friend, a little redly. 'He frightens me.'

'Huh,' said Louise. 'You should meet some of the men at Oxford. Pompous twits. They're really frightening.'

Clare squeezed her hands together. She wanted to stretch them out and grasp Louise, shake her, make her see the raft upon which she was stranded and drifting inexorably away from Louise's world of youth and parties and wonderful everyday life. The gap was widening between them, soon it would be too great to bridge. Help me, help me.

'He's old,' she said. 'Foreign. Terribly serious.'

'Not that old,' Louise said. 'Anyway, you should have come with me to University. Why didn't you? You could have. You had a brain or two, once upon a time.'

Clare stretched out the towel and flicked it quite hard at Louise's arm. Louise caught at one end and pulled. For a moment the two girls tugged and then collapsed together, rolling and squealing like puppies on the sagging bed. Louise propped herself on her elbows. 'Well?' she said, 'what's your answer?'

'I wouldn't have got a grant.'

Louise exhaled rudely. 'Of course not. So what? Your people are rolling.'

'Oh never mind. It's too complicated.' Clare shook her head and picked crossly at a torn nail. How would Louise, daughter of a merchant banker with a large but brand new house in the Home Counties, understand the ridiculous cash flow problems of the La Fontaines? Clare did not entirely understand them herself, she only knew that real money of the kind necessary to sustain her at Oxford or any other university, for that matter, was not on her particular cards. Higher education was Louise's privilege, not hers. The knowledge, obscure and hurtful as it was, shamed her, it could not be discussed.

Louise, watching her fiddle with her fingers, thought what rough going it was to have a friend like Clare. Easier at school, of course, where there were no men to undermine trust and everyone wore the kind camouflage of serge tunics and hideous woolly stockings but even then hard to avoid the pangs of jealousy. Those pangs were demeaning and yet how to face up to them without losing confidence? How could you be expected to admit, in the anxious teens, that your friend had everything? Beauty, brains, a title and money. And she made you laugh. Life could not be so unfair. Clare could hardly demand sympathy on top of all that.

In the short silence, Clare looked up and saw the pinpoint glint in her friend's eyes. 'Let's get pissed,' she said quickly. 'Raul left some champagne.'

'There,' said Louise. 'He can't be all bad.'

Her other women friends avoided the subject of Raul. Something about the intensity with which Clare spoke of him embarrassed them and, by contagion, her. The men they talked of were young, Clare knew them all, had even slept with one or two, they were no threat, they were hardly even men or not in the way Raul was a man, bringing with him the cold wind of power from an alien adult world. When they came, these girls, their arms outspread, their cheeks cool on hers, laughing and teasing, she was so pleased to see them that she pushed the thought of Raul far away, buying time from all he represented; sex, marriage, internment, separation. She was on remand, the women were her visitors and the judge had not yet passed sentence. But Nellie was a warder who abetted Raul, she preferred one man to many round her chick and believed he was protecting Clare, in spite of all Clare could say.

'You're a silly old trout,' Clare screamed once, driven to desperation by Nellie's — everyone's — refusal to listen to her or to understand the situation. 'You're a bad old mad old hag.'

'Sticks and stones,' said Nellie haughtily. 'What you need is a good tonic, my girl. You look all washed out, you're a real sight. It's beyond me what that nice foreign gentleman sees in you.'

It was beyond Clare, too. It was all beyond Clare. No man had ever behaved towards her as Raul behaved with that deadly combination of courtesy and threat that held her in a kind of thrall, aching to escape but waiting, always waiting for some storm to break around her and set her free. She told Raul that evening that she could not keep the emeralds, that he must take them back.

'I do not want them back,' he said. Then he said, 'I love you, Clare.' The words held their familiar power but she rallied.

'Raul, please, I don't love you, I can't love you.' She said the words almost lovingly and he gently replied, for he was very gentle when he had her to himself, 'My love is enough for both of us.'

'No. I shall go away.'

'Then I shall follow. I shall follow you to the ends of the earth. I shall never let you go.'

She believed him absolutely and a chill settled over her. Now there was only one hope. She would have to take him to Tucolston and get Ma and Pa to see him off.

[2]

Tucolston Old Hall was the La Fontaine seat and the hereditary La Fontaine burden. During all of Clare's lifetime its wide white gables, the sills and frames of its many high windows, its arched roofs and beams and its numerous outbuildings had crumbled silently about her ears, the ancient fabric eaten away by fungi and insects, the wear and tear of hundreds of years and the assaults of the La Fontaine generations. Outside, the once clipped and geometrical gardens, each separated from the next by orderly lines of box, had year by year pushed beyond their proper borders to merge in defiance of human plans. Dahlias encroached on the territory of roses, flowers invaded vegetable land, clematis coiled around the gooseberry bushes. The great circle of green lawn in front of the house, with its central plume of red hot pokers and pampas grass, was no longer incised from the gravel around it but extended exploratory fingers on every side, spotted with daisies. The peach trees spread against the south walls were barren for lack of pruning, the crab apples behind the stone balustrade creaked beneath their layers of woolly lichen, the cypresses that lined the avenue were blotched with brown, the great beeches bent in the winds and lost limbs that lay forlorn all summer, the parched leaves rustling sadly. On the outbuildings, the shingles split and slid askew and the doors hung open, yawning on empty straw where the nanny goats that had menaced Clare in her childhood with their slit eyes and needle hooves had pranced and munched. The skeleton of the conservatory, once a welter of green fronds, reared blackly now against the autumn sky from a fall-out of glass shards and broken earthenware. What little remained of the way things had been was kept going from month to month by Ma and Pa, both permanently welded into gumboots, and by old Fox, the only gardener left, that same Fox who had carved Clare stilts for her tenth birthday so that she could totter behind him, her head miraculously level with his frayed cap. The three of them had occasional help from an assortment of village lads and shifts of village matrons in flowered cross-over aprons, a fluctuating population drawn from the families who had always provided the staff for Tucolston, the Foxes, the Voles, the Snipes and (Clare's own nanny) Nellie, daughter of the Crows. Our Tucolston zoo, Pa called them. Clare knew all too well that to outsiders the La Fontaines must seem rich, last beneficiaries of feudalism, but being a La Fontaine herself and scarcely ever handling money in its primal form — pound notes and coins that could be exchanged for clothes and taxis and adornment — she was plagued by poverty. Even the farm children had a few coins to jingle. Clare vividly remembered her shame when she'd asked for a packet of crisps at the village shop and then couldn't pay and had to watch while little Alice with the ugly birthmark who trailed behind her everywhere like a devoted puppy dug in her pocket and pushed the necessary pennies across the counter, beaming. That pocket had once belonged to Clare – Ma handed down all her clothes to the tenants — but there'd never been a bean in it then. Though nothing was said in so many words, Clare was quite aware that Ma and Pa had placed her in the London house to find a husband, thus relieving themselves of her upkeep and enabling them to sell Flood Street and channel the resulting cash where all La Fontaine cash went, into the house and grounds of Tucolston. To that end, the husband was expected to be rich.

'Kind hearts,' the Countess Mamaine La Fontaine said in her vaporous voice to the summer morning, 'are more than coronets and simple faith than Norman blood.' She did not believe a word but thought it charmingly put. Fortunately, she had a coronet as well as a kind heart and her husband the Earl, who was presently shearing the box hedge round the vegetable garden, supplied both the simple faith and the Norman blood though he looked the very picture of an Englishman with his noble roast beef face, slightly underdone. The Countess took pleasure in the knowledge that her own faith, bestowed upon her at her marriage to Geoffrey, was not in the least simple. The intelligence that had found few outlets as the daughter of a Norfolk county family had blossomed nicely within the intricate closed system of Catholicism and Mamaine prided herself that few cradle Catholics could match her when it came to debating the finer points of a Papal Bull. The Old Religion had also provided her with a deep and abiding interest in the minutiae of ill-health and death-bed dramas. She saw rewarding signs of sickness in the most robust of people, she was an avid mourner at funerals and one of the most dedicated cemetery visitors in the county. Her tasteful wreaths, with their coroneted cards, were recognized by even the most grief-stricken to be a valuable introduction to the afterlife, whether Protestant or Catholic — the Countess was no narrow bigot. Nor did she direct her energies solely to other sufferers from disease. She carefully nourished her own occasional symptoms, hanging over them like a gardener over feeble but precious seedlings, and was mortified when they showed no signs of killing her or even of making her a permanent invalid. She inordinately admired one sister-in-law, after whom Clare was named, for having taken to her bed after the birth of her first-born son Percy and never rising in daylight again. It showed, she thought, a uniquely religious nature in these all too secular times. Mamaine herself had given birth once, after which she had scrupulously taken the necessary precautions. When a young and impertinent priest, new to the Cathedral, had commented upon her relatively childless state, she had been much offended and seen to it that he was removed to a more suitable working-class area. Liverpool, if she remembered rightly. At the thought, always nagging, of her only child, the Countess's broad, blunt and once beautiful features – now veiled by a fine cobweb of lines – contracted. Clare was a sore disappointment to her. She seemed determined to ignore her proper role in this or any other life. When had she last attended Mass? Was she fit to attend at all? If she were knocked down tomorrow by a car, Mamaine feared for the purity of her soul. And her underwear, of course.

'Geoffrey,' she called.

'What is it, old girl?'

'Clare will be here shortly with her Spanish friend. You will talk to him, won't you? Clare seemed a little distressed when she telephoned.'

'Absolutely,' said the Earl, squinting at his wife in the sunlight. 'Leave it to me, leave it to me, leave it to me.' He began clipping the hedge again, this time rather savagely. He loathed visitors.

Raul stood in the rooms of Tucolston like an emissary from another planet. He sat gingerly on the edges of the dog-haired chintz sofas, kicking surreptitiously at the dogs. The Countess's hand trembled as she passed his teacup, the Earl boomed with the bonhomie he reserved for those whose raison d'être he could not fathom; his eyes, crescented with pouches, blinked like a startled hen. Raul walked with him across the Lincolnshire fields in a razor-creased silk suit, carefully placing each glossy punched-leather shoe along the ruts left by the plough. He was seeking the right moment to ask for Clare's hand in marriage but opportunities seemed strangely lacking.

They paused under a dead oak, struck by lightning the winter before. 'Sir,' said Raul, 'about Clare . . .'

'Clare?' said the Earl and looked madly around as if he had heard an explosion. 'Beaulah! Down, girl! Heel!' He poked his stick at the labrador and set off in another direction.

Raul tried again on a second walk, the punch-holes in his shoes already blocked with mud. 'About Clare, sir,' he panted.

'Clare?' said the Earl. The dismay on his face was that of a family man pestered in his wife's presence by a dirty-postcard salesman. 'Bonny! Get out of that, dammit!' and he charged away after the dogs.

'Extraordinary cove,' he said to his wife later. 'Keeps on saying Clare.'

'Poor man, he looks rather unwell,' said the Countess happily. 'I expect it's the wretched climate.'

'What's wrong with the climate?'

'Of Ventura, dearest. Clare says it's very close.'

'Good God, how does Clare know?'

'Perhaps geography lessons, dearest. Or he may have told her. Clare doesn't look much better, white as a sheet.' She contemplated the roses in her own cheeks reflected in a pier glass and sighed.

Later the Earl cornered his wife as she played a melancholy air upon the grand piano. Its wide harp-shaped surface was littered with silver-framed photographs of the dear departed. Geoffrey looked hunted, Raul had begun saying 'Clare' again.

'Mamie, that man smells,' Geoffrey said in his most discreet boom.

'It's his scent. They wear scent,' Mamaine said. 'Such a sad tune.'

'Who do?' he demanded.

'Well, dearest. Foreign men.'

'How do you know, woman? Bloody queer, if you ask me. Prince Philip doesn't wear scent and he's a foreigner. Have you seen that gold watch he wears?'

'Prince Philip, dearest?'

'Not Philip, Mamaine.' The Earl's jowls quivered. 'Whatsisname.'

'That's unfair, Geoffrey. You have a gold watch.'

'Not on my arm, woman, not on my *arm*. Is he Jewish? He looks Jewish.'

The Countess tinkled away on two high notes. 'Spanish, darling.'

'Spanish Jew, then.'

'Dear one, he's a Catholic. These keys are sticking.'

'Dammit, Mamie. A queer Spanish Catholic Jew. What sort of company is that for Clare? Whatever happened to the Chedleigh boy? At least he was only a drunk.'

'But a Protestant drunk.' Mamaine closed the piano. Her daughter would not be permitted to risk her Faith for a mere Chedleigh.

Geoffrey's older maiden sister Florence, who dressed with Oxfam in layers of scratchy woollens with a fine disregard for the weather, sat in the unkempt rose garden and interrogated her sister-in-law. They got on well together. Florence looked younger than her years and Mamaine older, which gave them both satisfaction.

'He won't make old bones,' said Florence, pointing an accusatory finger across the lawn at Raul who was trying to talk to Clare who was trying to hit a ball through a rusty croquet hoop. 'Peculiar grey, his skin.'

'Yes, Florrie.'

'Catholic, is he?'

'Yes, Florrie.'

'The sort that gives us a bad name, I'll be bound. Gets his braces blessed at Rome, keeps coloured statues on his mantel, wears medallions, goes to Lourdes.'

'He doesn't wear braces, Florrie.' Mamaine felt a spasm of irritation with her sister-in-law who knew very well that she had passed many happy hours at the shrine of dear Bernadette. Still the old gap between cradles and converts. Raul would be a cradle. Perhaps he visited Lourdes. Perhaps they would meet there one day in wheelchairs, DV. As Florrie grumbled on, Mamaine watched her daughter move erratically about with that man her dark shadow. Anyone would think she was trying to shake him off but if she didn't like him – and Mamaine perfectly saw why she might not – why bring him home? Nevertheless, they made a handsome pair. Day and night. Clare was, of course, quite lovely, everybody said so, but a bit showy if the truth were told. Rather hysterical looks. Nellie had once called her highly-strung. My daughter is not a tennis racquet, Mamaine had said, but she knew what Nellie meant. It might be the way the child dressed. Or the hair. Or the bust. They would have to have a talk ...

'Mamaine.' Florence was tapping her stick. 'I asked, is he rich?'

'I imagine so.' Mamaine winced at Florrie's directness. 'He owns a lot of land in Ventura.'

'*Land*,' said the older lady with a snort of contempt. 'We all own *land* and look at us. Not a penny to rub together. Look at this place.' She poked her stick at a bunch of ragwort nestling companionably at her feet. 'Cash is what you need, you and Geoffrey, or you'll have the place round your ears.'

'It is easier for a camel,' said Mamaine sententiously, 'to go through the eye of a needle than for ...'

'Rubbish,' said Lady Florence. 'As far as I'm concerned, camels can go anywhere they like. I'm talking about cash. Find out if he's got cash and if he has, Clare had better marry him and the sooner the better, is that quite clear, Mamie? Otherwise the ceiling in my bedroom is going to bury me.'

'Really, Florrie, what a way to talk,' Mamaine protested. 'Excuse me one second, dear, I must tell Nellie to bring tea.'

On Sunday after Mass, at which Lady Florence dropped her handbag as she was wont to do with much noise and fuss whenever the officiating priest aired views from the pulpit with which she disagreed – this time he harped far too heavily on ecumenical matters – Lady Mamaine drew Raul aside for a little talk. Afterwards, humming a Gregorian chant in waltz tempo, she made her way to her husband's study where he had ensconced himself to read of the secret orgies of a Surbiton housewife in the *News of the World*. Three-quarters of an hour later she emerged, ran her hand absently over a damp patch at the edge of one of the windows in the gallery, stood deep in thought gazing at its mould-encrusted frame and then went upstairs and along the creaking floor of the corridor to Clare's bedroom.

There, while her daughter changed from her church dress into jeans, she launched a full-scale attack on Raul de Toro y Plata. He was, she proclaimed, an entirely unsuitable companion for any daughter of hers. This unsuitability consisted of being foreign, above all, and in quick succession after that a disturbing vulgarity of manner, dress, adornment, odour, behaviour and religious practice. Also accent – so American.

'Your father and I,' she said calmly and firmly, 'have your best interests at heart and this man is not for you. I don't wish to be crude but he smells of money and the corridors of power, not our sort of thing at all.' Mamaine's nostrils flared delicately. 'We expect you, my darling, to marry a man who is one of us. Steady, dependable, interested in farming and horses and dogs. A man who can be relied upon to uphold all we hold dear, our English traditions, our La Fontaine standards and values and our enlightened approach to Catholicism, so vital if the Faith is to survive in a changing world. A man . . .' said Mamaine, looking earnestly at her daughter, '. . . like Basil Beswick. We have invited him next weekend so that you may renew your acquaintance with him.'

Basil Beswick, heir to the Catholic Dukedom of Suffolk, was a short stout youth with a whinnying voice and the face of a disgruntled budgerigar. He had once pushed Clare into a bed of nettles, piqued because she would not let him play Joan of Arc on a bonfire.

Clare was outraged, she stood over her mother shaking visibly, pale with shock. How dare Ma interfere this way in her private affairs? Basil Beswick indeed! She would die first, if necessary on a bonfire like St Joan. Losing her temper entirely she shouted at Mamaine, accusing her of narrow-mindedness, authoritarianism, xenophobia, bigotry, an insular snobbishness and a wilful rejection of reality.

'Raul,' she said furiously, 'is worth ten times a wimp like Basil Beswick and layabout drunks like Freddie Chedleigh and all those other men you think so suitable. Horses and dogs, huh. Farming? I *loathe* farming.'

Clare was too angry to notice her mother's unnatural calm. She paced up and down, waving her hands, raging. Unlike these wimps and drunks, she said, Raul was a real man, he knew what he wanted and he went out to get it. He had power and great responsibilities and was immensely rich and if it came to a question of smells she, Clare, liked the smell of money a whole lot better than the smell of old wellies and wet rot that hung about Tucolston.

'If you and Pa think I shouldn't marry him because you don't know or care where Ventura is and you don't like his *clothes* for heaven's sake, then you've got another think coming. I'll marry whom I please and I shall be pleased to marry the President of Ventura, Raul de Toro y Plata. So there.'

At the end of this speech Clare's hair flared around her head and her cheeks were pink with exertion. She had never been so rude to her mother in all her life. Mamaine, rising in a dignified silence, thought that she looked more than usually beautiful and felt a surge of relief that such indecorous looks, with their inherent risks, would shortly be removed from under her nose to the distant fastnesses of South America.

'We shall see what we shall see,' she said enigmatically at the door. 'Your father will have something to say on the subject, mark my words.' Then she swept out.

Clare stared blankly after her mother. Her quite unaccountable defence of Raul left her dazed and deeply apprehensive. She had brought him to Tucolston and to her parents because nothing was more real to her in England than this place and these people. London was something else, a stage upon which was daily rehearsed an infinite variety of drama that required every sort of player for its continuation. In London you invented yourself and as long as you strutted and fretted against the appropriate backdrop, no one could challenge you, no one penetrate your chosen disguise. Those crowded streets were the proper containers for every sort of exotic bloom, natural or hybrid or of the purest plastic – indeed the more synthetic, the more entirely self-made you were in that DIY city, the more acceptable you became. Turning heads, flouting convention, was the name of the urban game.

By contrast, the countryside had far fewer theatrical possibilities and Lincolnshire almost none. The land here did not undulate, there was nothing dramatic about it. There were no mountains and no rich valleys, no lonely lakes nor waterfalls, no wild wind-blown moors, no secret forests. It was a plain place, agricultural rather than rural, down to earth. The fields were flat and serviceable, potatoes grew in them, not gleeful daffodils, and the flat domestic waters of rivers and canals, with the cargo of Midland trippers, did not invoke a single thought too deep for tears. Surely here, against such an unadorned backdrop, the gas that kept Raul inflated would begin to leak and he would hurtle about, a shrinking balloon making farcical noises, until all that was left was a rubber rag. The secret codes of family life, the sidelong glances, the dogs, the damp, the relentless ordinariness of everything, would all combine to puncture his posturings and reveal him brittle, one-dimensional, an insubstantial man.

Nor had her plan failed. Raul, in this setting, was indeed preposterous. Her parents, her aunt, the villagers too, had rejected him in a hundred subtle ways. She had watched their eyes, she had seen the polite smiles that concealed ridicule and disapproval. The very lawns of Tucolston upon which he walked in his glove-thin shoes seemed to heave against him as if its grass were fur and Raul an infestation.

Then why this outburst? By rights her image of him and the tenuous hold he had on her should – with her mother's outright condemnation – have cracked across like the mirror of the Lady of Shalott, leaving her finally free to say loudly and with absolute conviction 'Go'. What held her back? In spite of Raul's threat to follow her to the ends of the earth she was quite aware that if she were able to range every atom of herself against him he would recognize defeat and depart. Yet some rebellious part of her, some inner disorder, obstinately refused to lend itself to this highly desirable conclusion. It seemed to her that she wanted nothing more than to be in control of her life, at peace with the familiar, however apparently tedious. But against her will and without her sanction she was invaded by other possibilities. Another world was anchored below her mind and lay shimmering there like a great lake, its waters silken and seductive, waiting to engulf her in its mysterious depths. She could turn from it and walk away along the firm dry land whose every contour she knew or she could summon every morsel of courage, draw herself up and plunge in, to swim or to sink.

Clare tipped up the maple-framed mirror that stood on her dressing-table and gazed into it. With an odd dismay she saw that her face betrayed no sign of the turmoil within. The banality of beauty lay like a screen between her feelings and their reflection, giving nothing away. Absently, out of old habit, she posed at her image, tilting her chin and arching her eyebrows just so. Soft shadows slanted along her cheeks and deepened the blue of her eyes. Very slowly she smiled at herself, an ardent and consoling smile. Everything was bound to go her way, no matter what dangers she confronted. What harm could possibly come to a woman with lips that could break any man's heart?

*

That afternoon she dodged Raul, creeping past the library where he stood rocking forward and backward on his heels staring at a dingy oil painting of a fat white pig, and walked across the meadow at the top of the avenue to where a brook meandered between willows, marking the border of the first tenant farm. A girl sat hugging her knees by the water, fair hair falling over her face.

'Alice,' Clare said.

The girl jumped up and ran to her, small breasts bouncing under a too-tight dress, feet clumsy in schoolgirl sandals. 'Miss Clare,' she said, smiling with delight, 'you've been away so long. My Mum said you was back, old Foxie told her.'

'Only for the weekend,' said Clare. 'I'm going back to London tomorrow.' Poor little Alice. How pretty she would be, without that horrid mark.

Together they walked along the bridle path that ran beside the brook. 'What's new round here?' Clare asked.

'Nothing,' said Alice. 'Nothing ever happens in this old place. We had a ewe die yesterday. She just swelled up and died.'

Clare stopped and leaned her back against a sloping willow. 'Do you think I should get married?' she said, looking up at the sky.

'Oh.' Alice gazed at Clare leaning there. No one in the world was beautiful like Miss Clare. 'Oh yes I do.'

'Why?'

'I don't know.' Alice became shy. 'It would be lovely for us. You in a lacy dress and flowers and that, oh lovely.' She gave a joyful little sound.

'You could be a bridesmaid,' Clare said, twisting a leaf round her wedding ring finger and frowning at it.

'No,' Alice said, turning away. 'Not me, no.'

'Why not?' Immediately, Clare knew the answer. 'You're not worrying about this, are you?' Lightly she touched Alice's cheek where the dark red stained it. 'Silly. That makes no difference.'

As Alice stubbornly shook her head, Clare tweaked the long hair, more golden than her own. 'You'd be bored, tell the truth. You're only, what are you? Fifteen. What do you care what an old woman of twenty does?'

Softly Alice said, 'Don't tease us, Miss Clare. You know what you do makes a difference to me. It's life, what you are, if you know what I mean. What goes on at the Hall, that's our life, me and Dad and my Mum.' Only that morning in the village shop she had heard them all talking, Mum and Mrs Jarvis and old Foxie. Foreign, is he? Mum had said and old Foxie had nodded. A General, he said, or something of the like. He stands up that straight. Mrs Jarvis said she had seen him in the fields with His Lordship. Funny, he looked, she said. Oh a handsome one, right enough, but dressed a bit fancy for a walk in a field and on the old side for a friend of Miss Clare. And Alice's Mum had sighed a little and said it seemed only yesterday that her Alice and Miss Clare were making mud pies together and didn't time fly?

Clare said, 'I don't think being married will make me happy. Not to him.' She took Alice's hand and rubbed her fingers round the rough bitten nails. 'I'd have to go and live abroad. A long way from here.'

Alice let her hand lie patiently in Clare's. 'You don't love him?' she asked.

'I don't know,' said Clare. In what way that Alice might understand could she begin to describe the turmoil of feelings she had about Raul? 'In a way I do. He's not an easy man. Not a man you can easily understand, do you see?' Of course Alice could not see. Why did she bother to mention it? 'Alice, forget it. None of it is to do with you.'

To Clare's amazement, she saw bright tears gather in Alice's eyes. 'I can't forget it,' she said, her voice hoarse. 'It's silly, I know, but sometimes I feel that what happens to you will happen to me. In a way, I mean. Like if you find the right man, so will I one day, even with this ...' and she covered the stain on her cheek with one hand. 'And if you don't, I won't. I'm talking rubbish, aren't I?'

'Yes you are,' Clare said and meant it. Alice was sweet and a good friend in her way but she was a farm girl and Clare ... Clare wasn't. Nothing but a childhood in common connected their lives — to believe anything else was ridiculous. 'I'm joking, really. I'm going to be happy and so are you. Okay?'

Alice said 'Okay'. She gripped Clare's hands and said 'Okay' again.

Later that evening, Raul disappeared into the Earl's study while in the exquisitely panelled sitting-room that smelled of old boots and stagnant flowers the Countess, her thin shanks pummelled by the flanks of passing labradors, dispensed dry sherry to the Curtis-Whites who had come over from the New Hall a mile away across the fields. Tom Curtis-White, recently retired as Chairman of UK-Oil, had bought the near-derelict mansion four years ago and his restoration of it had caused his La Fontaine neighbours severe bouts of envy, so that Mamaine had avoided them whenever possible. They were, she often said, a dull couple of no conceivable consequence who would not rest until they had turned that lovely house into something resembling a Trust House Forte. People like the Curtis-Whites, she often said, did not know when to stop. Direly she predicted flock wallpaper in the flagstoned hall, rumpus rooms with wall-to-wall carpets, avocado bathroom suites and double glazing on the Georgian windows. Double-glazing, in her view, lay at the root of all that was currently wrong with England. Today, however, she surprised and delighted her neighbours by the warmth of her welcome and the vivacity of her conversation. Privately, Janet Curtis-White thought it rather unfortunate that Lady Mamaine's ebullience simply emphasized the dullness of Lady Clare who, though pretty enough, had clearly inherited no part of her mother's charm.

As the couple were saying their effusive farewells, the Earl came in holding the arm of a tall dark foreign-looking gentleman. Lord La Fontaine exuded cheer, his eyes blinked rapidly within their pouches as he looked around. The foreign-looking gentleman pushed rather rudely past Janet Curtis-White and made straight for Lady Clare. He put a hand on her waist and she smiled at the room. The Earl then informed the assembled company that he would like them to meet Don Raul de Toro y Plata, President of Ventura and his future son-in-law.

'Sir. Congratulations.' Tom Curtis-White gripped Raul's hand and pumped it up and down. 'Amazing, Ventura, an amazing place.'

Fondly, Mamaine said, 'It is Clare's decision. I have told her that Ventura may not bear much resemblance to Lincolnshire ...' she laughed wispily and the Curtis-Whites laughed too, '... but she will have it. A headstrong girl. Well, love conquers all, isn't that what they say?'

'That's what they say,' said Janet Curtis-White and bent to pat a dog, spilling the last of her sherry.

When the Curtis-Whites had been waved off, scattering the gravel untidily under the wheels of their Mercedes, Mamaine turned to Clare as they stood in the doorway and embraced her tenderly. Tenderly she drew the sign of the cross on Clare's forehead.

'Dear child,' she murmured, 'how we shall miss you.' She ran a hand down the flaking paint of a pillar, her cheeks wet with tears.

[3]

Three months later Raul flew back from Ventura where he had gone immediately after the engagement was formally announced and he and Clare were married at the Tucolston Church of Our Lady. The bride, ravishing in a cascade of Honiton lace thought as she knelt beside the bridegroom at the altar, I am now doing the worst thing I have ever done in my life but the money will help. The reception was held in the Tudor magnificence of nearby Burghley House – the walls of Tucolston having already been invaded by men in scaffold cages – and attended by five hundred guests. of whom the most distinguished were Prince Charles and his grandmother.

Once the wedding was over Clare determined to take each day as it came and enjoy whatever was sent her way to enjoy. She had travelled little hitherto, a school trip to Paris, a weekend in Rome at a cousin's wedding, and she looked forward to spending ten days in Egypt (Raul was impatient to return to Ventura with his bride) less from a desire to see foreign parts than for the luxury she supposed would be attendant on the visit. In this, she was not disappointed. The champagne and cosseting of the first-class flight to Cairo put her in a mellow mood and her first sight of the Mena House Hotel outside the city, with its neatly clipped well-watered lawns and flowering shrubs. pleased her mightily. The buildings were a wholly reassuring combination of the modern, with its hygiene and reliable plumbing, and the romantic – the hotel's situation at the foot of the Giza pyramids made immediately available to its clientele the ethnic backdrop it had paid for without any forfeiture of comfort.

The honeymoon suite lived up to the same criteria, indigenous pierced screens and shutters were tactfully Arabic without in any way detracting from Western efficiency and though the large double bed with its carved headboard, snowy pillows and adjoining – rather too closely adjoining – bathroom moment-arily lowered her spirits. the sumptuous public rooms cheered her. At least there she could rely on an appreciative audience for her new wardrobe.

Raul's continuing circumspection also cheered her. His sexual restraint during his courtship of her had contrasted oddly with his jealous possessiveness of her attentions and she had imagined, shuddering, that the marriage vows would instantly transform him into a slavering wolf. Thankfully, there were no signs yet. On their arrival at the hotel before lunch, he left Clare in sole possession of the suite so that she could unpack and change in privacy and suggested, with a proper concern for his bride's welfare. that they spend the rest of the day relaxing by the pool and dine at their leisure in the hotel's restaurant

'The pyramids ' he said, 'have waited three thousand years so that they may see you. They will wait another day.'

Clare thought that elegantly put. Admittedly, the sight of his almost naked body at the pool reminded her uneasily of what lay in store that night but there were compensations. Though his flesh was surprisingly white for a man who lived under a strong sun and the hair that curled down his arms and arrowed from his flat lower stomach to the bulge at his groin seemed rather tastelessly black in contrast (her eyes flickered away from the bulge), his appearance by the bright blue water occasioned enough admiring glances from other females to provide her with a mild fillip and Clare herself was happy enough with the male heads that turned as she passed in her silvery bikini. It was evident that to others they were an enviable couple and Clare stretched on the padded chair beside her husband with a sigh of satisfaction. He reached out for her hand and she surrendered it willingly, gratified by the softness beneath her back, the hot sun on her body and the fetching clink of ice in the cool long drink that stood on the table beside her. She was at last inhabiting that sensual paradise promised since childhood in a thousand television commercials.

They left the dance floor at midnight. She consoled herself as the lift rose and Raul's hand on her elbow grew firmer. Men were only men, after all, and sex was only sex, not so bad and little enough sacrifice for the life of luxury that lay ahead. To her surprise, she even felt a mild flutter of anticipation when Raul turned at the door of the suite, lifted her in his arms and swung her across the threshold, a rare smile upon his face. Freddie, she remembered, had been pretty useless as a lover, with his sour whisky'd breath and his headlong puppy-dog rush to ejaculation and the half-dozen other men with whom she had briefly shared a bed had left no other traces on her memory than an impression of clumsy weight and a fairly repellent stickiness between her legs in the morning.

Raul, pushing the door shut behind him with a shoulder, set her gently on her feet and gently put his arms around her as he had done at other times, holding her as if he were a Sotheby assessor and she a valuable Sèvres shepherdess. This time his lips, which had lingered only lightly before, sank around hers and took much deeper draughts and his tongue moved confidently into the soft membranes of her mouth. A sharp excitement, all the sharper for being unexpected, made her push him away and he let her go easily, stroking her hair. Flushed, with a little parting smile, she went into the bathroom and closed the door. To the mirror she smiled again, fascinated by the glow in her eyes. She made a sweet wet rosebud of her mouth and, seeing it, felt quite aroused. At the age of ten, standing in front of another mirror at school, combing her hair, a girl had stopped and stared at Clare's image and said abruptly, 'You are pretty, Clare,' and hearing that, gaping in wonder at the glass, her familiar features had shifted before her and made for the first time a delightful whole that meant something beyond their separate parts, like the angular limbs of letters at the moment they came together to form a word. 'I am,' she had said, surprised by vanity. 'I am pretty.' Now that she knew she was much more than pretty the fact did not overly interest her except when it came to sex. Then, the knowledge became crucial. What enjoyment she got depended on that cameo portrait of herself glimmering in the eyes of the man who looked down at her. It was his face that reflected her own perfection, his desire that fuelled her own. She laid herself out as a rich pasture for his grazing and his lust gave her such lust for herself that her limbs grew most satisfactorily weak.

She slipped the honey lace of a new nightdress over her head and watched it fall to cup the tilt of her breasts. She whispered to the bride that hovered before her, 'God, you're lovely,' and then, clowning, repeated what Pa so often said, 'It'll be better than a slap in the belly with a wet fish.' Thus fortified, she left the bathroom to embrace her fate.

Raul, to her relief, was modestly clad in a wine silk dressing-gown. She had no prudish dislike of male bodies, it was simply that the ones of her acquaintance had seemed a peculiar combination of belligerence and comedy – such muscled expanses of chest and limb to frame such a curious centre sunk in its nest of abrasive hair, alive and unpredictable, like a creature in a burrow that might be endearingly tame when it emerged or might inflict nasty bites. He took her hand, drew it to his lips, bowed his sleek head and kissed each smooth pink nail.

'My lovely bride,' he murmured, 'my Madonna.'

He let her hand fall and went over to where his suitcase lay on a brass-studded chest. As Clare watched, he rummaged within and straightened up with a nod, holding something to his chest. He walked over to the bed and, leaning across the pillows, took down the framed print that hung over the headboard – the Sphinx reddened by a setting sun – and positioned in its stead

[53]

against the nail a large crucifix upon which a pallid Christ writhed in wooden agony, a wreath of ceramic thorns welded to his head.

Astonishment made Clare mute. He came to her again and led her to the bed. Obediently, she laid herself on the white sheets and looked up at him. Incomprehension gave her eyes the myopic cast of a Siamese cat.

'You must not be afraid, little one. I will be very gentle. So,' he said and 'so'. Delicately, he took her arms and folded them across her breasts. Clare's mind was empty, somewhere inside her a bubble of laughter rose and silently burst as her heart gave a disconcerting lurch. Beside her, the bedsprings lowered as he extended himself. There was a short silence broken by small rustling sounds – was he undoing his pyjama cords? But no, he had no pyjamas on. Then Clare's contemplation of the ceiling ended. He swung over her and laid his hands along her temples. His face, very close to hers, was preoccupied; before she closed her eyes she saw that his were shut.

Minuscule dots danced against the light red of her eyelids. She was relieved that the moment had come. In Clare's experience, however botched the sexual act it broke barriers of awkwardness and inevitably some warmth, even friendship, ensued. She felt his hands moving her nightdress upwards so she put her arms round him and, accommodatingly, opened her legs. The gesture stilled him. Through her eyelashes she saw him look at her, a frown line between the fine hairs on his brow. He moved again, settling himself between her thighs. A swift plunge and he was inside her. She flattened her hands on his back and thought my husband, this is my husband; pleased.

And then, abruptly he pulled away, rearing up from her.

'What is this?' His voice was loud in the quiet room. Taken very much aback, Clare shook her head. Her nightdress was up, he was staring, pawing the inside of her thighs. Embarrassed, she pulled her legs together.

'You are not a virgin.'

'No,' she said and added, as an afterthought, 'dear.'

'You are not a *virgin*.'

'Well,' she said helplessly, 'not entirely. I mean, Raul, after all, I wasn't *married* until now.'

He did not speak, his head was arched back and his face was out of her sight. Clare pushed herself up on her elbows and, for the first time without his coaxing, kissed her husband on the tip of his chin. He jerked away as if he had been stung and rolled off her to the edge of the bed, where he sat with his head bowed. Bewildered, she reached across and tentatively touched his back.

'Raul? I didn't ... it isn't ...' She hardly knew what to say. It seemed ridiculous to apologize for something she wasn't in the least sorry about. Did anyone think it was wrong nowadays, except nuns and their ilk? Even Ma accepted it, though Clare's sex life was never discussed between them, naturally not. But of course Raul was a foreigner and foreigners obviously felt differently about such things. She sighed, swung her legs round and crawled across the bed to lean lightly against him. With some concern, she gave his back a little pat.

At that, he stood up, put on his dressing-gown, unhooked the crucifix from the wall and carried it back to his suitcase. An unaccustomed tightness constricted Clare's chest, though whether of anger or surprise she could not yet discern. Then Raul wheeled round, took two strides to the foot of the bed and spat at her. The gob of spittle struck her hip.

'Puta.' Raul's face was distorted, his lips were white and flat against his white teeth. 'Whore.'

Clare watched the spittle slide down her thigh to the bed and a convulsion of rage took hold of her, lifting her to her feet. Her cheeks burned. 'How dare you,' she howled, 'how bloody dare you.' Moisture blurred her vision, she saw his figure red and in fragments, bulky in the shadowy room.

'Whore,' he hissed.

Without thought, she swung her arm back and hit him with all her force. He grunted and grabbed her arm, twisting it behind her so that she jack-knifed with pain, pain that made her gasp aloud. Raul took hold of the back of her nightdress and ripped it away from her body. Clare cried out. He knocked her sideways then and she fell against the bed's frame and on to her knees. The fire in her scraped shin drove everything else from her mind, on all fours she crouched and stared at the carpet, dug her fingers into the pile. Her ears pounded. As the pain in her shin subsided, she began to tremble. I want to kill him, she thought, I want to kill him. She saw the knife plunging into the white flesh of his chest, straight into his pumping heart. Yet she knelt and stared at the carpet, trembling. The room grew quiet.

Eventually. she got shakily to her feet and, clutching her torn nightdress to her, began to move towards the bathroom. Raul stood before her. She stepped sideways and tried to go on but he reached out and took her chin. His face was awful, quite grey. the upper lip drawn paper thin, all the skin stretched so that the cheekbones were pinched into a ridge. He was smiling.

This time, dragging her back to the bed, he was not gentle. Clare found no refuge from his attacks upon her, she cried out and his hand clenched her jaw, she beat at him and he pinioned her fists, she kicked wildly and he clamped her knees between his thighs, she crawled away and he pulled her back. His smile, which never wavered, left her aghast. Exhausted, she fell back at last and, holding her shoulders down, lividly smiling, Raul assaulted his bride.

Afterwards Clare slept, tears making white tracks down her sun-pinkened cheeks. She woke once in the night to find his arm across her as heavy as a pillar of marble and she lay listening as he breathed beside her. It was incomprehensible that she should be in this dark room in the country of Egypt lying in a strange bed alongside a sleeping stranger who could call her his wife and hurt her. She was an exile from the world she knew and from herself as well, from her own familiar body. This flesh had betrayed her. In the violence of the night, brutally breeched, it had surrendered and opened and shamefully forced excitement on her. Unforgivable. Remembering, her gorge rose and she gave a short dry sob. That at least, she promised herself, clenching her fists under the sheets, would not be allowed to happen again.

In the morning, disinfected by the hot beams of the desert sun, the room looked ordinary and unalarming, a room among other rooms. Raul, already up and sitting by the window, was as he had always been, attentive and distant. Framed in glass, the Giza pyramids rose from the scrubby sands in majestic indifference. Camels, lugubrious and resigned, were already moving off with their burden of tourists. Barefoot boys in tattered pyjamas scampered beside them, shrieking their wares at the faces perched up above. The bones between Clare's legs were dreadfully sore and her shoulders throbbed but a curious indifference had taken the place of her anger. How many women had been raped in this place, in this city, in this country? The very thought tired her. Raul, seeing her stir, raised his voice and read to her from a guidebook.

'The Great Pyramid of Cheops, four thousand years old, was built of over 2,500,000 enormous blocks of limestone cut from the Moqattam. It has a height of 137.2 metres and a volume of 2,550,000 cubic metres.'

Suddenly, Clare felt extremely hungry.

Raul was indefatigable in his explorations of Cairo and of Clare. He walked everywhere because, he said, you cannot get to know a city from a car. He showed no sign of fatigue and in the great heat of the mid-day sun he did not sweat. Day after day, he ushered his wife through the cool precincts of mosques, along the narrow cobbled streets of the Islamic quarter and past the packed and dusty shelves in hall after hall of the great Egyptian Museum. The din of the streets, the shriek of over-stressed brakes and the hooting of angry horns, surged around them. Clare stared into the faces of the shawled women as they shuffled past and they stared back and sometimes followed her for a while, drawn, perhaps, by the bright beacon of her hair. She could not tell if they were hostile; when she looked too long they would catch an edge of scarf in their teeth and turn away. In the bustle of the bazaar the men and boys stopped work as she wandered by and grinned and gave guttural exclamations and patted their crotches. Raul remained impassive, his face as expressionless and aloof as any museum pharaoh. He dispensed information but, otherwise, was silent.

At night, in the hotel bedroom, he was also silent, but methodical. As Clare undressed, he folded her clothes neatly on a chair before taking her against a wall or bent across the bed or spreadeagled on the moroccan-leather table. Unimpeded by any further illusions as to his bride's innocence or maidenly modesty, he spared her very little and his onslaughts were bruising. Warmth and tenderness were not on offer and Clare was given no option but to accede to his demands. His violence aroused and sickened her in equal measure, so that the two emotions quickly became inextricably tangled. Afterwards, they did not talk or look at each other and the following day Clare ransacked the shops for rings and jewels and elaborately embroidered caftans. She refused to bargain and Raul did not demur, counting out note after note without looking at the roll, his narrow eyes upon her.

On the tenth day they returned to London and on the eleventh Louise Lawson joined them in that area of Heathrow reserved for private aircraft. Clare had not expected this favour to be granted but her husband, accustomed to chaperonage, had made no objection, greeting Louise courteously. The two girls fell upon each other, Clare ravenous for chat and a dilution of

Raul's presence, Louise hungry for the more general excitement of the Presidential Gulfstream jet and an unknown destination, though she did her best to remain cool, as befitted her image. Together, they flew to Ventura.

[4]

In Ventura they say that the man who spits out a pip on his way at dawn will not find his path again at dusk. Trapped under a glassy sky, the forest sweats in endless and gargantuan labour to bring forth monstrosities. The house plants familiar to Clare at Tucolston, perched in decorous clumps on window-ledges and watered erratically by her mother, were here pumped to elephantine proportions, swollen travesties of their English selves, their vast spread the sunless domain of shrieking parrots and hysterical flea-ridden monkeys. At Tucolston she had pinned four white orchids on a white organza dress for her Coming Out ball, a rare corsage whose cost had sent her beleaguered father into a rare rage. In Ventura, countless species of orchids, splotched and streaked and spotted in all the colours of the rainbow, frothed and fell from every branch and stem and there were many more in the forest depths unknown to botanists.

With Louise closely behind her, Clare descended the stairs from the plane into a maelstrom of noise and clammy heat. As she reached the tarmac, clutching Raul's arm, a band struck up, its brass as bright under the brilliant sun as the gold flags that hung motionless in the airless afternoon. 'Wave,' Raul whispered as he stretched his own arms high in salutation to the crowd and she waved, standing unsteadily on the molten asphalt that sucked at her heels. Anxiously, with her other hand, she guarded the limp folds of her skirt for fear that even in this windless place an embarrassing incident might occur. Louise, nearby, made tiny gobbling sounds in her throat to keep herself calm and underwhelmed. If she began to see all this as anything other than a comic episode she might have to alter her view of Clare and that would never do.

Smoothly, Raul moved both women through the official introductions – even the Airport Manager, Louise thought, was dressed up like a Victorian four-poster, all ruffles and tassels – and past the sweating faces of people who pressed inwards upon them rattling incomprehensible words of welcome to the eventual reward of an air-conditioned limousine that drew smoothly away towards Nombre Dios, the capital. In the car, Clare was silent, stunned by events. Louise exchanged politenesses with Raul. They drove along the only all-weather road that Ventura possessed and Clare, used to London's broad thoroughfares, saw with a little jolt of fright what a narrow beachhead it was against the high green sea of the forest that heaved on either side, its predatory fringe of thick and dripping leaves poised to suck intrusive humans into its dark maw. She could hear the soft scrape of vegetation on the roof over her head and see spiked green fingers at the window. She remembered with trepidation Pa telling her of Colonel Percy Fawcett who had vanished without trace into this same forest some sixty years ago. 'Eaten, I expect,' Pa had said, smacking his lips. Were the colonel's bleached bones, Clare wondered, lying somewhere near by, turned not to coral in those fathoms but brightest emerald green?

'What were those men in uniform carrying?' Louise asked Raul. 'Those funny sticks like long torches, do you know what I mean?'

'In English you call them cattle prods, I think,' Raul said.

'Oh,' said Louise. 'I shouldn't have thought this was cattle country, should you, Clare?'

Clare shook her head. Both women looked enquiringly at Raul. He tapped on the window and waved the driver impatiently on.

In Nombre Dios, at the Palace, the reception went on. Clare's outstretched hand was raised to a hundred lips and a hundred brilliantined male heads, pungent with perfume, bowed in homage. But she also glimpsed what lay in these male eyes, watched with increasing interest as time after time the unfocused official gaze narrowed to the pinpoint gleam of arousal as she smiled. Slowly, with little inner sweeps of satisfaction, she understood that these dignitaries of Ventura had awaited a woman quite other than herself, a demure and modestly pretty spouse to their ruler, a healthy receptacle for his seed, and were each and every one flummoxed by her, their masculine pomp visibly undermined.

Clare had long been aware of her assets, they were catalogued in her mind as dispassionately as the various lots of an auctioneer and she knew exactly how and in what way to display them, lit now and again by judicious beams of sexuality. At home she had used these assets with restraint, if at all, knowing that her physical beauty alone was as much as the market would bear without the additional strain of voluptuous movements or any other expression of sexuality. That too easily tipped over into caricature or aroused the antagonism of the observer. In England, the young men she knew found overt sexual messages not merely embarrassing but laughable, lapses from taste to be savoured in their pantheon of unreal women – actresses, models, dancers, tarts of one sort or another – but ridiculous in their female peers unless strictly confined to the bedchamber and even then, always a hair's breadth from a hoot. Sympathising with this view herself, Clare had carefully exercised the necessary caution. But here in Ventura it quickly became evident that there was no such ambivalence. These men who greeted her, blazing with gold braid, buckled into sharkskin, plumed and gloved and belted to absurdity, were so much tinder. She had only to flutter her lashes and they flared on either side as she passed. Their obvious combustibility heartened her. The power she had never felt free to use in England for fear of unpleasant repercussions was available here without incurring the slightest risk. As she progressed through those first days she grew hourly more delighted and more cunning, aiming her shafts so discreetly at a designated male that he was hit, as it were, out of the blue and could not lay his wounds at her door. She played the innocent for no more reason than that it pleased her and was easily done, a game of no significance that passed the time. Raul watched the stir that his wife's phenomenal silvery beauty created and thought that only he, of all that company, knew the taint, the corruption that beauty hid and saw the game she played for what it was. This knowledge he locked away in his mind, to be used when he saw fit. and in the meantime, his hand always at Clare's elbow, he played out his role as the proud groom.

Clare met the women, too, the wives and daughters of the grandees of Ventura, shy sloe-eyed girls who bobbed nervously in her wake and big-breasted matrons who sailed at her like funeral barges decked in black lace. At these women Clare smiled very sweetly and directly, confiding her hand to them with warmth. Women had always been her refuge and would be all the more important to her in this strange place. Men were her audience and their applause was delicious. For them she deployed her charms as artfully as she knew how – the sinuous sway of hips, the subtle jut of buttocks, the pout of moist lips, a pretty flurry of hair. But her own sex, she knew, had the name of this game and would be quick to ostracize her unless countermeasures were taken. Beauty was a two-edged sword, it wounded others and also its possessor, it had to be handled with consummate skill if it was to cut down men without cutting off women. She had learned that early.

'Today we shall start rehearsing *Tobias and the Angel*,' Miss Sutherland her English teacher had said, walking up and down between the desks. Clare was twelve and sat at the back of the room where she could best avoid censure for her frequent and uncontrollable fits of giggles. She was giggling as Miss Sutherland halted beside her. 'And Clare, if she can stop making that dreadful noise for long enough, shall play the Angel.'

At this pronouncement, the classroom became quiet. Clare, still flushed and shaking, looked at her best friend Louise sitting beside her and saw the laughter drain from her eyes and looked at all the other girls' faces turned towards her and saw a wall slide silently between them and she was outside, left alone. After the class she took Louise's hand but Louise fiddled with a plait and turned to talk to another girl. At lunch, Louise sat between other friends and didn't keep her a place. No one kept her a place and she had to sit wedged miserably in with younger girls from a different form and House. In the evening, lost and lonely, she tracked Louise down.

'I don't want to be the Angel,' she said, 'you be the Angel, I'll ask Miss Sutherland. Would you like some of my cake?'

'The Angel?' Louise said and gazed out of the window. 'Who cares about the Angel, silly.'

'But I thought ... I thought that was why. Louise? Isn't that why?'

Louise whisked round. '*Everyone* thinks you're big-headed. Pushy thing, you. Show-off.'

Clare stepped back from the heat of Louise and her friend whizzed off like a firework, banging the door. After that, for a week that seemed to last for years, Louise and the other girls made her invisible, they wouldn't talk, they wouldn't look at her and her insides ached all that time. She dwindled.

On the following Monday Miss Sutherland again presided over her weekly class. She saw Clare huddled at the back of the room behind her desk, which had become a wooden island cut off from Louise's desk and that of the girl on the other side. After a few introductory remarks, she walked down the aisle and halted by that isolated desk. The child smelt of honey, her hair curved in white hanks from her scalp like the hair on a Greek statue and the eyelids were fringed with gold. But when it came to the welfare of her beloved girls, Cynthia Sutherland, MA (Oxon), missed very little and so she also noted the blue shadows under the lowered eyes and the restless hands with their sorely bitten nails. Others might judge this child too fortunately endowed to require any sympathy but they would be wrong. Looks, as she knew better than most, guaranteed nothing, one way or the other. Regarding the descending expanse of her own sandbag body, catching a glimpse of her own thick legs and large flat feet, Miss Sutherland thought that she and Clare represented, at this moment, two extremes. Herself irretrievably plain but happy, the girl lovely but quite wretched. Inspired by that happiness she guessed at the cause of wretchedness. She coughed and addressed her class.

'Girls,' she said, 'I have changed my mind. I shall not have Clare as my Angel after all. Her face is unsuitable, her height not sufficiently commanding and her carriage leaves much to be desired. Don't take it too personally, my dear.'

Clare looked up and Miss Sutherland looked down without expression except for one eye that solemnly closed and opened again as the girls began to chatter with excitement. When the bell rang at the end of the hour, Louise bumped into Clare in the aisle.

'We're playing Monopoly in the dorm tonight. If you want to come, bring your cake.' She ran ahead and the fallen Angel flew beside her.

Late that night, rising from the clutter of paper notes and wooden houses, Clare and Louise and the other two girls tumbled squeaking and squabbling on to Clare's bed. There, buried, hardly able to breathe, smothered by the weight of pummelling limbs and choking hair, Clare succumbed to such a surge of delight in the comfort and closeness of the heavy friendly bodies as she had never felt before and was not to feel for years again.

Clare had never forgotten that lesson. Necessary as men were, addicted as she was to their praise and admiration, their sheer predictability, the thought of their company alone made her shiver. She craved the easy companionship and laughter of her own sex and knew that to ensure it she had to send herself up, decry her sexual assets to them as discreetly as she directed them at men. The throw-away shrug, the barely perceptible lift of an eyebrow, the quick roll of eyes to the heavens above, these were sufficient. Women quickly decoded that ancient female sema-phore which lulled envy and diverted hostility, the semaphore that said 'what else can a poor woman do, sisters, to make her way in a man's world?'

'Whew,' Clare sighed. It had been an evening of yet more handshakes and polite monosyllabic conversations, this time with the bemedalled brass of Raul's private army. Raul had wished the two women goodnight and left them at the door of Clare's sitting-room. She turned her back to Louise.

'Undo my zip, there's a darling. If I don't breathe soon, I'll pop.'

Louise groped at the tab hidden within folds of silk and the dress fell away. Clare moved herself from it and stood naked, except for the triangle of lace at her hips.

'Which is the real you?' said Louise, looking at the length of ivory on the carpet. 'That or . . . ?' She nodded with her chin at Clare.

Clare began jogging energetically. 'How can you ask?' she said. She dived at the dress and held it up, limp as a parachute. 'Look at it. A costume. Stupid.'

Louise smoothed her hands over her stiff beaded bosom. 'D'you like mine?' she asked.

'Bliss,' Clare said and poked hard at Louise's front. 'Is *that* the real you?'

Louise squawked crossly. 'Yes,' she said, 'mostly. What about *this*?' She tugged at Clare's dress, holding out the bodice. Tiny velvet-covered ridges were curved in rows under the silk cups. 'What are these for, Madam?'

Clare grinned and shrugged. 'We're both the same,' she said. 'We are ridiculous.'

'Speak for yourself,' said Louise. 'I bought my dress, that's the way they come, I can't help it. You had yours made, didn't you? Didn't you?'

'Ooh.' Clare knotted her hands together and stretched, yawning. 'Women. Look at us. We're clowns. All gluey faces and bits sticking in and out and silly walks. Thank goodness we can take it all off when we're together and be ourselves.'

'I'm always myself,' Louise said, twisting her neck. 'You're the one. Prink prink prink, whenever there's a man in sight.' She arched her back, stuck out her breasts and, pouting, minced across the room.

Clare ran at her, grasping an arm. 'I don't *do* that,' she wailed. 'I can't help men looking at me.'

Louise turned on her, sucking in her cheeks, wrinkling her nose. 'And they don't at me, is that what you mean? Huh. No wonder.' Her eyes fizzed. 'Hey, look at this,' she said in a baby voice, bouncing her beaded bosom at Clare. 'That's what *you* do.'

Half laughing, half protesting, Clare put out her arms. 'No,' she said, shaking her head. 'I don't, Louise, I don't.'

They swayed, close together, Clare hugging Louise. 'Okay,' Louise said maternally. 'I believe you, thousands wouldn't.' She patted Clare's hair.

At that moment the door opened. Both women turned abruptly. Raul stood in the doorway, looking slowly from his wife's face along her naked body. 'A thousand pardons,' he said, 'I am interrupting.' Behind him, the door closed with a sharp click.

'I have this feeling that I've overstayed my welcome.' Louise was staring at the door.

'No,' Clare said loudly. 'No.'

Louise departed the next day.

Soon, Clare had won the hearts of all the men and women who counted in Ventura. She was entertained well enough for some weeks by the admiration with which she was surrounded until the receptions in her honour began to repeat themselves. Already she was meeting the same people in the same places. It dawned on her then that though she might be Big Lady Frog, the puddle she inhabited was exceedingly small. Nombre Dios, the only town, had two main streets, one main square and a few thousand residents, most of whom were either stashed away in the corrugated iron and wooden boxes that honeycombed the encircling hills or eked out a living on the rafts roofed with palm leaves and sacking that were moored along the banks of the Amazon that ran along the southern boundary of the capital. These people were the anonymous poor and their faces watched unsmilingly as Clare passed by in the black Mercedes Raul had put at her disposal. On her way to a party in her honour given by Don Roberto Montalva, Raul's distant relative and trusted adviser, Clare saw through the window tinted against the sun her own face reproduced on a poster. Below it, in capital letters was written 'Bienvenida a Nuestra Dorada.'

'Welcome to our Golden Lady,' Clare translated from her minimal Spanish and giggled in the cool car. 'Honestly, Raul . . .' – he was beside her, staring ahead – '. . . isn't that rather over the top?'

His eyes were so narrow that sometimes she could not make out whether he was looking at her or keeping them closed in disdain or boredom or fatigue. 'Over the top?' he repeated slowly.

'Never mind.'

She looked out again and saw her own face pasted against the ochre-washed surface of another wall. This time women were clustered around it, talking and laughing. They wore battered straw hats on their dark hair and bundles hung from their shoulders. some knobbly with corn cobs, some round with babies whose slit Chinese eyes peeped above the sacking rims. As Clare watched, one of the women, her bare feet planted squarely on the flattened dirt of the road, heaved up a toddler and held it. grubby legs kicking, level with her likeness. The child's mouth opened wide, its face scrunched into a whorl of protest, its feet pedalled frantically. The women began to laugh, their arms doubled over their stomachs, their high cheeks creased with mirth. Clare saw the chauffeur ahead of her glance sideways at the women and saw below his grey peaked hat the high ridge of his cheekbone rise before he looked away. She straightened the white silk of her skirt over her knees.

'This street is filthy. Raul,' she said, her voice unusually sharp.

But soon enough the men and women of the town, sprawled on the kerbs, shouting from their stalls heaped with orange peppers, mangos and papaya, or squatting in the dirt outside their shacks, became no more than a backdrop to her excursions, screened on glass like figures in some ethnic documentary that could quickly be switched to another channel in her mind. When the facilities of Ventura's top citizens – those twenty or so families who owed their positions to Raul's protection and the small American business community – had been exhausted, Clare turned her attention to the rural parts of her husband's fiefdom. She spent every day of one week clambering in and out of the Presidential helicopter that took off from the strip behind the Palace and flew her over monotonous stretches of broccoli-headed forest to drop into identical dust patches where, already limp with heat, her white dress fast becoming grubby, Clare would stumble out on her high heels, shake the leathery hands of a few astonished old village men – the women remained shadows in the dark interiors of their huts – and re-embark with ever-increasing relief for the cool comfort of what she now supposed was home. At first, she asked questions of Raul or of the dour, interchangeable bodyguards he assigned to accompany her but the names of things were mostly untranslatable and when she tried to find out what she really wanted to know – who are these people, what do they do, what are they *like*? – the answers were either vague ('They are Indians, they are mestizos, they work the land') or too specific, full of dreadful words like 'cash crops', 'alluvial soil' and 'shifting cultivation' that made her feel she was back at school. Her energy was additionally sapped by a clammy heat that was like drowning in a vat of simmering cream. She did not visit the tin town that hung like a giant wasp's nest over Nombre Dios. Raul explained that there were no roads up there and that it was a hive of thieves and parasites who would not work but preferred to sponge upon the honest citizens below. Clare did not insist, the wind that blew from there over the town carried a malodorous burden.

On the last day of these trips she flew with Raul to a village at the very heart of the forest. Sitting in the helicopter's belly she thought how much happier she would be if she could pass all her time skidding and hovering in the skies above Ventura – it was blessedly cool up here churning through the blue and, oh, the relief of spiralling upwards from the stuffy confines of Nombre Dios to where there were far horizons and air and space and none of the human squalor of the town. Below her the forest lay like a great green shaggy beast with the brown river winding under its limbs and she stared down at its immensity, wishing never to land. They landed soon enough though – no journey took long in tiny Ventura – but when the roar and the grit had subsided, no one appeared from the straggle of huts to see what the skies had dropped in their midst. This village was desolate indeed, perhaps deserted, its inhabitants scattered into the trees that closed about the small clearing to hunt for food and a more hospitable place to set up their palm-thatched houses. The roofs of the huts here were gouged in as if by a giant fist, though two skinny dogs came barking at them, baring yellow teeth. Raul scooped up stones from the rocky ground and threw them and the dogs fled, yelping. Then he strode towards the huts with his guard and on an impulse Clare walked quickly away from the men, veering to where the forest reared up along her path, that mysterious forest that covered all of Ventura except for the rent in its seamless green that was Nombre Dios and into which she had never yet ventured. The forest was the country, perhaps within its reaches she would discover the spirit, the essence of the place. Bending under the low branches, trampling through a high net of undergrowth, she came into a space where the light fell away and found herself a Jonah swallowed into the belly of a living whale. The leafy rib-cage arched far above her head and from every side came the soupy sounds of mastication, the grumbling, sucking, squelching noises of an over-burdened gut with, here and there in the half-light, whistles and clicks and sibilant whispers and sudden loud whir-rings of wings. As she stood astounded in the watery gloom a frog slapped against her leg and tumbled to the ground. Stepping back, she saw a snake coiled along dead leaves and froze in fear and saw that it was a snake's skin given monstrous life by a squirming rope of maggots. The forest floor beneath her teemed with insects, an endless carpet of them crept and scuttled and rustled interminably; there was nowhere to set her foot that was free of them or where they would not swarm in a moment from the leaves under her feet to cover her feet and lap upwards in black waves until they engulfed her completely and she was a crawling mass in the shape of a woman. The thought made her gasp, the air, thick with decay, plugged her nostrils and some-where back in the steaming darkness a howling began, hollow and hideously sad, the lamentation of a soul in hell. Aghast

Clare whirled. Something flew into her hair with a dry buzz. Clapping her hands to her head, she crashed through the hammock of vines, stumbling and tripping until she could see the sun again and scrambled out to where Raul was calling her name.

She clung to him for a moment before he held her away, frowning at her dishevelment.

'Oh Raul,' she panted, 'in there . . . a terrible sound . . . someone howling . . . what is it?'

'Monkeys,' he said. 'I've been waiting for you. Come.'

She followed him, brushing at her clothes, combing her hair smooth with her fingers. The hem of her dress was damp. He led her behind the huts to where a line of men stood, short stocky men from the forest who wore orange loincloths and were as brown as tea. Nervously she approached them and they stared impassively ahead, their broad faces blank under schoolgirl bobs. On Raul's instructions she passed in front of each man, trying to smile as each of them, upon a guttural command, extended arms braceleted with beads to touch her hand. A stone lodged itself under her ribs. Those dark eyes that looked past hers to the forest were the eyes of prisoners forced into an officious charade, patient, waiting for release. She had never felt so remote from any human beings. They were divided – she and these Indian men – by every barrier that could divide human beings: race, sex, colour, language, customs, beliefs, wealth, authority, even mutual need, even time itself. Clare was chilled by that distance, it stayed with her as she climbed back into the chopper and turned her face to the window. As they took off she saw the brown men running for the forest. Not one paused to look up and see her go.

Early one morning after these visits had ended, she tied a cotton scarf over her telltale hair and slipped out of the Palace grounds through the gap left by a broken railing. She made her way along the unfrequented lanes that ran at the back of the big houses near the Palace and came eventually to the river's edge some distance from the harbour's crowded banks. The river seemed to swallow what light there was, its wide flat surface was colourless, it lay in loops like a dead serpent. On the far bank huge branches hung over the water and were not reflected. Where the river bent beyond her she could just see the blunt nose of a long barge swaying gently at anchor. There were no signs of a crew but she could hear the faint tinny music of a transistor; the Beatles. She loves me yeah yeah yeah, she loves me yeah yeah yeah. She stood there listening and thought that she could stow away on that barge and be carried down the river's coils under the swooping parrots and the chattering yellow-bellied monkeys to where at Belem on the coast the river opened in a belch of cool salt air to the sea and the sea moved on to England. Thinking of the friends she had left behind and the easy words of her mother tongue, the cool English rain, the diffident English sun and frivolous English laughter, she knelt beside the river and took her scarf off and wept into it for a while.

Then, scrubbing her wet face dry, she got up to go back to the Palace and saw that the barge was gone and where it had been a young boy stood naked in the water, his head bent, holding a spear in his hand. He stood without moving, his narrow hips aslant, and looked as if he had been standing there with the river at his flanks since its waters first rose at the beginning of the world. Clare watched him for a long time and the pain inside her eased.

[5]

When Clare had seen what was to be seen in Ventura and failed to draw any comfort from Raul for her homesickness and increasing boredom – he was offended at her feelings, they were an affront to him and to his country – it occurred to her that if this was where she must stay, she could at least feather her alien nest. The de Toro Palace, its two arms and central stretch embracing a wide cobbled rectangle off the main square of Nombre Dios, was as Raul had described, a scaled-down version of that Petit Trianon seen by his grandfather on a youthful visit to the Sun King's residence and it had many of the outward charms of that building. It was low and long, its walls were flushed with the pink marble imported from Carrara, its cool stone floors were of white tiles inset with panelled hexagons of black. But within, it had few comforts. The furniture throughout was heavy and ornate, the chairs high-backed and hard. In Raul's own suite of rooms the only resting places apart from his enormous four-poster bed were two narrow Napoleonic couches, tightly scrolled at either end and upholstered in a shiny brown leather that indignantly repulsed the human body. Clare's rooms were equally austere, unchanged since Raul's mother had died six years after his birth. Mahogany chests and armoires stood haphazardly about, the windows were framed in thick brown velvet and the bed, in a sole gesture to femininity. had a hideous padded velvet headboard and a stifling feather mattress out of which Clare had to fight her way each day, leaving behind her a damp outline of sweat. There was a bathroom off the bedroom, a hollow cavern of large white tiles containing a great eagle-footed bath, an uncompromising basin, huge taps like brass sentinels that were stiff and difficult to turn and coughed out, under protest, rusty gouts of water as if from lungs coated with nicotine. The corridors were long and bleak, hung with gloomy oil paintings of forgotten battles and lowering landscapes rent by storms, and the many formal rooms had a deserted air, like an unfrequented library or a museum closed for repair. Pleasure had no place there, there were no games, no badminton or billiard tables, no record-players or records, no piano, many frayed leather-bound books but nowhere comfortable to read them and no bright lights. Outside, in the gardens at the back, guarded by high walls, there were no tennis courts and – what Clare most longed for in the endless afternoons – no swimming pool.

'Living here is like being trapped in a tropical *Wuthering Heights*,' Clare told Raul irritably after a particularly tedious dinner party. She had been at least fifteen years younger than the youngest guest and reckoned that none of them had ever been young anyway. Raul's waxworks, she called them, and they did look waxy, like lilies at a funeral. How strange it was that they had been born under such a sun and yet were as pale as if they had lived underground all their lives, succulent trolls.

'Everything is as my mother left it,' Raul said. 'May her soul rest in peace.'

Several retorts rose to Clare's lips but she cut them off. Tact was necessary now if she wished to get what she wanted. 'She was a beautiful woman, your mother,' she said softly. It was nearly true. The painting that hung on the wall at one end of the largest of the two dining rooms showed an elegant woman of sombre countenance. Raul in drag, thought Clare, no wonder he thinks she's God's gift.

'She was a good woman, devoted to her family and her people. A faithful wife, a loving mother. A noble lady, a saint. Clare, that dress you are wearing, I find it immodest. You must take more care.'

Clare looked distractedly down at herself. The dress was sleeveless, it fell in gossamer folds to her ankles and rose to a cowl at her neck.

'Immodest? What do you mean?'

'I can see your legs. I can see your nipples.' His voice was harsh.

'Oh my goodness me,' said Clare, driven. 'What do you want me to wear in this bloody oven. Thermal undies?' She walked over and peered at herself in the muddy depths of an old gold-framed mirror. The image swam towards her, it wavered, she was a phantom mermaid in a haunted pool. She moved closer and flattened the thin fabric over her breasts. 'You can see nothing, Raul, you're imagining things.'

'Was Roberto Montalva imagining things? Was his wife? He could not take his eyes off your breasts this evening and Maria-Luisa suffered. She did not eat. You are wanton, Clare.'

Wanton? Clare tried to laugh at the ridiculous word but managed only a throaty gasp. Maria-Luisa was a nice woman, the nicest she had met, she had a warm laugh, spoke good English and treated Clare in a gentle, motherly way. Indignant and uneasy, Clare flared up.

'I don't know what you're talking about. It is ridiculous, the way your precious compañeros look at me. I feel suffocated.'

'That is not true, Clare. You like their eyes on you, I have watched you.' Raul moved over behind her and put his long fingers over her breasts. 'You flaunt yourself like a two-bit whore.' The Americanism sat weirdly within his guttural English.

Clare's throat closed. It couldn't be so. Oh, in those first weeks she had played with them a bit, those pompous men, with their moony eyes and quivering mostachos, but no longer. Now she was just herself, bored most of the time but polite. She had even made an attempt at dignity, holding herself very upright, never making jokes, trying earnestly to learn and understand their rapid Spanish. Yet Raul thought she was flaunting herself. She felt her head begin to throb.

Raul pressed his hands harder on her breasts, made scissors of his fingers and pinched her nipples between them. She flinched and moved away but he caught her arms and pulled her against him. 'Puta,' he whispered into her hair. 'Putita. You want other men, you would like other men to lie between your legs, many men have already had you, my little whore wife, but now I have you and I will have you whenever I like and however I like because that is what you are for.' His arms tightened across her back, hurting her, his voice became distant and drugged, as if he were talking in his sleep. With her face crushed against his chest, unable to move, she stood and heard above her a litany of abuse from her husband's lips for a female who bore her name, a female who obeyed his every command because she was shameless and insatiable and could not rest until each orifice was engorged with male flesh. It was grotesque. As her mouth began to tremble Clare tried to whistle but the old trick did not work. With a now familiar self-disgust she felt heat flicker along her thighs and a pulse begin to beat between her legs. It was a physical betrayal beyond her control, the treachery of a quisling body. Evidently Raul's disease was contagious and she too was sick. She drooped against him, grieving for something she had never known and was already lost beyond recovery. Raul's hand gripped her arm, he turned her round and moved her rapidly to the door.

He paid her, though. He usually paid her in one way or another for the use of her body, he seemed to want it so. Soon the Palace was under siege. A team of young men from England appeared in pale trousers and peacock shirts. Robin, the chief designer, stood in the entrance hall with Clare, looking around.

'Bliss outside, lady dear,' he said, 'but inside, well! The wreck of the *Hesperus*, really.'

'The *Titanic* before the iceberg?' Clare suggested.

'Just after, I think, don't you? But abide with me, Your Prettiness, rescue is at hand. The ferry man is here.' He tittered happily, rubbing his hands, looking with relish around him. 'Mind, it's a pity in many ways to dismantle all this. So macho. Frightfully erotic.' He saw Clare's face. '. . . to such as myself, of course, not to your sex, fair one. I get the feeling I'm very rare here. Amongst the rarest of all the rare birds, don't you think?'

'In my husband's house there are many closets,' Clare said and was surprised at the words that had popped out thoughtlessly. Robin laughed.

They all laughed a lot, one way or the other, it was like a carnival. The young men took over the dark silent rooms and corridors and filled them with life and noise. They stood with notebooks muttering at expanses of wall and window or sat with Clare poring over catalogues and swatches of fabric and drawings whose grandiose perspectives did not manage to make the huge halls look any larger than they were. Clare sang in the mornings, she floated about, the silliest jokes made by Brendan or Robin or Dave brought tears of laughter to her eyes. Raul did not interfere – his own rooms and offices were to remain untouched, out of bounds. He had greeted the designers courteously when they arrived, ordered his secretariat to issue them with identity cards – 'so exciting, my dear,' Robin had said, 'at last I know exactly who I am' – raised his eyebrows briefly at their curious attire and vanished. 'Count Dracula at sunrise,' said Robin and shuddered deliciously. Only once Raul came like a shadow into a room where Clare sat crumpled with laughter. Raising blurred eyes, she saw him. For a second he looked straight at her and his face was sad.

'I wish I could make you laugh like that,' he said in an undertone and went.

Three months later, when Clare's ships came in – four barges up the river from Belem loaded to the plimsoll lines with crates – half the town turned out to crowd the banks and the quay of the small harbour. The dock had no derricks, every crate had to be hauled off the decks of the barges and heaved on to waiting trucks by muscle power alone and over the ten days it took the river people swarmed in to tug and lift for scattered pesos. Barefoot children splashed and shrieked and swung on all the ropes that looped from ships to shore, cursed at by the sweating copper-backed men. Twice a carton packed with strange marvels slipped from its bonds and plunged into the water, to be winched up dripping with weeds as the people roared and pointed and the donkeys brayed in alarm.

At last, bereft of the young men, Clare gave a party when the work was finished, to cheer herself up. The great crystal chandeliers glittered on the gleaming floors and glowed over the long silky Persian carpets in faded raspberry colours. Everywhere there were sofas and day-beds and chaise-longues massed with huge embroidered cushions. On the walls, under the tapestries that had always been there, watered silk in the softest pastels, lilac, ivory, eau de nil, gave richness to the austere rectangular halls. The low lamps in one room shed pools of light on a billiard table and a full-size roulette wheel surrounded by stools and two gold embossed Chinese chest-on-chests were packed with the wherewithal for every kind of game from chess and back-gammon to spillikins. In another room, the music room, a grand piano was moved in from a remote corner of the Palace, one wall was stacked with shelves of records and cassettes, there was a built-in sound system and in the middle of the floor a large glass star was set that moved slowly round at the touch of a switch, the star shimmering through the colours of the rainbow. The place was transformed; only the guests, exclaiming as they wandered from one scene to another, were the same. Decorous and formal, the women always falling silent when the men talked, they offered Clare their compliments, waving about them at the various wonders, shaking their heads. In awe or disapproval? Clare, who had been happy as she gazed around her, waiting for her guests, stood sadly at midnight as they departed and a black shroud of depression settled over her. Two blue-jowled men smoking cigars, talking together an hour ago, looking around them, had said something in fast Spanish as she passed unseen behind them and laughed and made gestures with their fists. Something about the Palace, then the word burdel. Her Palace, a brothel? The words went round and round in her head like a tape that would not stop. Were they meant to go together? Was it possible they thought that of her lovely rooms?

'What pigs they are,' she said aloud, staring up at the bright sliver of moon.

Frowning, Raul said, 'You are drunk, Clare.'

'I wish I was,' she said and went to her bedroom, her new ivory satin bedroom where a new maid with a short sturdy body and muscled legs was laying out her nightdress and turning down the satin counterpane.

'Does it look like a brothel, this place?' she said to the maid in English. The woman turned, startled, and gave a little awkward bob. Clare went on, waving at the room. 'I think it looks lovely, cool and comfortable and welcoming. These Venturans are all closet queers, they kiss your hand and ogle you and hate you. They hate all women. We're either virgins or whores. There's nowhere in between to be human.'

The maid stepped back as Clare advanced on her.

'What is your name?' Clare asked in Spanish.

'Concepción, Señora, if it please you.' The woman had a husky voice with a coarse edge to it — by now Clare could distinguish such subtleties of accent. She laughed and, alarmed, the woman retreated again.

'Concepción. I love it. A good Venturan name if ever I heard one. That's the only thing women are allowed to do in this godforsaken place. Conceive.' Clare, wobbling a little, stuck her stomach out. 'How many children have you conceived, Concepción?'

The maid frowned anxiously. 'I have no children, Señora. I am not married.'

'Ah, *that's* how it's done,' Clare said. 'No marriage, no children. Neat, Concepción, so neat. Our Lord has organized things very well for women here.'

Concepción regarded her gravely. Clare giggled. Then the maid's face broke into a smile and she gave a snort of mirth. 'Eh, Señora, if it were only so.' Their laughter was friendly in the quiet room.

Before daybreak in the dark hut that smelt acidly of sweat Concepción ran through a forest where stiff sides of bloody meat were the trees and woke with a cry as her sister Dolores flung a dreaming hand across her face. Together they heaved themselves from the straw mattress they shared on Concepción's day off and brushed at their crumpled skirts. Crouched behind the sheet of corrugated iron that made the kitchen, Concepción lit the paraffin stove and put on top of it a jug of thick black coffee while Dolores moved out to sit herself on a tin drum at the hut's entrance and feed the mewing baby. As the three children woke, she shoo'd them out to squat in the gutter at the back. Already the tin city was stirring, its inhabitants – crammed together between walls of cardboard, cartons, sacking and iron – waking each other. Nearby a baby began to wail, a man's voice exclaimed in anger, women chivvied at their children, a dog yelped in the distance. The smells of paraffin and coffee and urine mingled and rose in the growing heat. Concepción sat back on her haunches waiting for the jug to boil and thought as she thought every Saturday of the white bedroom she entered each weekday to wake her Señora. Cool in this heat, quiet in this clamour, light in this half-dark. As well that José-Eduardo had never seen what she saw every day. He was wild enough as it was, running with his pack, playing at being a man, a guerrillero. This boy who was like her son because she had lugged him

[81]

everywhere with her since he was a baby and their mother had already coughed herself to death. Last night, climbing through the narrow alleys of the barrio from the broad streets of the town below she had determined to give him a piece of her mind, tell him straight he had no right on earth to expose his sisters and the children to the dangers of his macho games. Arriving at the hut, puffing for breath, she had stooped to enter and gone straight to the basket in the corner, pushing José aside as he greeted her. The basket was empty. In the doorway, José laughed at her.

'What have you done with them?' she said, turning to look at him standing against the light in his torn shorts, with his hairless chest and his moustache like a moulting caterpillar, a bony child on stilts.

Seven days ago this child had held up the lid of the basket and watched her with round expectant eyes as she peered inside. There she had seen the lethal fruit, muddy knobbled objects the size of mangoes. 'Is that what you do with the money I bring you each week for your food?' she said. 'No, I swear it, Concha,' the fool replied. 'I'm storing them for a week only, for los chicos, the boys.' Seeing her face, he flinched but Concepción hit him anyway, punching at his ribs in dread and fury.

Last night, at her question, José made a monkey mouth, twitched his shoulders up and down and grinned, dodging away from her as she came towards him.

'José,' she said, pleading now. 'Little brother, listen to me, please listen. Are they gone, those things? Are they out of our house?'

In the gutter, children screeched and shouted after a ball. José flapped his elbows at his sister and hopped on one leg across the fly-ridden mounds of rubbish flung up like flotsam against every wall. 'Gulla gulla gulla' he gobbled as if his brains had melted and jigged off down the alley, turning and leaping and making clown faces until he dwindled into the night. Concepción had spat with fury after him and then went in and searched the hut, pummelling the three mattresses, pushing her arms into the sack of dried beans, climbing on the tin drum to probe the layers of sacking that was their roof. She had found nothing and, panting, crossed herself with relief. Idiot though he was, José had listened to her. For once.

The coffee steamed and Dolores squatted down beside her sister to drink. Five minutes later, shouts from outside announced the arrival of Concepción's other sisters – Blanca, with the broad flat nostrils of their Indian mother, already thickening with the fourth child her shiftless husband had given her, and Ramosa, with hollows under her cheekbones and a yellow bruise that spread from her temple up into the wide-brimmed hat she wore. The women exclaimed with delight when Concepción gave them two bags of oranges, purloined after the last dinner at the Palace.

'And this? What is this?' Concepción held Ramosa at arms' length and nodded at the bruise.

'Ay,' Ramosa sighed and giggled behind her hand. 'You can guess, Concha.'

Concepción made a hawking sound in her throat. 'You were always fool, Rama. You could have come with me to the town and instead you stayed here in this heap of shit for the pleasure of being beaten by a husband who gives you children he cannot feed.'

Ramosa twisted her shoulders from Concepción's grasp. 'Keep your tongue off him, Concha. You haven't heard yet. Alfonso has gone. He left two days ago, after the soldiers came. They poked their guns everywhere and one held a pistol to his head. The children cried. It was very bad. Then Alfonso said he must go away for a while or the soldiers would come back and hurt me.'

'And Alfonso thinks only *he* should do that,' said Concepción sourly. 'Good riddance to him, I say. To both your men. They treat you like dogs.'

[83]

The two sisters moved against each other uneasily, clucking their tongues at Concepción's words. Blanca pushed at her shoulder in reproof.

'You are our oldest sister, Concha. You are good to us and we respect you. But you do not understand our lives any more. You live in the town and you serve La Dorada. You don't know what is going on here.'

Concepción cupped her hands against her chest and made a rude noise. 'What is going on here is what has always gone on here,' she said. 'Why do you think I went to the town in the first place, instead of marrying Hernández? You know what he did when I asked him what he had to offer me? This is what he did.' Concepción stuck out an arm, flexed it and hit it with her fist. Blanca and Ramosa burst out laughing but their laughter had a nervous edge and their eyes did not leave their sister's angry face.

'Laugh,' shouted Concepción, 'but there is no joke. Look at the two of you. Look at her.' She waved at Dolores who was washing her children's faces with rust-coloured water from a plastic jerry-can, her hair tumbling about her ears. 'You think it is funny, what those pricks of men have done to all of you? Stuck one child after another into your bellies and beaten you if you try to refuse them. Eh, Ramosa, am I right? I see that I'm right.'

'It is God's will,' said Ramosa sulkily. She began to peel an orange. The nails on her hands were ridged like the claws of a bird and ingrained with dirt.

Concepción threw up her arms. 'And if it is God's will, why is it not God's will for the Señora? She is married, so are the ladies who visit her. But they have flat stomachs and no children or maybe one or two, with time in between. It's true my Señora has bruises like you, Ramosa, now and again. That is men for you. But why does God not give her children? Why is she rich and educated and you poor and stupid? Is that God's will?'

Short and stocky Blanca, her black hair drawn back in a ponytail from her square face, stuck her neck out at Concepción. 'You talk like our brother,' she said, 'you talk like the men. They always say why are we poor, why are they rich, why are things so different between people?' She looked quickly around and lowered her husky voice. 'That's why they go, Concha. To fight. To take from the rich what should be ours. They are brave and we women must stand by them.'

'Bravo. *Cha*.' Concepción's snort was full of disgust. 'These guerrilleros of yours, I wouldn't trust them *that* far ...' and she snapped her fingers under Blanca's nose. 'You listen to José, our monkey brother still wet behind the ears? Where is he when there is work to be done? Where is he now, since last night? Playing with guns, somewhere, giving me gut-ache. Your precious guerrilleros, their courage comes out of a bottle. They point their guns at the soldiers, who are also shit, and they point their pricks at you. You think, if they win, they will give you anything? They will give you *nothing*. El Jefe down there, your Alfonso up here, the other men, they are all pigs. There is not *that* much to choose between them.'

'If El Jefe's men heard you, Concha, they would take you away.' Blanca's voice was low and angry.

A shadow moved in the doorway and the three women turned abruptly but it was only an old woman with a thatch of white hair, hunched over a stick. She peered vacantly in at the sisters, her eyes two watery marbles, her toothless jaw slack.

Blanca pointed at Concepción, her finger quivering. 'So. This time it is only the old witch. Another time, our visitor may not be deaf. Here, Tía, catch.' Blanca rummaged in the plastic bag, took out an orange and gave it to the woman. A skinny hand closed over it and held it, glowing, against the stained rags that covered her chest. 'Be careful, Concha, for God's sake.'

Irritably, Concepción pulled her skirt straight over her hips and tugged at the shawl round her shoulders. Why did she bother to argue with her sisters? She was so fortunate, compared with them. She had left the shanty town just in time, before marriage and children had made the move impossible, and her life with the Señora was good. She had enough to eat, a room of her own and work that was easy compared to theirs. She rubbed her hands together, feeling the soft palms. The hands of Ramosa, Blanca and Dolores were like the backs of snakes, scarred with whorls of rasping skin that would pull out threads on the thin silk of the Señora's dresses and mar the shining surface. How strange that it was her soft hands and the soft work they did that kept the family going, earning more pesos in a week than their useless men could find in a year. Some of that was her luck, of course. It was luck that Father Torres had liked her and let her run errands for him, luck that he knew the Cardinal, El Jefe's uncle, and through him had heard they wanted a maid at the Palace. Luck that she had learned to sew so well.

Concepción remembered that small hot room at the Palace where she had spent so many months bent over the ironing board. Her back had ached at first as the piles of washed and crumpled things mounted up in the mornings – men's shirts with their froth of lace down the front, the footmen's uniforms, the endless tablecloths and bedlinen and the frilly aprons of the maids that had to be sprayed with starch first and then dug at with the point of the iron to splay out the yards of frill – but the muscles of her back had slowly grown strong and the ache had grown less. And then, one day, Madame Gómez had come in with dresses on hangers, the new Señora's dresses, ghosts that swayed and billowed at the slightest breeze from the open door. Madame Gómez was French and very grand and she was, she told Concepción, leaving Ventura soon, so Concepción had been chosen to care for the Señora's wardrobe. Carefully, in broken Spanish, she pointed out to Concepción the tiny gap in a bodice where four minute stitches were needed and the place at the top of a pleat that required the most delicate reinforcement. She stood as Concepción eased the first fragile folds on to the board wrong side out, and spat little beads of saliva on to the iron until the first drop sizzled, upon which she must pull out the plug. Every piece of the Señora's clothing was either silk or chiffon, with an occasional blouse or evening suit in satin, and Madame Gómez had to teach Concepción to cover each item with damp muslin before she pressed. Shortly afterwards, Madame Gómez departed. For a while, Concepción continued alone, ironing and darning the Señora's ghostly apparel, and then one day was sent to prepare the Señora's room for the night. In that white room Concepción threw a dark shadow, her limbs felt coarse and thick, her feet in their leather thongs too heavy, likely to leave ineradicable marks on the velvet pile of the carpet. From the perfumed drawer of the rosewood chest she drew the wisp that was a nightdress and as she laid it on the bed, the door opened. It was the Señora herself, white as the sheets, talking. Talking to Concepción in a language she could not understand, her white hair swinging round her face as she walked in the room. Alarmed, Concepción bent her head. The Señora advanced and Concepción retreated.

'What is your name? Cuál es tu nombre?'

'Concepción, Señora.' A frog croaking in a lily pond.

Then the Señora had thrown back her head and laughed.

That was how it had started, her time as maid to the Señora, the good time. Looking back, she knew that the Señora had had too much to drink that day or perhaps too many of the white pills that she kept in the chest by her bed. Since then, Concepción had grown accustomed to the routine — two pills with the first drink in the morning and two at night, also doses of the yellow pills that she quickly learned to make sure were always in the tiny mother-of-pearl boxes that the Señora kept in every handbag. Concepción did not know what was in those pills and never asked — whenever the Señora took them in her presence, she put a finger across her lips and looked at Concepción like a bad child, so that Concepción knew it was not to be mentioned anywhere but in the privacy of the white bedroom. Before taking them, the Señora was often nervous and bad-tempered, snapping at Concepción and twisting her shoulders away in annoyance as Concepción brushed her silver hair. Afterwards, she was kinder but subdued. Sometimes she would sit for long minutes gazing at herself in the huge oval mirror that hung over the inlaid dressing-table, a faint frown marking her forehead between the blue eyes, as if wondering who that pale stranger was, regarding her, equally puzzled. On the few occasions that the Señora had been visited by norte americanos with their husbands, so oddly pink and large, she was much more lively than usual during the day and Concepción had her work cut out to keep up with the changes in clothes – swimming costumes for the pool, short flared dresses for the tennis court, long floating gowns for dinner and the dancing afterwards. Sometimes, Concepción followed her mistress down and stood at a doorway, watching the Señora as she swung round the floor in some gentleman's arms, hardly ever the arms of the President. When he was there – and he was not often there – his grey bulk seemed to muffle the usual gaiety and on those occasions Concepción was required late at night to come to the white bedroom, give the Señora one more of her usual white pills and stay beside her, massaging her temples, until her breathing eased and she was asleep, though sometimes tears squeezed from under her closed eyelids and Concepción was peremptorily dismissed. Now and again at such times, a knock at the door would herald the President himself. He never spoke. He would simply walk in and wait against the open door until Concepción got up and backed away into the corridor, bowing as she went, murmuring buenas noches. The Señora's eyes always remained upon her until the door closed. The poor Señora. She, too, was only a woman after all and like all women must submit to her man.

*

The old woman still stood holding her orange, gaping. 'Move, old one,' said Concepción. 'The sun is up and we stand here arguing. Come, Dolores, Rama. Stir your legs. We're going to the forest.'

Dolores, pushing her fingers through a child's tangled hair, looked up. 'The forest? It's an hour's walk from here. I have work to do. What do you want from the forest?'

Concepción put her hand flat on Blanca's swollen belly. 'We need plants. To help the baby in there slip out as easy as a little fish. And something for that ... She pointed at Ramosa's bruise. 'Blanca, you stay here, you are already too heavy to be of any use. Come on, let's go.'

'Ai,' Ramosa protested. 'We can go alone another day, Concha. You should rest on your holiday.'

'Without me, neither of you would know cure from poison. I have to show you what to pick. I am the only daughter our mother taught before she died, before we came to live on this rubbish heap. I know the medicines in the forest. You lot, you know nothing.'

The old woman hobbled forward, poking her thin neck towards Concepción. 'That was the Indian, your mother,' she croaked. 'Ah ha, I remember her.' The gnarled hands clutched at Concepción's arm. 'She couldn't talk to us, she spoke only her own language. Soon she couldn't speak at all, only make noises in her throat ...' the woman retched feebly and cackled, '... and then she died. Her medicines couldn't cure her.'

'Oh get on your way, Tía,' said Blanca. Ramosa came up beside her and together they half-carried the old lady out into the alley and set her down. She stumbled off, still cackling, the dogs yapping at her wrinkled ankles. 'Old fool.'

Ramosa pulled her shawl over her head and retrieved a battered basket from a corner of the hut. Dolores tied the baby on her back and shouted instructions to the other children.

'Ramon, watch your little sister. There are oranges and bread to eat. Stay around here and if José comes, tell him to stay, too. We will be back at sundown. Behave yourselves.'

She broke off wedges of bread and stuck pieces in her sisters' baskets. The children, their bare legs under tattered T-shirts already filthy, clustered around and were waved away. 'Shoo, go on. Ramon, get some water while we're away. The can is nearly empty.' Ramon, his peaked cap backwards on his black hair, made a hideous grimace.

Passing him, Concepción said, 'If the angel comes by, your face will stay that way,' and, patting his cheek, began to trudge down the hill.

[6]

The newly decorated Palace, for all its delights, remained largely empty. Except for the weekly Presidential dinners, few visitors came to sit on the comfortable sofas or chat over the card tables or dance or play the piano in the music room and it was mostly servants who walked down the corridors, dragging hoovers or carrying trays. Once Clare set the switch and stepped on to the glass dance floor, where she danced and twirled alone, her skirt billowing around her in reds, greens and yellows as the lights changed. When she had no appointments, she lay alone in her ice-blue bikini by the new swimming-pool, its bright blue waters spread beside a white terrace lined with orange padded chairs. The corseted wives of Ventura, though they had grown fond of their singular First Lady and showed her many kindnesses, remained firmly in their daytime purdah, refusing even to contemplate divesting themselves of their layers of clothing to reveal the plump white flesh seen only by their mothers until marriage and only by their husbands after that. These staid mammas also forbade their daughters such revelations, for might not prospective husbands refuse to take in marriage bodies that had been so immodestly spreadeagled under the sun for all to see? Clare was unique, an exception, an Englishwoman possibly licensed by the English Queen to lie like a starfish on the grass with every secret orifice ajar, showing even the brush of under-arm hair, even the cleft of buttocks, even a trace of pubic hair in the concave dip of the inner thighs. A First Lady could do as she liked because she was the wife of El Jefe but no other Venturan man or woman could afford to flout convention by keeping company with La Dorada and Clare's frequent invitations – 'Please just call me, just come round, I'm always here in the mornings' – were most courteously evaded. Only two or three of the American wives responded to begin with but they were dull too-polite women much older than Clare and their visits soon petered out for lack of any fuel.

Desperate for female companionship Clare telephoned Louise and insisted that she come for a visit. 'I'll send you the ticket,' she urged her sleepy friend – she never got the time right for long-distance phone calls and was always rousing Ma and Pa from their beds, spluttering in dozy incomprehension, Pa shouting 'Who?' over and over as Clare screeched 'Clare, Pa. Your daughter. How many daughters have you *got*?'

So Louise came and trailed through Clare's glistening rooms making acid remarks about costly refurbishments, prodding at this and poking at that, managing to combine – as she always had – a degree of rough criticism with pure green-eyed jealousy. Clare found her very bracing after the bland formality of Venturan grandees, though Louise's sympathy for what Clare thought of as her plight was kept to a stern minimum.

'I don't know what you're complaining about,' she said as they lay by the pool. 'What more do you want? A devoted husband, pots of money, eternal sunshine and trillions of peasants to run about after you, bowing and scraping and kissing your toes. Honestly, Clare, you're never satisfied.' Louise squinted at her hostess in the violent sun. Apart from anything else, the simple sight of Clare in a bikini was enough to wither a saint's charity.

Needled, Clare pulled herself up from the downy expanse of the chaise-longue, unaware that her golden breasts in their insubstantial cups merely confirmed the case against her to prosecuting Louise. 'He's *not* devoted,' she said. 'I hardly see him. Except at night.'

'Of course you don't,' she said crossly. 'Men have other things to do, you know. than hang over us. After all, Raul *is* the

[92]

President of this place. He must have a few odd jobs to do. other than ...' she coughed modestly and regarded her lobster-red arms. 'He's an attractive man. If you like that type, she added primly. George, her merchant banker, was fair and freckled and already running to fat.

'You don't understand,' Clare said. 'On our honeymoon he ... Well, things went a bit wrong. He was awfully miffed because I wasn't, you know, intacta.'

Louise screeched. 'He didn't think ...? Oh the poor love. My God, Clare, I thought everyone from Land's End to John o' Groats knew *that* about you.'

With dignity, Clare said, 'Raul doesn't come from Land's End *or* John o' Groats. You are rude, Louise.'

'No. Sorry.' Louise put out a placatory hand. 'I was only teasing. Is it really bad, the sex thing?'

Clare talked for quite a while after that as Louise stared upwards at the cornflower sky and struggled with conflicting images: the soft white body of George snuggling like a plump teddy in her arms, dark hard Raul holding Clare down, cold and silent. Afterwards, clearing his throat, George always said, 'Are you all right?', which was very proper and gentlemanly and the fact that Louise often yearned to say, 'No, actually, I feel like a sack left out in the rain,' was neither here nor there. Women, in Louise's opinion, got what they asked for and if they asked for a man straight out of Barbara Cartland they had to put up with muscles of steel and no chat and a lot of kinky asterisks. Still, Clare was obviously unhappy and Louise was fond of her, particularly since her description of Raul threw a warm glow over the George sort of man.

'So you don't ...?' she said to Clare at the end of the harangue '... well, to put it crudely, you don't *come*?'

Clare stood up and stretched. She gave as large and casual a yawn as she could, thinking hard. She had always told the truth to Louise and any other woman friend, that's what was lovely about women, you could tell the truth, certain that it would be accepted and echoed and laughed about or sympathized with, depending on its nature. Once you liked a woman and knew she liked you, the barriers were down, you could say anything and usually did. But this time, this time was different.

'No,' she said and made her voice snappy. 'Of course I don't. Would you?'

'No, of course not,' Louise said. Side by side, the two girls stared ahead at the sapphire waters of the pool. If a woman can't with a George and can't with a Raul either, who can she with? Louise asked herself, gloomily adjusting the plastic cone on her flaking nose.

'Perhaps you're a lesbian,' she said.

Clare's face swooped at her, scowling. 'Oh, thanks ever so, dear Agony Auntie. Go on, give us a kiss you gorgeous thing.'

'Only trying to help,' said Louise, flapping her hands at the mad face.

Clare relapsed on to the cushions. 'Sometimes I wish I was,' she told the sky. 'Louise. If you don't think much of men but you want to sleep with them and you love women but you don't want to sleep with them, what does that make you?'

'Normal,' said Louise, and gave an awful snort.

Met at Heathrow by George on her return, Louise hugged him with unusual vigour, kneading his spare tyre affectionately, delighted to see that he carried a wet umbrella.

'Well, well, well,' George said, straightening his tie. 'Didn't fall for any of those dagos, eh?'

'Certainly not,' said Louise. 'I'm not that sort of girl.'

George rested a leaden arm on her shoulder. 'Besides, you've got me,' he said.

'So I have,' said Louise.

Missing Louise, disturbed by that first failure to rid herself of a festering worry by confiding in a female friend, Clare turned again to Raul, determined to try and be a good wife. Unfortunately, she hadn't the faintest idea what being a good wife meant. Ma and Pa were not helpful role models. They saw very little of each other on the whole; Ma wandering about at one end of Tucolston's gardens smelling of wet dog, Pa shouting to himself in some copse. Ma didn't even wear a wedding ring, she said it brought her out in spots. As for their procreative activity, it appeared to be a case of 'tried it once, didn't like it'. They slept in separate bedrooms, which was natural enough, but Clare could not remember ever seeing Pa in Ma's room or Ma in Pa's, even in the daytime, and since Aunt Florence was a byword for insomnia and spent most of the small hours creaking along corridors dribbling interminable milk drinks, that put paid to the nighttime, too. Clare was aware that ordinary English wives spent a lot of their time clattering about in kitchens and she had heard that the way to a man's heart was through his stomach but all that was hardly applicable to a First Lady wife with a fleet of servants in a Palace.

At dinner one evening she said to Raul, making a vague stab at what she thought was conventional wifely conversation. 'Have you had a nice day, dear?' and felt rather pleased with herself, the words had issued from her lips as smoothly as little round pebbles. Raul, however, did not respond in any useful way.

'No,' he said, his eyes like scars. 'Por qué?'

He refused to speak English with her any more and though Clare's Spanish was improving nicely, it did not yet extend to chattering of the price of cabbage. Besides, she did not know the price of cabbage. Besides, in Ventura there *was* no cabbage.

In bed, they met physically but not intimately. The more Clare tried to change the ritual there, the more rigid it became. Her struggles to escape merely wove her more intricately into the web. If she offered tenderness, Raul visibly wilted. He was not the sort of man you patted and, Clare had to admit to herself, she did not wish to pat. On the other hand, what she did enjoy could not be called enjoyable; it was, at best, a travesty of the state whose occasional flame almost immediately flickered and died. If she did what she wanted and fought Raul off, the walls of the trap closed. He fought back with a grim pleasure and he won, in ways that were always humiliating to Clare, making her nervous and extremely irritable the next day and angering him. Thus they teetered back and forth, doomed, it seemed, to a series of explosions.

So Clare embarked on a massive correspondence with distant friends. Her two letters to Freddie Chedleigh were eventually answered from South Africa – an envelope stuffed with blurred newspaper photographs of His Lordship more or less vertical in the muscular arms of a series of underclad Johannesburg heir-esses without accompanying note. Freddie, it seemed, was not anxious to exchange these supportive ladies for a matron with a jealous spouse in a dump like Ventura. Others, however, responded more conventionally and in the second year the Palace began to be visited by leisured English friends and their various spouses, lovers and hangers-on: promising starlets, rising pop singers, *Vogue* models between assignments or sometimes on assignments, posing with haughty grace against Clare's silk walls or rising like glamorous storks from a group of shawled market women whose faces went blank with astonishment at the exploding flashes of light. These exotic inhabitants of another world flew in on Raul's private Gulfstream jet to cavort in as much of the sun, the fun and the entertainments as could be provided within Clare's walls. Sometimes they were flown up-country to view the flora, the fauna and the human specimens but the poverty they saw grew dreary and their tourist enthu-siasm was quickly squelched by the sticky heat and the ubiqui-tous mosquitoes. They took up residence again at the Palace, where they drank a lot, soon became bored and departed for more amusing spots. Waving one group off at the airport, feeling a melancholy made more piercing by one of many hang-overs, Clare slumped back into the Mercedes and closed her eyes. Even on her lids the forest impinged. When the car suddenly stopped, she opened them again and saw Manuel, the chauffeur, through the glass partition, pointing ahead, laying a finger across his wide mouth. On the road ahead two spidery fur-coated figures were copulating. Monkeys. The female crouched, gnawing without interest at a leaf, peering sideways with her small rusty eyes, the male, his lips flared out, beat against her rump, pumping in and out with absorption, snickering and grunting. Startled, Clare watched until the male pulled away, scratching his ear, and the simian lovers ambled to the edge of the road and disappeared into the forest. Manuel turned his stony Indian face and regarded her closely for a long second through the glass that divided them. Clare stared back. They he turned round, started the engine again and drove on. Puzzled, she looked at the smooth brown nape below his cap and the broad shoulders. Was he showing off the beauties of Venturan wildlife or making a pass? An affair with the chauffeur, was that what lay ahead for her? Quelle cliché.

It was shortly after this that Clare began on her ill-fated attempt to put Ventura on the tourist map. 'If Imelda Marcos could do it for the Philippines, I should be able to do it for this backwater,' she told Raul, buoyed up by a mixture of valium and Scotch. 'There's nowhere to stay in ND except that flea-pit near the river and there's nothing to buy. No one can even get hold of your precious gold and emeralds.'

'I dispose of them quite satisfactorily, thank you,' said Raul.

'But why not sell some here? The men who find them aren't allowed to sell them to anyone but you and no one else can take them out of the country. Let tourists take them out and you'll make more on them, you'll have cut out the middle men.'

'In a small place, it is often better to do things privately ' Raul said. He picked up the petal of a rose that lay under the vase beside him and rubbed it between his fingers. The diamond on his little finger gleamed.

'Illegally, you mean,' said Clare.

Raul looked at her. 'This country is my property I own it,' he said. 'Nothing I do here can be illegal. J am the law.' He flipped the torn petal on to the carpet.

Clare sighed irritably. She knew very little about Raul's daytime occupations, he came and went without explanation, his offices at the back of the Palace were terra incognita to her and when occasionally she questioned him his replies were vague and he quickly became edgy if she persisted. Mostly, she did not persist. Many of her questions worried her, they came unbidden from some well of unease within her and hearing them said aloud in her own voice was unsettling enough without getting even more unsettling answers. When Raul said brusquely, as he frequently did, that this or that subject was no concern of hers she felt relief.

'Well,' said Clare, 'but what about a hotel? A small one but with the proper facilities where the sort of visitors we want would be comfortable.'

Raul considered the proposition for a few days and then agreed. 'But one thing you must understand from the start, Clare. This is your project. I do not wish my name to be used in its connection. Is that clear?'

'You will give me the money, though?'

'The money will be provided.'

A wasteland of shacks put up by the nomad poor, an eyesore, a breeding ground for rats and flies, was demolished, bulldozed to a wreck of planks and household rubbish. Stones were thrown at the men in the bulldozers, women dug about in the debris wailing until they were herded on to trucks and driven away from the town, but on the whole the operation went smoothly enough and Clare was not informed of these minor incidents. The three-storey hotel, finished on schedule, fitted harmoniously in proportion and style with the other buildings on the street and contained every modern convenience, including a telex for the use of visiting businessmen. Clare cut the ribbon at the imposing entrance and named it La Dorada at Raul's suggestion, which touched her. Raul himself was not able to attend the ceremony since he was in Rio on business.

Enthused by this success, Clare persuaded Raul to finance further building. Under the supervision of a firm of American architects, four more sites at the edge of town were cleared and four more buildings went up in quick succession: an art gallery, a concert hall, a centre for crafts and artefacts (Indian carvings and beadwork, Venturan lace and silks) and a small casino. This time, unfortunately, speed did not pay. The top floor of the casino, designed as a roof garden and open-air bar that overlooked the river, collapsed late one morning under its weight of new earth and threw eight workmen to their deaths on the concrete slabs below. Clare, pale and all in black, laid a wreath on each of the wooden coffins at the funeral and was extolled by the officiating Cardinal, His Excellency Don Alfonso Guilberto de Toro y Plata, for her untiring efforts on behalf of the Venturan people. 'La nuestra Dorada,' he said solemnly from the pulpit, 'has a mother's heart, young as she is, and she weeps with you today for your loved ones who lost their lives in the furtherance of a great and patriotic endeavour.' It was true. Clare wept with the widows, holding their hands, while the men stood silently, their heads bowed. Raul was not present, he was detained in Bogotá on business.

With a vague idea of recompense, Clare embarked on plans for a hospital and watched it rise in its web of scaffolding at the edge of town with mounting anxiety; she had insisted beforehand to the architects that all safety regulations must be scrupulously followed. The topping-out ceremony, which she performed, went without incident and she breathed again. The hospital was dedicated to the Virgin of Ventura and though small it was equipped with the most up to date of medical facilities: laser surgery, a cobalt unit, a fine maternity ward. As time went on, the air-conditioned rooms and the gleaming operating theatre remained, for the most part, unused – even the richest of the Creole women preferred to have their babies at home with midwives in attendance and the rest of the population did not suffer the kind of ills that hospitals could cure. One day, four months after the hospital had opened, an inquisitive child who had strayed from the *barrio* nearby fell into a sewage pipe half sunk in the sand that had been dumped and left by the builders and for a day and a night the citizens of Nombre Dios stood while men in hard hats lowered each other on ropes to try and rescue the child. The first day, the child's voice could be heard sobbing and crying mamma. On the second morning it ceased and an hour later the small bleeding body was dragged into view. This time, Clare did not attend the funeral. She sent a wreath and spent the rest of the day, red-eyed, in the Palace, pouring whisky down her throat. Graffiti appeared on walls overnight, great letters dripping red and reappearing as soon as they were scrubbed off. 'Váyase a la casa, Clare' was the mildest of the slogans, but it was often repeated. Clare could not face going home to Lincoln, her parents would not provide distraction of the kind she craved.

'How would you feel if I descended on you?' she wrote to Louise, trying hard not to sound desperate. 'I'm rather lonely here at the moment, since Raul is always away, and the heat is addling my brains. Some things I've been involved in have gone a bit wrong and I'm not frightfully popular, strange to say. Louise, do say yes, I'd so love to talk as we used to do.'

Louise, married now, was expecting her first child. She wrote back with a vague sympathy but her mind was on breathing exercises and the hiring of nannies. 'You could come if you liked,' she wrote, 'though goodness knows what you'd do for entertainment, George and I are very dull these days and go nowhere much, I'm too fat and George doesn't like to leave me, bless him.'

It was plain to Clare that the last thing her friend wanted in the eighth month of her pregnancy was a disturbed First Lady mooning about, perhaps making eyes at her George. Instead, she packed her bags and flew to New York and did not return for three months, caught up with that roving band of rich gipsies that newspapers call the jet-set. Beauty, cash and the sort of inner disturbance that is only allayed by constant movement were the qualifications for entry into that exclusive band and Clare possessed them all, along with a growing dependence on alcohol and the fashionable drugs. With these talented or talentless or half-crazed drifters and their self-appointed court of gossip merchants, she moved across the United States and its luxurious offshore islands on yachts and private planes and cars like sharks, from Palm Beach to New Orleans, from Nassau to New York, from parties in Malibu to identical parties in Las Vagas, the Vineyard, Hollywood and Hyannisport, give or take tennis whites or mink. Waking up in strange rooms, often with unexpected bedfellows, her clothes in a trail from the door, a glittering stole here, a gold sandal there, a sequinned dress hanging on the end of the bed, Clare would reach for her bag, find the hip flask that was always with her and launch herself on the new day with deep swigs of Scotch. Then she would drag herself out of the sheets and carry herself carefully across the carpet as if she were a glass she might spill. In the adjoining bathroom she would be as neatly sick as a cat.

'Wassa madder, you pregnant?' Rocco Cacciatore was the sole heir to a State-wide dry-cleaning empire, a fact he did his level best to conceal since it did not enhance his *macho* image, carefully nurtured with a view to becoming a second and even more successful Sylvester Stallone. Rocco boasted of Mafia connections which gave his father attacks of painful angina. Mr Cacciatore Senior was an honest Milanese who had built up his business over twenty years of grinding work and despised all southern Italians as corrupt and in the pay of the uomini d'onore. It hurt his heart that his only son should admire those dirty Sicilianos.

Rocco stretched and yawned on the huge oval bed that Clare had just vacated. 'Hey, baby, I'm talking to you. Are ya pregnant?'

Clare rested her head on the cool porcelain rim of the lavatory. Drop dead, she thought.

After a while he said, 'You wanna toot?' He could see her through the open door, huddled, shaking her head. 'So okay, so wassa madder?'

Rocco swung his legs out of bed and walked across to the bathroom. Already, the heat of a New York summer had penetrated his Park Avenue apartment and he wanted a cold shower. He stood naked over Clare.

'How about a suck?' He waggled his penis at her and giggled girlishly. 'Aw, come on. See the magic lollipop. See what the doctor ordered.'

Clare pulled herself to her feet and went over to the basin. Rocco watched as she doused her face with water. He had to admit, she was one good-looking broad, the best he'd had and he'd had plenty. Poppa's money was good for that. He sang in a light tenor, 'You shoulda been in pictures.'

Clare dried her face and, ignoring him, walked out of the bathroom. She would keep going, taking no notice, and perhaps he would vanish in a puff of smoke, leaving behind him only a few strands of spaghetti.

He did not disappear, he followed her. 'Lissen. Hey. Lesscrew.'

Clare picked up her brassiere from under a chair and leant over, fitting her breasts into the lacy half-cups. If she dressed and got out of here fast, maybe no one at the Sedgwick house would know she'd spent the night away with this idiot beach-boy.

'Guaranteed all stains removed from items entrusted to our care, twenny-four-hour service.' Rocco gabbled his father's slogan, unaware of Clare's half-smile. He unhooked her bra again before she could wriggle away and caught her breasts in his hands, kneading them as if he feared to find a lump, pushing his stiffening groin against her buttocks. 'Come on, baby, fucky-fucky.'

Clare brought her heel down hard on his toes.

'Okay,' Rocco said, releasing her. 'So why don't you go back to that spic of yours in the jungle? You know why? Because you're a tramp. A high-class tramp, a rich tramp, but a tramp.'

He was crooning 'The Lady is a Tramp' and flexing his muscles in the mirror when she left. She'd had worse, at least he took no for an answer when it got through his thick skull. Back at the Sedgwicks, she wrote another letter to Raul, wrestling as always with the problem of showing him she wanted to come back without actually saying so. She was tired to increasingly frequent tears of this pointless wandering life, divorce was out of the question and Ventura, for all its myriad drawbacks, was really her only home. There, left in peace, she might be able to get herself together again and stop feeling as ill as she now felt most of the time. So far, she had had only the most formal responses to her letters, dictated via a secretary to save his face, she guessed, though the money she needed was always available in Raul's Miami account. Perhaps this time, she thought, licking the envelope, perhaps this time.

Exactly one week later the summons came in a card personally delivered from the Venturan Consulate by a man with too many teeth. El Presidente requests the honour. Celebrations for the five hundredth anniversary of Ventura's founding. Clare started packing immediately. Accompanied by several of her current friends at a seasonal loose end – she had grown too used to constant company to cut herself off cold turkey and she was apprehensive at the thought of seeing Raul again – she returned to Ventura.

Concepción was overjoyed to see her and embraced her as tenderly as a mother, pinching her pale cheeks in fond anxiety. Raul bowed over her hand on the cool marble stairs but his lips did not touch her fingers and his eyes did not meet hers.

'Darling, were you crazy, staying away from that?' said Mitzi van Haag, whose name was scrawled on the bottom right-hand corner of half the silk scarves sold in Europe. 'What a doll!'

Clare, sipping at an icy crystal glass, thought she had never heard so inappropriate a description of that granite man, her husband. That night she lay in her white satin bed and waited nervously for his knock at the door but it did not come. 'We are just good friends,' she whispered to the ceiling but this time the glib gossip column cliché wasn't true. She and Raul were neither friends nor good. 'Tant pis, Auntie's in the bathroom,' she said aloud and whistled in the dark.

The anniversary celebrations took the best part of a week — or rather the worst, Clare thought, standing hour after hour flapping her hand from the Palace balcony as Raul's soldiers marched by for the umpteenth time in their ceremonial white breeches and frogged jackets and plumed hussar hats, the bandsmen sweating as they drummed and blasted their way through the hot streets. Raul stood like a ramrod by her side and looked, she had to admit, quite grand and noble in his snowy uniform with its loops of gold braid and its gold epaulettes though what he had to be grand and noble about was much less clear to her. In spite of the pomp, the uniforms, the martial music, the flags that fluttered from every side, the bowing and saluting and hand-shaking, wasn't this tall man in the midst of it all with a face like a handsome skull simply playing a game with a toy army in a toy town in a hot little minibrick country? But the same sort of things went on in every country — was it only this scaled-down version that was absurd? Would she, Clare wondered, feel this confusion if she were watching a march-past from the balcony of the White House in Washington, D C?

In Washington, though, crowds would gather and cheer and wave the Stars and Stripes. Here, the people of Nombre Dios stood and stared in silence like cattle lifting their heads from a meadow to watch a train go by. Only when the gilded Virgin of Ventura was carried by on her flower-strewn litter under its fringed canopy did they come to life and run along beside the litter-bearers jostling and singing, holding up their candles to the Virgin's tapers as night fell. Then the indigo sky filled with shooting stars as the fireworks banged and crackled and Mitzi van Haag with the other guests oo'ed and aa'ed and the people sighed, gazing up at the fountains of light that gushed above the circle of hills where the shanty towns squatted in the dark.

'Bliss,' breathed Mitzi on the steps of the Palace but Clare saw her eyes and they weren't on the sparkling sky lights, they were on Raul's profile, dark against the glitter. 'Isn't it, darling?'

'Sure,' Clare said.

She tried to talk to Mitzi that evening as they sat in their nightdresses in her bedroom nibbling cheese footballs and swigging brandy. Crumbs cascaded into Mitzi's cleavage, brandy dribbled on to Clare's chin.

'Look at you, darling,' Mitzi shrieked, her words slightly slurred. 'Better tell your maid to bring a bib. Suppose your peasants saw you now.'

Clare wiped at herself and felt the sting of tears behind her eyes. 'It's awful, living here,' she said. 'You don't know.'

'Sure,' said Mitzi. 'Awful sunshine, awful palace, awful champagne and caviar and an awful awful husband. Poor Clare, I could weep for you.'

Blinking, Clare said, 'I haven't any friends. The Spanish women, even the Americans, they keep their distance because, you know, because of who I am. There's only Concha and that's impossible. She's a maid. Stay here a while, Mitzi. Please?'

'Honey,' said Mitzi, sighing in the soft down of her armchair, 'believe me, nothing I'd like more but I have a business to run for my sins. Anyway, you have your lovely Presidente. I can't think, now that I've seen him, why you stayed away so long. Wild horses wouldn't drag me if he was mine. New York's full of faggots, you don't know your luck.'

At the mention of Raul, the tears began to run down Clare's cheeks. 'Raul doesn't love me. I think he hates me. I wasn't a virgin when we married.'

'Big deal,' said Mitzi in a Donald Duck voice.

'He's never forgiven me. That's the way men are here, Mitzi. I can't cope. I can't even have an affair here, the place is too small, everybody'd know.' She dabbed at her face with the hem of her nightdress.

'So. You'll have to come to the States more often. You got your rocks off *there* all right.'

Clare wailed. 'That's not what I want. I want to *do* something. Something oh, useful. To forget it all. This heat, day after day, and the boredom, Mitzi, the boredom.'

Staggering slightly, Mitzi came over and flopped down at Clare's feet, cuddling her knees. 'Baby, baby. You've just had too much booze. It's coming out of your eyes. See?' She ran a finger along Clare's cheek and held it up. 'One hundred per cent alcohol. Sweetie, you're a living brewery.'

Spluttering, laughing through her tears, Clare gave up.

At the end of the week, Clare took her guests on the twin-masted *Rosa de Ventura* for a cruise down-river, to aid their recovery from the Palace ball the night before. They lay over cushions on the shaded deck, therapeutic cocktails a fingertip away and for a while peace reigned as everyone sweated their hang-overs away in the midday sun, inexpertly fanned by three river lads to keep off the mosquitoes. The *Rosa* sailed smoothly between the forest banks along the wide river that was green that day and drifted quietly round a bend. As they came to its furthest reach, the quiet was shattered. Raft huts were moored at the water's edge and from every raft transistors hung and blared across their bows. There were transistors, too, tied to the racks of the bicycles boys were riding up and down the forest path, banging out metallic sound. The guests awoke, dazed and disgruntled. 'God, darling,' Mitzi moaned, clasping her ears. 'Bloody hell,' said Perry Cathcart, propping his throbbing head on one hand and waving the other at the offending river bank. 'Thought it was unspoiled here. Yer come hundreds of miles ter punt down the Amazon and yer can't close your eyes for the screech of bloody wog boxes. Aren't you Queen of the May round here, Clare? Tell the bloody natives to stuff their muzak, why don't you?'

That evening, shaken by one of the nervous storms that frequently beset her, Clare screamed at Raul. 'You're supposed to be El Jefe. Get rid of those awful trannies, they spoil everything. *Ban* them.'

They were in Raul's study, no one was around. In the distance, the thump of percussion from the music room where the guests were dancing was just audible. Raul walked across to where Clare stood fuming and slapped her hard. She fell back but kept her balance, her mouth opening in shock. He slapped her again so that her chin jerked sideways and she reeled and went down on her knees. A shoulder string broke and the flimsy bodice of her dress sagged, revealing the mound of one breast. He laced his fingers through her hair and yanked her to her feet and hit her again. She put up her hands across her face, her eyes blank, and Raul broke the second shoulder strap. The dress crumpled to her waist and she folded her arms over herself, hunched in the heat of the room as if she were dying of cold. Both her cheeks were striped with crimson. Raul was breathing loudly, his face blotched yellow, the veins on his neck swollen and blue. 'You drag my name in the mud all over America, you bring shame on me and then you come back and tell me what to do, in my own country. You insolent slut.' He picked up Clare's wine glass and hurled it at the wall where the wine spread on the watered silk like a bloodstain.

Concepción in the bedroom wrung out a flannel and laid it gently on Clare's temple. 'Los hombres,' she said softly. 'President or peasant, they are all the same.'

A week later Raul issued an edict banning transistors, though the edict bore Clare's photograph and name. It suited him to do so. For years he had become ever more irritated by the excesses of the one element he could not control in Ventura — the airwaves. From the countries that bordered on his all manner of subversive rubbish filtered in via the transistors that were the pride and solace of every Ventura peasant and indio and in Spanish, too. Disembodied voices reported uprisings and the consequent fall of military juntas and dictators. Continually, they talked of elections and land reform and unsettling events in America and distant Europe. Priests whom Raul considered a disgrace to their cloth challenged American policies across his continent, attacked landowners and fed ignorant minds with the liberal nonsense of equality and the brotherhood of man. Some questioned the word of God Himself on the procreation of children and the place of women. These pernicious doctrines flew in the face of everything orderly, natural and ordained by the Lord, they were a poison, a virulent virus and it was his responsibility to protect the minds of his people. Under the steering hands of the de Toros, Ventura had been peaceful for five hundred years. While the rest of the Americas writhed and heaved with coups and counter-coups, while the peasants were manipulated against their own interests and leaders were shot like dogs in the streets, Ventura had remained an oasis of calm, a bulwark against Communism and a stalwart friend of the West. Raul was determined that this state of affairs would continue as long as he ruled his kingdom and owned every blade of its grass.

When the edict went out, groups of men gathered in the

streets of Nombre Dios, gesticulating angrily. Raul's men were instructed to destroy the transistors of anyone who disobeyed the edict and were heard using their sets. The few rich families remained undisturbed, muffled behind thick walls. The majority, the poor, who lived their lives in the open, wailed and shouted as their treasures were snatched from bicycles and boats and shacks and smashed against the nearest wall. A man was arrested for throwing a brick at a portrait of the First Lady in the Post Office, another was severely beaten by two policemen who found him urinating on a poster that bore Clare's face.

At the end of the week a bomb exploded under the statue of Vincente de Toro y Plata in the main square. Clare heard the dull punch it made in the air and the pretty tinkle of breaking glass as she lay on her bed in the silence of siesta. She sat up slowly, puzzled, turning her still-bruised face to the window where the sun shone under the slats of the blinds. Concepción ran in then, panting out the news. A minute later, the women heard the scream of sirens and the beat of helicopter blades in the white sky. At dinner that evening, Raul ate in his customary silence and when he had finished put his knife and fork neatly together on his empty plate.

'It was you, Clare, who caused that explosion,' he said, regarding his pale blunt nails. 'You realize that.'

'Me?' said Clare, shaking her head in bewilderment. 'What can you mean?'

'It was the people's revenge on you.' He leaned forward, his eyes fixed on a point just above hers. 'There was a doll in the wreckage. It had hair the colour of yours and a necklace of green stones like the emeralds you wear. It was horribly burned.'

'Dear Child.' Ma's writing was quavery and hard to read on the rustling airmail paper. 'I worry and pray daily for your safety. May Our Lady preserve you and Raul from the evil that has come to Ventura and may peace soon be with you again. The world is in a dreadful state, no one is satisfied with what they have, it is all money money money. Yesterday our faithful Nellie said she must have more money or she would have to leave us and that after *twenty years*. I am still shocked. She, of all people, must know how little we have. Your Father says it is the Communists.'

Pa had always said that. The first time she had ever heard the word had been from him. He'd been telling her the story of St George and the Dragon, leaping splendidly round the nursery with one arm curved behind him like Errol Flynn while she sat entranced by the huge brass fireguard and Nellie, her white hair brown then and tucked into a muslin cap, hovered with half an eye on the clock, ready to whisk her charge away to bed. Too soon, the story was over, Pa stood panting, the fiery dragon slain at his feet. Nellie moved forward.

Dodging her arms, Clare asked, 'Pa, what's a virgin?'

'What's that?'

Pa always said 'what's that?', pretending not to hear, when he didn't want to answer a question. 'A virgin,' she said again, pushing Nellie away, 'what is it?'

'A virgin is a good girl,' her father said carefully. 'It's what people call you when you're a very good girl.'

Clare sighed melodramatically. 'Then I'm not a virgin, am I? Nellie's always saying I'm a bad girl.'

Spluttering, Nellie advanced once more. 'Bed for you, Missie,' she said. Clare squirmed away and took her father's hands, gazing up.

'But Pa, in the stories, why does the dragon want a virgin? What does he want to do with her?' She tugged at his hands and he squatted down so that their heads were level.

'He wants to eat her, dumpling. Munch her all up and spit out her bones.'

'But *Pa*, how do you *know*? Perhaps he just wants to marry her and live happily ever after. How did St George know the dragon was bad?'

Her father rounded his eyes at Clare so that the whites showed. 'He just knew, dumps. He knew that dragons are wicked and he had to fight them. Like we have to fight the Communists today. They're the dragons and we're all St Georges.' He heaved himself up again, groaning comically. 'St George and Merrie England,' he said, 'bang bang bang. Off you go, my dumpling. Beddie byes.'

Fifteen years had passed since that evening in the nursery but Pa had not changed his point of view one jot. To him the word 'Russia' meant simply the Anti-Christ, a force of pure evil that had no roots in history and could not remotely be compared with other forms of government or ideology. Catholics, he often said, need not concern themselves with why Satan did what he did, that was irrelevant. Evil did not have a reason, it *was*, instantly recognizable and to be instantly confronted.

'We called it a dragon when you were little, dumps, but the dragon's real name is Communism. And ...' Pa explained, '... that's it and all about it.'

Brought up with these views Clare had nevertheless been upset when she first came to Ventura by occasional newspaper references to her husband as a fascist and a right-wing dictator. Embarrassed was perhaps the better word — such accusations drew the odd spiteful comment from her visitors. She soon came to see that these amateur critics of Raul had, in fact, no interest whatsoever in how Ventura was run and heartily disliked any sign that the democracy in their own countries might threaten inherited wealth or privilege. This did not stop their carping. They mouthed the word 'democracy' with much satisfaction, it proved that they were paid-up members of the civilized progressive West while the word 'dictatorship' meant backward countries, either flea-ridden and dreary or, at best, equipped with sunny beaches for an out-of-season tan. Pa, too, was made uneasy by the knowledge of his son-in-law's power. On a brief visit to Ventura, his first since Clare's marriage, he had paced about one evening after several brandies, his jowls puffed out.

'You ought to give 'em a say, my boy ...' (Who else but Pa would call that grim man his *boy*?) '... have to move with the times, more's the pity. I dare say they're not fit for the vote, can't read, can't write. But there it is, if you don't ...' and he pointed an arthritic finger at Raul lounging on the couch, '... you give every bleeding heart for miles around a stick to beat you with. They won't say you're too far to the right, oh no. Lefties nowadays are too smart for that. They'll say Ventura is no better than Russia, that's their tactics. Believe me. They'll try to smear you so you can't put a finger on them for what they are, fellow-travellers, parlour pinks, bloody Commies.'

He sat heavily down beside Raul, jerking his trousers over his knees. Mamaine sighed and fanned herself briskly with an issue of *Country Life* she had brought from England for Clare's perusal. Clare watched Raul's face.

'You'll lose nothing, you know,' said Pa. 'Look at England. We've had the vote for donkeys' years but do the people vote the Queen out? Course not. Worship her. More popular than all your P.Ms put together. And shall I tell you why?'

Raul's eyebrows lifted slightly and his jaw moved sideways as if, inside, his tongue was probing a painful tooth.

'I'll tell you why,' said the Earl, encouraged by these signs of life. 'Because people know what's good for them and people don't like change. Hate it. Oh, the socialists fiddle about a bit when they get in. Give out with the hot air. Tax the rich, free double-glazing for the poor, bomb Eton and up the workers, that sort of thing. But they can't change the fabric. Can't get rid of the people who really run the place. Voters wouldn't let them. Common sense. Change causes heart attacks, the medicine men will tell you. No, my boy, trust the people. Give 'em the vote. They won't do anything with it. Everything just the same.'

At the end of his long speech, Pa had subsided, mopping his brow with a large white handkerchief. Clare got up to ring for tea and Raul trailed idle fingers at the hem of her skirt as she passed. He seemed calm enough though he had never taken kindly to her own few attempts to question the running of his country.

'I see, Sir,' he said to the Earl, his eyes half-closed, 'that your daughter has not enlightened you on the way we do things here. Well, she is only a girl.'

He proceeded to remedy Clare's oversight. The peasants of Ventura did indeed, he explained, have the vote. Every five years they were given a list of candidates who would represent their interests on a General Council and on Polling Day they put their crosses exactly where they wished. Elected members were then free to raise with their President complaints or suggestions on any subject the electorate had at heart.

The short silence that greeted this exposition was broken by the chink of teacups as the maid deposited a tray glittering with silver at Clare's knee. She began to pour, fighting to keep her mouth firmly shut. Pa coughed and cleared his throat with several small explosions.

'Ah. Clare. Misinformed, both of us. Sounds a decent system. Perfectly adequate. What's wrong with that, dumps?'

Dumps tried and failed. The giggles broke out. 'It's just like Russia, Pa,' she spluttered. 'Just like the bloody Commies.'

Mamaine leaned forward, extending the delicate gold-rimmed Meissen cup to Clare. 'Delicious tea, dear child,' she had said in her light wispy voice. 'Lapsang Souchong, isn't it? Do you have it sent over specially?'

Clare finished reading her mother's letter and, putting it down on the blotter, crossed her hands over it and stared at the glassy sky opposite her desk. There was a clatter overhead and at the top edge of the window she glimpsed the bloated metal belly and the skimming blades of a chopper. The noise grew to a crescendo and slid away through the hot white sky towards the forest where guerrillas crouched peering up through skeins of lianas, stocky young men of the Fronte Liberacion Ventura in patched green denims who blended into the forest shadows along with the black stumps of their Kalashnikoff rifles. Men who, hearing her name, hawked and spat in the dust. She shivered at the thought. Why me, she silently protested, why me? It was so unfair, their hatred was misplaced. Raul ran Ventura, not his wretched English wife, so why was it for her that they reserved their real venom?

She often conducted these inner inquisitions now or wrote distraught pages in her diary, trying to sort out the facts of the charges against her from her growing weight of guilt, an emotion which was a foreign transplant in her and which every cell in her body fought to reject. *You did not concern yourself with the condition of the poor*. But nor had Raul or his Ministers or the Venturan rich or even Cardinal Alfonso, who infinitely preferred his imported bourbon to drinking fermented maize with his ragged flock – why, then, should she bear the burden of blame, she who came from the outside a few short years ago? She had been unhappy, lonely, too young to shoulder responsibilities that were anyway not asked of her. *You were stupid and greedy and frivolous, you drank champagne when the poor had no water, you ate caviar when the poor had no food.* No. Unjust. Their plight had not been drawn to her attention, they themselves had not protested. She had asked to visit the *barrios* but she had been refused, had accepted that refusal for fear her presence would be seen as an intrusion. They had no doors up there, no privacy, they might have resented her nosing around, peering into the women's cooking pots, eyeing the sick in their too-public beds. She remembered the Indian men in that village, lined up for her inspection, staring through her to the forest. They had wanted her not to be there, that had been obvious. She was not an English Queen to go about waving a gloved hand at her subjects and, besides, here they did not wave back. *Not waving but drowning.* That old tagline was inapplicable. It was. She could not swim herself, she could rescue no one, flailing about she would drown as well, drag them down with her to a useless death. *The eight men died, the boy died.* That grief merely proved her point. She had interfered then — why had Raul not stopped her? — and it had been a miserable failure. She had asked for a ban on transistors — why had Raul not refused? Best to let things alone. Look how the people were suffering now because a few ruthless young men refused to let things alone.

Clare remembered a history lesson at her boarding school. Fat Audrey Taylor — a scholarship girl they nicknamed 'Red Aud' for the portrait of Marx stuck over her locker and her constant hammering on the Marxist theme — was holding forth in her whining London accent on the glories of the Russian Revolution and the advances that had come to the Soviet people as a result. Miss Needham, the History mistress, had crushed her flat.

'There is no evidence, Audrey,' she said in her precise voice, 'absolutely no evidence that those advances would not have come about under the Czars, had the Czars continued to rule. The March of Time, girls,' she proclaimed, '*that* is the crux of the matter. More has been accomplished by the March of Time than by all your revolutions put together.'

Thinking of Miss Needham, Clare felt briefly more cheerful.

Surely that explanation worked as well the other way round? Perhaps revolution had come to Ventura because of that same March of Time and had no connection with anything she had done or not done. She looked at Raul's photograph in its heavy silver frame. That first bomb had been an amateur affair, hardly more than a Molotov cocktail, and it had merely added another patch of flaking plaster to a statue whose renovation was long overdue. Its real damage had occurred in some intimate recess of Raul himself, it had stretched his skin more tightly over his skull and jarred his eyes out of focus so that he appeared always to be listening to inner implosions beyond the range of other ears. He had boasted of Ventura's record of non-violence. There had been none since Raul's father, also called Raul, had ordered his men to disperse aggrieved campesinos who had gathered in the forest to march on Nombre Dios. Fourteen men had been killed. 'But that was an accident,' Raul had told Clare. His father had instructed the men to shoot above the peasants' heads, to scare them, and the killings, the 'incident', was a regrettable result of poor military training. 'Why were the men so badly trained?' asked Raul and answered triumphantly, 'because there was never any thought of them shooting anyone, *that* is why.' Whatever the reason, there had been no more trouble. With hindsight, Clare could only be surprised. All along Ventura's borders there was an almost constant rumble of unrest, with periodic flare-ups of insurgence, so that one government after another had come to accept guerrilla activity as a way of life. Raul, pointing out the contrast to her when they were first married, ascribed the country's stability to the stability of its ruling family.

'With us, the people know where they are,' he explained to his bride. 'Change for the sake of change leads only to evil. Our friends over the border will tell you and so will Americans, those who have power. You think Nixon believed in democracy? You think even Roosevelt or Kennedy did? Ah, they had to *say* so in their speeches but they ignored the people's wishes whenever

they could. Elections are simply ... how do you say it? ..
window-dressing. If American governments really believed in
democracy they would support it in other countries but they do
not. The Americans give me aid because they know I rule here
in Ventura and so I will keep the peace, which is good for
everybody. Besides, querida, change comes to us all, with or
without elections. In England, you vote a Prime Minister out,
here ill-health and death does the same job naturally and much
more cheaply. My father died and here I am. That is change
enough, no?' He had kissed her then. Those were the early days
when he occasionally kissed her and she sometimes argued with
him. Now his theory had been blown apart and violence was on
their doorstep. Sometimes a week would pass in peace and then
fighting would flare up again, so near that the metallic clatter of
rifles could be heard within the Palace walls and the maids would
stop what they were doing and stand like statues, only their
frightened eyes moving from side to side. The first bomb had
been followed by others that caused much more damage – the
old theatre had cracked under the onslaught and lay in rococo
slabs across the street, the cathedral walls were gouged with
bullet holes and the plate-glass doors of Clare's hospital and the
Dorada Hotel were concealed under sheets of protective corrugated iron. Outside Nombre Dios, tanks rumbled along the red
dust roads beside burned-out trucks, jeeps loaded with soldiers
were everywhere and gunfire cracked from the slopes where the
tin city clung. Overhead, day and night, helicopters rattled
across the sky, sending pedestrians scuttling into the shelter of
walls and doorways. As the terror mounted, Raul had tried to
get help from the governments over the border, convinced that
the guerrillas were being trained and armed there, but the hoped-
for allies had their own troubles and were deposed in their turn,
leaving him with worthless pacts signed by men who, if their
luck held, were safely holed up in Miami or Palm Beach.

He had returned from the last of these visits a fortnight ago and now stayed close to home. The once predictable routine of Palace life had changed. Before, he had worked in the mornings, shutting himself up in his office at the back of the Palace before Clare awoke and emerging as the heat built up to noon. These days he was often closeted behind the panelled doors until late in the evening. He took occasional naps, sending his secretaries away and stretching himself on one of the hard day-beds that he had refused to let Clare replace. Lunch was sent in to him, sandwiches, a thermos of coffee. Now and again, hungry for the sound of voices, Clare knocked at his door and entered unannounced. In the outer office, the girls turned from their typewriters or from where they stood at filing cabinets, their chatter dying away into silence. As they ushered her into Raul's room, he would get up from his desk to greet her or, if he were on the telephone – which he nearly always was – he would ask his caller to hold, put his hand over the receiver and wait for her to speak, his face a mask of courteous impatience. Every action was suspended, every voice silenced as long as she was present and in the hiatus anything she said sounded foolish to her ears, the aimless prattling of a pretty woman with not enough to do. As she was bowed out, as the doors closed behind her and she stood in the empty corridor outside, she could hear the sounds of working life begin again and felt a most conspicuous intruder. Quite often, as she went about in the Palace rooms, she would come to a stop and stand for a minute feeling curiously dizzy, as if the ground under her feet had suddenly sloped away from her. That part of the mansion she inhabited seemed to have become light and empty, a see-saw upon which she rose into a vacuum while the other end, where Raul sat with his aides, his secretaries and his stream of visitors, mainly Americans in crumpled seersucker suits clutching bulging briefcases under their arms, swayed heavily downwards, weighted by a gravity of matter that was mysterious to her and from which she was excluded.

*

There was a timid knock at the door and Luisa, one of the maids, announced that El Jefe was awaiting the Señora at the garden entrance. When the girl had gone, Clare moaned quietly to herself as she got up from the desk. In this one plan of Raul's she played all too central a part. For four years he had evinced no interest in becoming a father and had posed no awkward questions as to the reason for Clare's failure to become pregnant. Probably he was relieved, thought Clare, believing her to be an unworthy vessel for his heirs. Ma, of course, was under no illusions. Each time she sent the parcel with its several months' supply of the Pill she castigated her daughter for foisting upon her the burden of a mortal sin and pleaded for a grandchild to comfort her old age. But now Raul was obsessed by the wish for a son, another change that appeared to date from the detonation of that first bomb.

The car, one of three anonymous Fords that had replaced the Mercedes since the troubles, was parked below the steps by the swimming-pool. Manuel, his uniform replaced for security reasons by an open-necked shirt and light denim trousers, got out to open the door for her and she slid in next to Raul. There were some photographs on his knees. He put them in his briefcase as he saw Clare looking and barked instructions at Manuel. On the seat between them a pistol lay, at the windows little curtains in a jazzy design obscured the view, kept out the burning sun and concealed the face of the President and the shining hair of the President's wife. Manuel drove fast in the sweltering heat, bumping interminably down stretches of dirt track lined with the dusty green of the forest's edge. 'Oh God,' said Clare once, jolted into biting her inner cheek, 'this is ridiculous. Superstitious rubbish, Raul. D'you *hear* me?' Raul did not answer, he leaned forward in his seat and told Manuel to draw up. They had reached their destination, a gap in the forest, a pathway and, at its end, the skeleton of a ruined chapel, little more than a wayside monument with an arched entrance and a root held together by ropes of vines and the roots of ferns. Inside, in the cooler mote-filled dusk, Clare could just make out an effigy of the Virgin nailed to the stone wall. There was a bunch of dead flowers at Her feet, stuck into a rusty Nestlé tin. The rotting face, its wooden features worn and twisted, leered from beneath the remnants of a mantle which hung in shreds to where the round drum of a belly protruded with a knot of wood for a navel. Clare shivered in spite of the heat. Poor Lady, she could do with a good dose of Rentokil. More worms had tunnelled through her face than in the skirting boards of Tucolston. How Aunt Florrie would roar at this nasty fetish. 'What's *that* when it's at home?' Clare could hear her say. 'Go on Bonnie, Beulah! Fetch. Good kindling for the fire.'

On her shoulders Raul's hands pressed heavily down, pushing her to her knees on the jagged stone floor where tufts of spiky grass scratched her legs. 'Pray,' he said in a low voice. 'Pray to the blessed Madonna for the gift of a son.'

'Mumbo jumbo,' said Clare under her breath, 'bubble bubble toil and trouble.' Outside she could hear the car's engine revving over and over, setting the parrots shrieking. In derision, thought Clare, her head bowed. 'Eeny meeny miney mo wickety wackety woo.' Behind her by the crumbling arch, Raul shouted for quiet and as the engine died obediently away said again to Clare's back, 'Pray for fertility. Ask Our Lady to fill your barren womb.'

Woom boom. What a prayer in a country bedevilled by fertility, groaning with it. A hundred blood-smeared infants were probably pushing from their mothers' wombs right now and countless other women were poking themselves with sticks to empty out the jelly inside them before it could cling and grow. Ventura was sick with fertility, that much Clare knew, and here she was, driven through a forest in an uproar of breeding to kneel before a trunk of wood for the boon of others' doom. 'Obscene,' she muttered, 'onery twoery tickety boo.'

Raul said, 'Come.' He helped her upright and propelled her

towards the image. He rubbed reverently at the wooden navel. 'Kiss it, Clare.'

She twisted her shoulders in involuntary protest but Raul's hand pressed inexorably at the small of her spine. Manuel must know what was going on. He was only a chauffeur but still it was humiliating. Perhaps he was imagining her and Raul entwined at the feet of the idol, pumping at each other below the blind eyes. Shuddering, she leant forward and brushed her lips against the knot. Outside the monotonous chirrup of the cicadas rose like tiny jeers.

The chore over, fury gripped Clare. She stepped back and glared at Raul who stood staring without expression at the noseless face above him. 'And you?' she said waspishly. 'You should kiss it too, Raul. Even Our Lady needs two to tango.'

Raul turned and walked to the archway, where a dome of bright light shone whitely in the darkness. As he ducked his head he said, 'No. It is not to do with me that you are barren, Clare. I know that. I know that very well.' For a moment, Clare felt unease. He couldn't know about the Pill, could he? Of course not. Otherwise, why this journey, why this disgusting ritual? His fingers closed on her elbow, he led her back to the car. Manuel, his face impassive, slammed the door after them and then, leaning through the open window, dropped on Clare's lap three stems of a scarlet flower.

'For you, Señora,' he said in his hoarse Indian Spanish. 'These are good for what you seek.' Then he climbed into his seat, turned the car in the clearing and trundled back on to the track.

Raul scooped the flowers from her lap, unhooking one barbed leaf from the silk of her skirt. A sour smell filled the car as he wound down his window.

'But what are they?' asked Clare. 'What are they for?'

Raul shrugged. 'Who knows? Some tribal cure-all. The Indians have many.'

'Let me keep them, I'll find out,' she said, leaning towards him, her hand out. She was too late, the flowers tipped over the glass and fell along the forest border. 'They have something to do with fertility, don't they?' she said. Then she said, 'I'm sure they're at least as effective as that old bit of wood,' but Raul did not bother to reply.

At midnight, Raul came into her bedroom, his legs with their covering of black hair bare under the dark wine dressing-gown. Nodding gravely at her as she sat brushing her hair at the dressing-table he walked across to the bed, slipped off his gown, stood briefly naked – the black clump of hair at his groin, the pendulous flesh that hung under it making Clare move her eyes quickly to her own pale face in the mirror – and lay under the sheets. 'To what do I owe the honour of this visit?' she said but her voice cracked. She knew the answer though he gave her none. This was the conclusion of the day's fertility rite. She went about the room, opening and closing drawers and cupboards. She spent as long in the bathroom as she dared but when she emerged, Raul's eyes were still open, staring at her. Unable to postpone any further what lay ahead, she slipped out of her wrap and got into bed beside him.

Since the first weeks of their marriage, Raul had imposed a certain ritual upon his wife. He imposed it now. Clare arranged herself as he asked, legs straight and together, arms crossed over her breasts, her eyes closed. At times she had fallen asleep before he was ready and he had awakened her – he did not, Clare thought wryly, want her sleeping, he wanted her dead. The tremor of the mattress began. As the pace quickened – it was like being rocked in a cradle by an energetic nurse – Raul rolled against her and pushed at her legs, spreadeagling them. Fingers fumbled at her lower lips. There was a lull and she knew because she had seen before that he was examining her, his brow furrowed, his face clinical, a doctor in a morgue. The lips were stretched wider and she felt the hard pressure on the tender flesh within, probing. He pushed his fingers into her and moved them

[122]

inside, pressing this way and that roughly, as if to make room. A small sound of protest escaped her and, for a second, her eyes opened. Raul's face was grey between her legs, preoccupied. She closed her eyes again and lay blind as he pushed. Sometimes, against her every effort of detachment, Clare felt sickening excitement during this probing and moved her hips involuntarily up from the bed but Raul always withdrew, waiting until she lay still again. Once, when her excitement had become shamefully obvious he had withdrawn altogether, out of the bed, out of the room, leaving her wretchedly swollen, a lewd abandoned doll.

She knew tricks now to divert her mind. When she was a child, as a special treat, Pa would show her his legs. Slowly, as her face grew purple with laughter, he would edge his trousers coyly upwards and reveal two dead white sticks of celery topped by knees on whose pitted surface he swore you could see the Man in the Moon. 'Aren't they hideous?' he would say with modest pride as Clare quaked and rolled on the ground. 'The most awful legs in the world.' Then, to cap that, he would stretch out a monstrous tongue, moist as a sea creature, and touch the tip of his nose. By that time, he had Clare weeping and helpless, her heaving tummy sore.

The image of Pa's legs got her through the worst. Once the fingers were replaced by the blunt stab of the penis, there were only seconds to be endured. He heaved between her aching legs, his hands pinning down her arms on either side, his mouth tugging at her nipples as he thumped. A cry, a weight so heavy she could hardly breathe and the exercise was over. While her eyes were still closed the weight lifted, she felt him leave the bed and heard the quiet click of the door. When semen began to drip disconsolately from inside her to the sheet below, she rang for Concepción who came ghost-like in her calico nightie to raise her spirits with rude jokes.

*

There came a lull in the fighting. Day after precious day passed without incident, people gathered on the streets again to talk and sit rocking on their chairs and Clare slept without stuffing pillows around her ears. At dinner alone with Raul at the end of that week Clare said with unaccustomed light-heartedness to him, 'It's over, don't you think? Don't you think it's over?'

Raul sat rigid, his arms gripping the arms of his chair as if he were holding it together. He was paler even than usual and his face was hard and tight. He glanced at the window framed between its silk drapes and then at Clare, his eyes without light, impenetrable. Like the river, thought Clare, and shifted uneasily. The slight movement recalled him and a faint smile touched his lips. 'Over?' he said, 'oh yes, Clare, it is over. It is all over.'

That afternoon, he came into Clare's sitting-room where she was writing letters and standing at her desk asked in his formal way if he might interrupt her to talk of certain plans concerning Ventura's future.

'Naturally,' said Clare, unable to conceal her annoyance. His request seemed a reproach, implied that her interest in Ventura was minimal and had to be sought. God knows, that was near enough the truth. She had ceased her personal inquisitions, they had come to seem morbid and futile now that she was more alone than ever. What could one woman do anyway to reverse the inertia of centuries? She was Clare La Fontaine, not Jeanne d'Arc and even the man who owned Ventura was anxious only for the return of what had been the status quo.

Apparently the man had changed. For the next hour Raul talked and she listened in a near-incredulous daze, her eyes following him as he paced about the room, picking up an ornament here and an ashtray there, sitting again and getting up, his palms together in front of him as if praying for her attention. He admitted, wonder of wonders, that he had believed too long in the way the de Toros had managed things for generations and that he thought the time had come for new ways to be introduced. He said that Ventura possessed many riches, natural resources that could be harnessed for the use of the people, to provide them with work and a better living. He talked of distributing parcels of land to the peasants for their own cultivation, to grow food for their families and to encourage those who had migrated to the city slums to return with hope to the rural areas. It had been a mistake to modernize Nombre Dios, it merely encouraged more migrants and incensed the rebellious, it was in the forest and on the river that the work must begin. Dams, hydro-electric power, mineral resources, tree clearance for the planting of crops to feed the peasants – rubber, resin, hemp to grow and export, the potential was great and the work ahead hard but he was determined, with the help of American aid and American expertise, to drag Ventura into the twentieth century. He said this as if no one had said it before but Clare did not groan as she sometimes did when Raul whipped out a well-worn English cliché. She was too astonished at his outburst, she still clutched the pen that had been in her hand when he arrived. She released it now and saw crescent imprints of nails on the ball of her thumb.

'There is the question of the terrorists,' Raul went on, standing with his back to her at the long window. 'They must be isolated, dealt with. I am certain they are few in number, a small band of undisciplined malcontents who have no support among the peasants. But . . .' Raul turned on his heels to face Clare, '. . . their grievances will be used against us all, they will be supplied with arms, ammunition, training, encouragement by terrorists outside our borders, by Moscow, by Cuba. It is happening all around us and it will not stop here unless I take the strongest action now, before they regroup, before the fighting starts again.'

Unbidden, unheralded, before she could censor it, a memory of photographs came to Clare, glossy and ghastly, photographs seen on Raul's knees the day they visited the forest chapel and instantly censored from her mind. Twisted grey bodies splayed on a grey square, sewn to the ground by long runnels of darker colour, dead flies in a web of black blood. A painful thudding began inside her. 'Oh please,' she said in anguish, 'the fighting is over. Please don't start it again.'

'I?' he said, his face darkening. 'I did not start it.'

Clare went blindly on. 'The killings. I know your men kill, they go through the barrios at night, very late. I hear them, I hear the shooting. They say people disappear here, Raul, as they do in Argentina, they say there are bodies up there on the hills, that your men torture, kill women and children . . .' Her voice shook. She had tried ferociously hard not to think of these things and had almost succeeded. Why had she lost control now, of all moments?

In the short silence that followed, the clock on the main square struck four times, its chimes rusty and slow. There was a whirr of wings as the pigeons on the balcony outside scattered in alarm. Under Raul's eyes, the skin was puckered and yellow.

'What you say is most interesting.' He spoke softly. 'I tell my wife what I plan to do for my country and she repeats to me my enemies' slanders. She is on the side of the terrorists, she is against me.'

'No, Raul, no.' There was panic in her denial. 'I don't know why I said that, I know nothing about it. Something . . . I saw something . . . I misunderstood.'

'You have always misunderstood. You choose to do so. I cannot trust you, my wife.' He walked to the door and she went after him, taking him by the sleeve. She swallowed painfully and tasted tears. Was it true? Had she been wrong about Raul from the very beginning, from the moment they had met in that crowded noisy club? Ignorance and snobbery had made her despise him as a foreigner out of place in her constricted world, greed – her greed – had tied her to him. He had bought her with a handful of emeralds but she was willing to be bought. On their honeymoon he might have been gentle if she had been what he thought she was, what perhaps she ought to have been, what her God and Raul's enjoined her to be, a virgin until marriage. Her promiscuity had poisoned the roots of their union at the start and destroyed them utterly in those three lost months in America. She had been a rotten wife, she had injured her husband often and wilfully, choosing to make him into the monster rather than face her own sins and her selfish cowardly useless self.

'Raul,' she said in desperation, 'please listen. I was wrong to say what I said. Forgive me. I have been wrong about many things. I want to help you. Let me help you. I believe in what you're planning now, I know it is right. Let me be part of it.' This was her chance to do something useful at last, perhaps even a last chance to build a little love. Sombrely she looked up at his averted face, waiting and hoping.

He kept his face turned away but she saw his shoulders relax. As he opened the door he inclined his head and nodded in her direction. 'Then if you will wait here,' he said quietly, 'I will send Miss Carrington to you. She is new. She will assist you. She will explain. If you are willing to do what I suggest, I would be most grateful.'

The door closed behind him. Clare dropped her head in her hands, dizzy with relief. Something might be salvaged.

[8]

Ten minutes later Deborah-Jane Carrington ('Hi, ma'am, I'm Debbie-Jay') had turned Clare's desk into a drift of papers. As she dug into untidy files gripped between her knees, Clare surveyed her through the dark glasses that hid her reddened eyes. The girl was a year or so younger than herself, a recent addition to the Palace staff and, by those standards, an exotic bloom. She had a penetrating nasal voice, hay-coloured hair tied roughly off her face, a small swollen mouth and huge blue-tinted spectacles that slid constantly down her tilted nose and were constantly prodded back into position. Instead of the neat primrose dresses worn by the other women of Raul's clerical staff, Debbie-Jay sported a striped seersucker jacket, skinny jeans and white sneakers that were none too clean. Raul had recruited her on a visit to Sao Paulo where her father was something in the US Embassy. Fleetingly, Clare wondered if the girl was Raul's mistress. The question did not overly concern her at the moment but she liked to know where she stood, it avoided embarrassment or, worse, undue familiarity. Once, she had caught a sideways glance from a maid, a swarthy odalisque of a woman who, as she was smoothing down the sheets on Clare's bed, had seen a small stiff stain. Clare had had her transferred to the kitchens because she thought she saw complicity in that look and complicity could not be permitted. But this Carrington was hardly Raul's cup of tea. She talked too much, she looked too rumpled. Sadly Clare thought, she looks too alive.

'Found it, ma'am.' Debbie-Jay straightened up, pushed at her spectacles and dumped a typewritten document in front of Clare.

'Jeez, I thought I'd lost it.' It was a memorandum from Raul, from the Office of the President, asking for the co-operation of Señora de Toro y Plata. Two paragraphs were circled in ink. Leaning over Clare's shoulder, Debbie-Jay read them aloud in her nasal voice that smelt of mint.

'The objectives and requirements of the Venturan Rural Development Project must involve and rely upon the co-operation of the international community. To this end, assistance and funding will be asked of the relevant agencies in the United States of America in order that ecosystem suitability can be assessed and classified with respect to specified kinds of use and to make optimum use of all available resources.' Debbie-Jay paused to push up her specs. 'Gobbledegook, eh?' she said cheerfully. 'I'll explain in a minute.' She began reading the second paragraph.

'A Women's Co-operative will be set up throughout the rural areas of Ventura under the auspices of the First Lady. This project is specifically designed to benefit the women of Ventura's Indian tribes who are frequently overlooked in development plans. For the purpose of aiding ethno-biologists in assessing potential subsistence resources, the women will be offered a fee to collect from the forests species of flora and fauna that they have traditionally employed for nutritional, medicinal and other uses. These will be delivered to local centres for sorting and categorization.'

There was a note attached in Raul's slanting script. Clare slid it from under the paper-clip. 'Clare,' it said, 'hope you agree to take this on. Ask Carrington for details.' Smiling, she sat up straight in her chair. 'Fire away,' she said to Debbie-Jay.

The first paragraph, shorn of its verbiage, meant Clare was asked to entertain at weekly dinners the men who constituted 'the relevant agencies' of the memo. The first list was already drawn up.

'Barnum, John T.' Debbie-Jay read out. 'He's a mining consultant, he works out how much it will cost to bring whatever it is to the surface, that kind of thing. O'Reilly, Gerard, from Washington, DC, not too sure where he fits in, I'll ask the Chief. Sammy Levinson from LA, in fisheries. Pogrebin, B. J., potato expert from Idaho. Gary Lutz, Penn. State, in pharmaceuticals. Penowski, Alfred, from Oregon. Timber.' The list went on and quickly Clare took notes on the cards provided by Carrington, cards small enough to be handy for instant reference. These men were likely to be crashing bores, Clare thought, but entertained they would be. And well.

When the dinners had been sorted out to Clare's satisfaction, Debbie-Jay dived again into her files and came up with the notes on the organization of the Women's Co-operatives. Listening, Clare's euphoria began to ebb. She was required to visit the villages, talk to the women, gain their confidence, become – as Raul put it – their trusted friend. Unbidden, an image of Indian men rose before her, their hands limp, their faces blank. Meeting Indian women would be a hundred times worse, the barriers between them more blatant and distressing. She tried for a moment to imagine being a trusted friend of the shadowy female figures she had seen peering from the mysterious interiors of their huts and failed. She scratched nervously at a corner of the leather on her desk while Debbie-Jay's voice drawled on.

As it happened, Clare was soon afforded a perfect excuse to withdraw her offer of help with the Co-operative. Ten days after her meeting with Debbie-Jay Carrington, fighting broke out again. There was an explosion in the harbour area, a boatman was killed and a harbour policeman badly injured. Raul could hardly argue if she pleaded the danger of village visits, under these circumstances. But by then she had no such intention. By then she had already made her first visit to a village centre and met the women there.

*

That comunidad campesina was much like all the others that were to become so familiar to Clare: a dozen or so dilapidated adobe shacks straggling along the river bank, a few scraggy chickens scratching in the dust, two donkeys with their heads bent mournfully under the lash of the sun and several skin-and-bone dogs rooting in the piles of rubbish. As Clare clambered down from the chopper they ran yapping at her. Ruiz, the guard at her side, dispersed them with a well-aimed stone, shouting. His voice was loud in the silence and when it ceased, nothing could be heard but the suck of the river at its banks and the alarmed grunts of some flop-eared piglets bucking towards the trees on short stiff legs. Clare batted at the flies and felt threads of sweat trickle from her armpits. No sound came from the huts. The able-bodied men would be out working on the local estancia or digging their own rocky patches at its borders so the women must be crouched in those black caves, hands over their children's mouths in fear and suspicion of this unwelcome gringa dropped from the sky in their midst. Groping in her shoulder-bag, Clare took out a valium and worked it down her dry throat. Everything was as she had feared. Hostility, incomprehension, sullen faces, dead eyes and no language in common to bridge the gap. Clare cringed inside.

As usual, she was feeling dreadful and, this day, worse than usual. In spite of the heat, bouts of shivering had attacked her since early morning and a heavy dose of aspirin had failed to shift the steel band that squeezed her temples. It seemed a long time since she had felt really well, certainly not since she had taken off for the States and perhaps before that. Tears came easily and she had grown so used to vomiting that it had come to seem a normal part of each day. Was she suffering from some debilitating tropical disease or was her liver slowly silting to a halt, furred like an old kettle? Only Clare was aware of how much she regularly drank though Concepción must have some idea, since it was she who threw out the empty bottles from the cupboard by the bed and dusted the array of pills in her bathroom armoury.

She stumbled and Ruiz caught at her arm, steadying her.

'The Señora is not well?' he asked in Spanish.

'The heat,' Clare said and pressed her fingers to the sides of her head, where tendrils of hair were already matted.

'A storm,' said the guard, looking up at the low-clouded sky. 'There will be a storm. We should not be here too long.'

The second bodyguard, Felix, trudged from the chopper to join them and Clare walked between them like a prisoner under escort across the dusty track to the hut that had been designated the Women's Co-operative Centre. It stood a hundred yards away from the other huts, its one bare room buzzing with fat flies, its walls plastered with the posters that bore Clare's photograph and urged upon the women of the villages their participation in Raul's project and the benefits that would accrue to them if they did. 'CAMPESINAS! THE FRUITS OF THE FOREST ARE YOUR HERITAGE', announced thick black capital letters. 'COLLECT THE PLANTS AND THE CREATURES YOU USE IN YOUR HOMES TO FEED YOUR CHILDREN AND CURE THEIR ILLS. FIVE PESOS A KILO IS YOUR REWARD.'

Reading them, Felix made a small noise of contempt and spread his hands at Clare. 'They are indios,' he said. 'Uncivilized. They do not read. They do not even understand Spanish, most of them. Uh.'

Shrugging, he ducked inside the hut while Ruiz, gesturing politely for Clare to wait, set off towards the other huts, his pistol in its worn leather holster jouncing against his heavy hips. Clare waited. She breathed in shallow gasps. The air was so hot it hurt her lungs. Nearby, a donkey shifted on swollen legs and tossed its head. The flies rose and settled again, ringing its mournful eyes. Overhead, a bird squawked and flapped slowly across the muddy river, in the distance the sky rumbled. A rank smell of rotting vegetation stung Clare's nostrils so that her stomach gave an unsettling heave and she leaned against the peeling wall

[132]

and closed her eyes. In the distance, she could hear Ruiz's hoarse shouts.

Clare caught the whine of a mosquito and, opening her eyes wide, smacked at her neck and saw that the women were coming from the huts, urged on by the guard. They came in twos and threes, dumpy figures with babies on their backs and solemn small children, bare-legged, clutching at their skirts. Slowly, with reluctance, they approached, Ruiz moving amongst them growling like a dog herding sheep. The straggling procession advanced across the scrub to where Clare stood upright now, trying to smile, her lips stretched painfully across her dry teeth. She could distinguish faces now and the grape-black eyes that were fixed on her, without expression. The guard pushed the women into a semi-circle around her and Felix moved forward. His shirt had pulled away from his trousers and a white tyre of flesh protruded, its runnels damp. There was a dark vee of sweat from his thick neck and shoulders to a point at the small of his back. Clare took a step forward, felt her knees give and stood still. Felix began to bark out words to the women in a guttural dialect Clare could not understand. The women stared at him, immobile. Flies crawled on their flat brown faces. He waved a hairy arm at Clare and the women moved their eyes to her. Clare nodded several times in the silence and said, clearing her throat, how delighted she was to be a guest in their village and how she had come to help and encourage them to join with her, as women together, in this new Women's Co-operative. The words sounded in her ears like the rattle of stones in a tin. A creaking came from the river bank, the trees hanging over it were stealthily rubbing against each other, their branches swaying.

'The President asks me to tell you,' she battled on in her now fluent Spanish, 'that whatever plants or snakes or lizards or other living things that you bring from the forest to this Centre will be returned to you a hundredfold, for the benefit of you and your children. In the riches of the forests of Ventura, scientists will find secrets that will in the future provide you, the people, with food and health and a better life for all. This he promises you, as I do.'

She fell silent and Felix translated what she had said, or half-translated – Clare detected all too easily the burden of Spanish that larded his words. She glanced quickly around at the blink-ered faces. They didn't understand. They had been pushed out of their huts to stand in the sun while a gringa with gold round her neck bleated at them in a language they did not know but the sound of which they feared. The whole project was useless and badly organized, a farce. Please God let it be over soon and I will never intrude on these people again.

Felix of the fat belly went into the shack and came out with a chair for Clare, motioning her to sit down. She sat.

'What must I wait for now?' she asked him. It was all she had the energy to say. If only she could put her head between her knees, the ringing in her head might ease.

'The cartons, Señora.' He waved towards the chopper. 'They are bringing the cartons to hold what the women collect.' He saw Clare's face and raised two big hands consolingly. 'No, no, Señora. You will not need to come back. That is our job.'

The pilot appeared with Ruiz, carrying between them a hammock piled with plywood boxes. Nodding to her, skirting her politely, the three men went into the hut. Outside, Clare sat on and the women stood staring. At the edge of the group a tiny child, its belly hard and swollen under a ragged vest, sucked its thumb and gazed unblinking at Clare over its fist. She smiled hopefully, the child gazed and her smile became a rictus.

Then, out of the corner of her eye, she caught a movement, an odd gasp. A young woman with a dark scarred face ducked her head. Clare stared at the pale parting between her plaits. The sound came again, a strangled moan, an older woman clapped both grimy hands to her mouth and her little girl, yelping, dived into her mother's skirt, pulling it round her ears. Clare tried to understand what was happening but her mind refused to move. The noises became louder. On wizened legs a crone shuffled two steps forward and, opening the wrinkled pouch of her mouth, emitted three loud cackles. All at once the women exploded, shrieking and shaking. Laughter. They were laughing at her. She looked about, aghast, as two more women sank to their knees, slapping each other's broad shoulders, grunting at each other, convulsed. Then the crone came straight at her, one stick-like arm extended. Clare felt the rough scrape of the old woman's hand on her shoulder and put up her own hands to fend her off but there were hands everywhere upon her now. stroking her flesh, pulling at her clothes, hands on her hair, on her cheeks ..

Clare stood up, panting. There was a roaring in her ears and a scribble of darkness across her eyes, blotting out the sun. The faces shrank and dissolved into fragments as she crumpled at their feet.

Drowning, she fought upwards in a boiling sea, her lungs bursting for air. Her head had become a red-hot disc and flares of white light burst behind her eyes. Tossed helplessly across the burning waves she threw out her arms and moaned in terror. Her hands were caught and held, she clung on grimly until the next wave sucked her away. Her limbs were huge and the distended skin split and blistered, blubber filled her mouth and she gasped and choked and the same hands caught her again and raised her to drink ... a strong nutty liquid that ran into her parched body, blessedly cool. Cool cloths were laid on her scorching forehead and over her sore eyes and across her aching chest. The cloths smelt rancidly of the forest

When she opened her eyes at last and looked up at the grave faces of the women kneeling around her, their dark hair curtaining her crib of straw, weak tears of deliverance ran down her cheeks. The young woman with scars on her skin wiped the tears away, and the old woman leaned over her, baring her gums in an ecstatic grin. Then, wrapping skeletal arms across her shrivelled breasts, she began to sway and croon. To that hoarse lullaby Clare closed her eyes and slept.

On the flight back to Nombre Dios the guards, shouting above the engine's roar, told her that the fever had lasted a night and a day and that for some hours they had even feared for her life, so grey had she become, with blisters this big on her lips. But the storm had been too violent to risk flying her out and they had lost all radio contact with the town and besides, she had been delirious, babbling, hot as fire, best left to the devices of women.

'We had no choice, Señora,' they assured her again and again, their faces pained and anxious. 'Please tell the President, there was no choice.'

Clare looked out of the window along the torn shreds of the clouds that were all that remained of the storm and through them down to the broad brown loops of the river and the curly trees that stretched for ever on either side concealing, somewhere in their depths, that hut and those women, and she saw how perfect was this green cradle of the planet, how infinitely generous with its gifts and how in harmony the trees, the water, the creatures and the people who lived amongst them. She was wrapped, still, in the loving kindness of the women who had taken her, a sick and silly doll, into their home and with their skills cured her. Stupidly, she had feared them and shrunk from those rough hands that had been so gentle. Because of them she was alive and more than alive on this marvellous clean morning, better than she had felt for many months, better than she had ever felt in Ventura. It seemed to her that the women, nursing her on that pallet of straw and sacking in the dim heat among the flies, feeding her their medicines that tasted of the bark of trees, had returned her to a half-forgotten world of bliss from which she had been for too long an exile. Looking down at the swell of green surf below, she thought 'I am reborn.'

'Concha, why are you so ...' – Clare wanted to say 'cynical' but could not find the Spanish word, '... so hard? Those village women are marvellous. So kind and so brave, Concha. They have nothing and they work so hard.'

Concepción, her arms full of sheets, shrugged and sucked at her lips. The Señora's new passion made her uncomfortable though she couldn't say why. She fumbled at the handle of the door, said 'sí' to Clare and retired with her burden. Clare watched her go, puzzled for a moment. Well, Concha had her moods like anyone else. She went back to her letter.

'Oh, Ma,' she wrote, her writing sprawled upwards along the page, 'you cannot imagine how marvellous these Indian women are. Sometimes they stand as still as the cattle at home used to stand at sunset, a million miles away, dreaming by the river. And sometimes they push all round me and I can smell them, warm and steamy and sour-sweet. They are like those children who came at us on the bridge in Dublin, do you remember? Those tinker children, wild and dirty, with those wise eyes? There is no distance between me and them in spite of everything, they look so directly at me that I think they can read my thoughts, the ordinary barriers between people simply aren't there, none of those twitches and unease and politenesses that the so-called "civilized" have. And, Ma, they have nothing, less than nothing, and yet they are good and generous and so funny. They talk all the time in a kind of low roar and they make frightful jokes about men and sex and bodily functions and shout with laughter and haven't a shred of shame. I feel it doesn't matter what I do when I'm with them, they've seen it all. Ma, I think they may be saints, truly I do. Loud, hoarse, merry saints, the lot of them. They make me feel an inch high but they seem to love me, nevertheless, and I love them back with all my heart. I would do anything for them.'

[137]

This letter rather shook Clare's mother, reading it over the marmalade at Tucolston. 'Do you think the dear child is entirely *well*?' she said, passing the inky sheet to her sister-in-law. 'There's something feverish about this, don't you think?'

Lady Florence read in silence and raised her head. 'Road to Damascus symptoms. Know 'em well,' she said. 'Typical of Clare to go so overboard. Remember the hoo-ha there was at her first communion? We can only hope the good Lord has her well in hand. Otherwise, it'll end in tears.'

Clare's illness and her cure had, indeed, brought about a kind of conversion. She felt herself called to the women as a nun is called to her Saviour, she prepared to dedicate her life to them. Whatever they needed, whatever they wanted, she silently vowed to do all in her power to give them.

It was a task for which that first visit had hardly prepared her. She met the women of the next village with a new confidence and though most of them, too, spoke only their Indian dialect, there was one who knew Spanish and willingly acted as Clare's translator. There was always such a one. Soon the project was well under way and Clare could have curtailed her work, flying in only now and again to make sure Raul's wishes were being carried out. But by the time each place and each face had become familiar to her, the scale of the women's suffering had revealed itself and the project itself became secondary, merely providing a convenient excuse for her visits. Clare felt vaguely but strongly that without the raison d'être of the Co-operative, Raul would have raised objections to what was now almost an obsession.

Her visits had fallen into a pattern. After the women had emptied their baskets of the plants, insects and other small creatures they had gathered in the forest and Raul's men had sorted them into cartons to be loaded into the helicopter, Clare began her round of the huts, tugged from one to the other by women fearful that she might depart without hearing of their particular misfortune. True, she was sometimes required to admire a new baby born healthy and perfect, thanks be to Our Lady, or to praise the skill of a little boy who had caught his first monkey for the cooking-pot or to hear the latest gossip, relayed with much giggling as the women beat their washing on the stones by the river or ground dry beads of maize. Often, they appealed to her to judge a tricky situation and settle disputes.

But it was the litany of grief and misery that had taken her by surprise and appalled her, a litany that was endless and for which her help was endlessly implored.

'Señora ...' – Carmen's hands pulling at her elbow, '... my little girl has a fever, she has terrible fits, I have given her medicine but I think she will die.' And the child, motionless in the darkness of her mother's hut, her eyes dull, her body emaciated.

'Señora ...' Aída grasping her skirt, '... I have had five children and I am pregnant again. See, this is where my babies sleep. Will this one sleep there, too?' And the pitiful mounds under the trees, covered with palm leaves, swarming with ants.

'Señora, come with me ...' María's hands clasped entreatingly – 'for a week, our babies have died nearly every day but nobody comes. They get diarrhoea one moment, they are gone the next and the doctor is too far away. We are left alone. Señora, help us.'

They had cured her with their medicines but in the face of epidemics and life-long malnutrition, they could not cure themselves. With the women around her, holding her hands, Clare stumbled through one foetid hut after another along the tracks and clearings and river banks from one end of Ventura to the other and the sights that met her were always the same. Under a green Christ hung on the wall, His red heart swollen in His wooden chest, children lay whimpering in dark corners or curled like small dried leaves in what little shade there was. Children with weeping sores and suppurating ulcers that would not heal, children with rasping exhausted coughs who looked at her from the tunnels of their eyes, children with twisted withered limbs and grotesquely bloated bellies. As she stooped over them, the grey scabs on their sunken cheeks and round the sockets of their eyes seethed horribly and broke up into swarms of flies. She learned to judge the degree of sickness by the flies — they gathered most thickly on those who were nearest death, making a living shroud for dying bodies and a humming halo round death's little heads. When the sick were past hope the women covered them with sacking to keep the flies off because it was easier to endure the suffocating heat than the endless torment of those busy legs. The huts were ovens and terrible but the flies were more terrible. They clustered wherever there was pus or excreta and gorged and buzzed away to wipe themselves fastidiously upon the sores of another victim. Clare grew to loathe them with a wild fury and emptied can on can of spray into their ranks in the early days, before she had fully understood the intransigence of the woes that beset the villagers. She also learned that if she pressed hard enough with her fingers at the hinges of her jaw she could stem the useless tears.

There was always more suffering, it poured like a torrent from a breached dam. 'Señora, since my last child I cannot walk. Look, I can only crawl.' 'I bleed all the time, Señora, since my baby was born, my milk has gone, how shall he survive?' 'See these bruises, Señora. My man is good but he beats me when he is drunk and now he is always drunk.' In one village a woman led her away from the huts to the place where she kept her mad son and pointed, watching Clare's face with a pent intensity as if only Clare's feelings could release hers. Clare looked at the small crouched figure behind the stakes. The corner of a sack hooded his shaggy head, there was a string of spittle on his cracked lips and he stank like a wild goat. She pressed her fingers at her jaw and her throat closed.

Yet the woman were cheerful for the most part. It was rare

that they cried, though in grief they sometimes threw their heads back and howled like dogs, plucking at their faces and their breasts as if trying to pull away some leech of pain. They would squat beside a dying child and stare ahead without expression, waiting patiently for life to depart. But they laughed easily too, as the women had done on Clare's first day in the village, exploding into mirth, slapping their thighs and doubling up, their eyes vanishing into crescents of wrinkles. The only times they seemed simply sad with a kind of wrenching sadness was when they allowed themselves to think of what they could do and could be if things were otherwise. Hope was what wrecked them, the hope that someone, somewhere, might come and teach them just enough to let them struggle against fate. If they could read and write, if their hunger to know something of the world outside the forest could be momentarily assuaged, if they had just enough food, how different things might be.

'If only I could knit,' a woman said to Clare. She had buried her third child the day before, digging the small trench herself, tenderly cuddling the little corpse, and she had not shed a tear. The tears came when she said, gazing up at Clare, 'if only I could knit.'

On her visits now, Clare loaded the big-bellied chopper with clothing, blankets, mattresses for the sick, tinned food, packages of gruel. She recruited a nurse from Madre María who came with her to do what she could with medicine, bandages and injections. She distributed reading materials and boxes of pencils and set one woman in each village to learn and begin to teach the others. She taught herself to knit and showed the women, bringing wool and needles. Above all, she talked to them and listened and answered their endless questions as well as she could, emptying out to them any shred of knowledge or information that she had, about everything in the world from space exploration to how women walked in high heels – she brought her own shoes and

the women stuck them on their feet and staggered about screaming with laughter, Clare laughing with them at the ridiculous
pointed pointless things. And always, after all the others, the
same question would come. Shyly or giggling, pulling Clare
aside or whispering to the translator, the same question. 'Señora,
I have had nine children, I do not want more.' 'We have so many
children, year after year, how can we stop?' 'God rules, Señora,
but must we receive whatever He gives us, child after child that
we cannot feed?' 'We want to learn about these things, please,
Señora, teach us.'

In one village, sitting in the shade, encircled by the women,
Clare began to explain the technique of coitus interruptus, watching the women's faces as the translator passed on her words. One
by one, she saw them shake their heads.

'Señora, they say this will not work with their men.'
The translator's voice quavered. 'They say the men will not
permit ...'

Alarmed, Clare thought she was about to cry. Instead, she
giggled, one hand over her mouth. At that moment an old
woman with a face as quilted as earth seamed by drought
grabbed at a stick. Holding it menacingly at her groin, she stood
and waved it about, pretending drunkenness. The women
ducked and squealed. She weaved at them, ululating, and they
shrieked, crawling from her on their knees. By the tree under
which Clare sat lay the ashes of a fire and a blackened kettle, on
its side. The old woman galloped at it, the stick straight out in
front of her, pushing at the kettle's mouth. The first time, she
missed, amid guffaws of joy. Twice more she tried and the third
time the stick entered the kettle, hitting its back with the sound
of a gong. Triumphantly, the old woman turned, careering in a
circle, the stick between her legs, the kettle banging round its
top. The women cheered and clapped their hands, tears of
laughter rolling down their cheeks. Clare laughed with them,
giving up, her stomach aching. The old woman threw down the

stick, spat after it and stretched out her arms, the rags of her clothing hanging along her scarecrow bones. The women gathered beside her, one of them raised up her voice in a hoarse chant and they all started to dance, reeling from side to side around the dead fire. Hands beckoned to Clare and held on as she joined them and lurched with them, singing gleefully along with them in the hot sun.

'One is one and all alone and never more shall be so,' sang Clare, dancing away.

Afterwards, when they squatted again on the ground, panting, she tried to look solemn, straightening her face, beginning her lecture again. How strange they were, these women who suffered so from bearing children and yet laughed themselves into fits at a stick pronging a kettle. How brave, how admirable. But what, then, could she do for them?

Clare knew she would get no help from Raul or from anyone else in this Catholic backwater. Her mother begrudged Clare's own demands, she would hardly relish sending crates of the Pill to unknown Catholic women half across the globe, even if it could be arranged. Yet somehow it must be arranged. Clare saw with absolute clarity that some form of birth control was the only real freedom she could offer the women. What use were her tins of food when there were always more mouths to feed? What use was doctoring bodies undermined by constant pregnancies? The fear and the reality of childbirth hung like a vulture over each female from girlhood on, undermining their every effort to make the smallest change in their own lives and the lives of their daughters. And this burden was given them in the name of God, a God who was omnipotent to these poorest of His flock but had no dominion over nightly doses of progesterone.

Towards the end of the year Clare was squatting by a short arm of the river cuddling a brown frog of a baby while its mother, her rump in the air, gutted a fish in the water. From the village there came a ragged cry and then a burst of piercing screams that set the monkeys screeching overhead. The mother stood up, wiping her bloody hands on her skirt. Clare pushed the baby at her and began to run towards the huts, her hands over her ears. The woman raced after her, the baby jogging at her hip, and caught Clare's arm.

'No,' she said hoarsely, shaking her head, 'no es nada, no es nada.' The screams rose and fell and died groaning away and Clare stood trembling, clutching the woman's hand. Later, it was explained to her that Magdalena, a woman with a haggard handsome face and long flaccid breasts, had been pregnant and was no longer so. Flat stones lifted from the river had been laid on her stomach and the heaviest women had clambered on to the stones and stamped up and down. 'Sometimes,' they said, shrugging, 'it is the only way. Magdalena was sick, she could not feed the children she had. She wished it.'

On that day, cold with horror, Clare made her decision. From then on, she told the women in each village that she would shortly go away to England and when she came back she would bring with her pills and devices that would prevent children being born without pain and injury. 'Trust me,' she said to them, 'don't lose hope, something will be done, together we will manage. Things around here are going to change.'

Hearing her, the women were euphoric, their faces split in joyful grins, clapping and shouting the news to each other. They did not doubt her for a moment, their Señora could do anything, however magical. Clare was wracked with doubts but daily more determined that she would find some way to cope. She vowed to herself that she would convince or if necessary defy anyone who stood in her path — Raul, his Creole Establishment, the Church itself. The women, light-headed, whispered happily of the coming miracle.

Their gossip had an immediate repercussion. The following week, on a visit to the village of San Pedro, Clare was sitting with her arms round María-Aída, a young Indian girl with a twisted foot whose first child had died the night before and lay in a basket beside them on the lumpy straw mattress, a scrap of blue cotton hardly raised by its tiny body. María-Aída was fifteen and still had tears to cry, she sobbed and coughed against Clare's breast while her mother squatted beside them in silent distress, herself heavily pregnant. Clare held the girl, crooning gently. Suddenly, the dim light in the hut was extinguished. Two men stood at the entrance, their black boots caked with mud. They wore jeans and torn combat jackets, they had lines of bullets criss-crossing their backs and they filled the hut with the acrid smell of their sweat. Clare thought, her heart jumping, they are guerrilleros. Crouching, the men came in, looming over the women, and Clare saw that their faces were smeared with black. One was no more than a boy, a small scar ran from an eyebrow to the lid of a lightless eye and his lips rose full and red against the charcoaled skin. The other was older, his knuckles white against the heavy rifle, his face pockmarked and rough with stubble. He spoke bad Spanish, it stuttered out jerkily like rifle fire. He said Clare was perverting the women with her evil norteamericano ideas, he said all that his people had were their children and she must not come here again, filling the women's heads with wicked rubbish so that they would refuse to have babies and the Indian race would die.

'You,' he said, each word a bullet, 'you are a rich gringa, you sit in power over us, you and your husband, and you keep our land from us so that we cannot feed our children and they starve. It is because of your greed that they die. Yet you do not come here to offer justice, only to tell our women they must have fewer children.'

As the women huddled, he lunged across them, snatched the dead baby from its basket and swung it up. His hands were huge and brown over the waxen flesh, the little skull drooped against his wrist. Her mouth open on a soundless cry, María-Aída raised

[145]

her arms towards her child. The man shouted hoarsely shaking the shrivelled body.

'This child did not die because we have too many children. This child died so that La Dorada ...' he hissed the words, '... could eat and drink and grow fat from the land that is ours. *That* is the truth, la verdad, la verdad. Go away from here, leave us alone. We know what our women need and it is not you with your lies and your treachery. Go.'

His face was contorted, drops of sweat flew off him. The boy beside him wiped his mouth with his hand, smearing the charcoal. María-Aída began to sob quietly, fluttering her hands at the child who lay like broken porcelain in the man's hands, its eyelids violet bruises in the sunken sockets. Appalled, Clare stood up and pushed past the men to the door. In the distance, across the scrub, the helicopter that had brought her here gleamed in the sun. In the shadow of its bulk, the two guards squatted with the pilot, chatting, content to smoke and talk while their mistress went her way as always, hob-nobbing with the indios. As she stared across at them, the men shoved her aside and ran crouching and silently for the forest. A yard away, the young boy turned as he ran and spat at her, a wet coin of fury in the dust. Clare turned back and went into the hut again to comfort the weeping women. Her hands, she noticed absently, were trembling. She soothed the women and, together, they laid the fragile baby bones again in the basket cradle. A violent anger flared in her. Those men, so selfish, so past all words ignorant, worse than swine in their contempt for the burden of these women, her women. They called themselves revolutionaries but they were swine who cared only for themselves and treated their women like slaves, child-bearing chattels. *Things*. Nothing now would deter her. That very evening, she swore to herself, wiping the tears from María-Aída's swollen eyes, she would tell Raúl that she must go to England.

*

[146]

In the event, no arguments were needed to persuade him, he acquiesced without comment. Clare glanced sharply at him. Was there even a note of relief in his voice?

'You will be glad to see me go,' she said flatly Do you have a woman somewhere? Am I in the way?' She yawned with exhaustion, hardly interested in his answer. So much organization lay ahead.

'A woman?' Raul said. 'I have no time for women. There is a war here in Ventura or had you not noticed?' Then he softened. 'No, Clare, I shall be glad to see you go for your own sake. You have been working too hard in the villages and it is more and more dangerous. The people there hide terrorists, what if they were to kidnap you? I have thought about this for some time and I have already decided that when you come back, you should not leave the city again until the troubles are over.'

For a moment, Clare froze. That could ruin all her plans. She opened her mouth to protest and closed it again. Sufficient unto the day. When the time came, she would do whatever had to be done and no one would stop her.

[9]

'Ventura,' said the man on the television screen, his eyes sunk in corrugations of suffering or drink, 'is the smallest, least developed and least known country of the South American continent. It is, however, a loyal friend of the West and one of the few politically stable states in that unstable part of the globe.'

A map of Ventura appeared behind the man's head. It rocked for a second or two.

'Unlike its neighbours, for whom revolution is a way of life, Ventura has had no major uprising in its five-hundred-year history and during all that time it has been under the guardianship of one family of Spanish descent, the de Toro y Platas. With me now is Ventura's Consul in London ...'

The cameras moved back to reveal a short stout man in a tight dark suit. He wore glasses so thick that behind them his eyes swam like two fish in deep water. The two men's knees interlocked.

'Poxy bastard,' said Charlie, squinting at the screen through the conflagration of his roll-up. 'Looks like he's stuffed all the food in Ventura up his jumper. You know what, Ally? I saw this ad in a Yank magazine the other day. For lace from Ventura. Said it was so fine the women making it often went blind. On my life. Then they give us this crap about stability and having no nasty revolutions. Poor buggers. Probably can't see to pick up a shooter, never mind hit anyone.'

'Terrible,' Alice said, making chucky noises at the baby on her lap.

'Bloody right. And we sit here griping because we haven't got the readies for a cab.'

'I'm not griping, Charlie,' said Alice. 'Look, love, he's smiling.'

Charlie snorted smoke through his nose and stubbed out the disintegrating butt in a wilting Busy Lizzie. 'Not you and me, Ally. The rich, I'm talking about. The West.'

Alice heard the irritation in his voice and flinched. She seemed to irritate him quite a lot these days without meaning to. There was something about his ways of looking at things that bewildered her. Whenever there was anything nasty on television like a famine in India or people torturing other people or some big money scandal, Charlie acted like it was her fault, he blamed her, or sounded as if he did. Once or twice she had pointed this out to him but it only made him crosser. Do us a favour, Ally, he would say. Of course I know it's not down to you. I'm not daft. Then he would slam a door a bit harder than usual and open another can of beer. Sometimes Alice thought that if she could only join in with him and shout about the famine and the torture and the crooked businessmen he would calm down but she couldn't seem to manage it. One glimpse of children with sticks for limbs and puffed-up bellies, one mental picture, however fleeting, of torturers or the tortured, made her go cold all over. She had nightmares then, waking up with tears on her cheeks, feeling sick. On those mornings, the baby cried more often, his little face a wet mask of grief that she put down to gripe or teething if Charlie asked but that she knew was caused by her own unhappiness, caught by the baby, imbibed through her milk. Because of this, Alice tried quite hard to remain content, censoring out the horrors and even her own anxieties about how to pay the electricity and the rent but her efforts often misfired. Like now. Sighing inwardly, Alice pushed down one shoulder strap on her nightdress and the baby, scenting milk, blindly snuffled round the white globe of her breast until it found and fastened on the milky brown peak.

Charlie stood in the middle of the room and waved his arms at the poster-hung walls, the worn carpet, the white paper lantern hanging from the ceiling, torn in two places. He informed Alice that though she might think this place was a bog, the furniture a junk heap, the windows falling off and the kitchen falling down, it was a palace compared to what half the world had to put up with.

Alice raised mild brown eyes. 'I like it here, Charlie,' she said. 'It only needs that switch repaired, the one in the kitchen. It sparks when I turn it on and scares me.'

'A palace,' Charlie repeated, digging his fists into the pockets of his jeans. On the box, a man with a grey face and a diamond ring on his little finger was being treated with extreme courtesy by an invisible interviewer.

'Mr President,' said the disembodied voice, 'I wonder if you could explain, Sir, the priorities you have for the modernization of Ventura.'

The diamond gleamed as the man leaned forward.

'Looks like someone caught his face in a door and good luck to them.' A familiar bolt of anger shot through Charlie. Bastards, evil bastards. Men like this one ruled the world and nobody gave a monkey's. All that was left for the likes of Charlie was to sit on their deaf and dumbs and listen to the Mister Bigs run off at the mouth about how bleeding wonderful they were – or get their ponces in the media to do it – while they kicked the balls off any poor sod who got in their way. Stuffing their wallets while they did it. And what could Charlie do about it? Sweet Fanny. Watching the baby suck at Alice, he felt himself harden. Well, sod it, then. Fists clenched, he walked over and sat down beside her on the sagging sofa. After a while, he took her round the waist, pushed her so that her knees came up under her and lifted her nightdress. Her buttocks bloomed out, white moons. Silently, Alice shifted the baby so that it lay in front of her on the sofa's cushions, its mouth still fastened to the globe that now hung pear-shaped above it. Charlie unzipped himself and wedged one knee along the sofa's back. Carefully, he opened the mossy lips within the moons, put himself within them, tightened the muscles of his buttocks and, shoving forward, went into her. Alice, a torso between Charlie and the baby, felt several things. A tiny buzz in one nipple as the baby milked her, a twinge of pain from the little finger on her right hand stuck awkwardly out at an angle, dull jolts inside her as Charlie moved faster and faster, in and out. She raised her head. In front of her, the television screen glowed and flickered.

'Señora de Toro y Plata,' the sunken-eyed man was saying, 'will be greeted at Heathrow by the Princess, an old friend ...'

Behind her, Charlie grunted briefly and slumped. Sitting back on his haunches, he pulled down the hem of Alice's nightdress. She crouched, the baby still attached to her breast, staring ahead. A fine needle seared for a second, somewhere in her groin. On the screen, a tiny female figure with a cap of bright hair waved between pillars at the crowd below her. Flags fluttered, there were banners. The woman extended both arms in the air, as if she intended to fly.

'... known to everyone in Ventura as La Dorada,' said sunken eyes. 'The Golden Lady who has done so much for the women in particular, often visiting them ...'

'... in their gracious bijou slums,' finished Charlie. He patted Alice's head and ran his hand down the long hair that fell to her shoulders. 'You all right, Ally?'

'Fine,' said Alice and smiled awkwardly back at him. The baby's lips had fallen away from her breast and it lay sleepily, a thread of milk on its chin. Alice rearranged herself, rubbed the sore little finger and surreptitiously pushed an elbow into the side of her belly. The woman on the screen was in close-up now, bending solicitously over white iron cribs containing dusky children with flat unsmiling faces, her hair shining among the blue-black heads.

[151]

'Fascist tart,' said Charlie, standing to ease up his fly. 'Beats me how a girl like that can marry a villain like wassisname and queen it over some foreign cow-pat. She must know her old man's goons are cracking the balls of any peasant who does his starving in their road when they drive past in their bullet-proof motors. Just look at the two of them.'

Alice looked. 'Oh, Charlie,' she said, sitting bolt upright. 'That's Clare. Lady Clare.'

Charlie closed his eyes, groaning. 'Yeah, Alice. It is, Alice. You got wax in your ears?'

'You didn't say. I'd quite forgotten. Oh ...' Alice squatted by the screen, '... she looks lovely. Charlie, doesn't she look lovely?'

A dark man with a sallow face loomed beside the little woman. They both began shaking the hands of bowing men. One man took the woman's hand and raised it to his lips. Behind them, mirrors framed in gold glinted in a large room.

'That's the President. Clare's husband. He looks *older*.' Alice was breathless with interest, her nose an inch from the glass. 'Charlie, I know them. I mean, I never met him but I was at their wedding. She was my friend at home, when I was little. I loved her, Charlie. She was always good to me.'

'Yeah, yeah,' Charlie said, 'how many times have I heard that before? Doesn't matter what some people do. Torture, kill, cheat, lie, there's always someone like you, Ally, saying ...' he put on a mincing voice, '... she was always very good to *me*.'

Alice got up as if her bones hurt, not looking at Charlie. Doggedly she said, 'She *was* nice, Charlie. Clare wouldn't do any of those things you said. I know she wouldn't.'

'Feudal, that's what you are, Ally.' He clicked his tongue impatiently. 'If she's so lovely, what did she marry that monster for, then?'

'Because she loved him,' said Alice. 'She took one look at him and fell hopelessly in love and now she's doing everything she can to change him.' A memory of willow leaves and Clare came

[152]

to her but she swept them out. This story had to have a happy ending.

'No one gets the hots for a pig unless they're a pig themselves,' said Charlie.

'That's not true. I might have been a pig and so might you. We didn't know anything about each other when we fell in love, did we?'

'Yeah, well,' said Charlie, 'who are we? Two people without a pot to piss in along with three million other potless. Who gives a toss what we think?' He heaved himself off the sofa and walked across the room. Alice heard the thump of the refrigerator door, the hiss of a beer can opening.

'We've got the vote,' she said. 'More than they've got there, I expect,' and she gestured towards the television set.

Charlie came in again and set a beer can on top of the box. Alice looked up at him standing there skinny and angry and, loving him, wished fervently they could talk about other things. Charlie was all worked up again and what good did that do? Why couldn't he just accept that nothing they said in this room would make any difference to anything or anyone outside? It only affected the two of them. For a moment, Alice frowned at the television, hating it. All very well for that lot, blabbing their opinions, telling you this and telling you that, pontificating. She and Charlie weren't allowed to pontificate back. She and Charlie were only there as audience, viewing figures, footballs for practice kicks, having their feelings stirred up without any point, like children frightened by their parents quarrelling in the next room. And then, of course, taking it out on each other because they were all upset. If she had her way, she would only ever watch programmes like 'Coronation Street' or 'Call My Bluff', programmes Charlie despised. But what was the point of the programmes he switched on? Did it help a starving child, having Charlie and Alice watch it starve? Could she comfort a woman half across the world, weeping for her murdered son? Could either of them do anything? No. It just suited the television people to pretend they could so that they could go on poking their cameras where they had no business to be poked. Obscurely, Alice felt that the reporters blamed her just as Charlie did. They might not say it in so many words but she got the message. They were there among the burning buildings, the flooded huts, the hungry refugees and where was Alice? Alice was at home, unburned, unflooded, without so much as a pang of hunger, the smug cow. And then, when they'd succeeded in giving her nightmares, they brought on the man in charge to say that they were distressed, too, but, really, there wasn't that much suffering or that the people suffering were terrorists and had brought their suffering on themselves or some other wicked excuse or lie. As far as Alice was concerned, all the men were in it together, they ran things in whatever way suited them and she didn't want to hear their excuses or their lies. They only included her in the first place because she and Charlie were supposed to be 'the people' and the people were supposed to be included. She did not want to be included. She wished passionately not to be included. Her only freedom was ignorance and they spent millions of pounds making sure she couldn't get away with *that* one, so that when they did the horrible things they would do anyway, they could tell each other they were doing them in Alice's name. Why had she said that about the vote? She didn't believe it, any more than Charlie. She had just repeated what her father would have said.

'The vote?' said Charlie. His shoulders sagged. There. He was thinking how dumb she was and she couldn't bear that, for his sake. Putting her ideas into words never worked. She hadn't been trained for it like Charlie had. At home on the farm, she and her Mum and Dad had just sat around and watched the telly and then got up and gone about their business, thinking their own thoughts. It was better that way, at least they didn't take it out on each other, at least the men on the telly couldn't infect the likes of her Mum and Dad with their disease. Alice remembered a boy in her school, Tom Tulley. He wrecked every class he was in, fidgeting, tapping his ruler on the desk over and over, throwing bits of paper at other children, kicking at their feet, pinching them when the teacher wasn't watching. He couldn't sit still, he couldn't rest unless he was being shouted at or threatened with punishment, getting the teacher all wound up with him in his rage. Maladjusted they called him, old Tom, and it was true he had a rotten life, with Mrs Tulley trying to feed six kids on next to nothing and Mr Tulley always punching other men in pubs and Tom, too, when he got in the way. But at least someone had recognized there was something wrong with Tom, at least they'd sent him to a doctor to try and cure him. That was because Tom was nobody, just a farmer's son in hand-me-downs. If he'd been anyone important, they'd have stuck him on telly and let him wind up four million people with his maladjustment instead of only fifteen at a local parish school.

On the screen, the woman sat in a velvet armchair, her shining head inclined to one side, talking to an interviewer. Oh, Clare was gorgeous, Alice thought. Perhaps her gorgeousness would distract Charlie.

It didn't. 'Your Lady Muck,' he said, 'took one look at the pesos hanging out of Mr President's pockets and said I do. Someone should have shot them both at the altar and given Ventura half a chance.'

'Charlie,' she protested, hustling to the back of her mind a bright image of a younger Clare passing pennies from the grubby depths of Alice's pocket over a sweet shop counter.

The woman's face filled the screen, milky-pale, the blue eyes guarded under heavy lids. Her thin hands, ringless, lay flat and still on the arms of the chair. In the hollow of her throat, an emerald gave off a minute green light. In a clear voice she said she was immensely looking forward to her visit.

'And to meeting Her Majesty?' asked the interviewer.

And especially to meeting Her Majesty again. That will be a great honour and pleasure.'

'But the President is not able to be with you?'

'Sadly, no,' said the woman, briefly regarding the tip of a white satin shoe. 'My husband is a very busy man and, this time, he cannot get away. It is very disappointing for him but, as Head of State, the needs of his country must come first.' She smiled and the corners of her eyes turned down. For a moment, Alice thought she was going to cry.

'Busy my arse,' said Charlie, draining the beer can and crunching it up. 'She's a puppet, she is, you can see the strings. Her old man wouldn't leave Ventura to meet Jesus Christ. He knows if he did, they'd have another hatchet-face bastard waving from that balcony and he'd be stuck in his own nick, along with his missus.'

The screen blanked out and a tube of toothpaste, buoyed up on a plume of sparkling water, sailed over the heads of a group of children who had gone demented with joy at the sight. Baring rows of white teeth like a shoal of hungry piranhas, the children sang 'Say bye-bye to the dentist, bye-bye to the drill, hullo to Dento ...'

Charlie pounced, stabbing a finger at the recessed panel. A sudden silence hummed in the room.

'What's she coming here for then?' asked Alice, her eyes still fixed on the blank glass. In spite of herself, she felt unnerved, oddly bereft without the background chatter. The walls of the room edged perceptibly closer and the anxieties kept at bay by television images lined up at the horizon of her mind in wispy storm clouds. If you kept the set on forever, wherever you went, hooked up behind your eyes, you might just manage never to think about your own problems at all. A column of apprehension rose from her stomach and wedged itself under her ribs. She must have a talk with Charlie, she must.

Charlie said, 'You may well ask,' and stuck his heel on the beer can, stamping it into a threadbare patch on the carpet. 'What's this Government doing, wheeling out the Queen for the wife of a jumped-up bully boy from a country no one but Amnesty's ever heard of?' He pitched his voice to a high falsetto. 'My husband and I are chahmed to have you meet us. Do wash the blood orf your hands in the Royal bog and have a stuffed grape.' His voice dropped again. 'Maybe Princess Maggie fancies a slice of real estate out there. Maybe they've struck oil. Perhaps it's us saying ta ever so much for supporting Our Boys against the orrible Argies. Whatever it is, our Ally . . .' and Charlie bent over her, tapping the side of his nose, '. . . the Powers That Be will not confide in the likes of you and me. So you might as well come to bed, gel.'

Gently, he scooped up the sleeping baby and peered into its closed face. 'As for you, mate,' he said, 'you just don't care, do you? One look at your Mum's tits and you're out for the count.'

'*Charlie*,' said Alice.

'Charlie?' said Alice. She lay in the darkness beside him.

'Wha?' He was a hump under the faded pink quilt.

How could she put it best, so that he shouldn't think she was accusing him, whining, minding much at all? 'There isn't any money, dear.' Short pause. 'At the moment, that is. I wondered . . .'

'Oh Gawd.' The quilt flipped back. Near them the refrigerator clicked and began to buzz. The skimpy Indian bedspread hung across the window revealed, through chinks, the bloodshot London sky. Five storeys below, a car creaked across the gravelled parking lot, its engine revving and then cutting out. A plane droned faintly and was drowned in the clamour of a passing siren, police or ambulance. A long cry sounded in the distance, someone in mortal terror very far away. Alice was afraid of London. Even its silences were shot through with alarms. Charlie rose in a tent of blankets, threw them off and swung out of bed. Alice sat up in fright.

'What are you doing?'

'Ssh.' Charlie put a finger up. 'You'll wake the baby. It's all right. I shouldn't have stayed in the first place.' He was whispering. 'Kev might have something for me if I catch him early enough. Early birds catch worms, didn't you know? And Kev's nothing if not a worm.' He gave a low grunt of laughter, as if he'd been punched.

'You can get up early here. I'll wake you. I'll see you get up early.' Alice, ghostly among the sheets.

'I've got the stuff he'll want to see at home. I'd have to go back anyway.' He moved stealthily about, pulling on a T-shirt, slotting in a belt, smoothing his short furry hair. Alice said nothing. She might cry if she did and there was nothing to cry about. Everything seemed worse in the dark.

When Charlie had gone, touching her forehead with his warm lips, closing the front door quietly, Alice got up, cleared the drooping Busy Lizzie of Charlie's stubs and put on the television again, squatting in front of it, hugging her knees and rocking. Two men in swivel chairs appeared against an orange wall. The dark man with the big nose, wound in a white sheet, was talking.

'Verily, the whole world is Brahman,' he said squeakily. 'It contains all works, all desires, all odours, it contains all tastes, it encompasses this whole world. This is Brahman.'

The man opposite clutched his clip-pad and nodded solemnly. 'So, to you, the physical world is an illusion?'

'Exactly,' said the man in the sheet, switching his eyes smoothly to the new camera angle. 'There is no reason and no purpose in what goes on around us. Day and night, summer and winter, birth and death, they roll on from one millennium to another in meaningless monotony.' He looked very cheerful.

Alice, rocking, held one of her hands with the other. Charlie had said he'd got his stuff at home. Home. That was the word he'd used. Now he had gone and the baby was asleep, Alice allowed her eyes to overflow with tears.

A WELCOME FOR A GOLDEN LADY

Señora Clare de Toro y Plata is the First Lady of Ventura, wife to its President, Raul de Toro y Plata. She is also an Englishwoman, daughter of our soil in a very real way; her father, Lord La Fontaine, Lord Lieutenant of Lincolnshire and scion of one of our oldest Catholic families, farms 2000 acres of that county's land.

The La Fontaine family motto stems from Norman times and it is a simple one: *Je Sert le Roy*. They have faithfully fulfilled the strictures of that ancient promise. A La Fontaine fell at the Battle of Hastings in the service of the then French King and, ever since, La Fontaine descendants have served generations of English Monarchs. The present Earl is Advisor in Chancery to Her Majesty the Queen and his wife, the Countess Mamaine, was Lady-in-Waiting to the Queen Mother.

Five years ago, Lady Clare La Fontaine married Señor de Toro y Plata. At the time there were criticisms in political circles of this marriage. Ventura, a Spanish fiefdom until 1890, is a very small country but it shares many problems of poverty and disease with the rest of the troubled South American continent. It is also frequently labelled a dictatorship by those who lack a sense of history. While it is true that Parliamentary democracy as we know it in Britain does not pertain in Ventura, as it does not in many Third World countries, it should be remembered that conditions there resemble those now safely in our past, as in the past of all the industrialized nations of the West.

Ventura's medieval constitutional structure has led to the protests voiced in the House yesterday – viz. Mr Ronald Kirkpatrick's designation of Señor de Toro y Plata as South America's King Canute, a remark that drew predictable applause from the Left. Such inflexible self-righteousness concerning a so-called dictatorship stems in the final analysis from parochialism. The affairs of mankind are temporal and must be judged, as any historian will confirm, within the context of their time and though Britain, along with the rest of the industrialized West, rightly rejoices in a twentieth-century parliamentary democracy, within which our Royal Family performs the duties of Monarchy without its erstwhile power and prerogatives, that system is not necessarily appropriate to a country whose development parallels our own in the eighteenth century, when our affairs were conducted under the more or less absolute aegis of King James II and King George IV.

Much is being done by the developed world to speed Ventura's journey into the twentieth century. Last year, some $2 billion in American aid was assigned to her government to assist in the eradication of the worst poverty. A modernization programme has begun. The Virgin of Ventura Hospital in the capital city, Nombre Dios, is equipped with the latest in laser surgery techniques and possesses a cobalt radium unit, one of only three on the South American continent. Other building in Nombre Dios has, as its aim, the attraction of a potentially lucrative tourist trade. Rather more uniquely, funding has also gone towards the Women's Co-operatives initiated by Señora de Toro y Plata herself.

La Dorada, as she is affectionately called throughout Ventura, is an indefatigable worker for the poor of her adopted country and an object of near-worship among the peasant *mestizos* (half-castes) and Indian women whose rights she has championed. It is through her good offices that development funds, too often earmarked for male use, have found their way to women through the Señora's programme of education in the nutritional and medicinal uses of the flora and fauna of Ventura's fertile forest. Her Women's Programme is outstanding in development terms for its sensitivity to grassroots needs. For the past year, the guerilla activity that has long plagued Ventura's neighbours has spread to this previously peaceful country and its First Lady has become a particular target for terrorist venom, embodying – as she does – the ordinary Venturans' hope that change can take place without violence and without the substitution of a malevolent Communism for a benign feudality. We welcome the coming visit of Clare de Toro y Plata. May her brief sojourn here in her homeland give her strength to continue the peaceful struggle for change in her adopted land.

The Sun

GUESS WHO'S COMING TO DINNER!

The Queen is dusting off her best china for the Royal Dinner planned to honour one of the dishiest of our far-flung countrywomen – Clare de Toro y Plata, Ventura's Queen Bee, whose Anthony Quinn look-alike hubby Raul sent a flutter through Top Hearts on his last visit here.

Sorry, ladies, Raul won't be with you this time but your menfolk are in for a treat when Clare makes it solo. La Dorada, as Venturans call her for her white-blonde crowning glory, is a noted beauty who, as Lady Clare La Fontaine, was named Deb of the Year and charmed England's most eligible bachelors, including our own now happily-married Charlie. The Prince and the First Lady will meet again at the Buck House banquet and Clare, at twenty-five, can still charm even Royal birds off trees. Princess Di, you have been warned!

Vogue

LA DORADA – THIS SUMMER'S GOLDEN GIRL

She comes to us in June, a white rose bred in the English shires who has taken flourishing root in that Latin Garden of Eden called Ventura. With her classic features and her extraordinary silver hair, Lady Clare presents the perfect portrait of an English beauty whose ivory complexion remains miraculously untouched by foreign suns. For inspiration under cooler suns, we show you exclusive photographs of Lady Clare at home in her palatial Nombre Dios mansion wearing some of the white 'n wonderful outfits she has had specially designed in the traditional Venturan mix of chiffon and silk for her coming visit. The material, light and gauzy as a butterfly's wing, has become Lady Clare's sartorial trademark and symbol of her devotion to her new country. Is it any wonder that she was described recently by our own Poet Laureate as 'a white taper, alight, before a dark altar'?

The chopper touched down in a tornado of dust and noise. It was hotter than hell, mid-summer, and the landing strip was dry and brown in the encircling green of the forest. Clare breathed in shallowly, the air was like hot milk. This was to be her last visit, there was so much to do before she left for England and no real need to snatch this time from a crowded schedule simply to return to the village where the women had cured her of her sickness. She had been back many times since and nothing could be accomplished, no further progress made, until London had furnished her with the expertise she needed; the goods.

Nevertheless, the unease with which she had woken that morning was with her still, the hangover from a sweating nightmare in which the ground she had walked on was shaken and split, pitching her into a parched underground cavern where the roots of the trees over her head had shrivelled and died, loosening the earth they held to fall around her. She had come awake choking, her nostrils, her throat plugged with the rank and powdery stuff, her lungs heaving and had felt very little relieved to find herself safe on her white bed with the stolid figure of Concepción bending over her, smoothing back the hair from her sticky forehead. Concha had given her one of her pills with a glass of cool water and Clare had clutched at those hard and capable hands.

'Am I late? I have to go to the campesino. What time is it?'

'But, Señora, surely not.' Concepción stood with her hands on her hips and shook her head. 'Those visits tire you. Why go again, so near your departure? You told me yourself you could do nothing more for those indios until you got back from England.'

'Never mind that.' Clare's voice was sharp. She slid out of bed and stood up. She had grown thinner over the past year, her stomach was concave under the satin nightdress and there were blue bruises under her eyes. She looked at Concepción, her shadow moving with her in the sunny room. 'Por favor, Concha, go and make sure Carrington has organized the flight.'

Concepción reached up, drawing the nightdress over Clare's shoulders. 'Send her, Señora. Señorita Carrington. She has the time.' She was grumbling now, a mother with an obstinate child, trying to chivvy Clare across the room towards her bath. 'You should have a fitting with Señora Marquez this morning. Do you want to meet the Queen of England with your dresses looking like this?' and she tugged her own skirt askew, wagging her head in comic reproof. She was well used to coaxing Clare out of dark morning moods, it was a familiar part of her job. A joke, a little bullying, a little pill, that was the formula and it worked. It did not work today. Clare turned at the door of the bathroom and scraped back her hair.

'Concepción. Do as I say. Go this minute to Carrington. That helicopter must be out there waiting in half an hour. Finito.'

As they landed in the village and Clare climbed down from the chopper into the day's heat, she became instantly aware of a strangeness around, her skin prickled with it. The thwack of the propeller blades came to a halt, the engine died in a final cough and the dust settled. Clare glanced at her watch, it was exactly noon. She nodded at the two guards who had climbed down with her and walked from them across the landing strip, her feet in rubber soles noiseless on the sandy soil. The cluster of shacks a hundred yards away was ringed in hard shadow, the sun blazed directly overhead. As Clare neared the first hut, the high whirr of the cicadas cut out abruptly and her heart began to beat uncomfortably fast. Something was wrong. The panic of her dream returned. The women were always waiting for her, summoned by the first far drone of the chopper to gather by the strip, chattering and waving. Where were they today? Why was it so ominously quiet?

The thin mewling of a child came from behind the shacks, a forlorn cry that rose and fell away. Running now, Clare threaded her way past one empty door after another until she came to where the houses ended in a broken clay wall and three trees cast a circular shadow. The women were there. Three of them were not even in the shade, they had crawled to where they lay on their stomachs with their backs to the broiling sun and flies rose in a buzzing swarm from the trickles of vomit behind them on the ground. A baby's fist waved from a pile of sacking nearby, it was from there that the whimpering came. Four or five other children, their hair wildly tangled, their faces stony beneath the grime, squatted beside the slumped women and turned their heads as Clare approached, their eyes huge and vacant. Sick with foreboding, Clare knelt by the wall where a woman was hunched, her head hanging over her splayed legs, only the parting between the black plaits visible. 'Please, God,' Clare said and felt for the woman's chin, tilting her head up. It was María-Luisa. Her eyes fell open as her head lolled back and her jaw sagged in a stupid grin, gusting at Clare the sour stink of liquor. Clare pulled her hand away. María-Luisa was blind drunk, they were all blind drunk. How could they, how could they? She shook the Indian woman violently, smacking her scarred cheeks, shouting her name. María-Luisa fell over sideways, muttering, and began to retch. Clare jumped to her feet, revolted. All around her the women sprawled, limp rag dolls too drunk to wave away the flies that crawled upon them or respond to the children who tugged hopelessly at their drink-sodden clothes. Bottles were everywhere, upturned and dripping. With fury, Clare saw that two of the little boys had been drinking too, their bodies looked squashed and vomit smeared the loose corners of their lips, while under a bush old Tia lolled, an ancient debauched slut, her dirty blouse torn across the flaps of her wrinkled breasts. Broken glass winked in the scrubby grass.

Clare stood in their midst, batting off the clouds of flies, and heard the heavy tread of boots. The guards appeared behind the wall and stood for a moment, staring at the flung bodies. Then María-Luisa's feeble retching was drowned in raucous laughter. The guards punched each other, roaring. One of them, his chest heaving, stepped over the wall and tucked the toe of his boot into María-Luisa's back. She pitched over and lay flat, groaning. He bent over her, sniffed, picked up the bottle beside her and held it up to his companion. They guffawed and began to reel between the women in a parody of drunkenness and the children ducked their heads into their mothers' skirts and cried with fright.

'Stop it.' Clare exploded. 'Stop it.' The laughter died away. She stormed towards them, holding up a bottle. 'Miguel. Fernandez.

[164]

What do you know about this? Look, this is bourbon, American bourbon. How did it get here? How did the women get hold of it?'

Miguel shrugged, glancing at Fernandez. 'Beg pardon, Señora, but how can we help laughing? We heard you cry out, we thought something was wrong, a guerrilla raid, something. But this ...' he gestured contemptuously around him, '... who wouldn't laugh? These Indian women ...' He made an ugly sound in his throat.

Clare placed herself squarely in front of him and held the label of the bottle to his eyes. 'I am asking you, Miguel, how did this get here? The women didn't buy it, someone brought it in. Look ...' she pointed to the wall of the nearest hut, '... there is the carton. One dozen bottles of imported bourbon. Maybe more. How? Why?'

Miguel shrugged again, backing from her, his hands spread out. 'I don't know, Señora, how do I know?' His mouth dragged down to conceal a grin. 'The indios, they have their ways, they bring things in over the border, they smuggle them, eh Fernandito?' The other guard, attempting seriousness, nodded. 'The Señora should not concern herself. These people are degenerates, they have always been so. They love to drink but they cannot hold it. Everyone knows that about the indios.' The two men looked at each other and Fernandez puffed his lip out, shaking his head.

Disgust in Clare was replaced by confusion. 'No,' she said loudly. 'That is not true. I have visited this campesino very often. The women are good, hard-working. Respectable. The men drink, yes. The women, never.' Niggling doubts made her fierce in the women's defence, the knowing faces of the two guards angered her. She turned away from them and went over to the crate. It was half torn open and beside it lay a basket that bulged with lank fronds. They had been working, then, the women, they had been out in the forest that day. She bent over the crate. On

[165]

its side was stamped JIM BEAM SOUR MASH WHISKY, PRODUCT OF THE USA, and half over the stamp was a label. She tore it off and stuck it in her pocket. Then she went over and picked up the baby from its sacking bed. 'Come on,' she said to the men, 'there's work to do.'

In two hours the women had all been chivvied or dragged or carried back to their huts and cleaned up with copious ladling of water from the jerry-cans that stood about. They would have their work cut out tomorrow to replace that water, Clare thought grimly. The guards were put to boiling up jugs of coffee and Clare forced as much as she could into each slack mouth. She brushed and wiped and comforted the children and burned the vomit-stained clothes. Outside, the guards covered the trails of vomit with fresh earth and gathered up the glass and bottles – Clare was determined that all should be normal by the time the first of the men returned from their work and watched as, little by little, sense returned to the glazed eyes and some control to the limp limbs. She left with the guards as the women began to look round with recognition and stumble to their feet. She was filthy, wet and exhausted but the village was stirring again and the women coming to themselves. Before she left, she knelt beside María-Luisa again and took her hands.

'María, listen to me. Where did you get the drink? Who brought it? María?'

The Indian woman, the only one who could understand her Spanish, held her head in her hands. Her eyes were still glassy and the liquor was strong on her breath. Clare smoothed the tangled hair off the wide brow and patted the dark scarred face that had looked so gravely down at her in her fever, composed and wise. The palms of María's hands were scratched and a flap of skin at the base of one thumb frayed from a weeping sore. She extended them suddenly in front of Clare.

'See,' she said, 'I have been stealing from the forest.' Her tongue was thick, her speech slurred. 'We have all been stealing from the forest. For you, Señora, for you. So he punished us. We took what was his. He is angry ... angry.' Her voice trailed into a mumble.

'What man is this? María, you must tell me. Who was angry? Who?'

'Curupira,' the woman muttered.

'Who?' said Clare, bending near her.

María-Luisa sniffed and bit her lip. 'Curupira,' she repeated. 'He came and took our souls.' She had a furtive air, she kept her voice low. After that she would say no more.

On the flight back to Nombre Dios, Clare stared sightlessly out of the window. She could make nothing of María-Luisa's words but someone had brought that drink and perhaps an American, since the bourbon came from there. Was this an attempt to sabotage her project? Had it happened in other villages too? But if whoever it was didn't want the women's plants any more, why not just tell them? Why not tell her? Raul couldn't know, he would be furious, it was his idea in the first place. Below her, the curled green stretches of the forest gave way to buildings and more buildings as the town rushed in. Lower and lower they came over the dingy rooftops and the wide white arms of the Palace swung beneath with its green lawns sunk between high walls. The helicopter sank and the grass blew flat. At the double bump of landing, Clare was already scrambling from her seat.

The women in the outer room of the Presidential offices looked dismayed as she burst through the heavy mahogany doors, their clattering typewriters fell silent and they murmured in surprise.

'Señora.' One of the older women was on her feet, bustling to where Clare stood. 'But, Señora ... what has happened? Your clothes ...'

'I want to see my husband.' She moved fast between the desks towards the door of Raul's inner sanctum and the woman moved with her stuttering, her hands reaching for Clare.

'The President is in a meeting, Señora. Can I ... please let me ...'

Grasping the thick brass knob, Clare pushed open the door. Faces turned as she entered, there were men lounging in the leather armchairs that stood about the room and a smell of cigar smoke hung in the air. Bars of brilliant light, sliced by the venetian blinds that lined the two long windows, lay across the thick carpet and across the girl who sat on the edge of Raul's desk so that, at first, Clare did not recognize Carrington in her zebra-striped garb. From the other side of the desk, Raul rose to his feet.

'Gentlemen, please. I have to talk to my husband,' Clare said.

When they had gone, giving her puzzled nods as they went, she told Raul what had happened. As she talked, her words falling over each other, he walked to the window and slotted his fingers through two blinds, pushing them up.

'Did you know about this, Raul? What does it mean? I shall find out, I promise you.'

'You need do nothing more, Clare. Calm down, go and change your clothes and continue your preparations for England. You have done too much already.' Clare stepped towards him to protest and he put up his hands. 'I will make the relevant enquiries and, I assure you, whoever is responsible shall be punished.'

'You didn't know?'

'Of course I didn't know, Clare. I have no possible interest in drunken Indian women. I am mortified that you could even imagine ...'

Clare laid a grubby hand on his ivory silk sleeve. 'No,' she said earnestly, 'of course not. But Raul, who could it be? One of the women said something about curu ... a name I couldn't catch.'

'Curupira,' Raul said, 'a superstition, a forest ghost.'

He walked back to his desk and stood, twiddling an onyx pen in its stand. His face was thoughtful.

'I think the episode was a joke.'

'A *joke*?' Clare's voice rose.

'You must know, Clare, there are many people in this country who look down on the Indians, who think them less than human. Animals. Dirty lazy animals, good for nothing.'

'But it's not true,' Clare said, outraged. 'My women are wonderful. They work hard, they have nothing, they are so poor. Oh Raul, how can you allow it? The women always pregnant, the children hungry and sick. Too many children. It's wicked. When I go to England, Raul, I'm going to find ways of stopping those endless pregnancies, I don't care about the Church, I don't care what *anyone* says.' Her eyes filled with tears and she blinked them angrily away. 'I won't allow anyone to stop me, not you, not your Cardinals, not anyone. And I'm going to see that my project works and the women get the benefit of the plants they pick. I'm going to talk to people in England who know ...'

Raul banged his fist on the desk and Clare stopped, startled. For a moment, his face was drawn and then it cleared. He came over to her and put a finger lightly on her shoulder.

'If you will let me finish,' he said. 'The bourbon must have been brought in to make the women drunk, to laugh at them when they were drunk. It comes from boredom. Maybe. Who knows? People despise the indios.'

'*Oh*.' Clare's exclamation of disgust rang in the room.

'Leave it with me. I will find out who was responsible and I will see they regret what they have done.' He was already ushering Clare out, his hands on her back. She turned at the door, scrutinizing his face and he nodded again as he held it open.

'Forget it, Clare. Leave it with me.'

[10]

Alice, humped in a scoop of orange chair in the white-tiled precincts of the local Health Clinic's Mother and Baby Unit, her own baby wedged between her feet in his red carry-cot, stared absently at the white face and white hair of Clare on the cover of a *Vogue* that she had picked out from the table beside her as suitably thick to write upon.

'Dear Mum,' she wrote. 'Here's hoping you and Dad are well and my birthday card got to you in time only it's a bit hard, sometimes, to get to the post. Me and the baby are well. He is sweet now and smiles if you tickle his chin. You would like him, Mum, if you saw him, he looks like you, it must be his curly hair, mine is straight. I expect you remember that!!!'

Strands of her straight hair trailed over her eyes and she pushed them back. They were remnants of the fringe she had cut one evening, alone in her bedroom, tipping the mirror on its swivel to catch the light from the overhead bulb. The mirror would not stay still and her face continue to elude her, it floated towards her and away, as wavery in the surrounding gloom as the face of a drowned girl might be, seen by the light of street lamps from a bridge. That morning, Alice had read in a newspaper about a Dutch girl who had tied her newly born baby to her chest and plunged into the canal, where they had both drowned. The canal ran between boats and roads two blocks and five flights of stairs below Alice's own flat. Alice had been caught up by this event, happening so close to her. She had imagined the baby's face sinking beneath the brown water, its mouth opening to cry and staying open, filled with leaves and twigs and rivulets of oil from the boats. Had the Dutch girl known her baby was dead before she herself sank to the scummy bottom that clinked with the beer bottles thrown from tourist barges? The tourists, waving and whistling from Jason's red and yellow painted boats (TRIPS EVERY HOUR ON THE HOUR) must have crossed several times above the two of them as they swayed. bound together, in the shadow of the keel, the mother's hair drifting like water weeds, the baby's tendrils lifting in a halo round its pale scalp.

She wondered where the man was, father of the drowned baby. Perhaps at this very moment telling his mates in some pub about the girl he'd had with the big knockers and what he'd done to her and his mates roaring, sucking the beer froth off their red lips. Or to give him the benefit of the doubt, perhaps he was Dutch himself and back now in the village where he was born, standing over a bike with one foot on the pedal and one on the flat road, watching a heron motionless beside a high canal, knowing nothing of an English canal that had just drowned a girl he barely remembered and a baby he never knew existed. The heron stands still among the still reeds, one yellow eye absorbing him. How beautiful it is, he thinks, maybe. How beautiful it all is, the grey long ribbons of water beside the green long strips of fields along the grey sky that rises from below his eyes to flood that flat Dutch world. Alice's only trip abroad had been on a package tour with her Mum and Dad to Holland, to see the tulip fields.

'Philips, please. Valerie Philips?'

The voice from the Reception Desk, loud, commanding, broke up the layered netherlands of Alice's imagination. A fat woman pushed her mottled yellow legs across the carry-cot and Alice hooked it with her feet further under her chair and wrote again.

'Mum, I don't like to ask this, I never have before and I wouldn't now if it wasn't for the baby but could you and Dad see your way to sending me a little money? You always said

[171]

neither a borrower nor a lender be and that is a good rule and I made my bed and I must lie on it but, Mum, things are so hard now. For everyone, of course, not only me. It's just that Charlie was laid off last month from the Park, it wasn't his fault, and we are that strapped because I can't work, due to the baby.'

Now Alice found herself stranded in another desolation. She'll think why can't I get a job and Charlie look after the baby. Bad enough I had it. What would she say if I told her Charlie's moved out? She saw her mother reading the letter, wobbling her head away from the words, preparing herself as she always did with letters in case bad news formed suddenly out of the writing and came at her in her basket chair, causing her glasses to crack, her perm to straighten, the milk in the dairy to turn sour, the heavy udders of the creamy cows to dry up and the land to harden in drought. People who lived on farms believed in magic, the black kind that cursed your best efforts. Storms, floods, snow, hail, wind, sun, clouds, the sky that curved above the land that was your living delivered its gifts and its punishments at random, indifferent to the merits or otherwise of the human ants below who toiled and dug and ploughed for their survival. It had not, therefore, surprised Alice that her parents had withdrawn in self-protection from the ill-luck she had brought them, getting pregnant first go by an itinerant guitar-player with a London group, down for a mid-summer pop festival in the meadow that ran by her father's fields. Those who couldn't rely on a natural order had to compensate with order in their own affairs. Alice, vomiting quietly in the barn where she went each morning to leave milk for the barnyard cats, woken early by her nausea and the cats' mating yowls — *they* didn't care — was not sorry for herself. She knew the reason for her sickness and kept it a secret only because her plight did not deserve sympathy; she had broken the rules, made her own disorder and must now tidy it up on her own. The happy mirage of a marriage to Charlie had faded fast in those first few weeks of her blood ceasing to flow (he'd told her he wasn't the marrying kind). It ebbed away at the same time as her heart filled up with love for this ragged scarecrow who had pushed her skirt up to her waist among the white flowers of her father's crops and gone where no man had gone before, a fact Charlie hadn't believed, hadn't thought even to check.

As he pressed her down, covering every inch of her, butting at her with the hard knot at his groin, she had seen his seal-smooth head, black and featureless against the white sky, loom over her and had quickly turned the bad side of her face and pressed it against the earth, out of his sight. The consequence of that and many other encounters over the two weeks of the festival were inevitable. Charlie's arrival had been unheralded, he had come in unto her, Alice thought, like Gabriel to Mary and behold, she was with child. Anyway, even if she had had some warning, how could she have steeled herself to enter the fusty leather-smelling front room of Dr Mullaly's house and ask the man who delivered her, the man who drank her Mum's lemon tea most Saturdays in her Mum's kitchen, to write out a prescription for the Pill? And then hand it over the counter to be filled by Mrs Pennyfoil at the chemist's who had known her since she was, as Dad used to say, knee high to a buttercup. There was only one person she would like to have told, because she was not that much older and wouldn't have talked and always made you feel easy and girls together, but she was far away. Not that she could have done anything, being RC. Also, there was the matter of her face.

'Billie got a spell for his warts,' said the four-year-old Alice, peering into the chipped mirror propped over the sink. 'His Auntie did it. She put meat on them and Billie buried it and the warts magicked away. Put some meat on my face, Mum.'

'Don't you be silly.' Alice's mother, scrubbing her back, scrubbed more fiercely.

'Don't you be silly,' her father echoed, lighting his pipe with a spill from the grate. Sparks flew round him. 'That mark's with you for life, my lady, and you're none the worse for it.' He sucked noisily at the stem, his head bent.

Large tears hung on Alice's lashes, she winced away from the harsh flannel and mewed in protest. Her back was flaming. 'You hurt me, you hurt me, Mum,' she whined.

Then her father was out of his chair, a mountain towering above her, ugly and frightening. 'Don't you blame your Mother, d'you hear me, girl? It was no fault of hers, that mark, so get that in your head for good and all.' Behind Alice, her Mother gave a sob and in fear and incomprehension Alice wailed. Her father had swung her up and she was on his lap by the fire and the cat jumped on the arm of the chair and she watched, comforted, as her father held its little head towards her, his thick fingers making it as sleek as a fish.

'There,' he said. 'See this moggie? She's got a black mark all over her nose and she's not crying. She don't care. Same as that old Daisy, same as our Beauty and you don't see 'em mooing out the barn, making a fuss cause they've got a patch here and there. No sirree.' Alice, leaning back in his arms, wiped her tears away on the roughness of his jacket, still confused but cheering up. 'My Clare don't mind,' she said. 'My Clare don't care. Can she come to tea?'

'One day.'

Fifteen years later, Alice knew that there existed no one in the world to whom she could say 'I am pregnant' without catching, far back in their eyes, the flicker that said 'You pregnant? You with that mark on your face?' She didn't mind for herself, simply she wished to avoid that mutual embarrassment. No one had ever been cruel to her about it, even at school. Tom Tulley, the worst and biggest of the four Tulley boys, a raw red clan who scavenged and scrimmaged their way through life, regularly outraging the village with some act of outlawry, even Tom, famous for driving a tractor straight at Farmer Belton so that he had to jump in the river to escape, had never said worse to her than that she'd be one person better off for turning the other cheek and he hadn't laughed all that much when he'd said it, though he usually brayed like a donkey at his own jokes. Alice was duly grateful for this considerable mercy and showed a proper diffidence when she was with the other girls. She felt her shame and was grateful for their tacit sympathy. They in their turn were kind to her, including her in all their games and gossip about boyfriends because she was kind herself and the mark that reddened her left profile from the delicate edge of the jaw to the temple was a relief to them, their antidote to the envy that would otherwise have been aroused by the wide spacing of her features, the astonishing buttery skein of her hair, the soft curves of her body and the skin that shone everywhere upon her except where the mark clung, as if trying to draw attention away from its horrid failure there. Beside Alice the other girls might too often have felt themselves heavy, earthed and functional, without grace, but when they saw the familiar flinching away of her head they forgave her readily and basked in the warmth of their own generosity. The boys and men around her felt their own burden – the constant itch of lust – lighten a little in her presence, allowing the least adept among them to remark upon her sexiness without the obligatory edge of ridicule or anger.

Thus the natural kindness in all young children was preserved in Alice to adulthood, though it left her without practice in deceit or in the careful manufacture of a carapace of malice, wit, vanity and the other tactics of self-preservation. The flaw she carried with her and was forced to reveal wherever she went, despite her best endeavours, was the outward and visible sign of a fallibility that everyone possessed but could conceal, erecting structures around them of a marvellous intricacy to disguise inner deformities. Alice's flaw had no hiding place and though she grieved often over it, she could not pretend it was not there; no moral system, no power base, no carefully nurtured delusions of a just world could protect her and so she had none.

When Charlie, thin as a rake, his smooth head bound in gaudy rags, twanged the strings of his guitar at her as she stood in the festival field with the music grinding at her bones, a great bird fanned its wings inside her and she fell in love immediately, too far gone in those minutes that she watched his lips singing, to pretend the slightest indifference or play one single mating game. A half-hour later, his day's gig over, he sought out this girl and found her already retarded with love, rendered thick as two planks by the bliss of his presence. As he stood in front of her, she turned the bad side of her face towards him, saw his eyes fall for a splintered second and was rewarded for her gamble by his smile, made grateful beyond thanks because the smile contained no pity and only a hint of disappointment. At that moment her idyll commenced, her magical Indian summer during which he kissed and stroked and hugged her silly, so that she lay at the centre of the spinning earth with her thighs spread open, quite beyond knowing if she worshipped the blazing sun or the black shape of Charlie that swung across, obliterating it and her.

The consequence of all this required unaccustomed calculation. Like the mark on her face, the beginning of the arch of her belly could not remain unconcealed but, unlike the mark, it could be removed to a place where it would not excite comment. Alice knew that what caused it could also be removed but the mechanics of that process defeated her from the start and seemed, anyway, to have no remote connection with the fever of love that consumed her. The word for what she would have had to undergo was chilling and ugly and happiness made her obstinate, she did not want to follow that barren road to the freedom she had no wish to feel. It did not occur to her even to discuss the choice with Charlie when he came back each weekend, roaring down the motorway from London, and he, seeing the glow that enveloped her as she ran to embrace him, did not know how to discuss it, either. He lived from day to day, always had, and was happy for her happiness, all the more so because he knew it would not last, being more informed than Alice and streetwise and thoroughly accustomed to shrugging off a future that had always been unpromising. He was a child of the Welfare State and believed they would get by somehow.

Alice left the ramshackle farmhouse and her room with its sprigged wallpaper cellophaned with posters of pop groups and photographs of the Sting very early one autumn morning at the beginning of her fourth month of pregnancy, disturbing only the few red hens that mumbled in the yard. Well out of her parents' ear-shot, in that stretch of the road from the village where the cats' eyes began, she tied her few belongings on the back of Charlie's motorbike, climbed upon the saddle, clasped her arms around his beloved body and leaned in utter confidence against him as they rushed to London and the paradise of Charlie's damp, peeling, cheerless Paddington flatlet, leaving behind her a letter begging forgiveness and offering the consolation of her joy to her mother and father.

Installed five flights above the dirty streets, Alice slowly swelled, stuck the stolen flowers Charlie brought back from his work at the Park in the dark green stubby bottles emptied more and more frequently by Charlie of Ruddles beer, and waited for letters from her mother that did not come. She wrote to her parents about London life, of which she saw nothing and bought what she could for the coming child: a red carry-cot, a bundle of nappies, four plastic pants, two small blankets, four sheets, two safety pins and five cotton vests. As her belly mounted, Charlie moved behind her and, holding her hips, went invisibly into her while she closed her eyes and imagined his face. Towards the end of her pregnancy, Charlie was occasionally drunk and pushed himself into her much less than gently, so that she curled her hands protectively over her belly. One bad time, when they had bickered all day about what lay ahead, both of them suddenly bereft, he had shouted at her angrily and that night straddled her face with his thighs. For the first time apprehensive, she watched a penis that descended upon her too quickly to turn her face away, as she usually did, to bury the mark on the pillow. Astonished, she opened her mouth round the stiffness and was infinitely relieved by its removal within a minute and its insertion between her legs, in that slit Charlie called her honey-pot and loved, he said. Cunt-struck, he called himself, which was strong language to Alice, who had only ever heard the word 'cunt' used twice, by angry men against each other, and had thought Charlie angry the first time he used it. That was back in August. They had been lying on dusty bags of grain in the old shed at the bottom of Belton's field, in semi-darkness, the daylight sifting through broken slats and lying in strips on Alice's thighs, bare and loose with love.

'Open them,' Charlie said after minutes of stroking the soft blonde fuzz between her legs and nibbling at the hairs as Alice, weakly protesting, tried to lift his head towards her. Then he pulled himself up to his knees and began parting her legs.

'No,' said Alice, at once appalled and dizzy, but Charlie, his hands flat on either side of her, lent down and sent a bolt of such pleasure through her that her body arched. His tongue, rough as a cat, probed the lips apart and his mouth began sucking and lapping at the pink flesh within, where the soft hairs gave way to the moist inner folds. Alice, who had not dreamt that such things were possible or permissible without God striking you dead, obediently nearly died as waves of ecstasy lifted her up and threw her against the peaks of cliffs, again and again, until at last she lay exhausted. Then the same tongue licked the tears that seeped from beneath her closed eyes and the salty odour of them mingled with the salty smell of herself on Charlie.

'I'm cunt-struck, I am, my lovely girl,' whispered Charlie's voice in the dimness and, putting his lips to her ears, he confided to her many details of the delights that lay between her legs and how they all belonged to him and no man but him, so help him

[178]

God, while Alice stared blindly up at the cobwebbed rafters of the old shed.

Nine months later, Alice lay with her legs apart in the same way and, this time, three green-garbed strangers gazed between them as she heaved and groaned, the sweat running down her face and along her veined and swollen breasts. Stretched beyond all possibility, bound on a rack, 'look,' said a green person and with a hand on the nape of Alice's neck swung her up and doubled her over and there she saw herself giving birth, the waxy half-head of a rising son.

Alice folded her letter, revealing the magazine cover beneath. Once again, Clare looked up at her with a little smile. 'P.S.' scribbled Alice, 'fancy our own Miss Clare, coming home again and to meet the Queen! Maybe you'll see her, I wish I could. I did love her.'

She leaned back and sighed. Oh how long must she wait in this anonymous green room?

Clare scrutinized her reflection in the gold-carved mirror. She smiled but the eyes above the smile remained detached and observant. Behind her, Concepción brushed her hair, her dark head bent over the silver strands. Clare thought about the puzzle of her own beauty. It was like wearing a mask. Comforting in one way, a kind of passport that she had in common with thousands of other beautiful women, you held it up and at the sight of those perfectly symmetrical features, familiar from the pages of every glossy magazine, they let you go wherever you wanted, honorary citizenness of the world. But in another way beauty cut you off from the human race with its bumps and flaws. Out of envy or a simple lack of imagination, ordinary people refused to believe that skin and bones arranged in a certain order, conforming to a certain standard laid down by mysterious rules, did not in themselves protect their owner from the common anxieties and tragedies that beset all human beings. Clare felt imprisoned by the very faultlessness of her disguise, it sealed her off behind a glacial wall through which no sound penetrated, no scream of protest carried to the outside world. A heavy penalty to pay for a face and body that had been imposed without a by-your-leave. Inherited money, an inherited title, could be rejected. The genes that formed a small straight nose and all the other accoutrements of beauty could not.

Concepción, her arm moving rhythmically up and down the pale gold curtain, felt the sweat soak into wider and wider arcs under her arms. She brushed hard to drown out the fears that invaded every part of herself, dried her throat, hurt her ribs, churned up her stomach. That stupid little ape, José, had been gone too long. On her last day off, she and Dolores had trudged from one shack to another asking endlessly if anyone had seen him. No one had. If anyone could guess, they would not say. They shrugged, they patted the women with anxious sympathy but that was all.

And now, thought Clare, I am going to England. So much work lies ahead and so many battles. She had felt really well, full of energy, this whole year since the women had cured her fever but now worries crowded around her and she was tired, very tired, propped up on pills and drink again after the shock of that last village visit and the new rift it had made with Raul. In the mirror, her eyes met the eyes of Concepción and they smiled briefly at each other. How lucky she is, Clare thought. How lucky she is, thought Concepción.

'I know what you bloody want.' Judith downed her third half-pint and rubbed her hands under her breasts as the beer sloshed down. 'Don't tell me. Out of my vast journalistic experience, let me guess.' She wore a grey sweat-shirt with the letters she had ordered herself printed over her bosom – PRESS. Her joke. 'You want me and this visiting fascist lady to talk girl-talk about her clothes, right? Goodness, Lady Clare, what a smashing pair of knickers. Hand-embroidered, you say, by twenty slaves from the slums of Nombre Dios? You can't find work like that here in England any more. The unions, you know. Dead set against producing exquisite handiwork like that, they are. Commie bastards.'

The Red Lion was packed at lunch-time, expense-account businessmen in the back with their shrimp cocktails and steaks diane and working people like her and Andy, Features Editor on the *Chronicle*, crushed at the bar keeping their strength up with potato chips.

'Jude.' Andy's weary voice cut through her diatribe. 'Say whatever you like, only please say it round five photos of Lady Clare's wardrobe, that's all I ask. We've spent the whole of this last month pouring Scotch down the throats of advertising agents so let's not bugger up a possible breakthrough. Okay?'

'Advertisers,' said Judith. 'If I had my way, I'd shoot them all. Even our own advertising department hates us, Andy. They sneer at everything we stand for.' She swayed belligerently towards him. 'Advertisers are the unacceptable fucking face of newspapers. Right?'

'You got a better face?' said Andy.

They argued across the road to the paper. 'What's wrong with subsidies?' yelled Judith, halfway through the hooting cars. 'Political control,' shouted Andy, grasping the hem of her denim jacket. 'The Beeb manages,' said Judith, leaping like a gazelle to the pavement. 'Yeah, and they pay for it, all that so-called *balance*,' said Andy. They stood on the other side in safety, clutching each other. 'Is that what you want? BBC balance?'

'Fucking unbalanced, the Beeb,' Judith snorted, switching her argument as she pushed through the swing doors. 'Last time I went on the ghastly James Finn show he came on like I was some sort of KGB bull-dyke, on account of I said I didn't fancy the idea of getting nuked. Whereas a twit of a brigadier was allowed to go blethering on about Our Boys and Fortress Falkland and defending the Free World till the cows came home.'

'My point exactly.' Andy pressed the lift button. 'That's what we doctors call political control.'

'Yeah,' said Judith as they trundled upwards. 'More like what we feminists call men getting their rocks off. On telly or off, what men really want is a fight. You're all quite happy to bow and scrape to the next one up the ladder as long as when your turn comes you can put the boot in. Male politics, left or right, is only another word for a bit of aggro while they push the ladies out of the ring.'

The lift shuddered to a halt and Andy stepped out. Judith followed and touched his arm. 'Listen, Andy, I can't cope with the wardrobe bit, honestly I can't. Get Lizzie to do it, it's her thing. Then I promise I'll do a lovely profile of Her Fascist Ladyship for Features. Okay?'

'Anything you say, Jude.' Ahead of her, Andy sighed loudly, grinning to himself. Without the red herring of the fashion piece, Jude would never have offered a profile. One up there, man.

At Judith's desk at the far end of the clamorous Features Department, the phone was ringing. It was Min Holroyd, Judith could hear her bracelets clanking as she said hullo. When she'd worked with Min on the *Star* eons ago, disentangling Min's bracelets from her typewriter keys had been an occupational hazard. That armful of gew-gaws was Min's way of proclaiming she was not one of the boys.

'Judith?' Min's voice was up in the high Cs, another way of asserting her non-existent femininity. 'You doing anything on this Lady Clare caper?'

'Christ, Min, I've got to,' said Judith, scrabbling in her hand-bag for a light.

'Haven't we all,' squeaked Min. 'I've got to set up a women's prog and, so far, the Venturans are co-operating. Yes ma'am, no ma'am, three bags blah. But the catch is, Cheryl's down with a bad case of the zits. If we get Her Ladyship, could you present it?' At the other end of the telephone, her bracelets clashed in frenzied appeal.

'A nice little yak about Clare's undies, yes?' Judith said, making a scornful face at Lorna, the efficient Features secretary whose desk backed on to hers.

'No, Jude.' Min's squeak went up a register. 'We've moved on a little since you were here or don't you watch the box, now that you're not always on? It'll be about the women of Ventura. Legislation, birth control, status, rights, equality, that sort of thing. What does Her Ladyship think women most need, you know.'

'I know,' said Judith. She put on an excruciating Mexican accent. 'I am a woman of Ventura. What I most need is that Señora Clare and our beloved President stop shooting at me and drop dead themselves, pronto.'

'Two fifty,' said Min.

'Done,' said Judith. The women made an appointment to meet and Judith dropped the receiver into its cradle from a height. If I don't do it, someone else will. Classic excuse for knavery. What was the female for knavery? Sluttery. Slaggery. Still, it was true. Min doubtless had her index finger poised over her contact book, ready to call up Mandy Brice or, worse, that fat cow Linda Reeves who would slaver all over Her Ladyship on the off-chance of a freebie to Ventura. At least she could rely on herself to lash out with a couple of sharp questions and on Min's prog that was two more than usual. It was about time women stopped muttering sweet nothings at each other and started some healthy bouts of sister-bashing at appropriate moments. Hanging about waiting for all women to get the feminist message would only put a female finger on the button instead of a male. Look at Mrs T. Look at this dictator lady. What did they have in common with other women? Nothing but their ... Even in her thoughts,

Judith had no word for that part of the female anatomy. The proper anglo-saxon had been degraded long ago by men and she refused all substitutes as too coy by half. She'd once had a boyfriend who referred to it as her 'yoni'. What's that, a Swedish punter? she had asked him rudely.

Judith took her notebook and went across the corridor to the library. There, she found the file she was looking for: 'Ventura', subtitled 'de Toro y Plata', and settled down to riffle through the contents. A couple of items on the discovery of a hitherto-unknown species of fungus in the Ventura forest, a bit about Nixon visiting, a longish piece from the *New Internationalist* about the effects of long-term malnutrition on Venturan Indian children and a mention of the death of Vincente de Toro y Plata, the old dictator. Then came the marriage – Don Raul to Lady Clare of Tucolston Old Hall de dum de dum. The bride looked a treat in her great grandmother's lace veil and some lip-licking lines about how rich the groom was: THEY CALL HIM EL DORADO said one headline. Judith, peering at the blurry news-print photos, could make out only the dark cross his features formed on the long square of the face, the long bone of a nose. Tasty, though. In the battle with newsprint, he had fared better than his wife. The Señora came across as a greyer shade of pale, her hair and face and clothes a smear of light, like the bright edge of an eclipsed moon. There was a year's gap and then some *Homes and Gardens* stuff about Clare's refurbishment of the Presidential residence, a quarter of a million pounds that cost. No wonder the Venturans called her 'La Dorada'. El Dorado, La Dorada, a music hall turn. Pix of the two of them waving from a curlicued balcony. Hullo out there, ta for the lolly, awfully kind of you.

After that, a bit of American gossip – who was with whom at whose party in Palm Beach, Nassau, LA, NY. Mrs de Toro, it appeared, had stuck her hands in Ventura's coffers and flown out to classier beaches. Then nothing for a year or so and a fresh outburst of gush. Wonderful Clare building wonderful things, half a million on a concert hall – a *concert* hall in the back of beyond? – another quarter on a crafts centre for ripping off the natives. And the Virgin of Ventura Hospital with a pic of Our Lady herself cutting the ribbon. The *Chronicle*, Judith was glad to see, hadn't deigned to write a word about all this. What clippings there were came from the *Express* and the *Sun*, idiot headlines like GOLDEN GIFT FROM A GOLDEN GIRL and OUR OWN LADY BOUNTIFUL GOES INTO ACTION, as if she weren't doing it all for her own prestige and probably using American aid to do it. What's more, she'd obviously scrimped on the nuts and bolts because the roof of the casino fell in on top of eight men. She made it to the funeral though, looking simply ducky in a little black number. Noblesse oblige.

'Glad to see our star columnist at the grindstone.' Andy appeared beside her, his chin balanced on a pile of books. He put them down and leaned over her shoulder. 'Wow,' he said, 'what a corker, eh? Cor.'

'You're as bad as the readers,' said Judith crossly. 'Do you have to be so predictable?'

Andy said in a campy voice. 'It's El Presidente I'm talking about.'

'God,' said Judith ignoring this, 'that's just like a man. One look at a pretty face and your principles hit the dust. What would you say if I thought Pinochet was cute and I couldn't wait to screw him. Or the Ayatollah?'

'I rather fancy the Ayatollah. So stern, so thrillingly patri-archal. After you, dearie.'

'Andy. The woman's a monster. She's just out for what she can get, at any price.'

'And there's a million men out there would pay it,' said Andy. 'So long, sunshine.' He gathered up his books and went off, grinning.

Judith sat and burned. Bloody hell, there wasn't even equality in evil. If a woman had eyes, nose, tits and bum in all the right places, she was forgiven everything. She was also the ultimate distraction. The male half of the population thought of nothing but fucking her, the female half nothing but being her. Put pictures of women like Clare all across the front pages and politicians everywhere could stop their charade of party politics and get on with what they really wanted to do, blow up the world, while their sex-crazed underlings sang 'Isn't She Lovely?', crouched under their kitchen tables waiting for the Bomb.

At that point in Judith's angry inner monologue, another file was deposited in front of her. 'Ventura, Part Two,' said the librarian, 'thought you'd like to see it. We're a bit behind with Third World stuff.' Thanking him, Judith opened it. Articles from some Latin-American press agency, loud with praise for Lady Clare.

The once poverty-stricken peasant women of Ventura have new hope today, thanks to a scheme inaugurated by Señora de Toro y Plata, wife of Ventura's President. The Venturan forests are rich in nutritive, medicinal and profitable species of flora and fauna but the traditional knowledge of their use was dying away as peasants moved to the town. Now, the Women's Co-operative project is aiming to reverse this trend. In a recent interview, the Señora outlined her hopes for this enlightened campaign . . .

Judith read on. The scheme sounded good. Was there more to this brittle lady than met the eye? Had she seen some light on the road to Damascus? Why had a jet-set Queen with the finest collection of emeralds outside Buck House suddenly decided to play Lady Bountiful to a lot of half-starved Indian women? The answer, Judith knew in her bones, was that she hadn't. Or rather, that there was something in it for her, something that made it worth her while, putting on an act. What? Ah yes, here were the clippings about the first explosion in Ventura and the continuing guerrilla activity. The Women's Co-operative was an exercise in public relations, that much was obvious. Impress the uncommitted Venturans that your dictatorship was benign and flexible and impress the Americans so that they kept up a constant flow of aid. Manipulative capitalism, at it again. And what more successful way than a beautiful woman showing her bleeding heart to other women? That touching scenario could be relied upon to obscure all other nasties like the President's men rounding up peasants and whipping them away in the middle of the night, to be tortured and dumped in some convenient swamp. Shake a shapely tit and everyone would look the other way. Aaaah. A fresh burst of bile washed through Judith. Was there no end to the perfidy of women? You put your trust in them as a refuge from an insane male world, you devoted every working hour to bettering their conditions, you had faith in them as the future alternative to the sterile violence of masculine values and they betrayed you, they connived in the violence and the horror, they went hand-in-hand with the men for their own aggrandisement, their own greed, to save their own pathetic skins. Men were monsters, God knows. In a million hideous chambers across the planet they practised their tortures on howling victims for no other reason than their own pleasure in power and pain and their own hopelessly deformed idea of what life was about. But what did women do? They sat in front of mirrors, just out of hearing of the victims' screams, primping. Pouting out their lips the better to put on Estée Lauder's Autumn Range of Jewel Lipsticks. Poncing up and down wittering about the length of hemlines in the Paris Collections. Trying on the latest in sexy lingerie so that their menfolk, after a long day's pillaging, could lay their heads, bloody but unbowed, upon the lace-edged cleavage and pay for more sexy lingerie, more unbelievably expensive fur coats off the backs of endangered species. Even women with no vicarious power, whose husbands and sons were only cannon fodder for other men's wars, even they did nothing more constructive than throw up their hands in despair and sob and bind up wounds instead of gathering up all their children and stomping out and refusing to come back until the men had stopped playing their wicked games.

She slammed the file shut, dumped it in the retrieval basket and snapped at everyone for the rest of the afternoon. At five o'clock she swung her bag over her shoulder and left without saying goodbye to anyone. Down in the car park, she slid into her battered CV. The seat was warm from the day's sun, she could feel it on her thighs through the cotton skirt. What was it that idiot girl had said at school, whispering behind her hand in the art class, her bunches wagging? 'Do you know if you sit on a seat where a boy's been sitting and it's still warm, you'll get a baby?' Judith cricked her neck round, backed the car out of its narrow parking place and drove up to join the traffic on the main road. She'd gone home after that to ask her mother was it true, did you really get a baby from a warm seat, but her mother couldn't answer. She was there, lying crooked on the kitchen floor, with tiny worms of blood around her closed eyes. Glass crunched under the little girl's feet. The air in the room was thick with silence and the smell of her father. Standing at the door, clinging to her satchel, terror turned her stomach to water. She had shat herself.

Judith stared blindly at the dust on the windscreen, lines of cars stretched ahead. Fear, humiliation, the neighbours running to her shrieks, the pity in their eyes as they looked at her and a queer joy too. While they mopped at her mother's face and her mother stirred and groaned, the child stood helpless in her own stink and writhed in an anguish of hatred that left her shaking and screaming until they brought her mother across to her. Judith blinked, squeezed her eyes shut and opened them again but her mother's face was still there, bending over her in that hot kitchen, her swollen lips trying to smile. Her skin yellow, one eyelid drooping, the lovely brown hair matted on her neck. The child looked up into that battered smile, saw the tears

[188]

shining and was smitten with such an agony of love and loathing that she managed only to sob out 'I hate you' before her breath went and she sagged into her mother's arms.

'Jesus wants you for a sunbeam' sang Judith loudly at the wheel, grinding along the Gray's Inn Road. Why, mother? Twenty years with that bastard and hardly a week without a walloping. Mother's face was the end of the rainbow, yellow, green, red and every shade of violet, a free Technicolor ticket for every prying social worker in the borough of Hackney who happened to be at a loose end and fancied throwing their weight about with Hackney's Number One Problem Family. How many times had Judith tried to pull the stupid bag out of the door? How many times had she packed a suitcase, yelled 'we'll manage, come on Mum, come *on*?' But Mum clung to her house of horrors like a limpet and, Christ, a kid can't manage on her own. *Why*, mother?

[11]

'Pathetic leader in *The Times* this morning about that Clare woman.' Ruth Maryschild (editor of *Smash Patriarchy*) lay flat on her back on the floor of Judith's sitting-room, frowning at the ceiling.

'Useless,' Judith said, washing glasses in the kitchenette.

'I suppose we'll soon see the balance redressed by you in the *Chronicle*?'

'Something like that,' said Judith. 'Red or white?'

'Red, ta.' Ruth rolled over on her elbow and stuck out her hand for the glass. Judith sank on to a bean-bag which immediately excreted several small pellets from a slit in its side.

'That bean-bag's incontinent,' said Ruth. 'Cheers.'

'Cheers.' Now for the Inquisition.

Ruth drank and put the glass down with her hand over it, as if to say not another drop till we get things sorted out. 'May we ask what angle you'll be taking?' Ruth was a lecturer in Russian Studies at the School of Slavonic Studies when she wasn't smashing partriarchy and withdrew in moments of stress into an oblique Iron Curtain conversational style.

Judith wondered whether to fence some more and decided against it. Her piece would be wrapped round chips this time next week. 'I'm going to give that broad what's coming to her,' she said in fake American. 'Straight between the eyes.' She shot her cuffs in a Jimmy Cagney imitation.

'Cut it out,' said Ruth. She swung her legs to a sitting position and pursed her mouth. Judith thought how plain she was, really aggressively plain. If you had a face rather less charming than an uncooked currant bun, did you have to compound the error of your ways by refusing all adornment, all mitigating cosmetics and hack your hair under a pudding bowl with pruning shears? Ruth exposed her face to others as primitive tribes expose their bottoms, to spread alarm and despondency. Then shame bore in. This was her besetting sin, a kind of fascism of looks. At school she had committed a never-to-be-forgotten act of childish cruelty. Infuriated by the bumpy features, spotty skin and bad breath suffered by an unfortunate fellow pupil, she had egged the other girls on to send her to Coventry, as they said in those days. For a week, no one had looked at or talked to Hilary. Alone with her halitosis, the wretched child had shuffled about the school corridors, turning her pitted face from side to side in hopeless appeal to the Judith-inspired throngs who carefully skirted her.

Judith gave Ruth a warm smile to make up for Hilary but it cut no ice with Ruth, who practised not smiling on principle. In her view, women smiled altogether too much, hoping to appease and divert male wrath, and she had long ago decided she was not prepared to go about grinning like a loony at her oppressors. 'Go on,' she said, raising a cold eyebrow.

'Okay,' said Judith. 'It's straightforward enough. What we see in Ventura is a male dictator and also a female dictator, because that's what this Clare woman is. Assuming that she's not mentally retarded, she must be aware that her luxurious life, her palace, her wardrobe, her emeralds all come from the exploit-ation of the poor. She must also know about and condone the fact that her husband orders the arrests, tortures and killings of anyone in Ventura who is fighting for change. If her husband is a monster, then so is she and I'm not going to let her off the hook because she's a cute popsie or because she's a woman and I'm a woman and sisters in their little nests must agree. She's no sister of mine, over or under the skin.'

In the short silence that followed Judith's speech, the bean-bag rustled drily and disgorged more droppings from its innards. Ruth heaved herself up and helped herself to more wine.

'And what about this Women's Co-operative?' she said. 'Or will that be left out as not fitting in with your thesis?'

'Window-dressing,' said Judith, 'a confidence trick. Looks good on paper, gives her prestige, costs next to nothing. Propaganda.'

'Very interesting, your reading of the situation,' Ruth said. 'Bears an uncanny resemblance to the medieval practice of scapegoating. Don't attack bossman, drag in some female he employs and put the boot in her. It'll change nothing but it's safer and it feels good. All part of the thrills and spills of patriarchy.'

Judith heaved a melodramatic sigh. 'Ruth,' she said, her voice low and exquisitely patient. 'I cannot go on about patriarchy *again.*'

'Of course not.' Ruth nodded amiably. 'You've done patriarchy. The fact that it's ruined women's lives for thousands of years is neither here nor there because to write two articles about it is one too many. Boring, right? And you cannot afford to bore your readers. After all, we journalists are in the entertainment business, aren't we?' She warbled, spreading her arms. 'There's no people like show people, they smile when they are low ...'

Judith regarded her. Carefully, she set her voice on an even keel. 'Much as I wish I could live on air,' she said, 'I am forced to earn my money, regret it though I may. And I have to earn it within patriarchy. I am paid to catch readers and my employers are none too particular how I do it. Nor are they fascinated by my girlish scruples. I have had to come to terms with this admittedly unsatisfactory state of affairs in order to put food in my stomach.' Ruth's eyebrows were nearly at her hair line and to forestall her, Judith added, to the ceiling, 'I also have a mother to support.' That should do it. Nor was it wholly untrue — she paid her mother's telephone bills, didn't she?

'No need to look so put-upon,' said Ruth, noisily cracking

some of Judith's rather expensive pistachio nuts. 'We at SP have commitments too but, obviously, working as part of a feminist collective doesn't appeal to you. You couldn't afford this flat for a start on the pittance we pay ourselves. There is an alternative to working on the capitalist press but you just don't fancy it.'

Judith folded both arms across her stomach. Why did talking to her Sisters always give her galloping indigestion, not to mention incipient ulcers? Other women drew support and encouragement from their women friends. Half the books that arrived on her desk every day contained fervent messages from the author to other females. 'Without thee help of my Sisters in the Collective I would never have found the courage to write this book', that sort of thing. Whereas in her experience contact with her Sisters invariably brought on an acute attack of writer's block. Of course, a tame psychiatrist would say that this was due to an unconscious recognition of the truth of what women said and the truth did not make you free, it made you extremely tetchy. Judith had frequently examined this possibility in a spirit, she felt sure, of humble inquiry and a brave readiness to yield if the case were proven. But it never seemed proven.

'Maybe you're right,' she said. 'Maybe I am in the business of selling my soul for a mess of extremely expensive pistachio nuts ...' she glared at Ruth's pecking hand, '... raised by emaciated persons in the Third World.' Ruth's hand wavered. Good. 'Maybe everything else is a rationalization. But the unconscious mind isn't the only truthteller. Rationalizations make sense, too.'

'If you don't want me to eat your nuts,' said Ruth, 'just say so.' She collapsed on the floor again, in an attitude of patient resignation.

'Oh shut up,' said Judith, warming to her theme. 'I'm serious, Ruth. Who cares what people's inner motives are, as long as what they *do* works out for the best? Your precious purity usually ends up like that early Christian Father, squatting on top of a pillar in the desert, doing no one any good except the vultures.'

Ruth sighed heavily. Judith leaned towards her. 'No, look,' she said. 'I think you and the Collective are great, I do. I admire you all. I know I couldn't do what you're doing and what you're doing is first-rate. I mean that sincerely.' A reluctant twitch of Ruth's lips at the cliché encouraged her. 'But I've got reservations. If I didn't, I'd really have to join you. The thing about you lot is, you preach to the converted. I've no quarrel with that as such.'

'As *such*,' Ruth echoed, rolling her eyes about.

'Yeah.' Judith refused to be deflected. 'The converted need strength and solidarity and fuel for the crusade, fine. And I won't even mention some of the criticisms I have, like you don't half moan on a lot and you never, but never, celebrate any gains you've made or draw the slightest distinctions between shades of grey. With you, it's all either the blackest of black or the whitest of white when, in fact, all we've got is what's in between. But what does get me, now and again, is that I support and admire what you're doing and you do nothing but point the finger at what *I'm* doing. You're a bunch of squealing virgins.'

'Wise virgins,' said Ruth. Judith took no notice.

'Unlike you, I live in the real world, mate. Out there where the going's tough and the only way to survive is by stealth and cunning and compromise. You're not given anything, you just grab what you can and, by God, you're grateful for what you grab.'

'Thank you, John Wayne,' Ruth said. 'Don't call us, we'll call you.'

'Scoff all you like.' Judith was quite carried away by now. 'The women I write for live in that real world, too. I don't give them any of your undiluted theoretical feminism because they wouldn't read it if I did. But I do get in the occasional glancing blow, the odd nudge, the once-in-a-while shock horror sensation that starts them thinking and you couldn't care less about that. Sometimes I think you couldn't care less because you'd rather sit about smugly patting yourselves on the back for the loveliness of your own lifestyles than mess with ordinary women and get your hands dirty.' That's telling 'em, fat lady, she thought to herself, invigorated by her eloquence. It was bad for you, keeping things in, it ate at your stomach lining.

Ruth swung herself up, crossed her legs and brushed nutshells off her lap on to Judith's carpet. 'You don't understand, do you? You never have, Jude. You can't trade with the enemy without some mud sticking. If you write for women and you write it in male language in the male media, your message gets distorted. In fact, it becomes a lot worse than useless. What you actually do is provide an excuse for men to say to women, look, you've got some Judiths barking on, what more do you want? You're nothing but the vent in a kettle, Jude. Every week, millions of women read you, let off a little steam and then go and wash their husbands' socks, feeling better. Big deal. Contented slaves instead of uppity ones. Is that what you want?'

'The old Trot tune,' said Judith. 'Hum it and I'll play it. Don't plaster over the cracks, don't make a few lives worth living, don't put out a hand and prop up a crumbling wall. Just hang about and the proles will get so wretched they'll storm the barricades for you and you'll have your revolution. And I wouldn't give an ice cube in hell for their chances afterwards, stuck with you moaning Minnies.' Delving in the leather bag by her feet, she pulled out a lipstick and pursed her mouth. 'Excuse me,' she said, 'while I plaster up my cracks.'

Ruth made a nasty crowing noise, stretching out her neck. 'You'll betray us all one day, see if you don't,' she said. 'I've got to go, Jude, I've got a meeting and I'm late.'

'God, you're a pain in the arse,' Judith said.

Ruth smiled modestly as she struggled into her anorak. 'What I say is true, pet. One of these days you'll sell out women for thirty pieces of silver and you won't even know you're doing it, you won't even notice.'

'Bollocks,' said Judith.

'We'll see,' said Ruth.

At Judith's door, squat Georgian, painted red, architecturally-listed, the two women kissed briefly. 'We mustn't fight,' said Judith, feeling suddenly affectionate. Ruth was so dauntless and her hair so awful. 'We've only got each other.' Ruth, halfway down the steps, her parachute bag bumping on her hips, turned and came up again to put her hand on Judith's arm.

'Remember what I said about the de Toro woman,' she said earnestly. 'Whatever she's done, it's not her fault. She's a victim.'

'Right on,' said Judith.

'A victim of patriarchy.'

'Power to the Mothers,' said Judith. She watched Ruth then, walking briskly away, shoulders hunched well over her feet. As she reached the corner of the street, she collided with another woman coming the other way. A pack on the other woman's back swayed and a baby whimpered. Judith had seen the woman before, noticed her because one side of her face was red, as if someone had thrown ketchup at her. Poor thing, thought Judith. Whoever made her pregnant?

Clare in silk and emeralds among the Sèvres and Waterford stared into the gilt-edged specs of Gary Lutz from Chambersburg, Penn., in pharmaceuticals, wondering how Mrs Lutz could bring herself to touch those blebs of lips. It would be like kissing a small pink jellyfish.

'That is something we consider of very great importance, ma'am,' he said. 'The staff at our Pittsburgh unit are constantly made cognisant of the inter-relatedness of the research situation. It is an integral plank of our executive policy that the corollary of all research must be global responsibility.' Lutz nodded slowly, four times, to indicate his profound agreement with his statement.

'How wise,' said Clare. With a discreet click she unhinged her jaw like a python and moved slowly over his rubbery head and torso until he was no more. On her left, Al Penowski from Oregon, in timber, tucked away Kodachrome snapshots of Mrs Al Penowski and pulled out Kodachrome snapshots of Al Penowski Junior, waiting eagerly for Clare's renewed attentions.

The men at the long table shone greasily in the candlelight; only Raul at the far end was his customary dry grey self. Clare imagined herself gliding unobtrusively down the rows of carved mahogany chairs, sinking her vermeille knife between the shoulder blades of each occupant. The blood, seeping out, would make interesting batik patterns on the lightweight suiting. She was murderously bored.

Chewing his steak, Raul glanced down the table at his wife. She was hanging on every word of that fat peasant, the dog-faced Lutz. He could see the inviting shadow between her breasts, she looked as soft and sugared as a marshmallow. What a sham it was, that beauty. So apparently innocent, so feminine. But barren. Worse than barren, corrupt. The memory, always painful, of the night in Cairo came back to him. All those months of worship, of wanting her so badly and restraining himself because he had thought her his virgin madonna, a white candle burning with a pure flame on the altar to which he bowed down. And then to find his idol was rotten at the heart, soiled with the semen of other men, no more than a hole into which half the males of London had emptied themselves. How they must have jeered at him, those cool superior Englishmen who knew his wife so well. How they must have laughed in their London clubs when the news came that some dago fool had promised to love and to cherish what they had all had free. The mocking faces haunted him, his dreams were made bitter by their drawling sneers.

Wiping his fingers on a napkin, he thought of the preparations that were now being rehearsed at the airport and some of the bitterness eased. Revenge, to be truly sweet, must exactly fit the crime and also benefit the avenger, payment with interest and in kind. The Lord had not said a tooth for an eye, He had said an eye for an eye. But the American beside him was talking again. O'Reilly.

'We have contacts in Mexico, Mr President, sir. They'll handle the Stateside cargo. The European operation could be a little tricky but Lutz is the expert there, he'll advise you. There'll be no problems with the stuff *we* want.' O'Reilly gave a modest smile and lined up his fork and knife. 'You haven't ratified with CITES yet, is that right, sir?'

'Right.' Raul wiped his mouth carefully with his napkin, his mind still on his wife's departure. Deborah was fixed but that maid of Clare's?

'Fine,' O'Reilly said, draining his wine glass. 'Then all we have to do is alert our men. No documentation needed for the Mexican end but ...'

'Tomorrow,' Raul said. 'We can discuss the details tomorrow, Mr O'Reilly.'

'Of course, sir, I understand.' O'Reilly put his glass down and followed the President's gaze. 'The Señora is looking particularly charming tonight, if I may say so. The British will give her a warm welcome.'

'I hope so,' Raul said. 'I hope so.'

For a whole four minutes afterwards, Alice's heart beat against her ribs like a small animal trying to break out of a cage. Sunk in her thoughts, the smack of the woman's shoulder against her own had sent her into a spin of fright, thinking stupidly, over and over, it's the arm of the law. Daft, she had to admit, as out of breath and sweating, she scuttled into the doorway of the flats. Police-women didn't crash into you on the pavement coming the other way, they crept up behind you and put their hands on your shoulder. Or so Alice supposed.

The letter had been lying on the doormat that morning when

Alice got up. It was the only letter she had received in the eight months she had been in London and it was from her mother, she recognized that round uneven hand from the recipes in the kitchen drawer, painstakingly copied from women's magazines.

I am glad you are well and the baby, Alice. You fairly broke our hearts when you went off like that without a word. Your Dad was that angry he didn't let me write. I have done a lot of crying since you left, dear. The whole village knows and it is hard and I miss you. You were a good girl till then. That man should have talked to Dad and marry you, not gone off so far. Alice, you could come back. We could sort things out and look after the baby but not with that man. He should marry you, that is the least he could do.

Alice, reading, pulled her eyes wide to stop the tears. Marry you, marry you. The words blurred.

Alice, you wanted money. I have put five pounds in the envelope, it is all I can spare. You didn't notice anything before you went but things are hard for us. Dad lost all his potatoes down Five Acre. His Lordship too, everyone has. They got a blight and none of the farmers know what it is, the leaves got black spots. Uncle Craddock up to Bath, he has the same, it was in the papers. So that looks like half our money gone this year and it has left us not knowing which way to turn for a penny. Parson Lavery had special prayers in Chapel last Sunday but prayers are no good to stop potato rot. Alice, you will have to manage, that man has a duty to you. I bought Rhode Islands to make up the money but they are not laying yet. I will pray for you like always but I can't help you more. A kiss for my grandson and hope you are well. Love from your Mother.

There was an added note, 'They are all of a dither up at the Hall, with Miss Clare coming.'

In the bedroom, the baby's cries were loud and rhythmic, like an engine. Alice stuck out her tongue and licked the salty drops from her upper lip. They said sin blighted the crop and fornication was a sin. Lying there in her father's field, clutching each other in fornication, had she and Charlie spread disease along the

[199]

earth, poisoning hidden roots, drawing the good from each plant so that they withered on paper stalks? Black birds flapped across her eyes and her legs ached. The baby's screams beat at her eardrums and filled the air with anguish.

All the morning, Alice stayed in. She dusted every surface, she scrubbed the small linoleum square of the kitchen floor, she cleaned the rectangles of glass at the windows and wished she could clean away the grey sky beyond. She fed the baby, staring down at its tiny face, touching the delicate red wings that rose between the two fair eyebrows as it sucked. Twice, she became suddenly dizzy and sat down with her head between her legs, feeling sick. Perhaps it was just hunger, she thought. She didn't think she was hungry but when she tried to remember her last sit-down meal, she couldn't. Cornflakes and bread and apples, that was about the size of it, and most of that gone to the baby through the funnel of her breasts. Alice ran a finger across her front teeth. A tooth for every baby, her mother used to say but they seemed steady enough. Where was Charlie? Where was he ever, these days? His absences left an emptiness in her that hurt almost all the time, so that she had grown used to it mostly, and it wasn't his fault. That summer she had made him happy, a grinning lanky capering figure full of joy, and even when she had first moved into his flat and he had sobered, his face less smiling, his eyes sometimes sad, the same joy had often swept him up again, so that he would rush her down the stairs and push her on buses and they'd trundle off to somewhere green, Hampstead Heath, Victoria Park, once as far as Kew, and he'd whirl her around on the green grass and then they'd lie close together under the trees, smiling at each other. But now he was usually miles away in his head and his smiles were few and far between. Somehow, he seemed smaller, shrunk into himself and he drank too much – there were often five or more green bottles lining the kitchen counter when he'd left her in the evening and his eyes were blurry and he bumped against the wall as he went out.

Things had begun to go bad when he lost his job. He was already unsteady on his feet when he came back to tell her, and she only a week out of the hospital with the baby. 'Last in, first out, story of my life,' he'd said, grinning, but he stopped grinning when Alice gasped, 'Oh Charlie, *no*,' and clung to him. He'd pushed her arms away and said, 'Lay off, gel, it's not the end of the world, something else'll turn up.' But nothing had turned up, or not yet, and Charlie's redundancy money hadn't kept them long. After that, there'd been his dole but Alice had a hard time managing on that. It was meant for him alone and wouldn't stretch and she worried that her body wouldn't provide enough to keep the baby healthy.

'You'll have to go up the Social, Ally,' Charlie said when the quarterly rent bill came in. 'There's nothing else for it.'

'But Charlie,' wailed Alice, turning from the cooker with a saucepan in her hand, her eyes shiny with alarm, 'you said to me, you said, they wouldn't let me have anything because we're living together.'

'Yeah, well, that's easily settled. I'll move out. Bloke I was with at the Park says there's a room in his squat. It'll cost me nothing.'

Alice stumbled past the chairs and the table to him, flung herself against him. The saucepan tipped from her hand and spinach fell in dark green gobbets to the floor. She wept on to his chest. 'Please, Charlie, please don't go. I'll die without you. I love you so much Charlie, Charlie.' Then, despairingly, straining back her head to look up to his face, hers as wet as someone drowned, 'Oh marry me oh Charlie or you'll break my heart Charlie.'

He was gentle and rocked her and dabbed at her tears, smoothing back the damp hair from her forehead, and when she was calm again he told her about the girl who was now in Holloway, the girl he had married when they were both seventeen just for dumb kicks, she'd said let's do it, Charlie, that'll learn my old man, meaning her father who kept feeling her up. So there it was and painless, really. Alice quite cheered up, after a barrage of questions – no he'd never loved her, yes he'd get a divorce when she was out, three years for kiting cheques and GBH, she was a hard one – and dived after the spinach, scrubbing away at the fibres stuck in the coconut matting with energy renewed.

'You should have said before, Charlie.'

'You never asked.'

'I didn't like to,' said Alice. With a face like hers, you didn't ask questions. In case you got answers and the bubble burst.

'You're daft as a brush,' said Charlie and happiness flowed into every part of her.

It receded again, of course. Nothing would change Charlie's mind about moving out, he insisted it was the only way and it would mean nothing, she wouldn't even notice the difference and the money would be ensured. But from the evening he took his guitar, his razor and his few clothes, Alice was undone. Until then, those first moments of waking in the morning had flooded her with delight, so that she lay still between the sheets in awe that she should be thus blessed. Blessed art thou among maidens, she thought, and shivered and smiled to herself at the blasphemy because she was no sort of maiden now and Charlie made a very peculiar Holy Ghost, lying there beside her fast asleep with his cap of hair smooth as a seal on the pillow. At the sight of him, human in every way, snoring a little, Alice was daily transported. Often, she could not resist leaning over him and covering his face with kisses, every millimetre of it, the little trough between his lips, the curve of his nostrils, up the bridge of his nose and along the silky eyebrows that frowned as he woke. Once, apprehension had gripped her as he frowned, she had forgotten what he saw when he looked at her, the mark that dripped from her left eye in bloody rivulets. She had not turned it away from him soon enough, as she should, to protect him from her imperfection.

'I am ugly,' she said then, ducking down her chin. She yearned fiercely as she had not yearned for years to have the mark vanish, as a gift to him.

'You are beautiful,' said Charlie in a sleep-sodden voice, pulling her down to him and nuzzling across the mark. 'There is nothing ugly about any part of you, old darling.'

It was true that for some weeks after Charlie's official change of residence there was no very obvious alteration in Alice's life except, as Charlie pointed out when she got her Social Security money, for the good. He stayed overnight in his room at the squat only now and again 'in case,' he said, 'the Social are keeping tabs,' and for the rest of the time things were as they'd always been. Almost. For a while. Then Charlie began to stay away. Imperceptibly, an hour's absence turned into an afternoon, an afternoon and evening. An occasional night at the squat became two, became four. He had to see a man about a job, he met a mate he hadn't seen for yonks, his motorbike wouldn't start, it was too late to come over, it was too early, he'd been with her all yesterday, he'd be with her all tomorrow, he swore it on his mother's grave (his mother was alive and well and living in Peckham). The small black wedges of the hours on the face of the clock on the kitchen mantelpiece imprinted themselves in Alice's mind, the clock's ticking sliced her days and nights into leaden minutes. Sometimes she protested, mostly she did not, afraid that remonstrations would drive Charlie further away, afraid to ruin her precious rations with him, afraid when she saw that even when he was present, part of him was not.

And now, for the past fortnight, she had been almost completely alone. Whole chains of days passed and she saw no one but the baby and the flickering images of unknown people on the television screen coming and going, talking and arguing, claiming this and denying that, debating and discussing events as remote from Alice's four walls as a distant long-dead star. When Charlie came, they watched the screen together. The heads, the truncated bodies, seemed to have reality for him, he laughed with the laughter that came out of a tin, he talked back at the mouths opening and closing, he was involved in that shadow world, he reacted as he had last night to Clare, apparently knowing why she was coming and why she should not. Alice tried to enter the jumpy, boxed-off life behind the glass but succeeded only in seeing a drift of dust at a corner and fingerprints smeared on the surface, yet she watched with Charlie and even more without him. The television was their bond, it sat glimmering in front of them like a precocious only child, absorbing its parents with antics because they had ceased to be absorbed in each other. Alone, Alice needed its synthetic chatter to keep at bay the glacier that was moving, inch by inch, inexorably towards her. She did not question Charlie's absences in any way except as they pressed upon her. The idea that they could have to do with a transference of his love and desire from herself to some other woman never entered her head. She often felt that he deserved better than her, because of her mark and also her ignorance of the world he moved in so confidently, but she had been chosen and though she was sad and growing sadder and Charlie's absences bewildered her, they could not stem from outside interference. She knew in her heart and her bones and her blood that Charlie loved her because if he didn't, she was dead.

Nevertheless, the icy practicalities of living nagged constantly. She felt the weight of herself and the baby heavy on Charlie's back, dragging him down; she tensed her body often and drew in her breath as if, by doing so, she could lighten his load. Today he had been held up, he hadn't arrived with the tenner he'd promised and there she was, dizzy in the late afternoon, with a five-pound note from her mother and nothing in the kitchen cupboard or the fridge but an opened tin of baked beans and half a packet of shredded wheat. No detergent for the baby's nappies, no washing-up liquid even and the Vim had gone on the scrubbed floor, the last of it lay in gritty whorls under her feet. So she zipped the baby into his back-pack, strapped him on her shoulders and walked carefully, rather stiffly, to the supermarket two blocks from the flat. There, her head ringing with the clash of trolleys, she collected from the shelves a box of detergent, a carton of Vim, two rolls of toilet paper, two cellophane-wrapped pork chops, a tin of corn and three pounds of pale scrubbed potatoes, which she put in her trolley and paid for at the check-out point while the middle-aged female cashier wagged three fingers in greeting at the baby slung behind her. Then she pushed her way outside with her plastic bag of purchases and moved one foot after another along the pavement that led towards the flat. The dust of the streets, the screech of traffic, the rise of passing voices and their falling away did not impinge, she did not notice the plastic handle of the heavy bag cutting at the base of her fingers or the blare of drills at the edge of a road that made the baby jerk at her back. She stepped across and around and through them all, behind her own glass like a figure on a television screen, until a woman collided with her on the corner and dislodged her heart from its resting place, sent it crashing through her body and banging at her ribs, so that sweat burst out on her forehead and under her arms and she ran the last few yards to her front door and up the endless stairs and pushed in the key and stood in her own narrow hall, panting with fright.

In the kitchen, when her breath had been restored, she put the plastic bag on the table, unhitched herself from the back-pack and took the baby in her arms, looking down at the collapsed canvas in which lay a toothbrush, a tube of toothpaste, six flat envelopes of powdered soup, two packets of powdered whip and a box of baby aspirin.

'I had better get work before it's too late,' she thought in the silent room.'

*

'What work?' said Charlie that evening, stroking her buttery hair. 'You can't type, you never had a job. Not a lot of call for chicken-feeders in this neck of the woods. Forget it, Ally.' He began to tell her about his day. An hour queuing at the Job Centre, a half-hour's bus-ride to a hotel where there was a job as a night porter which had gone by the time he arrived. Then he'd talked to a man on a building site who'd said to come back next week, there might be something. Later, he had done the rounds of the local pubs, registering himself as a likely replacement for bartenders on holiday and later still, acting on information given in the pubs, trekked over to a West End office where there was a gig going for the lads a fortnight on at some street party.

'Big deal, that was,' he said as he helped Alice fold nappies from the clothes horse that permanently dripped over the small, yellow-stained bath. 'Three of us and they offered twenty smackers. Less than seven quid apiece. I said to the geezer, turn it in. A poxy twenty? Don't cover the juice for the guitar.'

'Still,' said Alice, 'someone might have been there and heard you play and offered you something better.'

'Yeah? You mean Paul McCartney might be kicking his heels at the Myrtle Crescent street party in Bethnal Green?' Morosely, he stuck his chin on top of the pile of nappies and went to the bedroom. Alice followed, uncertain of how to react. Charlie didn't like her being cheerful about his failures but, then, he didn't like her being depressed about them either. It was hard to know what to do for the best. In the bedroom, Charlie was talking.

'It comes easy for some,' he said, stacking the nappies on the dresser. 'There's a bloke got a photography business across from the squat. I met him in the boozer with a bird and she was no oil-painting. He drives a Jag and wears camelhair coats so he's doing okay and he pays her thirty quid for a couple of hours' modelling. All right for some.'

Alice thought of many things to say and said none of them.

Then Charlie said, with a sour little smile, that he had been promised three days' work next week and no questions asked, cash on the line.

'I got to put on me cor blimey trousers and be a dustman. It's on account of your Clare woman's visit, you know? They want her route cleared to the Palace so she don't have to see anything unpleasant like she sees at home, starving bodies and that. And we've got to put up the Ventura flag in front of Parliament and the Palace.'

'What's the flag?' asked Alice, sticking to the safe question.

'Search me,' said Charlie.

'What if I go down and see this photographer?' said Alice quickly. 'You could introduce me, Charlie. He might have something and I could take the baby, so it wouldn't mean you staying in. What about it, Charlie? Charlie?'

He leaned over the baby's cot and made noises at it. With his back to her he said there wasn't any point, the bloke had probably got all the models he needed and, anyway, he was a slag.

'You don't want to do business with a ponce like that, nice girl like you.'

'What you mean,' said Alice softly, 'he'd take one look at my face and ...'

Charlie swung round on her and glared. His voice was loud. 'Right,' he said. 'What d'you want me to say, Alice? London is full of girls ...'

'... without birthmarks.'

'... without birthmarks, right. So forget it. Put it out of your bonce. These are hard times. They don't want nothing from me but muscle and they don't want nothing from you but sex. We're in a recession, sunshine, and that means the lowest common denominator from everyone, see?'

Alice put her arms around him and leaned her face against his chest, bad side inwards.

[207]

'Never mind, love,' she said, her voice muffled. 'It doesn't matter. None of it matters if you love me. Do you love me, Charlie?'

Charlie put a hand on the side of Alice's face and held it gently against him. He looked across the room at the window, the pale stretch of sky. An oblong of wood framing nothing.

'I love you,' he said.

[12]

'Press Office, please,' said Judith, one hand over her left ear to shut out the babble in the Features Department. She had already spent ten minutes trying to get through to the Venturan Embassy. Obviously, most of the hacks in town were on the line and Judith was in the state of frustration that always hit her when she had to start rounds of telephone calls. She hated the telephone, which was not a useful trait in a journalist, and by now she hated the Venturan Embassy and all it stood for. Damn Clare the Lady Fascist. She could stick her Women's Co-operative and her rotten white clobber.

'Come on, get *on* with it, bloody inefficient twits,' she growled to herself at the mouthpiece. Adrian, passing, grinned.

'Hullo,' she bellowed. 'Press Office? Thank God. Look, this is Judith Gill, *Chronicle*. I'm fixed up to interview Señora de Toro y Plata for a Thames programme on Friday. The "Women Talking" programme at noon.'

The voice chattered some more.

'That's it. But the thing is, I need to speak to her as soon as she arrives. For that programme and for a profile I'm doing of her for the *Chronicle*.'

Chatter, chatter.

'I realize that.' Judith puffed a plume of belligerent smoke from her nostrils. 'I'm sure she's up to her eyes. Yes. Well, what about fixing that? I could drive down with her from the airport. In her car. She might like having a chat then, it's a boring drive to Claridges. Could you? Yes, I'll hold.'

Covering the receiver, Judith pulled a pad towards her. Across the desk Lorna, the Features Secretary, held up another telephone, eyebrows raised at Judith. 'Thames for you,' she said. Judith leaned across and took the phone.

'Min? I'm holding on for her this minute. Yes, for the prog. I'll ring you right back, okay? Ciao.'

Her own receiver squawked and she dropped the other telephone in its cradle.

'Oh great,' she said, smiling with relief. 'I understand, yes. That's perfect, fine.' Hunching up a shoulder to grip the receiver, she scribbled on the pad. 'Señor Astiz. One p.m., VIP Reception, Heathrow. Right, I've got it. You'll let him know I'm coming, will you? Fine, fantastic, thanks a lot, byee.'

'Got her?' asked Lorna.

'Got her,' said Judith.

Two miles away, up three flights of stairs in a dingy room above an Indian take-away in Notting Hill Gate, Ruth was on the telephone too.

'I know about the Press Conference,' she said, keeping her voice sweet. 'Friday, six p.m. But I'd like to talk to Señora de Toro personally, before or after that. Yes. Ruth Maryschild. Mary's child. We're a feminist paper. Feminista, comprendo?'

The voice stopped. Ruth sat still, the receiver clasped to her ear. The room's walls were covered in posters. FAT IS A FEMINIST ISSUE. Fat is a Feminist Tissue, thought Ruth. Always would be, if you tried to eat for the benefit of Third World Sisters. Nuts and pulses and grains weren't slimming. How unfair it was that a diet meant to help starving sisters blew you up like a balloon, made you the very one people pointed at as an example of over-consumption in the West. Ruth farted quietly in memory of her last meal. We must all have that in common, at least, she thought. In front of her, pinned over her desk, Monica Sjoo's drawing of a squat and Gauguinesque woman, massive thighs bent, framed an emerging head. God Giving Birth.

The telephone voice came back. Ruth's voice rose. 'You can't? But I'm sure Señora de Toro herself would want it. She's very interested in women, isn't she? The Women's Co-operative and all that. Yes, I'm sure. But the nationals won't give anything like the space we would to her peasant women project. They'll just write about her clothes and her private life. Gossip.'

The voice squeaked. Ruth glowered. 'She'll be sorry, too,' she said finally and crashed the receiver. 'Bloody hell,' she said to God Giving Birth.

A thousand miles away, Raul de Toro y Plata talked into a telephone, drumming his fingers on the large glass-topped desk in the Presidential Office in Nombre Dios. The air vibrated with the low buzz of air-conditioning machinery wedged in each long window. A thin man with blue-grey hair stood by the President's desk watching him, his chin tucked in as if he were playing a violin. 'Madre mía,' snapped Raul, banging down one of the five ivory telephones. 'My orders were crystal clear.' He stood up and pointed at the man behind his desk. 'The Señora will not speak to the Press. I want no interviews with stupid women who want to know about her clothes and her private life and I don't want the Señora talking to anyone about the Women's Co-operative, is that understood? She goes as my representative, the representative of Ventura, and it is a private visit. She will meet the Queen, she will spend some time with her parents and that's it. Entendido, Bustalieri?'

Bustalieri, Chief Press Secretary to the President and an old hand at deflecting the attentions of inquisitive visitors from the problems of Ventura with judicious applications of the excellent wines in the Presidential cellars and bourbon recently donated by Research Development, Inc. (US), was frankly out of his depth here. What they did in the London Embassy was beyond his normal scope.

'Mi Presidente,' he said, siphoning the words out of one

corner of his mouth, 'London has already fixed three television interviews and several appointments with A–B readership newspapers. They have, of course, sifted out the unimportant.'

'Sift them all out,' barked the President. 'They are all unimportant.'

Bustalieri departed. In the outer office, he buttonholed Miss Carrington. The President's orders were conveyed and Miss Carrington attached herself to the telephone. As Bustalieri left to soothe himself with a bourbon – a taste he was happily acquiring – he could hear the nasal voice drilling its way across the ether, cancelling the Señora's appointments. 'No way,' she kept saying, whatever that meant in English. 'No way.'

The ad hoc Ventura Committee was holding a meeting in the upstairs room of the Prince of Wales on the Kentish Town Road. Tankards of beer stood dotted about the floor, making new arrivals tread warily as they picked their way to vacant chairs. A woman in a jacket and frayed jeans handed out leaflets at the door. The leaflets bore a scratchy drawing of a peasant in a straw hat flattened under a big black boot and said SMASH THE FASCIST DE TORO! FREEDOM FOR OUR VENTURAN COMRADES! GIVE OUR BROTHERS BACK THEIR LAND! AND JOIN THE MARCH, HYDE PARK, SATURDAY!

Ruth Maryschild, with Judith beside her, pushed carefully through the swing door with two full tankards and looked down at the pile of pamphlets.

'Don't like that,' she said to the woman in the jacket.

'Pardon?' said the woman, staring.

'It says Brothers. Typical left-wing chauvinism, that is.'

'Point taken,' said the woman, turning her back on them. Judith nudged at Ruth. Behind her, the swing doors were half open, framing a tall skinny man with close-cropped furry hair, also balancing a tankard.

The woman turned back. 'D'you mind?' she said to Ruth and

Judith, 'you're blocking the entrance.' The man was now pressed up against Judith and a trickle from his glass splashed on her shoulder.

'Sister,' said Ruth, unbudgeable, 'the word Brothers should be changed.'

The man muttered an apology as Judith brushed at her shoulder. People were pushing in around them, they were jammed together. She looked up at him. He had a boy's face, wide, with spacy blue eyes that turned down at the corners as he half-smiled. She half-smiled back. The jacket woman poked her chin at Ruth. 'Look,' she said, her voice rising, 'Sister. Believe it or not, there are some things more important than a word on a leaflet. The Venturans are fighting a war, you know. They're being murdered right now, tortured right now. Men *and* women. First things first, okay? Now *please* move on.'

'First things first,' said Ruth loudly, addressing the trapped crowd, 'that's the history of women. There's always something more important than our struggle. We're *never* first. Right, Judith?'

'Yes, yes,' Judith said. 'Move on, Ruth, do. I can't breathe.'

'I'll bring it up on a point of order,' Ruth said in the direction of the combat jacket and was borne ahead, sloshing beer. They found chairs and plumped themselves down. The man sat beside Judith. 'You aren't much help,' said Ruth, frowning, 'as usual. You must support me when I bring it up again.'

'Okay,' said Judith, 'but honestly, Ruth, is this the time or the place?' Really, Ruth had no sense of proportion. There were times when she was plain embarrassing to be with. Judith shot a sideways glance at the man. Not at all bad.

He leaned towards her and nodded at them both. 'I'm with you,' he said. 'I agree. I agree with women's lib.' He grinned amiably into Ruth's stony face and a small crescent-shaped dimple appeared just above his chin. 'Name's Charlie.' He shook both their hands.

'Judith,' said Judith.

'The reason I'm for it,' Charlie said, pulling his chair closer, 'I like independent women. It's good for men. Like, if a girl leans too much, it gets very heavy for the man. Believe me, I know.'

'Uh-huh,' said Ruth. Charlie turned to Judith.

'I got experience,' he said. 'This woman I lived with. She was fantastic in lots of ways, you know, and I really liked her. But she was brought up in the country and she's old-fashioned, know what I mean? To her, what a woman does is look after a man and have babies and such. Nothing wrong in that, mind. But for the bloke, if he loses his job or something and these days anyone can, it's a worry. It preys on his mind.'

'I see that,' Judith said softly, her head turned away from Ruth. She liked his eyes, they were friendly but not too friendly, they had a certain light.

'She's never worked, you know. Only on the farm and that. She can't type. I wanted to introduce her to a photographer I know, so she could do a bit of modelling but she didn't want to know.'

Ruth leaned across Judith. 'Modelling?' she said. 'Exploitation.'

'Nah,' said Charlie. 'You make a lot of money, modelling. I wouldn't mind having a go but it's not me they want, is it? I do what I can but what's wrong with her bringing in the odd penny? That's what I say.'

Judith thought he could be a model. Not the conventional kind, not smooth and probably gay. He certainly wasn't gay. His thigh was against hers now.

'Nothing wrong,' said Ruth. 'But modelling reinforces the stereotype, doesn't it? Women as ornaments, women as nothing but bodies. It denigrates us, having the silly blank faces of models staring down at us from posters and ads and stuff. As if that was all we were good for.'

'Not faces,' said the man, quickly. He stared down into the dregs of his beer. 'Not faces.'

'What, then?' said Ruth sharply.

'Well. Hands, maybe. Legs, for stockings. Bras. With the head chopped off so no one would know her.'

'Bras?' said Judith to him. 'Who wears bras any more?'

Charlie's eyes flickered downwards to where Judith's breasts mounted in heavy globes under the T-shirt she wore, the round indentations of her nipples protruding. His smile vanished and he looked up again, straight into her eyes. A thin volt of the purest lust snaked between them. A moment later, they both straightened up and turned towards the platform, where several men and the woman in the combat jacket were taking their places at the long wooden table. The woman stood up and held up her hands. The scraping of chairs, the hum of voices died away.

'Comrades,' said the woman in a gravelly voice. 'Brothers and Sisters.' She glanced at Ruth and looked away. 'We are here tonight because of the coming visit of Clare de Toro y Plata, the wife of the Venturan dictator. An Englishwoman, to our shame. Invited here by our government who thereby sanction an evil and fascist regime. We protest!'

Ruth's voice rose above the noise. 'I protest, too,' she said. Her chair legs screeched on the wooden floor. 'I protest on behalf of Venturan women.'

Forty faces screwed themselves round to stare at her, the platform gazed. Judith scrutinized her hands. 'These leaflets,' Ruth waved one, '... they talk about Brothers. They say give our Brothers back their land. What I'd like to know is this. When the Brothers get their land, will they give it to the women they stole it from in the first place?'

Someone yelled 'Siddown'. Someone else shouted 'Bloody Trot'. A woman on the other side of Ruth glared through glinting spectacles. 'Silly bitch,' she spat. Ruth lifted her voice over the babble, her cheeks flushed.

'The fact is,' she shouted, 'the fact is that under tribal law the

Indian women in Ventura own the land. The *women* own it. By matrilineal decree.'

The room exploded with laughter and hissing. 'Matri what?' Charlie whispered, his breath warm on Judith's hair. She shook her lowered head. Oh Ruth, sit down, sit down.

'So I move,' Ruth shouted, digging her fists further into the sagging pockets of her baggy cords, 'that the word Brothers be struck off the leaflets and the word Sisters substituted.' There was a burst of ironic applause and jeers. The woman in the combat jacket banged on the table with a hammer.

'We've had thousands of those leaflets printed,' she yelled, 'and it cost us money we haven't got. And the protest march is Saturday, so forget it. Women like you have no sense of proportion.' Smoke rose thick about her and hung in a cloud below the tar-stained ceiling.

Ruth wheeled round, a finger pointing accusingly here and there at her attackers. 'It's women like you and you and you who've got no sense of proportion.' She flicked at Judith's bent head. 'Women were being oppressed in Ventura long before the de Toros took over.'

'What about Clare?' asked a man in front of her, glowering. 'Señora de Toro is a woman and she's right beside her husband, murdering and oppressing and ...'

Ruth shook the back of his chair. 'You can't get out of it by blaming one woman, mate,' she spluttered. 'Clare is what a patriarchal society has made her. It's *men* doing the murdering. It's men everywhere. Rape. Torture. Killing. Men do it.' Her voice cracked. The man in front picked up his chair, turned it round and stood towering angrily over Ruth. His sleeves were rolled up and there were tattoos on his arms. As if at a signal, two men at the end of the platform table plunged through the crowd and took hold of Ruth's arms, one on either side. Judith stood up and her arm was gripped too. Charlie shoved at one of the men, who shoved back.

'Please,' screamed combat jacket, hammering furiously. 'Quiet, *please*. Remember why we're here, comrades. We've got important business to discuss.'

In the sudden silence, Ruth and Judith were propelled to the swing doors and pushed through. A woman nearby stood up and sat down again. 'On your way, Sisters,' said one of the men. 'Don't come again.'

In the cool passageway, Ruth leaned against the wall, panting. Her hands trembled. Stupid oafs. What price revolution when its supporters were already revolting? Stick to women, that was the message. All other causes were tainted, fatally flawed by masculine blindness. Judith came up behind her and put an arm round her shoulders. Above them, the man called Charlie appeared through the swing doors. Ruth shrugged Judith away and plodded on down the narrow staircase. At the bottom, she banged on the iron bar of a door marked EXIT and disappeared through it, in a blast of cool air.

'Come on, I'll buy you a beer,' Charlie said, catching Judith as she wavered at the door, 'I got troubles too.' The dimple was there on his chin as he took her arm, she felt the light movements of his hand against her breast and let herself be led towards the bar. Really, Ruth was obsessed, paranoiac about women, she'd find something anti-feminist in a discussion on the merits of Marmite. The others were right, the Venturans were fighting a war, that was the priority. In the dim light, the man's eyes had paled to the colour of water. In them, Judith could see a tiny image of herself.

A clock somewhere among the buildings spread out below struck twelve. Alice had waited all evening, huddled in her dressing-gown in front of the television. The screen was grainy and shivered now and again, like wind blowing over sand. Pink faces bled through their outlines, the edges of hair flared suddenly sulphurous, for fractions of seconds bodies became disjointed and connected, broken and mended and broken again. Men in suits and ties talked and other men in suits and ties frowned and moved the words around. 'Are you saying that you're opposed to the scheme in principle?' asked a man with a beard and a line on his forehead that ran from the widow's peak of his hair to the centre of his brow. 'In other words,' said a man to a fat black man, 'you're prepared to sanction the use of force, am I right?' 'Are you saying? ... in other words you're saying? ... that is not what I'm saying ... is that what you're saying?' the men asked each other and the words passed like putty between them, rolled up and pulled out and indented and smoothed and broken and stuck together again. 'You should see my wife,' said a small man in boxer shorts and an audience shrieked. A woman leaned across him, her breasts bulged, he ducked and the audience howled. Men with guns ran stooping across rubble, the guns rattled, a smoking building turned into a box of detergent and white clothes waved in a country garden. Women in rags mourned beside graves of heaped sand and the graves curled over and became Cornish pasties in a gleaming oven as a woman with red lips smiled and a man galloped from her mouth who was John Wayne among the flat-topped mountains of Arizona and the man hanging at his back on the horse was Alice's uncle Billy with the bushy eyebrows who had frightened her as a child when he burst from a cupboard with a paper hat on and a woman like her mother with a bruised face and bare feet wept under a banana tree with little letters jumping beneath her that said her son had been found bleeding two miles from there in a ditch and was dead now and a woman called Judith came out of the banana tree and said that working women earned £77 weekly gross pay on average and were 4 per cent poorer in real terms at the end of this year and Alice thought I've seen that face before and a man with his hair braided into tiny plaits sang I don wanna dance with you and a man with a low voice like a gong said that, in essence, God's purpose for our lives was that we saved our own souls. The word 'soul' came out deep and hollow and the screen trembled and the man opposite nodded, the bags under his eyes adding weight to his solemnity. 'Thank you, Father,' he said and lowered his head in prayerful dismissal at Alice.

He must be tired, thought Alice, working at this hour and she switched him off and stood a moment at the side of the baby's cot, where he lay half-buried under his blue quilt, still as death, and she climbed into bed where she lay under the grey blankets and imagined Charlie's exhaustion after looking for a job all day, which was why he hadn't come, and resolved that tomorrow she would find that photographer and make him give her work, he could use her hands or her legs or her feet for shoes or her hair if he shot the back of her head and she saw the back of her head, shot, and it was the head of the woman who wept under the banana tree and the tears ran from Alice's eyes and soaked into the pillow.

In the morning, with a head pounding and a tongue in his mouth that felt and tasted like a piece of old felt, Ronnie Garston turned the key in the door of his basement office. The door opened a couple of inches and stuck. Jeez, what now? Bending, feeling around the splintered edges, Ronnie tugged out an envelope wedged under the frame. The door swung open and the acrid smell of nicotine hit him. A pox on that slag who was supposed to clean up, when was she going to get her old bones together and do what Ronnie paid her £2 an hour to do, clean up behind him? At the one window that looked out on a rubbish-choked well sunk three feet below the pavement outside, Ronnie zipped up the blind. Bare boards rose in the dusty half-light, circled here and there with cigarette stubs in a spray of ash and snaked across with cable. Opposite the window, one peeling wall was hung with a roll of parchment paper, four sets of 2K lights stared blindly at it. In one corner, a bentwood stand was draped with an assortment of objects: large-brimmed hats, fringed shawls, a feather fan, a bouquet of dried flowers, bits of lace, a spangled mask. Beneath the stand stood a bulbous brass parrot's cage, a folded garden chair and a large dull green Monstera deliciosa, woody tentacles sticking hopefully beyond its ochre pot, feeling in vain for rooting possibilities.

Ronnie switched on the central light and, standing under it, ripped open the buff envelope. Christ, another bill. Second instalment on his annual £700 rates. Add to that a quarterly £370 for lights and heat, a monthly £400 for processing and telephone, a weekly £200 rent, a dozen other unavoidable expenses and top it up with the dud cheque for £2,000 from *Skin* magazine, gone bust two months ago. Where did that leave him? Ronnie moved over to a nearby table and, sitting down, did a few rough calculations on the back of the envelope. Just as he thought. In the shit, in the bright red final demand shit. He'd have to hustle a lot more than usual for the next little while or R. Garston, Prop. Garston Pix Limited, would be a new addition to the dole queue. What a fucking awful place England was, where a bright lad like himself could work his ass off and still end up screwed. There was the Jag, of course, but hell that was part of the image, like his £250 Pierre Cardin suit and his gold cufflinks that had set him back a couple of ponies even from the back of a lorry. You weren't going to hit the big time, associate with the David Baileys of this world, if you turned up for assignments looking like crud, were you? A man had to look prosperous to get prosperous in this dog eat dog world. Rip off the next guy before he ripped you off, con him before he conned you. Ronnie pushed back the cuff of his silk shirt and glanced at the gold face of his watch, strung between alligator straps. Dammit, where was that stupid bird? Nine on the dot, she'd said, and here it was twenty to ten. Ten minutes later, after a quick broom round the floor and the lights moved into position, the doorbell rang and the bird appeared.

For the next two hours, Ronnie was fully occupied taking shots of the bird's legs for a well-known stocking firm. The girl was basically a dog but her legs — too skinny by half in real life — were exactly right for the lens. Perched this way and that on a high stool in front of the parchment roll, the legs gleamed under the lights, made even slimmer by the pair of black spindle-heeled sandals stuck on the bobbin ankles. She was a dummy all right, about all she could manage in the way of conversation was the odd 'Pardon?' and a titter behind the hand but she knew how to dangle her pins to the best advantage and that expertise, plus the quick fumble he got at her crotch as she stretched up to get her coat, put Ronnie in a better humour.

Two beers at the Prince of Wales and a tenner win at the crowded betting shop on a nice little filly called Chequers, a two-year-old whose form Ronnie had followed since he'd won on her at Princetown a year ago, cheered him further, so that when he was back in his dark room that afternoon, lifting the legs film out of the tank with his headphones turned on full blast, he didn't hear the door open and the film was ruined before he saw the bird and he didn't strangle her on the spot like he should have. He just took off the headphones, dried his hands and gave her a two-minute bollocking she wouldn't forget in a hurry, which included four painful things she could do to herself, two she could do to her mother and one that he would do to her if she ever again did what she had just done to him and his two rolls of 35 mm film. Then he pushed her out of the dark room into the studio lights. Christ, what have we here? Not only was there a baby strapped to her back which, now that the radio was off and he'd stopped giving out with the threats, started shrieking fit to bust his eardrums but there was something wrong with the stupid bird's face. It was frightened, he could see that, the mouth gaped, the eyes popped. But it had blood on its cheek. For a moment, Ronnie felt slight shock. He could swear he hadn't done more than shove her, so how come the blood forchrissake? Then, as it stood like a statue in his way, he understood. Rough purple tears, three of them, dropping across the peach of its cheeks from the corner of the left eye to the tilt of the jaw. Relief calmed him. Silly cow.

'All right,' he said, hands up, defensive now. 'Forget it. Sid-down. Here, take a pew.' He scooped at the legs of a chair with his foot and watched her as she backed wordlessly into it, pulling the baby round, extracting it from the canvas straps and clasping it to her, all this without taking her huge blue eyes from him. The baby stuck a wet fist in its mouth and the shrieks stopped.

'Look,' Ronnie said, 'I dunno who you are and I dunno why you're here but coming in like that, fucking up my photos, I blew my top, right?'

'I'm sorry,' said the girl. 'I knocked first but ...' she shook her head, 'I'm sorry.' Pity about the birthmark, thought Ronnie. Apart from that, she was a looker. Nice hair, good features, what looked like a great pair of boobs under the loose T-shirt, smash-ing length of leg and that buttery skin that he knew from experience came across glowing on film. Yeah, pity. Still, judging by the little 'un, some guy had put his leg over in spite of it. Probably put a paper bag over it when he was on the job. Ronnie then received a vivid mental image of this girl flat on her back mother-naked, being humped, and felt his groin stir.

'Wanna cuppa tea?' he said. Still rocking the baby, she nodded. Ronnie took the grease-streaked kettle off the table where it stood, plugged it in by the door and squatted on his haunches beside it, waiting.

'Charlie said you might have work for me,' the girl said, moving herself round to face him. She had a soft buzzy sort of accent. Not a Londoner, then.

'Charlie?' said Ronnie.

'He knows you from the pub.'

'I'm with you,' said Ronnie. So some bloke over there was screwing her. Ronnie didn't blame him.

'Well I thought I'd ask you, anyway. You don't get anything ...' she said in a nervous rush, '... if you don't ask, do you?' Then she turned her good side to him, tipped her chin up and smiled a little.

'Very true, that is.' This one wasn't so shy as she'd made out. The way she was looking at him. Definitely a come on. Definitely. The kettle whistled.

'So what did you have in mind?' Ronnie circled round her collecting mugs from the sink, putting in the tea bags, filling them up. He beckoned her over to the stained table and she came, carrying the baby. He knew what *he* had in mind all right and he reckoned by the way she ducked her head and looked at him sideways on that she had the hots for him too, the sly little scrubber. And now that he'd had a good eyeful, those were two gorgeous tits she had on her. Doughy soft with hard little teats. Ronnie was a tit man himself. He liked playing with them. Swinging them as he lay underneath and the cow crouched over him on all fours, reaching up and sucking at them, pulling them into his mouth as if he were a calf at the udder. Every now and then, he'd get carried away and treat himself to a bite or two. One of them with boobs to put your eyes out had carried on as if he was killing her or something. Squealing all over the shop which hadn't stopped him, no. Once he'd begun, Ronnie wasn't easily stopped, he'd got her arms pinioned behind her and munched at her boobs till they were red as hams and he'd come. She knew which side her bread was buttered. She'd been back for more, hadn't she? And this one must be used to it, she'd got a kid chewing at them, getting her hardened up. Like he was hardening up right now. Jeez, this was embarrassing.

'Modelling,' said the girl.

Ronnie looked at her, taken aback. He'd expected an offer to clean the joint, do typing, carry his gear, something like that. But modelling. How did she figure that one?

'I know,' the girl said, shifting herself. 'I know I can't ...'

Quickly, a hand went up to her cheek and fell away. 'Only Charlie said you did ads and I thought if there was a shampoo, well, my hair is long and there's my hands. See?' She held them out to him, long fingers, thin and golden, the nails short but a pretty oval.

Ronnie stared at the slender hands spread out on his grubby table. Beneath them, in between the fingers, he could see the red print of a Final Demand. The electrics, this time, threatening to cut him off. Into his head came a snatch of conversation. Some fat guy in a white raincoat with fur at the collar. Beaver, he'd said, and stroked the fur and stuck an elbow into Ronnie, winking. Oh yeah. He looked from the hands to the girl and smiled pleasantly.

'What's your name?'

'Angela,' she said, face down, cuddling the baby, a quick glance up.

'Telephone?' She gave him a number and he scribbled it on the edge of the LEB bill.

'Can't promise anything, Angela, things are tough all over. But I'll see what I can do, okay? Won't be your straight modelling on account of, well, you said it yourself. What we call a discrepancy. Still, I might be able to steer some money your way. For other services rendered, know what I mean?' Of course she knew what he meant. Shampoos, hands. He wasn't fooled.

The girl lit up like a sparkler. Even with the mark, Ronnie freely admitted she was a right little dazzler when she smiled. She thanked him all the time she was getting herself fixed up with the baby on her back again, ready to go. At the door she turned, bobbing her head, flirting at him openly.

'Whatever you say,' she said, 'anything. Really, thank you and I'm sorry about the . . .' Her hands fluttered.

Ronnie stood at the door, nodding. She gave a little wave, moved her shoulders to settle the baby and swung her boobs at him before she trotted off. He watched her go, then closed the door and went to the telephone.

Charlie left Judith's flat, letting himself out of the front door a bit cautious, her place had turned out to be too near Alice's for comfort. He patted his chest absently as he stood on the steps looking round, he moved his legs up and down and humped his shoulders briefly. He ached nicely. At the thought, he grinned. That Judith, she was something. It had done him good, to screw her, did her good and all, by the look of her. They'd been at it like rabbits, up half the night. Or down. He grinned again and wiped a hand across his mouth. The tension had gone for the time being, his chest felt easy, he could breathe deep. Last night's drinks were all fucked away and that was how it should be, how it had been, before. Wham bang, thank you ma'am, and no problems later. That's how she wanted it, too, she'd made that plain and thank the Lord for it. There was a lot to be said for these working women. Charlie handed it to them. A good screw and on to other things, none of that do-you-love-me lark. Love. Charlie, halfway down the street, thought of love and of Alice and the lad and a familiar weight slowed his pace. In a rush, anxieties swarmed around him in a cloud, buzzing. The day dimmed. Why did a face as sweet as Alice's put the sun out? She didn't complain, she didn't complain half enough, alone in that flat as she must be now, waiting for him, always waiting for him. She was a good girl, his girl, and he was lucky to have her. Worth ten times the Judiths of this world and more.

Charlie stood still on the kerb at the corner of the street, fists stuck in his pockets pushing the jacket apart, and saw himself on his motorbike racing down a wide empty road, on and on and away. Away.

The telephone rang. Alice lunged for it, nearly tripping on the torn rug. 'Charlie?' she said into the receiver, 'Charlie?'

[225]

It wasn't Charlie. 'Oh yes,' she said politely, 'of course I do. Yes.' Then she listened. She was there quite a long time, holding on to the receiver, saying only once, 'Yes, I'm here.' Slowly she hunched herself over the black telephone, her hair slipping slowly over it, over her face, a silk screen. 'How much?' she said eventually, almost whispering. 'I see,' she said. 'All right,' she said. 'Tomorrow, ten o'clock.' She put the receiver back in its cradle and raised her head, looking at the wall. 'Thank you,' she said.

Charlie came round in the early evening. He carried a Sainsbury's plastic bag with their supper in it – sausages, baked beans and a gooey cake oozing real cream. He also took two ten-pound notes out of the top pocket of his anorak and put them on the kitchen counter.

'For you, me darling,' he said. 'I done some work on this geezer's motor.'

Alice looked at the money. 'You keep it, I don't need it,' she said and began to cry. The tears on her left cheek grew pink as they slid over the purpled skin.

She weeps blood, thought Charlie, chilled. 'Don't,' he said. He wrapped her in his arms and rocked her gently. 'What's this, then? Didn't know there was two babies living in this place.'

She stood still against him, her head resting on his chest. She wiped at her face with one hand. 'I wish I *was* a baby, Charlie,' she said, muffled.

He bent sideways and peered up into her lowered face. He grinned. 'Yes sir, she's my baby,' he croaked, 'she's my baby doll.' Taking her hand, he held it out and jigged about the room. 'De da rum bum bubba, whoop dee, baby dollie.'

Alice let her arm move up and down with his but her body remained stiff, she clumped awkwardly, following him. 'Smile when you're feeling low,' crooned Charlie and touched the corners of her lips. 'Go on, lovely. Smile for Charlie.'

[226]

Alice smiled, widening her eyes to hold back the tears that lay in them.

'Charlie is my darling,' sang Charlie, clicking his fingers. 'Am I your darling eh?' He bumped her with his shoulder.

'You are my life,' said Alice.

Later, things were better. Alice fried the sausages and heated up the beans while Charlie sat with the baby on his lap and tickled its lips with a teaspoon of mushy peas. The baby stared at him fixedly and pushed its tongue against the spoon. The peas splattered on his jeans and the baby stretched its mouth in an aerated grin. 'Bad one,' said Charlie, wiping himself.

'He's full,' said Alice. 'I fed him before you came.'

On Charlie's knee the baby stiffened, its hands closed in fists against its chest, its eyes glazed and dreamy. Small creaking noises made themselves heard.

'Here, Alice, what's up? He's going all red,' Charlie said sharply. Alice giggled, leaning over the sofa.

'Guess,' she said. The baby creaked. Tiny beads of sweat erupted on his forehead, above the eyes the skin flared pinky-white. As they watched, he slumped and his eyes closed.

'Phew.' Charlie coughed in stagey bursts. He picked up the dozy body and held it at arm's length.

'I'll change him,' said Alice.

'I don't mind,' said Charlie but she took the child from his arms and laid it gently on a towel on the bed. She looked intently down. Poor smelly bundle, she thought. One little eyelid drooped, the button nose was grainy with minute yellow spots, the blonde fluff over the head showed patches of a darker colour here and there. Cradle cap. Tipping some oil out of a bottle, Alice rubbed it on the scalp and combed. Immediately, the scalp turned pink and the baby's face crumpled. Alice stopped at the restless squeaks.

'Go on, let me,' said Charlie from the sofa and began to get up.

'No,' Alice said. It wasn't that she loved the baby any more than Charlie did. The baby wasn't so much hers as her, part of her, like an arm, another limb. In a way, she was indifferent to it, as she was to herself. If she looked into the mirror, nothing happened in her heart, she didn't feel love or even interest. She merely inspected the various features to see that they were presentable, clean, reasonably tended. Her birthmark did not dismay her when she was alone – pity only ever came through other people's eyes, she felt none. In her teens, she had made attempts to disguise it, smoothing on thick foundation with a sponge and, once, smearing on calamine lotion to whiten it out but it looked much worse than before, as if her cheek had a crusted hand laid upon it. She had tried these concealments so that others, who had to look at her, would find it easier, would suffer less shock. In the same way and for the same reasons, she often put herself between Charlie and the baby, to disguise its imperfections from him, for his sake. Now, using her back as a screen, she deftly unpinned and folded back the nappy, stained with yellow curds, and wiped clean again the shrunken little bottom. What a sad scrap of her bones and flesh lay there below her. She would die for him, yes, but in no heroic way, she would not need an atom of courage. If your hand was burned, coming too near a flame, you pulled it away, that was all there was to it. Self-preservation. What she thought of her baby was neither here nor there, to tell the truth her mind was a blank on the subject. She was afraid only of what other people might think, so the little – what was it that horrible man had said? Discrepancies? – must be made as acceptable as possible to them, by her. No one else was suitable for this task because no one else saw the discrepancies as pitilessly as she.

When Alice had settled the baby on its tummy in the cot, she and Charlie ate their supper and he switched on the television and they sat as they always did now, drinking their mugs of grey instant coffee, watching together. In the days before the baby's birth, when Alice had hopes and Charlie had his job at the Park, the evenings passed to their talk. Now, talk was dangerous. It had to be steered away from too many topics — jobs, money, the way they felt, the future. Best to watch television, listen to other people talking, talk about that. Tonight, above all nights in her life, Alice did not want to think.

[13]

'Tres bien, Madame, tres jolie,' Deborah Carrington said with the nasal drawl that turned her French and her execrable Spanish into purest Texan. She twisted again in a whirl of white gauze and smoothed her hands down the billowing skirt. The sneakers she wore gave her the look of a down-at-heel ballerina. 'Señora Presidente will be the best-dressed woman in the UK, thanks to you.' Mathilde Márquez, a plump middle-aged Frenchwoman with delicate hands and feet, her greying hair in a neat chignon, shrugged modestly and looked at her watch.

'And now I must be off,' she said. 'I will be here tomorrow at eleven. The Señora will not cancel this time, I hope? Concepción, you will make sure?'

Concepción, easing the wings of fabric over Deborah's head, assured the Señora through a mouthful of pins that she would indeed make sure of Señora Presidente's attendance and Madame Márquez departed, her heels clicking down the Palace corridor at a great pace.

Pulling on her jeans, struggling into her T-shirt, Deborah stuck her glasses into place and looked at Concepción.

'Okay,' she said, 'Vamos. Manuel is waiting.'

Carefully, Concepción unhooked the hangers of three dresses from the rail, each one in its transparent plastic cover and slipped the dress Deborah had worn among them.

'She'll wear one of these, will she?' Deborah said.

'Si, Señorita.'

'Good. Then bring them along.'

In the car, with the sliding glass partitions closed between them and Manuel as he drove along the straight tarmac'd road to the airport, Deborah explained to Concepción the intricacies of a VIP arriving in England.

'We will be with her, of course, you and I, Concepción. You will dress her on the plane before we arrive. But we have to practise. We have to rehearse before, so that nothing can go wrong. We do not want to bother the Señora with all this so I shall wear the dresses and pretend that I am her. You understand? In London, at the airport there, we must make certain everything goes smoothly. There will be cameras. There will be Royalty. When the Señora steps out on to the plane stairs, they will take many pictures of her. That is why we must rehearse.'

'Si, Señorita,' said Concepción. She stared ahead through the window, watching the green banks loom up and slide past, watching the red dust fly. Her mind was splintered into many pieces, each one grasping for her attention. So much to do before she went. Fear gripped at her stomach when she thought of the flight that lay ahead, she, Concepción, up in the sky, flying in the air to an unknown place called Eng-land where she would probably never arrive because the plane would fall out of the air and scatter her in a thousand pieces on the ground far below, ah miserable Concepción, what a terrible punishment for mixing with gringos, to die alone among strangers and lie in an unmarked grave, forgotten by Dolores and Ramosa and José-Eduardo ... José-Eduardo. He was her worst anxiety, beside which all others faded. She saw him leaping away from her down the alley, heard the stupid boy's jeers, that night before she and Dolores and Rama had set out to collect plants from the forest. Since then, he had not reappeared. So many days and no sign. Dolores, too, had been round all the neighbours, asking. No one had seen him, no one knew anything about him. José, her pet, her baby, with his foolish bravado, his pretence that he was a man when he was only a silly half-grown boy playing games with guns, bang bang, you're dead, the idiot. Oh, when he came back, how she would beat him for scaring them so. He understood nothing, that one, but he would understand when she had finished with him, madre de dios, he would. In anticipation of her brother's imminent maturity, Concepción discreetly crossed herself, praying for his salvation and thus for hers.

With a grinding of gears, the car slowed down and stopped. A barbed wire fence held the forest back and reached to a gate and a shed, from which men in uniform emerged. Papers were exchanged and Manuel drove on and Concepción saw the heavy snub-nosed planes – Herkies, Miss Carrington called them – standing on either side as their car passed over ground that was now smooth and black and over which they glided smoothly to a final halt by a wide building where more men in uniforms swarmed. This time, the man who approached them was in civilian clothes, creased cotton trousers, a cotton shirt, with the sleeves rolled up and a hat with a wide peak pulled over his pink face. Letters printed on the peak said THE REAL THING. He tapped on the window where the women sat and Deborah Carrington leaned across Concepción and wound it open.

'Mizz Carrington?' he said. He was American. Concepción was used to that nasal drawl, she could distinguish it easily from the clipped sounds of the Señora's English.

'Hi,' said Deborah.

There followed a brief conversation. Squeezing past Concepción, Deborah got out of the car and turned at the open door.

'Right,' she said in her broken Spanish. 'I'll take the clothes. You and Manuel wait here for me. You understand, Concepción?'

'Sí.' Concepción detached the dresses from the hook where they had hung and passed them out to Deborah, who draped them on her arm. 'I should come with you, Señorita Carrington. I can help you to put them on, I can take care . . .' she looked

[232]

anxiously at the pale chiffon and silk lengths that were already blowing out in the faint breeze that whispered around this empty space.

'Don't worry,' Deborah said. 'Just stay here. I shall be back soon with everything just as it is now.' And she was off. Concepción watched her loping along beside the American until they disappeared behind the building. The Señorita, she thought, might be just the same size as Señora Clare but she moved like a creature from another world. America must be a strange country, to have women in it like Mees Carrington, with voices so loud and flat and a man's walk and men's trousers always hiding their legs. Ai, perhaps it would have been better if she had never left the barrios and her sisters. Their life was hard but no one expected them to fly through the air and leave behind them everything that was safe and familiar. Well, familiar at least – Ventura was not a safe place any more.

The minutes passed. Concepción was used to waiting, she could turn off her mind and sit thinking of nothing like a beast in a field but, today, the thought of José haunted her. Slowly, her chest grew tight and a hundred questions tormented her. If he didn't turn up soon, then what? Should she go to the police in Nombre Dios, join that queue outside the battered building where women with frightened eyes and crying children were always waiting now? Should she ask the Señora for help? But the Señora was too busy now and in two days they would both be gone. The journey ahead that filled Concepción with apprehension became more threatening than ever – how could she bear to be thousands of miles away when José might be in terrible trouble?

Brooding, she did not notice the glass partition slide back. She looked up only when a hand came through it, holding a can of beer.

'Quieres?' Manuel asked in his guttural Spanish. His voice was friendly, though his face was in shadow under the peak of the grey chauffeur's cap. The car was hot and Concepción realized that her mouth was dry.

'Gracias,' she said. He zipped off the top and she took the can, licking the froth off her fingers. For a moment they watched together as two more Americans – they must be Americans, so thin and tall and red – walked past the car and headed for the corner where Miss Carrington had disappeared. They were loaded with cameras, one of them held the biggest Concepción had ever seen up on his shoulder, like a man carrying a child.

'You are going to England with Doña Clara,' Manuel said. It was a statement, not a question, but all Concepción's worries rushed back at her.

'Alas, yes,' she said, sighing heavily.

'Alas?'

There was no harm, surely, in telling him of José's disappearance, if she voiced none of her fears.

'So,' she ended, 'a silly boy of seventeen has run off somewhere and gives much pain to his poor sister who brought him up. I don't want to go while he is still away but, there, it is probably foolish to worry. Maybe he is staying with friends, maybe he went into town to make a few pesos. Who knows what idiocies a boy can get up to?' She gave a half-laugh and looked at the chauffeur. He did not smile. He looked briefly around him and back at her.

'Was he with los chicos?' he asked, his voice low.

At this, Concepción became very alarmed. What did she know about this Manuel? That he was a chauffeur, an indio. That he worked for the Palace, as she did. They should be on the same side, then, but what did that mean? She had no side, she cared only for people – the Señora, her sisters, her nieces and nephews José. Manuel was a man. If he had a side it would take no account of people, only of guns and bombs and words written on walls. Quickly, she pulled herself together.

'No,' she said. 'He is a child, my José. He knows nothing about

[234]

such things, cares not at all. Football, that is all that is in his fat head. Football and the pesos he can wheedle from his poor Concha. Los chicos, huh.' She flipped at her cheek in a gesture of contempt and sat back in her seat. Between her shoulder blades, the sweat trickled. A pulse beat sickeningly, somewhere in her stomach. Why was this man still staring at her?

'If you wish,' he said in the same low urgent voice, 'I will make enquiries while you are gone. I have many contacts in many places.'

'No.' The word snapped out before Concepción had time to think and wretchedness engulfed her as the chauffeur turned away with a shrug. Of course she wanted help but how could she trust this stranger, with his 'contacts'? In Ventura these days, you kept your mouth shut if you were clever and trusted no one. Perhaps she had already said too much.

When more time had passed, Manuel started up the car and drove it into the meagre shade afforded by the iron roof of an empty hangar. There they sat in silence for what seemed to Concepción hours until she dozed off and was awakened by a clatter of footsteps and voices. Deborah Carrington was there by the car, chatting to the Americans who had gone by before with the cameras. Getting out, Concepción carefully scooped the dresses off her arm and smoothed a reproachful finger down a crease that ran to the hem.

Deborah said, 'Just a little touch with the iron' to her, pushed her glasses up her nose and got in beside Concepción. 'Ciao,' she said and waggled her fingers. Then she knocked on the partition and they drove slowly off the airfield onto the bumpy airport road back to town.

'Did everything go well?' asked Concepción politely.

'Muy bien,' said Deborah Carrington and said no more.

At the steps of the Palace, Manuel opened the door. Deborah collected her bulging briefcase, thanked them both and leapt up the steps two at a time. Concepción, her arms full, followed her awkwardly and stood a moment beside the chauffeur.

'Thank you all the same,' she said quietly. 'For your offer. I mean.'

'De nada,' he said. He fumbled in his pocket and pulled something out. It seemed to be a square of white cardboard, torn at the side. 'Hey, look,' he said furtively. 'I went for a little stroll while you slept. Look what I found in a litter bin.'

Concepción took it. The white cardboard framed a colour photograph. As Manuel held the tear together, she made out the figure of a woman. It was Señorita Carrington standing at the door of a plane, on the stairs, in a dress Concepción recognized.

Manuel pursed his lips and gave a low whistle, nudging her. 'Our Miss Carrington, she has legs like other women after all, eh?' he said.

He was a coarse man, this indio. Concepción raised her eyebrows, tossed her head and flounced off with her precious burden. She turned and looked over her shoulder at him for a second as she went.

'Los hombres,' she said.

That evening, guerrillas ambushed an army patrol twenty-five kilometres up river from Nombre Dios. They crashed from the sombre recesses of the forest, fourteen FLV men in tattered clothes with headbands tied round their hair, a band of pirates leaping and shouting as they scrambled over the frontier of the forest on to the earth road, guns held high. For one minute, then, the twilight silence was ripped by their firing as they riddled with bullets the five soldiers ambling along behind a jeep and glass exploded and screams echoed over the trees and flocks of green and yellow birds screamed as they tore up through the branches to the sky. At the end of the minute, silence fell. In an arc of spent cartridges the soldiers lay where they had fallen, limbs flung out, and blood began to seep through jagged rents in the grey uniforms. The raiders vanished as suddenly as they had come, leaving only one of their number, a young lad, sprawled athwart a ditch at the edge of the road, bleeding and moaning quietly, his thin hand still gripping a knobbled grenade the size of a mango fruit.

On this day of all days, Concepción had failed her, had not come in to throw up the blinds and wake her. A whole half-hour more went by before Madame Márquez appeared at the door to check if the Señora Presidente required any last-minute advice or help and found her still heavily asleep in the dark room. Two seconds later, Madame was scuttling back along the corridor, scattering hairpins in her wake, little hands patting the air as she went in an ecstasy of bustle.

Clare stumbled across to the windows and heaved the wooden slats upwards. In the white sky a helicopter throbbed and span away towards the forest, the light and the noise stunned her. She knelt at her bedside cupboard, tipped out a valium from the enamel pill-box there, broke off half and swallowed it, coughing. Oh God, was this an omen, this rotten start to an all-important journey? Where the hell was Concha? She stabbed again at the bell beside her bed and struggled out of her night-dress, kicking its folds aside. In the huge pier glass across the room her white body rose and fell, an agitated phantom. Outside the door, a cacophony of voices grew in volume.

'Pasen,' Clare shouted. A panting Madame Márquez stood against the entrance and two of the downstairs maids clattered in, Julia pushing the breakfast trolley set with a fringe of lace and Maria-Luz, her starched cap askew on the black frizz of her hair, running behind.

Madame Márquez burst into bad but rapid Spanish. 'Calm yourself, Señora, you must be calm,' she gasped, her lacy bosom heaving. Frantically, she fluttered her hands at Clare.

'Maria-Luz, my bath.' Clare pointed. 'Julia, take out the cork.'

[237]

Julia scrabbled at the foil round the neck of the champagne bottle on the trolley; in the bathroom water sloshed from the taps. 'Madame,' she turned to Madame Márquez, '*please*. Now slowly. Where is Concepción?'

'Ah, where indeed, where?' said Madame, appealing to the ceiling. 'Her bed has not been slept in, nobody has seen her. El Presidente also, he is not in the Palace, they say.'

She gave a little scream as the champagne cork popped. Julia, red-faced, poured froth into the glass and held it to Clare. 'Señora, if it please you,' she said nervously, 'there was some trouble last night, on the forest road. Soldiers were killed. Los chicos ... oh, excuse me ... the terrorists ...' her voice tailed away and she looked at the floor. Another helicopter drummed across the sky. Clare drank and Julia sprang to pour another glass.

'Madame. Please go and find Mademoiselle Carrington, she will be in the President's office. First, tell her to telephone the airport, our arrival there may be delayed. Then she should inform Manuel and our escort to hold on outside. Last, ask her to find out where my husband is and also Concepción. I want to see Carrington when that has been done. You understand, Madame?'

The head of Madame Márquez bobbed. Maria-Luz emerged from the bathroom, a towel in her hands and Clare moved towards her. 'I will take fifteen minutes for my bath and I want to be alone.' Her headache had reached a crescendo of pain which she knew from experience meant it would soon feel better. 'At a quarter past eight *exactly*, Julia, you come back to do my hair if Concepción has not been found and Maria-Luz, Madame, you will please return to help me dress. Now, all of you, go.'

On a sibilant wave of 'sí, sí, sí', the women went. Clare stepped into the bath and sank herself in the warm bubbles. What had that girl said? Trouble on the forest road. Well, there was nothing new about that. And it was just as well if Raul were away when she left, she had avoided him as much as possible since the episode in the village. Nothing had been done, of course, and she had immediately regretted her outburst about the women. Not that Raul was much around these days anyway, he seemed always to be either closeted in his office with his beloved Americans or away from the Palace on some government business and he looked at her oddly when they did meet. As if ... as if ... what? Clare's thoughts became a little blurred. Her head felt light and, for the first time since the idea of her journey had come to her, excitement tingled. She had a lot to do in England but there would be a little time, too, for enjoyment. Clare ran her hands down the silky curves of her breasts. It had been almost a year since she had given much thought to her appearance. The women, her work, had driven all that out of her head but now, for two short weeks, she could wear her lovely dresses with a clear conscience and knock their eyeballs out. Clare grinned to herself and slapped the side of the bath. Knock them sideways, yes.

'Señora?' It was a man's voice, guttural and husky, behind the half-open door of the bathroom. 'Señora?'

Calmly, regally, Clare answered. 'Sí,' she said. The whistle of the sound amused her. 'Sí sí sí,' she said.

'It is Manuel,' said the voice urgently. 'Please, Señora, there is not much time. I have something for you.'

'Ah ha.' Clare almost giggled. Thank God for the gift of valium and of champagne, hey hey. 'Pasa, Manuel.'

A brown hand came round the door. It gripped a curious bouquet of roots and sticks and dried twisted leaves.

'Flowers? For me?' said Clare in English, putting a soapy hand dramatically to her chest. She giggled aloud. She had almost forgotten how weird this place was, Raul's dotty estancia that they called Ventura. Everyone in it was mad as a hatter, when you came to think about it and they'd almost got her at it, too. Now, with her journey upon her, she could see clearly for the first time in years. A potty little hothouse full of crazies, a seething cauldron of every stupidity under the sun: priests, Indians, jungle, fish that tore your flesh off, snakes that crushed you, spiders like plates that poisoned you, drunken villagers, a necrophiliac husband, guns and blood and torture and swollen-bellied children and sweating Americans clutching briefcases and insects big as reptiles and reptiles big as birds and birds big as monkeys, all clamouring and screeching and shooting and killing each other and she, Clare, was Queen of the Nuts, a girl from England dropped amongst them like Alice fallen down the rabbit hole. And now there was a man in a chauffeur's breeches and a peaked cap offering her a bunch of old twigs while she lay in her bath. Perfect.

'Come in come in come *in*,' she called, scooping the suds around her. He has something for me, does he? Ho ho, let's have a peek.

He stood in the white-tiled room. He bowed, not looking at her, his face with its broad flat cheekbones impassive, his narrow eyes veiled. He laid the bunch of dried stems carefully down on a chair, his head in its grey cap lowered.

To the floor, he said, 'Your pardon, Señora. It is very important. I beg you to take these to England with you. There, if you ask ...'

Smiling angelically, Clare rose from the water. Her body gleamed. Bubbles clung to the tips of her breasts and to the soft gold curls between her thighs. The chauffeur kept his head down but his voice grew huskier.

'The plants, Señora. The plants that the women gather ...'

Naked, gleaming, Clare floated to the door and turned the brass key in the lock. 'Now,' she said. The room was hazy, her body felt extraordinarily light and her voice sounded far away in her ears, 'I would like you to fuck me, Manuel.'

Manuel sat down hard on the edge of the bath as if he had been punched. Dreamily, Clare began to undo the buttons at his neck. A pink nipple brushed his face. Galvanized, he bent down, pulled off his boots and his grey jodhpurs. Then he stood, his heavily muscled legs smooth and bare, his penis rising purple from the paler scrotum. He took two steps towards her, put his hands, dark against her wet white skin, on her waist, turned her towards the bath and bent her over. Then, as she gave a small groan, he spread her buttocks and drove into her. Stumbling, trembling, she hung on to the bath's edge, her hair streaming down into the water. Six times he went into her, fast and then he paused, his penis just inside her, its bulbous head wet in her wet lips. Convulsively, she moved against him. He held her hips, lifted her off her feet and went into her in swift strokes. Clare moaned with pleasure. He turned her to him and took her gently down with him on the slippery floor. As she sank, her thighs opened. Between them, he lowered himself, his arms protecting her from the hard tiles. Gathering himself, moving to widen her thighs, he thrust fast and deep. She gasped twice, rolling her face sideways. Her eyes fell shut, she reared towards him and cried out. Furiously, he moved in and out, made a low sound in his throat and was still. For an instant, he let his dark head rest on her white beasts and, in a single movement, lifted himself off her. Dizzily, she lay and watched the room spin around her. Then, already fully dressed again, he pulled her to her feet and raised one hand to his lips. His narrow eyes on her, he spoke, gesturing at his strange bouquet.

'Señora, you will take them with you? For the women, Señora.' And he was gone.

When Madame Márquez and the two maids returned, Manuel was standing outside the bedroom door of Señora La Presidente, cap in hand. He was told to wait and the women bustled in. Clare rose from her bath as they entered and Maria-Luz wrapped her in a towel.

'Everything is arranged, Señora,' panted Madame. 'The President will say his farewells to you at the airport and Concepción is coming up now. The bad girl says she went to say goodbye to her family, early this morning, but ...' she shrugged eloquently and rolled her eyes at the vagaries of servants. 'Come, we must dress you.'

The light silk fell over Clare's shoulders like a breath of wind and slipped down her body to flare at her hips. She turned slowly and the skirt belled out. She stretched herself up and whisked across the room in a silken swirl. She felt wonderful, wonderful. The omens were good after all, the journey would go well.

'Champagne, Madame,' she said, still spinning. The French-woman giggled with relief and filled up two glasses.

'Cheers,' Clare said, smiling, in English.

'Succès, Señora,' said Madame Márquez, beaming. 'Bon voyage et tous de bien en Angleterre. Bon chance, Madame.'

Over the brim of her glass, Clare saw a dark shape in the doorway. Concepción, at last. How pale she looked, almost green. It was the lipstick, slashed like a wound across her mouth. Concha never wore lipstick normally and it did nothing for her. She looked, Clare thought, like death. Guilt at her lateness no doubt. I shall say no more about it.

'Happiness, Concha,' she said and smiled forgiveness.

On the broad white steps Miss Carrington in navy, a bow at her chin, the normally tangled fair hair smoothed back, squinting alertly from side to side through her owl glasses. Concepción in black, holding a white vanity case, fingers at her throat flat against the gold cross beneath, lips moving soundlessly. Clare between them, white on white, perfection. At their appearance the doorman, plumed with the feathers of a bird of paradise, raised his hand. Six outriders on the drive below, black leather spacemen with domed heads, kicked their motorbikes to a roar, smoke belching at their backs. From the left of the colonnades, three limousines glided, two black Mercedes and a white Rolls, the white and gold flags at their prows still and furled in the windless heat. Four men in dark suits and pale ties jumped out and stood, hands clasped at the hems of their jackets. The guardians of her body, thought Clare with an inward smile and descended slowly towards them as they opened the car doors. At the white flank of the Rolls she turned and waved and the Palace servants gathered above waved and cried out blessings. Que se vaya con Dios, go with God. Farewell.

The forest rolled at them in breakers of green, a glossy tide. 'Down in the forest, something stirred,' said Clare amiably but the chattering Deborah chattered on. *Something* stirred? In this forest everything stirred – and screeched and crawled and slithered and whinnied and hooted and jumped and flew. The primeval forest, she thought, a land-locked ocean waiting to drown the unguarded traveller in its depths. Full fathom five my father lies, his bones of red ants made. Orchids cascaded over a bank of vines, horned and waxy. Along the ditch, the trunk of a fallen tree sprouted pink-gilled carbuncles, a leprous rash. Gaudy birds darted from frond to frond, butterflies hung and floated on muslin wings, dragonflies sprang about, weaving invisible rhomboids in the air and in the eternal twilight in this ink-green world that surged a thousand miles across and around and over the wide brown skeins of the Amazon river, feathered, scaled, furred, winged and leafy life boiled and churned and fought for survival.

'I'll be glad to get out of this heat,' said Deborah, fanning herself. 'It gets pretty hot in Houston but this place beats all. My, I'm looking forward to seeing London. My Daddy did a tour there before he was . . .'

Through the glass ahead, Clare could see the blue-black of Manuel's hair curving in a smooth cap to the nape of his neck. Her head steady now, she frowned at the memory of their tangled limbs, the two-backed beast on the bathroom floor writhing and pounding, First Lady and manservant plugged into each other. A picture of monkeys edged in, hairy pumpings on this very road and she had thought then, with Manuel's face at the glass, please God not the chauffeur, but the chauffeur it had been, oh yes, trust her. Hell's teeth, if Raul found out? She moved her shoulders and sighed with fright. But who would tell him, who knew but the two of them and one an Indian who owed everything to his job? It was all right, it was over and done, think of it no more.

'... in Grosvenor Square,' Deborah said, 'is that how you pronounce it, your English spelling is really weird, Gros-venor Square?'

'No,' said Clare. Manuel's strange bouquet. It would still be there on the bathroom chair or cleared away by the maids. Forgotten or half-forgotten. Impossible to take it to England and why had he asked? It didn't matter now. Light flooded over her, the forest dome had opened.

'Here we are, and on time,' Deborah said. The motorbike riders fell back and spread alongside them on the wide tarmac, revving rhythmically, black gauntlets moving like pistons over the handlebars. The guard at the front beside Manuel jumped out of the half-open door and ran alongside, his jacket flapping, the black nub of a holster revealed. The Rolls came smoothly to a halt, tailed by the two Mercedes, and a dozen doors sprang open. As Clare got out, a camouflaged jeep jolted towards her and behind the dust-streaked windscreen she saw her husband's face. He wore an ammunition jacket loose over the green and beige dappled combat uniform, his face was drawn and the bristles on his chin and upper lip scraped her hand as he brushed it in greeting. They looked at each other without expression and nodded formally.

Ten minutes later, in the roped-off VIP lounge, Raul dismissed the bedizened officials that clustered around them bowing and clicking their heels and, for a few minutes, husband and wife were alone.

'You look very beautiful,' Raul said. His voice sounded almost regretful.

'What happened last night?' asked Clare. 'There was trouble.'

He shrugged and rested a hand on the thin stuff of her sleeve. 'Señora Márquez has done well. That is a lovely dress.'

'Raul. Why do I have to hear things only from the servants? I want information from you.'

'What servants? Concepción?'

'Not Concepción. It doesn't matter. Simply, I never hear anything from you. I don't know what is going on in this place. In Ventura.'

'Five of my men were shot by terrorists, in an ambush, up near San Pedro. Just another incident. Clare,' he drew closer to her. stroking her shoulder. Then his hands slipped down her breasts.

An involuntary shiver of revulsion ran through Clare. She backed away, anger tightening her throat. Before she could control herself she was stammering accusations.

'Just another incident. Is that what murder is called now? Another incident? Raul, those were human beings. They had mothers and wives and children and now they are dead. And the men who killed them, the guerrillas, they will be dead soon, too. Perhaps they already are. Caught and tortured to death by other soldiers who will be killed in their turn by other guerrillas and on and on and on. But they're the same men, Raul. It's you who divide them. You who put uniforms on some and pay them to kill their brothers who grew up in the same slums, with the same hunger. They all need the same thing — land to grow food — and you took it away, you own it.' Suddenly, Clare recalled the faces of the two guerrillas in the hut, the pockmarked man, the boy who had spat at her as he ran to the forest. The dead baby, held aloft. 'You turned them against each other for your own gain.'

Sharply, Raul said, 'Pull yourself together, Clare.' He walked over to the buttoned-velvet bar, feeling in his breast pocket.

She called after him, tears in her eyes, 'And what did you do about my women? Who pushed that drink on them? You promised me you'd find out and punish them. Did you?'

'Drink.' Raul put a balloon of brandy in her hand. His eyes were covered now, concealed beneath wraparound dark glasses. He looked like a prisoner facing execution.

Clare coughed as the brandy went down. 'Did you?'

'Yes,' he said.

'And who were they?'

'As I told you,' he said. 'Riff-raff. Fools having a joke with the Indians. They have been dealt with.'

'Dealt with?' Clare gave an unsteady laugh. 'What does that mean? If they were your men they got a flea in their ear for being found out. If they weren't ... well.'

She stared through the glass wall, screwing up her eyes against the glare of the sun's rays that glinted off the fifty-foot Gulfstream 2 standing a hundred yards away across the tarmac. With its yellow and white body paint, its curved beak and its jutting tail, it looked like an exotic forest parrot. At the foot of the aircraft steps among a knot of officials, Clare could distinguish the dark figure of Concepción clutching her case. As she watched, the Gulfstream's engines roared to a high whine and the air shivered.

'Have you been talking to Concepción?' Raul asked, his blind-folded eyes on the window.

'No. Why should I?'

'Servants gossip,' he said and rubbed his unshaven chin. There was a knock at the door and the airport manager sidled in, bowing as he came.

'If you please Señor, Señora. All is ready. It is time to depart.'

The brandy burned in Clare's stomach. She nodded at the manager and placed a hand lightly on Raul's proffered arm. They walked together through the door.

'I know who brought that drink to my women,' Clare said quietly to Raul.

'Yes?' he said.

'Yes,' she said.

[246]

Raul let his arm fall to his side. 'Be careful, my dear,' he said, 'be careful.' As Clare looked up at him, he pointed at the stairs. 'Very steep. Very dangerous.'

Delicately, she set her heel on the first step and walked slowly out to the plane.

[14]

The brilliant edge of the sun cut a crescent in the clouds above Westminster. The pavements were warm and scattered here and there with London debris: shards of plastic beakers, empty cigarette packs, newspaper pages adrift in the gutters. Usually the men were on the barrows, sweeping up the muck. Nine to five, a bevvy at the Star and Garter and a bus back to the Elephant. Today however, Barry Barking, Ray Dooley and the new bloke had been set to do the flags outside the House of Commons.

'Don't like the look of them poles,' said Barry. They were sitting on the bank of grass beneath the line of flags, smoking roll-ups and watching the morning traffic coil slowly from the river around them, waiting for the Department van.

'Nor me,' said Ray. 'I've got no head for heights. It's something to do with me ears.'

'The pair you've got there,' Barry said, 'halfway up and you'll take off.' He wheezed like a concertina and the new bloke laughed.

'No lip from you, mate.' Ray punched the new bloke's shoulder and Barry wheezed again. 'What's it all for, anyway, this flag lark?'

'Search me,' said Barry, spitting shreds of tobacco. 'Some darkie visiting, I suppose, or some Ay-rab geezer come to put up the price of petrol in person.'

'You don't know where from, then?' asked Ray.

'Course I don't,' said Barry. 'The place was only invented this time last Tuesday. Them as lives there don't know what it's called yet, never mind us.'

'Here, said the new bloke. He stuck out a newspaper and flicked at it. 'She's the one coming, see?'

The two men screwed up their eyes and scrutinized the grainy photograph. 'Women,' Barry said, 'they're taking over the world, they are. Half the top jobs is women. I tell you, men have had it, no I mean it. Our day is gone.'

'She's the dictator, her and her husband.' The new bloke folded the paper and stuck it in his pocket.

'Still,' said Ray. 'That one can dictate to me any time she likes, eh Barry? With them tits, she's as good as Page Three.'

'Like to stick your flagpole up her, see how she flutters, would you?' The two men guffawed. Above them, Big Ben began to strike, raising a cloud of starlings, and a yellow van inscribed Department of the Environment drew up at the verge. Twenty minutes later, the new bloke caught a button of his overalls on a nail in the ladder he was climbing, missed his footing and fell in a flurry of white and gold flag. He sustained a Colles fracture of his right wrist.

The note was stuck in Judith's typewriter when she got in. 'Jude,' Lorna had scribbled, 'the Venturan Embassy telephoned, 6.00 p.m. They've cancelled your interview with Señora de Toro. She's not giving any, apparently. Sorry.'

'Can you believe it?' asked Judith of no one, since no one had yet arrived in the Features Room. '*Now* what do I do?' Easing her jacket over the back of the chair, she scrabbled in the depths of a large canvas bag and hauled out her contact book. She dialled, her eyes on an open page, and waited. Busy. God, it was going to be one of those days. She dialled again.

'Min? Judith. Listen, my Clare interview is off. The Embassy phoned. I don't know. Could you phone the studio, see if there's a message for you. Looks like no prog. Yeah, I'm at the paper.'

Lorna appeared, put down her usual array of carrier bags and went to get them both coffees from the corridor machine. The phone rang. Min's voice came at Judith in an agitated tremolo.

'There's a message for me, too. They must have snuck it in after I left yesterday. Cancelled. What are they up to? I can't get through to the Embassy, it's busy all the time. Jude, I haven't got anything else in the can, you'll have to do the programme anyway.'

'Oh yes?' said Judith. 'You want me to jump from chair to chair, whipping a blonde wig on and off?'

'No but honestly, Jude, we'll have to think up something. Look, I'll be in the studio in a half-hour. I'll have a chat there and come back to you.'

She rang off as Andy passed Judith's desk with an armful of books. 'Top of the morning,' he said.

'It's the bottom of the morning,' said Judith, swivelling her chair towards him. 'Madam Ventura's finked out. I can't see her.'

'Oh come on,' said Andy, dropping the books on his desk. 'I'm counting on it.'

Judith flared. 'It's not my fault, she's cancelled all round. Orders from the Embassy.'

'Okay okay,' he said, flapping a hand in her direction. 'But *why*? That's the story now, isn't it? Why has the First Lady had second thoughts? You'd better get down to Heathrow anyway. The telly boys will be there, she's coming in live. You can try a question or two on the spot. You might still get into the car.'

'Well,' Judith said, 'but . . .' She hated pushy assignments like this. It wasn't her style.

'Try it,' said Andy. 'Show the chauffeur a bit of cleavage, wiggle your hips, pout your lips, say the car chat's been arranged, he may not know different. If you're sitting there waiting when the Lady gets in, she might relent. This is scoop time, Jude.'

'More like poop time,' said Judith but she glanced at her watch. Two hours to landing. 'Right, And, I'll have a go. Lorna, when Min Holroyd telephones, tell her yes, whatever it is, and I'll be in touch this afternoon.'

Outside, her yellow CV had collected the first parking ticket of the day. 'Shit,' said Judith. She chucked it on top of two others on the floor and turned the key in the ignition.

'I don't want him in the same room,' said Alice. She stood on the bare boards staring down at the baby in the carry-cot at her feet. 'Perhaps it's silly, but I don't.'

Ronnie Garston was sweeping the small platform with the stool on it. 'You're the boss, Angela. Don't know what you're on about but we'll do it your way. I'll put him in the dark room and close the door, all right?'

She bent down, thrust one arm through the two straps and heaved up the cot. With elaborate gestures Ronnie ushered her across to the dark room door. Inside, the air was sharp with chemicals.

'No,' she said, stopping at the threshold. 'It smells in here.'

'Developing stuff,' said Ronnie, 'nothing to hurt him.'

'No,' she said.

Ronnie turned back into the studio and spread his arms wide. 'Angela, what do you want? This isn't Buckingham Palace. I can't offer the west wing for the use of Little Lord Fauntleroy here. Couldn't you have left him with someone, eh? This is a job, you know, not a baby-sitting service.' Was she trying to get out of the modelling, was that it?

'What's behind there?' she asked, pointing at another door. Her hand shook very slightly.

'Broom cupboard,' said Ronnie.

She opened the door and looked in. It was dark and musty but there was space enough. 'This'll do. I'll put him in here.' She lugged the cot over. He heard her muttering for a few minutes and then she emerged, leaving the door ajar.

'Anyone would think your kid was a peeping tom,' he said,

'the way you carry on.' She said nothing. Nerves. Ronnie made an effort to sound cheery. 'Right, then, darling. You get your things off behind that screen and we'll start when you're ready. I've got enough fires going to keep your tootsies warm.' He rubbed his hands and chuckled noisily, holding them over one of the paraffin stoves.

She took a deep breath and walked stiffly over to the three-piece hardboard screen covered with pictures of rubbery nudes. Oh Charlie, she thought. She'd left him setting off for the Job Centre but what hope did he have, with his arm in a cast? Then she thought, fifty pounds. Ten, twenty, thirty, forty, fifty. She tugged the blue T-shirt over her head and struggled out of her jeans. The static of a radio started in the room and a male voice blared, I can't give you anything but love, bay-bee. She could hear Ronnie humming. At home, she'd be feeding the chickens about now. Just the click of the catch at the kitchen door and they'd come shrieking from the yard, bouncing from one starry foot to the other, necks stretched as if someone held a match to their tails. Gingery, with little plumes of feathers like fountains. Round yellow eyes in wrinkled scrag and their combs flapping from side to side. Better go.

'Fine, fine,' Ronnie said briskly, his eyes carefully on her face. 'Come along, darling, settle yourself down on the stool. Like a cushion, would you? Don't want to numb the old bum, do we?' Quickly, he turned up the volume on the tranny. Anything to make them feel at home and this one was worth the effort, oh yes. I have to hand it to you, Ronnie boy, you can certainly pick 'em. Gorgeous pair they were, mounds of whipped cream with cherries on top. He ran his tongue across his lips as he felt a satisfactory leap at his groin. Guaranteed good photos, that did. Waste not to get a few shots of the titties first.

She was sitting awkwardly, staring blankly ahead, the purple tears dripping down the face. Well, what did that matter, with the long legs and the little waist and the pert bum and that downy crotch? 'Right, darling,' he said, trundling the floods forward. Then he heard her voice, shaky but clear.

'Please,' she said. 'Don't call me darling.'

He was motionless for a minute, rocked. What about that for chutzpah, a scrubber telling you not to call her darling? Oh man, too much. But he kept his mouth shut. She'd pay for that later, yes indeedy, but business was business, he'd keep her sweet now.

She looked down at the dusty floor. The thing about feeding chickens, you had to watch your hands. Those heads went back and forth like pistons, pecking, pecking. She remembered how they used to scare her when she was little, how she'd stick her hand out with the grain on it and pull back as the hard curved beaks advanced and the round eyes blinked, how they'd chase her as she ran away.

Ronnie adjusted the dials on the console and turned down the barn doors. For the next ten minutes he clicked away, shouting instructions over the babble of the tranny. 'Bend forward Angie, that's it, arms behind you. Now, breathe in and hold it. Lovely. Okay, arch your back, yeah, great. Put your hands across 'em, Angie, open your fingers. Now push 'em up and let the nipples show through. Lovely, lovely.' He was in an ecstasy. Look at 'em hanging there, bloody great gongs. The bells are ringing, for me and my gal. Ding dong dell, pussy's in the well. Wowee.

She did what she was told. She moved obediently. She stroked herself, she handled her breasts as she was instructed. She felt her nipples harden and whisked her mind away. She'd buy something for Charlie with the fifty pounds. Something for his bike. This wasn't happening, she was nowhere and this was nothing.

'Right,' Ronnie said. He was out from behind the camera now, at the edge of the platform. 'Move over, Angie.'

She stood aside with her arms folded across her and watched as he dragged a mattress to where the stool was and moved it away. Then he covered the mattress with a wine velvet spread, bunching it here and there, arranging its folds.

'Now,' he said, adjusting the reflectors. 'Lie down with your legs towards me. That's it.' This was it, the commission, and how could he go wrong? She glowed on that background, a living honey sandwich. He could eat her and that was a promise. 'Relax the knees, Angie, there's a good girl. Bit further. Pull the ankles up, yes, yes. Terrific.' He moved one hot light and then the others, closing the shutters to focus the beams. 'Hold still, now.'

The tranny cackled. '... and there's the Princess now, they're taking her up to the VIP lounge ... only another fifteen minutes ... that's quite a creation she's wearing ...'

'Terrific, terrific,' said Ronnie.

'... white feathers in a cockade, curling round the brim of the straw and just brushing the cheeks ...'

She listened hard. White feathers, like those birds in the hangar she'd been in once, playing with the Straker girls. She'd gone in to hide, entered a dark cavern and crouched behind the door. She couldn't see much to start with, her ears strained to catch the footsteps of the searchers, padding stealthily behind her in the grass. But then they died away and she was alone in the dim light or thought she was alone until she heard those sad defeated sounds and looked up and saw the bird spectres stretching away from her in barred lines of cages and went closer. And there they were, row upon row, with their maimed beaks and hanging combs and sore plucked skin, packed inhabitants of a penal colony who gazed at her with their dull hopeless eyes so that she ran as if these ghosts were after her into the sunny afternoon clutching the last pretty remnants of childhood around her. Battery hens, said the Straker girls and gave misery a name.

'Wider, can you?' came Ronnie's voice and she obeyed him and 'yes, hang on to that so I can bracket' and she lay spread out on the kapok lumps and the voice from the tranny said the

Princess is waiting now, there they are by the red carpet and beside her the Lord Lieutenant of Lincolnshire, Lord La Fontaine, and the flowers look marvellous, blue and red and Ronnie's voice said spread 'em, darling and a round black eye stared blindly at her, at the pink soft parts that looked like a sad cock's comb and in Alice's mind the cock with the white tail feathers raised itself on two forked feet and screamed with its neck stretched out and she's coming, crowed the tranny, we can see her in the sky now coming . . .

Ronnie switched off and Alice landed wet and quaking into a London basement with a man crashed between her legs heaving and panting and she howled, fighting him off, hitting him with her fists until he cursed and rolled off her. As he lay there, she flew into her clothes, grabbed the carry-cot and opened the door and went and Ronnie shouted after her, 'You can't fool Ronnie, you little tart. You *liked* it.'

The plane was a small chrysalis suspended in the dark sky. Behind it lay the Azores, last stop on the flight to London. Inside, Clare was cocooned in a mohair blanket on the rear cabin sofa, gazing drowsily up at the low curved roof. Soon I shall be a butterfly again, she thought. Buckingham Palace, Ma and Pa, parties, friends, as it used to be. That time seemed eons ago, in another life that was lived by another woman, a straw woman whom she hardly recognized as herself. So much had happened since she had flown out to Ventura as a bride on this same plane. For a moment, a tremor of nostalgia ran through her. How peaceful to be empty-headed again, with nothing more on her mind than herself and her own comfort. But that — she turned restlessly under the blanket — that was memory playing its usual tricks, bathing the past in an artificial glow. She hadn't been happy then and she wasn't happy now but at least now she had something worthwhile to be unhappy about. The thought made her smile ruefully. Hard work lay ahead after the social round, talks, meetings, organization. Her plans must succeed, she must not fail the women.

The dry air scraped at her throat, her eyes itched and she closed them. Later, lost in time and space, she half-woke, struggling to escape from the dreams that tied her down. Somewhere near by, she could hear Carrington's nasal drawl and Concepción's husky Spanish voice that seemed to plead. Then Concepción was leaning over her, one black plait swinging.

'Qué pasa?' Clare mumbled the words, rising through layers of discomfort, pushing the blanket away.

'You cried out, Señora,' Concepción said. 'I have brought you tea to soothe you.' Concepción's face swimming over her was an odd blur of colours, the skin greenish yellow, the eyes bloodshot, the lids puffy and red. Clare pulled herself up on her elbow. On the table beside her, a steaming cup chinked faintly in its saucer. The hot liquid eased her throat.

'Now, Señora.' A hand extended itself, cupping in its palm three elongated capsules, grey and yellow. Time capsules, Clare thought, my very own time capsules. H. G. Wells had to invent a machine so that his hero could traverse the fourth dimension. All she had to do was to place these pretty sweets upon her tongue and swallow.

'Gracias, Concha,' Clare murmured and lay back, drifting. She heard Concepción give a little cough, almost a sob.

'Don't thank me, Señora. Please don't.'

The cocoon closed around her and she sank gently into its soft warmth, too sleepy to think any more. She carried with her, traced on her eyelids, an image of tears.

Judith, nosing the CV through clotted traffic, took the wrong turning off the roundabout at Shepherd's Bush and was half way up the Goldhawk Road before the absence of little planes on signposts set up alarms in her automatic pilot. Shit oh *shit*. It took twenty more minutes weaving through the backstreets of W.11, line on line of identical Victorian cottages elaborately frontis-pieced with birds and fruit like biblical bookmarks, before she curved back on to the roundabout and headed first right to Heathrow. In a hurry now – the plane was due in at 11.50 a.m. and it was half eleven now – she cursed her way through Chiswick, always behind the sort of driver who slows down at green lights, and sighed with relief as she hit the Hammersmith flyover. Then she put her foot down and, as the road slipped under her, relapsed into a favourite daydream. There she was bobbing up and down in a sea of media people, all camaraderie gone as they strained towards their target, notebooks out, biros quivering, cameras at the ready and, this time, she would not be put down by any bloody twit attached to a television camera who thought he was God with special privileges far above and beyond mere pencil-pushers like herself. The cheek of telly people passed all limits. She remembered a time when she had spent six weeks visiting a woman in Holloway prison, a notorious murderess shortly due for release. Six weeks of carting in meals, a radio, books, letters and countless messages, six weeks of running the woman's endless errands, liaising with her solicitor, phoning up hostels to find her a place, all to make sure that when the woman walked out, free, she'd talk only to Judith. And then what had happened? The wretched creature had ap-peared under the Holloway arch and this great lump of a cameraman had blocked her way with his spongey prick of a microphone and the rest of his television musculature and said would you mind, lovey, your head's in the way. And pushed her aside and shot his film and gone off with the woman, who'd hardly deigned to glance in Judith's direction, so ga-ga had she gone at the sight of the camera. Well, she wasn't about to let that happen again, no siree. This time, Madame Whatsit would appear from the plane to the popping of flash bulbs and look down and her eyes would alight on Judith and a spark of the purest sisterly appreciation would pass between them, so that after the various ceremonies were over, Madame Thingie would make straight for her, brushing aside the importunities of other reporters. Together, arm in arm, they would walk across the tarmac, already chatting like old friends, and dive together into the cool upholstery of Madame's limousine, where Judith would touch a button at her side and a darkened window would silently glide upwards, screening out the red frustrated faces of less talented media folk. Oh ho and *then* she'd have a story because all the way back to London, soothed by Judith's sheer niceness and obvious trustworthiness, she would pour out every intimate detail of her life and feelings and hopes and fears and bingo, three thousand riveting, revealing and exclusive words would appear in the *Chronicle* next day, the only story that summed up exactly where Ventura and Madame Tiddlypush and her dictator husband stood in the political spectrum. And then the lady would gladly consent to participate in the television interview – for you, Judith, anything. The final coup.

Judith gave an involuntary sigh of satisfaction, suppressed the fleeting thought that the story and the interview were unlikely to be compatible, and zoomed into the outside lane. There was a slight stiffness in the joints of her thighs. The penalty for sex, she thought with irritation, and he hadn't been so great. What was his name? Gone.

In his office, Raul de Toro y Plata poured bourbon from a frosted decanter into the glasses of Gary Lutz and Gerard O'Reilly and tossed his own glass back, baring his teeth. The two men raised their glasses at him and drank. Then they sat talking quietly and watched the small black digital clock that sat on the President's desk. The clock ticked audibly and its thin black hand moved forward in infinitesimal jerks.

Two kilometres from where the men sat drinking, up in the steamy barrios, Concepción's brother José-Eduardo lay with his eyes closed. His face had never been really clean in all the seventeen years of his life but it was clean as a whistle now. Soapsuds clung to the tendrils of hair at his temples and a thin line of dried foam followed the curved recesses of his brown ears, there were tiny flecks of it on his smooth upper lip. Even his neck, even the hollow at his thin throat was scrubbed clean. The inky fringe that swept his forehead was combed into smoothness over the dark smooth eyebrows and his hair neatly framed the ovals of his cheeks and swept down to touch the white line of the sheet that crossed his shoulders.

José-Eduardo was dead. Abandoned, with a knee-cap shot away, he had lain helpless in a ditch among the bodies of the soldiers while flies crawled on his wound and a vulture, attracted by the sweet stench of blood, hung motionless above. The boy and the vulture waited. Eventually, other soldiers came. They stood over him, blotting out the sun, and kicked him in the side. When he moaned, one of them bent forward and eased the grenade out of his slack hand. Then the soldier brought his boot down on the hand, stamping on it again and again. Another boot ground down on the other hand. The boy screamed for a minute or so in a high falsetto and then became quiet, by which time there only remained two bloody gobbets hanging at the ends of his arms. They would have killed him then but orders came to preserve him until further notice so he was loaded on to a jeep with the corpses and passed twenty more hours of a kind of life, conscious and partly conscious, until further notice was given, whereupon he was shot several times in the belly and dumped from a car at the foot of one of the alleys that led to the barrios from the town of Nombre Dios. At twilight, his body was delivered by neighbours to the shack where he was born and his sisters Dolores and Ramosa wept as they tenderly washed his dead face. The boy's eldest sister, the one who had carried him everywhere with her when he was a motherless baby, did not yet know of his death. She was with her mistress in a plane that was coming in to land at London Airport.

'Alice?' Charlie was shouting now, his lips at the door's letterbox. Through it he could see the faded green hall rug, frayed at one corner, and an envelope lying upon it which he recognized as the rent demand. Shit, he should have had a key cut. Now he'd have to go all the way down the stairs again and come back later, when Alice was there. Later was tricky and all, what with saying he'd meet that Judith in the Star and Garter when it opened for a quick early evening bevvy. Where was Alice, anyway? She must have left before the post arrived and that wasn't usual. He worried about her. Last summer she'd been so cheerful all the time, whenever he looked at her she was smiling fit to bust. Merry as a cricket, that's what she'd been, his funny girl. She'd changed, though, the past two months. Sometimes he didn't want to look at her no more, her eyes were so sad. She took too much to heart. She didn't understand about life, well how could she, shut up with her Mum and Dad on that rackety old farm, nothing but a bunch of hens for company. Still, she'd cheer up when the plaster came off his arm and he got work again. That was what he had to make Alice understand. You didn't get a job watching telly with your bird and your nipper. You had to go out, meet people, make contacts, have a few jars in the boozer, keep your ear to the ground, otherwise you were dead.

Never mind. He'd have another go at her in an hour or so, when she got back, make her see his point of view. Then she wouldn't mind him popping off again for a little while. Charlie slapped the letterbox closed, got up from his knees and tramped down the stairs.

The burning leather seared the thin shanks of the little girl who sat alone, her feet dangling at the edge of the car seat, inches above the floor. The windows were dark, dark shapes moved past outside. Ahead of her was the shadow of a man, his back. Pushing herself off the seat, she stumbled to the glass and banged her knuckles against it. The man's back remained stolidly turned. Tears of frustration leaked from her eyes and fell hissing on her hot cheeks. She clambered again on to the slippery heights of the seat. Dread made her limbs heavy. She pressed her face at a window but the murky glass showed her nothing. Clutching the tiny diamond from its chain round her neck, she began to scratch it on the glass. The diamond screeched, black flakes peeled off, leaving a transparent web. Dropping the chain she put one eye to the flaky hole and peered out. A dusty earth track lined with trees. Red earth, red trees. Then she saw that the trees were not trees but sides of butchered meat in lines as far as her eyes could see and the meat ran with blood, gouts of blood dripped down the sides and splashed on the earth to make it red. Hands flat against the glass, the little girl put back her head and screamed and screamed.

'Señora. *Señora*.' Concepción, patting Clare's cheeks, paused as the blue eyes tipped open and stared blankly at the roof of the cabin. Oh, poor little Señora, to lie there so crushed and frightened, the golden hair matted across the pillow, beads of sweat on her brow. Concepción wetted a sponge at the basin as voices rose outside. The door of the front cabin slid open and a man's head appeared.

'Get her going, you,' he snapped at Concepción in Spanish, 'get her dressed. We've got twenty minutes to landing.'

There were grey marks under Concepción's eyes, she had not slept for two nights, inside she trembled, watery with fear. But there was no choice, the job had to be done. Reaching down, she slipped an arm round Clare and pulled her to a sitting position, where she slumped like a rag doll. So heavy, too heavy. Madre de dios, how could she manage?

'Meez Carrington,' she called at the open door. 'Meez

Carrington.' Her cry was echoed by a male voice up ahead and, a minute later, Deborah Carrington appeared, standing at the arch. In two strides she was beside Clare slapping lightly at her cheeks.

'Water,' she said. At its cold touch, Clare's eyes opened again and she looked dizzily around.

'Okay,' Deborah said. 'Come on, Concepción.'

Together, the two women heaved Clare off the bed and marched her between the swivelled chairs into the tiny rear bathroom, where they sat her on the lavatory seat. Behind her, Concepción slid back a cupboard door and took out a diaphanous white dress on a hanger, which she passed to Deborah. There was hardly room for the three of them in the cramped space.

'Am I drunk?' Clare said plaintively, swaying on the seat, holding on.

'Of course not,' said Deborah soothingly, 'not a bit. Just tired, Señora. It's been a long journey. Hurry, Concepción.'

Opening drawers in the cupboard that lined the narrow corridor, the maid retrieved the rest of Clare's clothes and lined them on the counter by the basin. White silk court shoes, white handbag in tissue, pale stockings, a brassiere, a wide white straw hat looped with chiffon. Deborah handed back the dress and helped Clare to her feet, where she stood unsteadily, her face loose.

'Just tired,' she said to Deborah and nodded. 'Just very tired.'

'No problem,' said Deborah briskly. She took hold of Clare's nightdress and obediently Clare stretched her arms up like a child. She kept them there as Concepción put on her brassiere and lifted her feet, one by one, as the stockings were rolled up her legs to their garter tops on her thighs. Then the maid sponged her face and dried it gently.

'Now that lovely dress,' Deborah said. The yards of fabric floated over Clare's head and slipped softly down her body to a swirl of skirt at her knees.

'Well isn't that something,' Deborah asked and turned Clare to the mirror set in the wall over the basin.

Clare peered at the little she could see of herself – face, shoulders, a square of white bodice. 'Lovely,' she said, focusing carefully. 'Lovely. Concepción?'

'Está muy linda, Señora,' Concepción said and put one hand on her heart.

Deborah glanced at her watch and clicked open a small purse that she took out of the pocket of her neat jacket. 'Now, Señora,' she said brightly, 'a couple of these and you'll feel just fine.' She held out a glass of water. 'Here.'

'What are they?' asked Clare, poking at Deborah's hand.

'Carrington's Specials,' said Deborah with her amiable grin, 'guaranteed to banish jet-lag, separation anxiety, hangovers, halitosis and butterflies in the stomach. The real thing.'

Clare took the glass, put the pills in her mouth and swallowed. 'Bottoms up,' she said and was faintly surprised at the edge of hysteria in Deborah's laugh.

Twenty minutes later, the throb of the engine roughened and the carpeted floor of the cabin took on a slope. Up front, the ground engineer snapped up his seat behind the cockpit and walked through to adjust the women's armchair belts. Through the open door, Clare could see the four chunky dark-suited security men buckling themselves into their swivel seats. The Captain's voice on the intercom kept up a constant barrage of incomprehensible flight information and the men talked in gruff undertones to each other. There was a clunk as the wheels disengaged and the growl of the engine sunk another octave.

A gust of euphoria swept over Clare, her heart thudded and her mind raced, she felt her whole body lift and buzz as if a swarm of bees were rushing through her veins. She was going to carry off everything wonderfully well, she knew it. I am an actress, she thought, a beautiful talented famous actress and the stage is out there and the audience is waiting breathlessly, all eyes fixed on the great velvet curtains that will soon swing back as they frantically clap and there I shall be with the spotlights upon me, glowing like a golden flame, their idol, their Queen. She flushed with the pleasure her image inspired, waves of applause roared in her ears, she inclined her head regally and her eyes shone. And who was that dark woman beside her, drinking in her every movement? Why of course, it was her dear devoted Concha who never left her side, who would lay down her very life for her mistress and who was at this very minute praying ardently for her success.

Clare smiled sweetly at Concepción and leant over to pat her knee. 'There, there,' she said in English. 'Don't worry, dear Concha. Everything's coming up roses.'

'Oh Mary, Mother of God, pray for us now and at the hour of our deaths,' whispered Concepción under her breath. The beads of the rosary clicked as they slipped through her fingers, her eyes were huge and glazed.

'Everything's coming up roses,' Clare sang quietly. Deborah swivelled towards her, pushing back her spectacles.

'Sí sí sí sí,' said Clare, 'doh ray me fah so lah ti si.' She smiled radiantly at this tousled woman who was regarding her so intently. 'Cheer up. Chirrup. Tweet tweet tweet.' She laughed uproariously at her own wit and the four men in the cabin beyond fell silent, watching her. One of them pursed his lips and raised his eyebrows at Deborah. She tapped Clare's knee.

'Señora. Please concentrate. We'll be landing at Heathrow in just a few minutes.'

'Good-oh,' said Clare brightly. The man with the moustache unbuckled himself and came over, staggering on the vibrating floor. He bent and whispered to Deborah, who nodded several times looking irritated.

'Our Lady, Mother of God, pray for us now and at the hour

of our death,' mumbled Concepción. Her face was grey. The man exhaled abruptly, shrugged and went back to his seat.

'I am very happy,' said Clare in a light clear voice, 'very happy indeed to be back here in my homeland again.' She gave a gracious little wave in Deborah's direction. 'Your Highness, my countrymen and women, I bring with me the greetings and good wishes of the people of Ventura and of Ventura's President, my husband. There has been a long tradition of friendship and co-operation between ...' Her voice rose over the low mutterings of Concepción as she addressed herself to the four men opposite. They listened politely and uncomprehendingly, shifting their feet, to the end of Clare's speech.

'... in these difficult times,' Clare said, her voice richening, 'I know that this will continue to be an example to be cherished and an inspiration to us all. Thank you.' She looked modestly at her lap.

The men glanced uneasily at each other and back at Clare. 'Thank *you*, Señora,' said one doubtfully. Deborah's face had cleared, she clapped.

'Word perfect. Bravo, Señora. But don't worry, the speech will be there on the rostrum, just in case.'

At that moment, the plane tipped and lines of small houses swam into view, framed by the windows opposite like so many postcards. Concepción gave a despairing groan and her lips moved rapidly. A burst of Spanish crackled from the intercom, the plane evened out, grass and grey tarmac rushed past, everyone held the arms of their chairs and with the faintest of bumps the wheels touched ground.

Concepción swallowed and two tears trickled down her cheeks. 'Mamacita Dios, tráeme a José otra vez. Protégele,' she prayed to the ceiling.

The gold and white plane, motionless now on the grey tarmac, roared to a crescendo once more and died away. In the blessed silence, Clare snapped off her seat belt and leaned to the window. The colours of England were pale, a soft sun, a mild breeze, an undemanding landscape. Sentimental tears came to her eyes, home was a watercolour, restful and benign, gone was the cruel glare of Ventura, a punishment to be endured and this a happy release. Home, so very sweet home. Nothing would go wrong here that could not be solved. When she talked to her own people, they would understand, they would give her what she needed without argument because what she needed was reasonable and, in England, reason ruled, the quiet oases of the mind reigned over the harsh flamboyance of the emotions. Morality, in this gentle place, was tuned to gentle rhythms, the natural commonsense requirements of ordinary human beings, it had no link at all with the fierce glow of a golden Virgin whose topaz eyes turned her subjects to slaves, lashed by the whip of faith, driven to attempt the scaling of impossible heights, their every human need ignored for the goal of a coldly glittering heaven where the God on the glittering throne so closely resembled the God, her husband.

Outside, Clare saw the wide carpet, a scarlet T across the tarmac, edged with neat rows of blue lobelias, red geraniums, white carnations, and the men with cameras, already jostling, and the discreet knot of people gathered below, blue and grey and red and a woman in blue with white feathers on her hat, fluttering in the breeze.

'Breezy,' Deborah said, peering out through the window. She looked pleased and bit the side of her thumb. Concepción, her face lined and sallow, dropped her rosary into her handbag. Clare stood up, swayed and nearly fell. Something in her head moved like the blade of a fan and left her short of breath. Behind, Concepción put out a hand towards her, a curious gesture, half pleading, half protective. She began to say something, a whisper in Spanish that faded as Deborah moved between them and the four men near the cockpit rose, straightening their ties, pulling at the hems of their jackets. There was a thump, a long hiss, the door at the end of the cabin opened, and cool air flooded the compartment. The Captain, resplendent in blue and gold braid, walked stiffly up the aisle and bowed before Clare. Behind him she could see the first two steps of the staircase below the open oval and hear the low buzz of voices rising. She held herself steady with her hands braced against the cabin door. The four men moved to stand on either side of the stairway, the Captain extended a courteous hand and Deborah came up close to her. Concepción folded into a chair as if her knees had given way, her fingers tightly meshed. Clare put her hand in the Captain's palm and they went forward together to where the creamy sunlight streamed in. To her right she could see into the cockpit where the co-pilot still crouched with his headphones on, talking. Outside there was a low rumble and one of the men framed in the door put up his thumb and then backed in, nodding at the Captain. He released Clare and she felt hands on her back, propelling her forward.

'Now,' said Deborah and she stepped out on to the first small stair in the sun, carefully straight, chin up, smiling. The faces below her shimmered, smiling up.

'Wave,' hissed the voice of Deborah as Raul's had once done and she lifted her hand above her head and waved and heard the hushed whirr of cameras and saw out of the corner of her eye the grey shape of another plane taxiing slowly past and felt the gust from its slipstream curl round her ankles and, gathering strength, spiral upwards to rise in warm blasts over her flesh.

'*Christ*,' the OB cameraman muttered back in his throat. With an effort, he kept his shoulder steady. The tin voice in his cans whispered urgently.

'Pete. Pan up to face. Zoom in on *face*, Pete.'

In the silver Outside Broadcast van parked to the side of the Gulfstream jet, the light voice of a woman huddled in the cabin paused for a fraction of a second and talked on as the Princess a hundred yards away walked forward, her mouth slack, her famous blue eyes stony. '... very pretty blue silk two-piece and there behind her I can see Lady Clare's parents ...' – she clasped her cans, squinting furiously at the tiny monitor – '... Lord and Lady La Fontaine, how thrilled they must be ...'

The OB director spun his index finger under her nose and she wound up in a rush – 'and now, back to the studio for the rest of the news' and, together, they pulled their headphones off.

'Whew,' the director said, pushing the damp hair off his face. They stared at each other in delighted alarm.

'Did I see what I thought I saw?'

'Oh God,' he said, 'you and four million others. Well. That'll make the Beeb's Christmas film.' Then they collapsed.

As Clare floated down the stairs, the crowd stood as quietly as beasts before a storm. Gratefully, she breathed the sweet moist air, still now after the wind, and stood on home ground. Then the people came alive. How wrong Raul was to complain about the coldness of the English. All around her a babble of voices rose in welcome, the eyes of the men and women who surrounded her winked and glowed, their faces flushed. A little primrose of a girl in palest yellow cotton bobbed at her knees, pushed a posy of flowers into her hands and turned away into her mother's arms with a trill of charming laughter. Guided by Deborah at her elbow – why, her hand was trembling, how odd that Carrington should be nervous – Clare went towards the unmistakable Royal figure plodding between a corridor of bodies and curtsied gracefully before they both touched cheeks and the Princess murmured 'Welcome home'. She looked a little distrait, Clare thought, but how nice she was, how kind they all were.

Then, through the hustling knot of photographers she glimpsed her father – Pa! – as bedecked as a Christmas tree in his gold-braided blue-sashed Lord Lieutenant's uniform and Ma, dear Ma, beside him, clinging to his arm. For a brief second, Clare received the impression that they were almost holding each other up, they clung so. Poor darlings, she thought, they hate all this and then she was in her father's embrace, held hard against his buttoned chest and then bundled to her mother, who pressed her papery cheek to Clare's and said in a whisper, 'My child, my child.'

'Ma,' Clare said happily, 'you're crying. You mustn't cry, I'm here,' but Ma merely shook her head and the Princess came to them and Ma curtsied and Pa bowed. Two Special Branch men in dark blue suits and skinny ties spoke into their intercoms, frowning. The metallic scream of a distant plane cut in and, briefly, a hiatus fell. Clare was ushered towards the small rostrum and there she stood like a porcelain angel and gave her speech to the whirring of cameras and the muffled clap of gloved hands. She stepped down, radiant.

'Señora de Toro, Lady Clare.' A man with fiery ginger hair and a battered leather jacket, hump-backed with bags, held the pear-shaped sponge at her face. 'How did it ... can you explain ...?' He looked down, apparently unable to get the words out.

Helpfully, Clare came to his assistance. 'How is it to be back in England? Wonderful, really wonderful.' She beamed. For several minutes then, as the Princess and Clare and the La Fontaines moved from the runway, other men and women pushed towards her, sticking their mikes hopefully at her. Clare answered their questions as best she could, unable to stop smiling. 'Wonderful,' she said. 'Thrilled to be back ... greetings from Ventura, from my husband ... so sad to miss all this ... matters of State ... her Majesty, yes ... of course, wonderful, wonderful.'

Beneath her arm, a young woman with streaked curls and a pale mouth sprang up, a notebook in her hand.

'Señora, welcome home. It's been arranged, I'm coming with you in the car to London. May I help you with anything?'

[269]

Clare inclined her head. Behind the reporter she saw Carrington's nacreous specs. She was talking rapidly to one of the Venturan security men and her skin seemed creased in some way. Oh and there was Concha at last, between two more men. What a poor black mourner she looked among the festive crowd with her yellow face and her red-rimmed eyes. Dear Concha, still so frightened. We must get her quickly home to Tucolston.

'I really don't know,' she said to the girl with the streaked curls, biting her top lip enchantingly. 'I'm sure someone will . . .' Her eyes darted merrily about in the bustle. Everything inside her was pulsing and fluttering with the pleasure of the day and the admiration she saw in the men's eyes. Delightful!

Then Carrington was there, interposing herself between Clare and the reporter, using her briefcase to push at the woman.

'Señora, Your Highness, Lord La Fontaine,' she said. The Special Branch men began to edge the photographers back. 'The cars are waiting . . . if you please.'

In the sunlight, murmuring to each other, they walked to the long black limousines. There were farewells and to a burst of clapping, the Princess drove off.

'Señora, I'm coming with you.' Streaked Curls was again beside Clare. '*Daily Chronicle*. It's settled with your Embassy. A short chat on the way to London and . . .'

A hand shot out and gripped the woman's shoulder, pulling at her. Deborah Carrington, amiability gone, said loudly, 'The Señora is not going into London. Her plans have changed.'

'But . . .' said the woman urgently. 'I assure you I was promised . . . I'm . . .'

And then Clare was in the car with her parents and drawing away. Peering through the back window, she saw two security men close in on the reporter as Deborah bundled Concepción into the car behind. In the distance, two men bent to roll up the red carpet and more men lifted and trundled away the troughs of lobelia, geraniums and carnations. As the limousine rounded the corner of a hangar, the runway was cleared. Nothing remained.

Turning back with a sigh of pleased anticipation, Clare found beside her the slumped figure of her mother, hands covering her face, sobbing quietly.

[15]

'Oh fucking hell,' said Judith, sweating with rage as she watched the car disappear. The guards let her arms go as she twisted away. Around her, a group of cameramen screwed covers over their lenses, talking and laughing. One of them, a leather-jacketed fellow with tousled hair, grinned at her.

'How about that, then?' he said.

'How about what?' said Judith crossly. She felt frustrated and humiliated and if this bastard was about to crow, she'd have his guts for garters.

'It's all in here,' he said, smiling hugely and smacking one of his bags. 'Man, that's a dishy Head of State and caught bang to rights. Better than Marilyn Monroe, that was.'

'Yeah,' said another cameraman. 'Wait till they get on eyeful of *this* at the paper.'

'Eyeful of what?' said Judith. She was still seething. Made it in time, after all that, just as Lady Clare had walked on to the tarmac, and then pushed away by that sodding American tart.

'Come to think of it,' said tousle-head, his face falling, 'they'll never use 'em. They'll have a D-notice slapped on 'em by the time we get back to town.'

'So what?' A third man in the group hoisted his bags on his shoulder. 'There's ways and means. *Gente. Stern. Paris Match.* Don't you worry, lads. There's money at the end of this rainbow.'

Together, guffawing, they shambled away. Judith ran after them. 'Here,' she said anxiously, 'I'm from the *Chronicle*, did I miss something? What are you on about?'

'When did you get here, then?' asked tousle-head. When he heard her answer, he slapped his thighs. 'Did you miss something! You got a *Chronicle* man here, a photographer?'

Judith shrugged. 'I think so. Yes.'

'Ask him,' he said. 'Unless he was up late, too. Hey ...' he called to the men in front, '... La Dorada, they call her. The Golden Lady. Now we know it's true, don't we? All over, huh?' The men roared, shoving at each other, sharing some private joke.

Worried, her head beginning to ache, Judith walked away from the noise of the men to find her car.

Mrs Adelaide Harker, Lancashire housewife and mother of four, put her elbows on her neighbour's garden wall, carefully avoiding the strands of flowering jasmine. 'Hullo, Mrs Simpson,' she said and then, formalities over, 'did you see her on the telly? Well, I couldn't believe my eyes. I said to our George, well, I said, whatever next. A lady like that, meeting the Queen, and there she is, standing there and I couldn't believe my eyes ...'

Nigel Weston, starting his Citroen GSA in Virginia Water, caught sight of his neighbour Tim Laidlaw-Hardy in the rear view mirror and rolled down the window. 'Tim,' he said, craning round, 'did you see what we saw on the box?' Already, the other man was nodding, coming closer. 'That Lady Clare arriving? What about that, eh?' Tim's face loomed at the window, moustache quivering. A low rumble emerged from beneath it. Seconds later, they were both bellowing with laughter.

Mrs Harker, Mr Weston and Mr Laidlaw-Hardy were not alone. In pubs and pool halls, in shops and offices, in garages and schools, on the floor of the Stock Exchange, in the canteen at the Houses of Parliament, on street corners and on village lanes, four million television viewers asked each other had they seen

[273]

what they thought they'd seen or nearly seen or been told about by others who had seen or thought they'd seen and told each other, over and over again, that they couldn't believe their eyes and expressed to each other their shock or laughed shockingly or were shocked into laughter, according to their natures. The air of England hummed with telephone calls, buzzed with the scandalized chatter, vibrated with guffaws and titters and all manner of expletives. Some people even went back to their morning newspapers, turning the pages and staring in frustration at yesterday's photos as if they expected them magically to change and put a seal on what had glimmered for a tantalizing moment on their screens. Everyone who could kept their televisions on, waiting for someone official, someone behind glass, to confirm that, yes, they had seen what they knew they had seen, to make it certain, to make it real.

'Will it be on again?' a small freckled secretary recently hired asked her harassed boss, the producer of 'News At Six'.

'Will it hell,' said the producer, running his fingers through his hair for the eighteenth time that day. 'What do you think we run here, sweetie, a soft-porn show? The lady is already on the cutting-room floor.' As it happened, he was wrong. The offending strip of film was carefully sealed in a jiffy bag and on its way to Station RIA in Rome, where the Floor Manager of 'News At Six' had friends.

Nearby, at the *Daily Chronicle*, the central table in the News Room had its horribly gouged surface covered by still-wet contacts. A small crowd of reporters jostled round them, and as the word spread more were pushing through the swing doors. Judith ran up the stairs two at a time, still jingling the keys of her car. All the bloody Sunday drivers in the world had packed the road back from Heathrow, the drive should have taken a half hour and here she was, an hour and a half later. As she erupted through the doors cursing her luck, Andy, looking distinctly less languid than usual, turned and saw her.

'And here she is,' he said loudly over the hubbub and the ringing of telephones, coming towards her. 'Judith, the *Chronicle*'s Woman on the Spot. Where were you, madam, when the crotch hit the fan?'

'What?' said Judith panting, pushing the hair from her eyes. Andy gestured at the table and she walked across with him and looked down. After a pause she said hoarsely, 'I don't believe it. It's not possible.' She picked up one of the contacts, looking from it to Andy, stupefied. 'When did this happen?'

'When did it happen?' Andy's voice rose. 'You were bloody *there*. The whole bloody world must have seen it. Don't tell me you didn't.' He stared at her, noticing for the first time her bewilderment. 'Fucking hell, Jude. Did you get a splinter in your eye at the vital moment or what? You were supposed to *talk* to her.'

Judith moved slowly along the table, pushing between the men to stare at each glossy contact. Impossible, incredible but there she was. Lady Clare, a wraith in the sun at the top of the plane's steps with a drift of gossamer skirt billowing upwards and below, a shockingly white expanse of skin, a gold triangle, white thighs cuffed by gartered stockings, graceful legs, high-heeled shoes. The gloved hand held high, waving, the smiling face half-hidden, the gold triangle wholly exposed. Oh God, Judith thought, hurting for her, the poor woman, the poor idiot woman, poor thing. As she gazed, whiffs of sweat assailed her, the men hemmed her in nudging and shoving, pawing the prints, punching each other, guffawing.

'Always said those South American dictators were twats.' Laughter.

'At least she's got no knickers to get in a twist.' Laughter.

'Freudian slit, eh?' Laughter.

'Wow, that's one Fascist I'd like to get up.' Laughter.

'Ventura's First Cunt Reveals All.' Cunt, laughter, laughter, cunt.

The word hammered unendurably, all round her and Judith exploded, the tensions of the day boiling from her guts. 'Fuck off, all of you,' she shouted, throwing herself at the table and scooping the prints nearest her in a wild sweep on to the floor. 'Bloody pigs. Haven't you seen a cunt before?'

The men's faces swam before her, hot, red, contorted, damp. Hateful, hateful men.

'Come on, Jude.' Andy's voice was rough. 'Cut it out, you lot. Bugger off, for God's sake, the show's over.' Judith stood breathing deeply. She scrubbed at her face, smearing newsprint across her forehead.

'It's all *right*,' Andy said, patting her impatiently. 'Forget it, forget them. What did you expect? We won't use the photos anyway, you know that. No one will.'

'You wanna bet?' said Judith, mopping her eyes. 'In a world full of male pigs, someone will print them.'

'Abroad, maybe.' Andy held the contacts in a fan in his hands.

'Here,' said Judith.

'Such a kerfuffle,' said Elizabeth Regina. She gazed across the tops of the trees in Green Park, the ivory telephone at her ear.

'It was frightful,' said her sister, a tinny voice in the receiver. 'I mean, it's happened to us all at times, hasn't it? Can't entirely be avoided. But at least one makes sure one is suitably clad. You remember Anne last year, all over the papers, of course, but naturally she had taken the proper precautions. Those bloomers looked rather Arctic I thought but ...'

'I didn't see the arrival myself,' the Queen said. 'I was in Whitehall. Philip told me when I got back, said Sir Michael couldn't bring himself to inform me of the details.' She pursed her lips to counter a small smile and deepened her voice. 'My dear, how could Clare have been so remiss?'

In her Wedgwood blue sitting-room ten miles away the

Princess shrugged. 'Really, one can't begin to guess. She was always, well, prone to scandal but I cannot imagine ...'

'So she was.' Elizabeth's mind flew back. What was that rather unsavoury episode to do with Clare's clothes, or rather the lack of them, when Charles was ... well, it didn't matter now. 'However, I have to make a decision about the dinner. There's really no precedent. One can't trust the newspapers not to publish and, besides, so many people must have seen it happen on television.'

'A diplomatic illness is called for, I think,' said the Princess, smoothing her own heavily petticoated lap with some satisfaction – no danger there of an errant breeze causing an Incident.

'You're quite right, that is surely best. I'll get on to Sir Michael immediately and he can talk to the La Fontaines. Poor Mamaine, I feel for her.'

The Queen let her hand rest briefly on the receiver as she put it down and then picked it up again. There were problems with Diana, of course, but thank heavens not of this sort. What a *foolish* gel. She permitted herself a small, rather irritated snort of laughter and began to punch buttons.

'*No.*' In the car, Clare's hands had flown protectively to her breasts, had crossed themselves there, warding off this evil that had splintered her happy day. 'It isn't possible. Ma? Pa?' Her face was imploring. 'Oh no, no, *no.*' By the time Clare knew the answer was yes, they were on country roads and the Earl was able to signal for the car to draw up by a discreet hedgerow, where Clare was copiously sick.

Mamaine could honestly say she felt most unwell herself. At Tucolston, in her own sitting-room, she tweaked viciously at the brown edge of a dying fern. Minutes after their arrival home the expected call had come from the Palace. Most sympathetic and very final. Her heart bled – she could feel it leaking under her ribs – at the thought of the small fortune she had just spent on that Givenchy dress, still in its tissue paper upstairs. What had she done to deserve such disgrace and such a daughter? Where on *earth* was Geoffrey?

'For heaven's sake stop crying, child, you'll make yourself ill.'

The monotonous sounds coming from Clare grated nastily on her nerves. The girl had always been a trial, her cross, always, but this time she had outdone herself. Unforgivable, really unforgivable. And how unprepossessing she did look, with those black runnels all down her face and her lipstick horribly smeared. Mamaine flicked with the toe of her shoe at the rumpled edge of a rug and began to pace up and down the room. She quite saw now why the Queen had not approved. A sixth sense; inherited, no doubt, a part of the Royal DNA. Just imagine if Clare had been the Princess of Wales and this had happened.

'Get out of it, Beulah! Nellie. *Nellie.*' Mamaine's voice, normally so modestly pitched, blasted Beulah's tail between her legs as Nellie, bewildered beyond measure, scuttled in and hauled the dog out. Clare did not stir.

No, of course, such a thing was unimaginable. Royal skirts did occasionally rise, the wind being no respecter of rank, but it took Clare to co-operate so fully with its importunacy. Worse, though she herself found no atom of humour in the situation, Mamaine was well aware that humour was inherent and one could fight anything but laughter. The Princess might well be laughing at this minute. The Queen herself could be having a quiet smile. At the thought, her cheeks grew mottled. This was a hot flush that no amount of time would cure. Oh damn Clare, damn her.

She paused in her nervous prowling and inserted a handkerchief none too gently between Clare's hands. As she did so, Lord La Fontaine came through the door and stood frowning at the two women. He was out of uniform now but his face was still a dull crimson.

'Been trying to get some sense out of that maid of yours,' he said to Clare's bowed head, 'but she's in no better state than you are and she can't speak a word of English, anyway. Clare. Pull yourself together, girl. We've got to talk.'

'Geoffrey.' Mamaine's voice soared to a high quaver as she leant against him. Her husband drummed impatiently on her back.

'No good moaning, woman. We've got to get to the bottom of this.' He paused and looked uneasily at his daughter. 'Dammit. No wonder we're a laughing stock. Can't say a word without some double meaning.' He put his hand heavily on Clare's shoulder. 'Were you drugged, girl? Was that it?'

'I can't remember, Pa.' Clare's face, raised to his, was streaming, she howled the words. 'I can't remember a thing. I was asleep, I woke up, the next thing I was walking down the stairs. Oh God, I wish I were dead.'

There was only the faintest trace of regret in the Earl's voice as he said, 'Well, you're not.' He sat down. 'But you are ill. Very ill. Far too ill to attend the Buck House dinner or fulfil any of your engagements while you're here. Probably best if you go back to Ventura as soon as possible. People forget. It'll be a nine-day wonder. We'll send you off from Cardiff or Northolt or somewhere and that'll be an end to it.'

'And Raul?' Clare whispered. 'How shall I explain what happened to Raul? He'll be ...' The thought of Raul suddenly terrified her. Nothing could have been so perfectly calculated to outrage him. She could hear his voice as if it were in the room. Puta. She shivered.

'I should think he knows already. He'll have heard from the Embassy. You'd better get on to him now, that's my advice. Now.'

Clare turned her blotchy face to her father. Her eyelids were so swollen that she could hardly see him. 'How could they have let this happen, Carrington and Concepción? Concha. How could she have let me go out there, how could she?' Piteously she said, 'I thought she was my friend.'

'She's a maid,' said the Earl and his eyes closed as if in prayer. 'And a foreign one, at that. It's your responsibility in the end, Clare, no getting out of it.' He shook his head as if a cloud of flies surrounded him. 'But that's not important now, blame. We'll just have to batten down the hatches and wait, lie low for the time being.'

'Where is Carrington?' The very name made Clare feel ill.

'That American girl? In London, I imagine. At the Embassy. Doing what she can to straighten out this mess.' The Earl turned to his wife, nearing the end of his tether. 'Mamaine, could we for the love of God have something to drink?'

After her outburst, Judith had gone home, diving down her basement stairs like a rabbit with a ferret on its tail. She was horribly aware that she'd made an exhibition of herself like that stupid Clare and she was going to have to come up with something to redeem it. When Charlie rang to say he was nearby and could he drop in, she began to say no but her voice was drowned in the call-box pips, so he came. By then, she had fortified herself against the day's misfortunes with several undiluted fingers of Scotch.

'You were there, eh?' Charlie said as she let him in. 'Here, what was it like? Fancy you being there.' He looked at her admiringly. That made a change, Judith thought sourly, but her battered ego rose to the bait. Walking over to her briefcase, she took out the contact she had stashed in it and watched him while he scanned it, drawing in his breath. When he looked at her again, his eyes were shining.

'Wow,' he said, 'ain't that something?' Holding the contact, he came to stand close to her. 'Come on,' he said, 'let's play games.' He bent down and eased off her shoes. When she was bare-footed, still wooden with surprise, he knelt and reached up under her skirt, pulling down the scrap of lace she wore.

'Women shouldn't wear panties,' he said, nodding at the photograph. 'She doesn't.'

'And look where it got her,' Judith said and giggled. Things were looking up in more ways than one. What a dirty beast this Charlie was. Men were. Oh, what the hell.

'What did you do to your wrist?' she asked. He took no notice.

'Turn round,' he said, 'go on, give us an eyeful.' He put his hands on her waist and spun her and she went on spinning, rising on her toes, her skirts flaring. She felt better, the air was cool, her thighs made a soft whisper as they brushed against each other. Then, off balance and dizzy, she fell against him. He held the photograph between them.

'You hiding something under there?' he said sternly, twitching her skirt.

'Me, sir? No, sir. Please, sir.' Games.

'You're telling fibs, ain't'cha? Go on then, up with 'em. Lessee.'

She stood still and a good ache began inside her. Slowly, she flounced the hem of her dress. He knelt and on his knees watched as she raised it.

'This one likes to show herself.' He stabbed a finger at the print. 'You like it too, don't you?'

'Never,' she protested. She looked down at his seal head and felt herself grow moist. She wanted violently to fuck.

On the bed, he put a pillow under her hips and carefully lifted her skirt to cover her face. Then he moved her thighs apart.

'Naughty,' he said. 'All wet. You want it?'

'No no no.' Her voice was muffled, her lips trembled with anticipation. Charlie's face, what she could see of it, bore a wolfish grin. The photograph, she saw, was still in his hand.

'Make room for me then.' Now she saw he held a candle in his hand, one of a pair he must have whipped as he passed from the dining-room table. 'Go on, games.'

'Dirty devil.' She gave a false shriek and turned her head away,

[281]

nursing her lust, afraid only that she would come before he entered her.

He put the candle in her hand and, staring at him, watching his flickering tongue, she pushed it slowly into her. The room was silent except for the rasp of his breath. Judith closed her eyes and moaned.

'Oh please. Now. *Now.*'

Then his tongue was flickering on her. 'This is the cunt that ought to hit the headlines,' he whispered once, his lips glistening. 'This one here.' His furry head plunged again and Judith sank into delicious darkness and gently came and then he was in her and she held his smooth head and shouted as he shouted and the games were over. He left her lying flung out on the rumpled bed and she slept and when she woke, she saw that the photograph had gone. The room in twilight looked bleak and rather dirty, there were thin strands of cobweb hanging from the ceiling and the air smelt of ash and the nauseating fruity odour of uncapped Scotch. Judith, trying not to think of what had happened to that woman and her own outrage and then her own games, felt suddenly extremely depressed.

'It's amazing,' Charlie told Alice in the flat later. 'You wanna see the photo? There she is at the top of the steps, not a gold hair out of place, except her skirts are round her ears and she's mother-naked and the whole world's getting a dekko at her little bush.'

Alice, moving heavily about with a duster, said, 'What, Charlie? What bush?' She tried to sound interested.

'Alice, where have you *been* today?' He frowned briefly and wiped his mouth. Then he explained. Clare. Heathrow. On the steps. Skirt up. No knickers. On the telly. 'Everyone's talking about it,' he said. 'The Princess was there and all.'

She stopped dusting and stood twisting the yellow cloth. The skin of her face flushed almost as deeply as the mark on her cheek and then she was white. 'Oh, my poor Clare,' she said. 'How terrible for her. In front of the cameras and everything. How will she ever get over it?'

'Well, it's down to her, isn't it? A State visit, all those maids she must have running round her and no knickers. She must be a nympho or bonkers or both.'

'How do you mean, a nympho?' Alice put a hand on the back of the sofa, looking intently at him.

'I mean,' Charlie said, doing his Groucho Marx lope round the table, stroking an imaginary moustache, growling, 'I mean, my girl, she must be kinky about wearing no knickers. It must turn her on, meeting all those VIPs., having all those cameras pushing up against her and knowing there's nothing more between them and her than a smidgeon of silk and under that her bare cunt. That's what I reckon. Only this time they've called her bluff.'

The heavy stone that had lodged itself in Alice's stomach seemed likely to break through her ribs. 'What do you know?' she cried. 'She's been shamed. Perhaps her life is ruined and all you can think is she likes it because *you* like it. Sitting there licking your lips, having a free peep show. And there's probably millions of men like you, gaping at her in her shame, getting erections. You're disgusting, all of you.'

'Alice.' Charlie's voice was half amused, half concerned. He couldn't remember when she'd made such a long speech and been so vehement. 'Don't carry on, lovey.' He went to her and, tipping up her chin, wiped at the tears. 'What's my little girl doing, saying rude words. Erection? You never said that before.'

Alice turned herself away from his arms, still crying. 'I'm not a little girl,' she said and put up a hand to push the tangled hair out of her eyes. 'You don't know, Charlie. You don't know me any more.'

'What don't I know?' He tried to hug her again but Alice shrugged him off. 'Here, what's wrong? What's the matter?'

'Nothing,' said Alice. She went across to the window, stared out a moment at the fluorescent sky and tugged the curtains closed. 'Nothing, Charlie. I'm just tired.'

Women were funny creatures, thought Charlie. You never knew what might set them off, even Alice, sweet Alice. He'd better watch it. He could be a crude bastard at times, he knew, and little Ally was still the prim country girl, in spite of having a nipper and all. He didn't want her to change, either. Primness was sexy. But then, he ruefully reminded himself, what isn't sexy to you, Charlie-boy? That Judith isn't prim, not by a long chalk, blimey no, but she wasn't half sexy. Acknowledging this — a quick vision of a dark room, white legs, red lips engorged — stirred and then vaguely upset him. He loved Alice, that was different. Her and the boy. They were his family. He gave a deep sigh and walked to the fridge. Maybe Alice had a beer in for him.

'Hey.' Charlie held the fridge door open and his eyebrows shot up. Inside, in its lighted cavern, the shelves were packed. Juice, yoghurts, several cheeses, a chicken, frozen veg, cellophane packs of various kinds — mince, kidneys, even a chunk of what looked like steak. Usually the light merely emphasized the empty wastes. 'Looks like Tesco's in here. Beer, too. Carlsberg. What did you do, win the pools?'

'Yes,' said Alice. There was a short, enquiring pause. 'Mum sent me some money.'

'Well good on Mum,' said Charlie. He took out a beer can and lifted off its metal flange with a discreet hiss. 'And I've got a bit of work, came up to tell you this morning but you weren't in. Must get a key cut. Yeah, a bloke I know wants me to spell another geezer on holiday. Doing bills at a garage.'

'How much?' said Alice from the bedroom.

'Seventy-five the week.'

Alice thought of the fifty one-pound notes Ronnie had stuffed in her pocket as she'd struggled out with the baby. She couldn't think further back than that, her mind made little forays and recoiled in revulsion. Ronnie had said 'tomorrow, then?' as she left. She had avoided his eye but she had nodded. If she returned, she would make a hundred pounds for two mornings' work. She held on to that. A hundred pounds, three weeks' rent. But how could she return, after ... after ...

'Seventy-five,' said Charlie loudly. 'Not too bad, is it?'

'No, Charlie. That's fine,' said Alice brightly.

Later, after Charlie had fried the two steaks and made a salad, a really posh salad of lettuce, spring onions, tomatoes, a whole avocado chopped and a nippy dressing, they sat on the sofa together, Charlie giving occasional small burps of contentment.

'Ta, Mum,' he said and Alice smiled. Then he glanced at his watch and switched on the television. 'The news – let's see if they show that Clare again.'

They did. A woman's powdered voice talked down the shining dot in the sky. The plane stood gleaming. The door opened. For an instant they saw a fragile white figure. Then she was in the crowd, shaking hands, kissing the Princess, chatting at the bobbing microphones.

'You and your fantasies,' said Alice. Her voice was happier now. 'You're not careful, they'll come and lock you up.'

'They've cut it out,' said Charlie, leaning forward. 'They've hopped her off the stairs where it happened.'

The woman's voice droned on, picking out the dignitaries as they came to greet the visitor. 'The Princess,' she said, 'looking chic as always in a charming feathered hat and there is Lady Clare's father, Earl La Fontaine, Lord Lieutenant of the ...'

'I've got the photograph,' he said. 'Right here in my pocket.' He patted his side, scrabbled at it. 'Look, Alice ...'

'I don't want to,' said Alice.

On the screen, the little figure turned and waved to the cameras and was replaced by a man's face, sad and baggy-eyed. 'Unfortunately,' he said earnestly to Charlie and Alice, 'that looks like the last glimpse we will have of Lady Clare on this visit. In a bulletin issued from Buckingham Palace this evening, the

Queen expresses her deep regret that owing to the sudden indisposition of Señora de Toro y Plata the dinner planned in her honour has had to be cancelled. Lady Clare is now resting at her parents' Lincolnshire home under medical care.' Papers crackled dryly on the newsdesk. 'And now ...'

Charlie pointed excitedly at the screen. 'You see, Ally? I told you. She got the wind up, literally. They've had to pretend she's ill. And I've got the picture. There's money in that, Ally, I can smell it. Tell you what, that photographer bloke in the pub, he'll know where I can sell it. The one I told you about, does the modelling stuff. I'll find him in the morning, get a good contact in Italy or somewhere. Money, money, money.' He almost danced, rubbing his hands.

A wave of fear flashed through Alice. There was a dead taste in her mouth. If Charlie got into that studio ... the thought made her physically sick. She'd counted on the fact that even if, by sheer chance, he saw those photos in a magazine, he couldn't possibly know it was her. But if he went to Ronnie's place, went into that dark room where the photos were pegged out to dry, they might show all of her and he'd know and then what?

On the screen now was a large man in a dog-collar. 'The ordination of women,' he said in a stringy voice, clearing his throat, 'is one of the main obstacles to the reunification of the Churches. Catholics continue to feel strongly that ...' He had a small sparse beard and a wisp of a moustache. Between the two, his lips showed red and rubbery. Alice put her hand across his face and switched off.

'Beddy-byes,' said Charlie. He stood up in the dark room and put both hands round Alice's breasts, kneading them gently. His thumbs touched two moist circles on the front of her dress and he pressed himself to her, fumbling at the buttons that ran from the collar. A warm full breast pushed through, a brown raised nipple with a bead of milk at its tip. He bent, fastened his mouth upon it and sucked greedily. Alice's knees began to shake, the

[286]

tiny pulse in her breast sent tendrils of sweet pain flowering in her body. But dread kept her alert, Charlie had to be stopped from meeting the man. She pulled away and made an angry face.

'You mustn't, Charlie.' Her usually soft voice was hard.

'Aaah,' he said, cushioning her breast.

'I don't mean *that*,' she said. 'You mustn't sell the photo. It's wrong. She's my friend, I won't let you make money from her. What must she be feeling now – and poor Lady Mame?'

He took his hands from her breasts and frowned. 'Come *on*, darling. Your friend? What did she ever do for you, up there in her castle? You was just one of her peasants, she doesn't give a toss for you. It was her fault, the whole thing and we need the cash.'

'No,' said Alice loudly. 'You don't know some things, Charlie, for all you think you're smarter than me. She had no side, Clare, anyone at home'll tell you that, not with us that she knew, any rate. She and me, we played together like any two kids.'

'You *were* any two kids,' Charlie said. 'Did you think she was better than you, being a Lady with a big L? I don't know. You're a funny lot, you country bumpkins. Back in the Dark Ages, you ask me.'

'I'm not asking you.' Alice buttoned herself up, facing him. This was as near a real quarrel as they'd ever had and the thought crossed her mind that she mightn't have stood up to him for Clare's sake alone. She was mostly doing it for herself. For them. 'Promise me,' she said, 'promise you won't do anything with that photo.'

'Alice.'

She uttered a final threat. 'I'd love you less if you did. I would, Charlie.'

'Okay,' said Charlie. 'Okay.' He didn't look at her. He went into the small hall, pulled on his anorak and shouldered the canvas bag he always carried. 'I'll be off, then.'

Alice, at the door, put a hand on his arm. 'It wouldn't be right, Charlie, earning money that way. You see that, don't you?'

'Oh sure,' he said gruffly, 'better to sponge on your Mum, right?' Then he went, not kissing her, not looking back.

In the silence after his departure, Alice stood looking down at the baby in his crib. He lay so still, so quiet, he could be dead. She leaned down, picked up the swaddled body and hugged it to her, rocking herself to and fro. She pushed her nose into the warm neck and inhaled the milky baby smell. Oh baby, baby, what is your mother doing, telling such lies?

The baby's eyes blinked open, his arms jerked out, his head wobbled, he gave a shriek of alarm. Five flights below, Charlie heard his son cry and looked up. The windows of the flat were dark. He ground his fists deeper into his pockets and crunched away across the gravel, head down.

A terrible day, a worse evening. Raul's voice, as clear as if he had been standing over her had been measured and cold, without pity. He had mocked her. Remorselessly, he went through the shameful details, almost as if he had been there. Evidently, he had been well briefed. She had brought shame on him and shame on his country, she had dishonoured a people, she had dragged the name of Ventura through the mud. He had always known that she was a whore, now the whole world knew. There was no repairing the damage. Her project with the women was finished, they would soon hear of her shame, their precious Dorada, naked in London, naked in front of the British Princess, in front of the British people. The women of Ventura would not want their own honour stained by her dishonour. She was ludicrous, unfit, an embarrassment to everyone who had put their trust in her. She was nothing. Nothing.

She had tried to hold back the glacial tide with explanations. The episode had been due to circumstances beyond her control – that familiar official phrase Raul so often used himself.

'The wind, perhaps,' said the cold voice, 'but not your clothing.'

'Raul, you yourself insisted that my whole wardrobe for this trip be made of silk. You said I should promote Venturan silk. It has chiffon in it. Fine, very thin ...' her voice trailed sadly across the ether.

The excuse was laughable and he laughed. 'I do not talk about the dress. Did you wear under it what every woman who is not a whore wears under her skirts? No, you did not ...' The tirade continued, there was a kind of triumph in his anger. Clare pleaded travel-sickness, dizziness, jet-lag, but he did not listen. When he mentioned her project, the women, Clare fell silent. A clot of misery began to bleed again inside her, draining her strength. She rocked on her feet and sat down.

'And Concepción?' She heard Raul say the name through the vacuum in her head.

'Concepción?'

'Where is she?'

'Here, with me.'

'Get her.'

'But Raul, why? I'll deal with her.' Clare roused herself from numbness in a vague alarm. 'It was not really her fault, she was ...' The voice of her husband crackled on. 'I know, I know, but she was truly so frightened, pitifully so. It was too much for her, that flight, she should not have come, she is still very shaken ...'

'Get her.'

Shivering, Clare put down the receiver and, pulling her satin dressing-gown around her, slipped out into the corridor and knocked on the next door to her own. 'Concha. Come quickly, rápido, rápido. El Presidente va a hablar.' Almost immediately, Concepción was beside her. Her thick black hair, unplaited now, sprang in a dark halo round her broad face, she wore a skimpy nightdress, her eyes had a yellow tinge and her skin was no longer smooth. Clare hustled her to the telephone. Concepción stared down at it as if a cobra were there, coiled to strike. Clare put the receiver against her ear and gestured. 'Speak, speak,' she whispered. Concepción looked despairingly at Clare. They were two women, trapped. Help me, said the black eyes. Help *me*, said the blue. Concepción crossed herself and gripped the telephone.

'Aquí Concepción, Señor Presidente,' she said softly. Clare watched and waited. She could hear the faint grate of Raul's voice, she could not make out what he was saying. She herself had screamed at Concha that morning, hysterical with nerves, blaming her for everything, threatening to fire her that moment and Concha had remained silent, her head bent, her rough hands clasping and unclasping, saying nothing in her own defence, only 'Forgive me, Señora. Forgive me.' She was silent now too, immobile, rigid. The room grew cold, the silence was almost audible, only the telephone buzzed like an insect enraged. Then, as Clare watched, Concepción sank on to the chair as if the bones of her body would not hold her erect any more. Never before had she sat in Clare's presence and now she sat and seemed in that position, no longer a maid, familiar yet somehow anonymous, but a woman like Clare herself, in a nightdress, suffering. Clare, looking down, saw the tiny black hairs that curled at the nape of Concepción's neck and the darker line of pigment that gathered there, saw for the first time with dim surprise that despite the fine puckers around her mouth and the pendulous breasts that hung low under the calico and the scarred hands, Concepción was still a young woman, perhaps only a few years older than herself.

With an angry click the telephone ceased buzzing and lay dead in Concepción's lap. Clare took it and clamped it back in place. Concepción did not move, she sat as if she could never move again. Beyond the velvet curtains in the velvet night, an owl made its comic, lonely sound. Uneasily, Clare touched Concepción's hand; it did not move. She picked it up and it lay a dead weight in her own, cold and unresponsive. Blank as an

Easter Island statue, Concepción stared ahead, her eyes hollow. Tremors rose in Clare. Stridently in the silent room she said, 'Well, Concha? What did he say, the President? *Concha.*'

Heavily, Concepción got up. She stood for a second with her arms hanging at her sides and then like someone walking in sleep she moved past Clare to the window. Mechanically she pushed the thick folds aside. Her face made a pale disc on the cloudy glass; she was looking at the sky but there were no stars that night, no moon. Clare suppressed a new surge of hysteria, covering it with an attempt at anger. Obviously, Raul had fired the woman and naturally enough that was a disaster to a peasant like Concha who had, Clare supposed, relatives to support besides herself, they all did in Ventura. Why was it that she knew so little about someone who had looked after her for so long, who had brushed her hair and run her baths and towelled her dry afterwards and smoothed her bed? And laughed with her and teased her out of sadness and soothed her when she was upset. Concha's face it was that she saw on wakening; her face the one upon whom she closed her eyes at night. Like a mother, a mother whom she had just discovered had once been young; discovered it with the same startled surprise as had come to her on seeing, for the first time, a girlhood photograph of her own familiar ageless mother and realizing, with a little shock, that she had a life, a history, dreams, friends of whom she knew nothing. But even so — Clare steeled herself — there was no need for Concepción to behave quite so eerily, like a tragedy queen, and at a time like this when she, Clare, needed help and consolation more than she had ever needed it before. Concha was still *her* maid, whatever Raul had said, yet she seemed to have forgotten that her mistress existed. She had brushed past her as if Clare were a ghost, invisible, insubstantial, in another dimension.

At that moment, Concepción turned from the window and walked back across the room, soundless on her bare feet. As she put out her hand to the door Clare said, sharply, 'Concha.'

Concepción stopped, her hand still outstretched. 'Concha,' she said again but this time, despite herself, her voice cracked into a plea and tears blurred her eyes. She blinked several times, quickly, but there were too many, they would not go away, they spilled over and fell along her cheeks. The fears of the day caught at her throat, clamped her brow, put heavy weights on the lids of her eyes. A lump at the base of her throat threatened to choke her. Anguished, hurting, she gave a low cry and put out her arms. Then, Concepción was holding her tight, patting her, rocking her, pushing back the sticky hair from her temple, putting a hand on Clare's hot forehead, a hand as cold as ice. The lump in Clare's throat eased, dissolved away, melted by that cold hand.

'It will pass, Señora. Mi querida Señora. It will all pass.'

The Spanish words in Concha's husky voice gave Clare peace. It would pass, it must. Her body, tense and strung, began to relax, muscle by muscle. In this bedroom in this house among the trees she knew so well, held by Concepción, calm invaded Clare. Once again she was a small girl going to sleep in a large four-poster bed with the clamorous future far ahead, unreal, unlikely, uninteresting compared with the joys of tomorrow, the picnics, the games, the soft muzzle of her pony and buttery crumpets for tea. The garish image of Ventura dwindled, a distant star. She tried to recall her husband's face and could not. The very word 'husband' seemed wooden, remote, ridiculous. The dressing-gown slipped down, eased by Concepción's gentle hands. The white sheets were drawn back, she lay between them, breathing the comforting smell of fresh linen, and Concepción tucked them round her tired body. She lay with her head sunk in the downy pillow, her hands folded at the sheet's hem and sleep engulfed her.

Some time – minutes? hours? – later, she heard in a dream the murmur of Spanish, saw in a dream Concepción kneeling at her bedside.

'Nuestro padre que está en los cielos santíssimo sea tu nombre ...'

Low and feverish, the words poured out and Clare looked into the redness of her closed eyelids, listening and not listening. A faint movement, a breath on her cheek, a flutter of a hand that passed over her, touching her hardly at all on one side, on the other, on her throat and her chest. The Cross, dreamed Clare, the sign of the Cross. Her eyes opened very slightly and looked into Concepción's eyes, black, impenetrable, unblinking. Slowly, Concepción nodded twice and her cold fingers closed Clare's eyelids as old women close the eyes of the dead.

'Goodbye,' she said softly. 'Adiós.'

Clare slept. In the branches of the great elm outside the bedroom window, the hunter rose on muffled wings and glided quietly out of the wood.

[16]

Swaying in their trucks on the 7.55 a.m. to Waterloo, the packed
herds opened their morning papers. A few turned to the letters
in *The Times*, some read with disappointment of 'an incident' at
yesterday's State visit. Lady Clare had been taken ill after this
'incident' the *Guardian* reported, and the dinner planned in her
honour at the Palace had been cancelled. But the many who had
bought the *Daily World* sat up suddenly, jostling their neighbours, alert and grinning. There was a buzz of voices, bursts of
male chuckles and female laughter. Rustling filled the carriages
as the *World* (in convenient tabloid form) was passed from hand
to hand.

In the space usually sacred to beaming and busty blondes
was a grainy blow-up of Señora de Toro y Plata, bisected
by a headline in bold caps that said DARK SECRET OF A FIRST
LADY. The 'A' framed and neatly blocked out the area between
the thighs. Above, an inverted convolvulus of skirt rose
on an errant breeze; below, long legs sheathed in stockings
tapered to high-heeled shoes. The layout was a triumph of
prurient prudery.

'We make no apologies,' announced the copy that ran down
the side of the page, 'for printing this photograph in a
family newspaper. The chickens of Fleet Street may squawk
but we on the *Daily World* believe in exposing dark secrets.
Our readers can take it. And what is Lady Clare's Dark
Secret? Not the one revealed here by a ghost of wind, oh no.
Her real secrets are the thousand Venturan citizens who lie
far beyond the range of the photographer's lens, beneath the

ground. Do not waste sympathy on her. Spare your tears for her victims.'

Poring over the *Daily World* spread that morning, eighteen national newspaper editors fumed.

'Can you beat it?' said Judith to Andy. The *World* lay on her desk, folded to the offending page. 'What about that for mega-hypocrisy? The *World* wouldn't know a dictator if he hit them with a rubber hose. Only last week they were gushing fit to bust about Lady Clare's loveliness and her exquisite silk frocks and how lucky we were to have her visit our humble realm. And I swear they had a travel piece, too. Wonderful country, Ventura, full of exotic folk, perfect for family hols. Honestly, their readers must be raving schizophrenics. Or are they blessed with instant amnesia?'

'Predictable stuff,' Andy said and smiled his tired smile.

'How can you be so calm about it?' Her early breakfast was curdling inside her. 'They don't have opinions, those twits. Just a series of unconnected farts.'

'They'll have a good fart after a beanfeast like this,' Andy said, slapping his hand on Clare's picture. 'Does wonders for the circulation. Judith, my love, I must leave you. I've got the editorial meeting.'

'So what are we going to do about it?' Judith trailed him to the door of the Features room, clutching the *World*.

'What do you suggest?' Andy paused in the corridor.

'I'll write something.'

'Around the picture.'

'No. Not around the picture. Andy, we're not using the picture?'

He shrugged and walked away.

Judith wandered back to her desk. The phone was ringing.

'Jude.' Min's voice was a bat-like squeak. 'You've seen the *World*?'

'The world has seen the *World*,' said Judith.

'That photo's going to be everywhere tomorrow. We've got to do the programme around it.'

'A *Which* Report on cunts, something like that?' Judith felt suddenly exhausted. She wished she was on a beach somewhere, as far away as possible from Fleet Street. Gold sand, blue sea, a blissful quiet. In her ear, Min's voice slid further upscale, it had all the seduction of a dentist's drill.

'Do you think it's funny, exploiting a woman like that?' Min said. 'Is it doing society some kind of service? That de Toro family have had their jackboots on Ventura since the year dot but the *World*'s only seen it since they looked up Clare's skirts. I tell you, Jude, it's a classic example of the way men use women's bodies to flog whatever nasties they've got up their sleeves at the time. Right?'

Judith sighed deeply. 'Since when have you been such an all-fire feminist, Min?' She held the receiver an inch from her ear, screwing up her face as she listened. Then she said, 'No. I don't think so, Min. A programme like that is just another way of getting your pound of flesh. If you'll excuse the expression.'

The telephone hummed angrily and clicked. Judith put it back in its cradle. Gloomily, she wondered just how much the Women's Movement had cost her over the years in lost wages. Other women on Fleet Street had grown fat on it, paid small fortunes by misogynist editors to sell their own sex down the river because sticking the knife in female backs was so much more effective when done by female hacks and the men's hands stayed sparkling clean. And here was she with a tax bill of over a thousand pounds lying at that moment on her dining-room table, giving up two hundred and fifty quid for the sake of a woman who probably spent more than that on nail polish. It didn't make sense.

'Hey,' Andy said. Judith swung in her chair. 'Popped out to

tell you A.K.'s given the go-ahead, the pic'll be in tomorrow. Better late than never. He wants you to write.'

'The exploitation of women by the media, no doubt.' She bared her teeth in a ghastly smile.

'Got it in one.'

Judith exploded. 'Jee-zus. The same fucking hypocrisy as the *World*, only arse to elbow.'

Andy popped his lips twice and frowned down at his clipboard. 'Look, Judith, we'd better get something straight. You're a first-class writer and we're all glad to have you aboard. But how many times do I have to remind you that we're running a newspaper here, not a W.I. house organ? I can't keep nursing your conscience, I haven't got time. I let A.K. know you had scruples about this and you wouldn't have cared for the look on his face.' He cleared his throat and looked down at her. 'What it comes down to, Jude. If you can't stand the heat, get off the pot. Or whatever.'

In the room, typewriters rattled, telephones rang, people shouted down them and across to each other. Bedlam. Judith thought of her first job, typing in a solicitor's office. The dusty air, the silence, Miss This, Mister That. The days had seemed endless, the people papery, thin stooks of bones moving through the years to the gold watch at the end of the tunnel and the Chairman's speech, cut short so that he could catch the 6.25 to Epsom and his tightly permed wife. She thought of Ruth and her dismal hair, the stern faces of the women in the pokey two-room offices of Smash Patriarchy, smelling of curry from the Indian take-away below. They wouldn't have her, free. On the few occasions she'd gone there to meet Ruth they'd eyed her dourly, with quite unwarranted suspicion. Or was it jealousy? Militant females like the SP lot despised talent because they hadn't got any themselves. They'd print anything, however turgid and boring, if it toed their particular party line, like the bloody Russians.

[297]

'Here comes the Star,' Ruth's friend Stella had said once, seeing Judith enter. She had hidden her hurt. 'You don't like stars, you better change your name, baby,' she'd said tartly but her quip was wasted, Stella merely looked blank. Those SP women were always ranting on about the wonders of collectivism – collective action, collective effort, the collective voice. It was their insult, to call another woman a star. 'Her? She's too starry,' they would say, their faces twisting with disdain, about any even mildly successful woman who had made it on her own, without the support of her sisters and without reflecting some collective view hammered out at endless dreary meetings till every thought, every word came out flat as a pancake or translated into a jargon that made your teeth ache to read. The other ploy they used was to treat you as a freak whose work and ideas, because they hadn't been consulted, were rootless and irrelevant, meaningless. Unless you continually waved the flag of some approved women's group, they cut you off. With them, it was all or nothing and if you wouldn't conform, you were nothing. They refused to see an obvious truth, that every effort, every book or painting or poem or piece of music or newspaper article done by an individual was also, by definition, collective because no one lived in a vacuum. The unconscious itself was collective; hadn't Jung called it the *racial* unconscious? The Women's Movement itself had coined the phrase 'The personal is political', yet now they sneered at the personal unless, of course, it came from the correct quarter in the correct way, which meant, Judith thought crossly, from a bona fide working-class woman who could hardly string two words together and had never heard of the Women's Movement. That was fine, that was o fucking kay, that triggered off an orgy of support and respect from Ruth and Stella and their ilk. But please don't come around with something good, something polished, something likely to be successful in the outside world because that sealed your doom with the fucking sisters. Would they never understand that every individual voice spoke from the depths of a shared mythology and the ancient brew of dreams?

Thinking, staring at Andy, Judith felt the hair on her arms rise in anger at her so unsisterly sisters. Briefly, Ruth's face came into her mind, shadowy and blurred and then it wasn't Ruth's face any more but her mother's, with little lakes of blood where her eyes should have been.

'Come *on*, Jude.' Andy's voice was tense with impatience, he stood over her rocking on his heels, one fist batting at his clipboard.

'Okay okay okay okay,' she said. 'Please sir, I'll do it sir, three bags full.'

He said carefully, 'That was in no way an ultimatum. Don't misunderstand me.'

'Of course not,' said Judith and smiled brightly. She stuck a pencil in the dial of her telephone and whirred it rapidly. 'Min? Wrong side of the bed this morning. Sorry. Will do. Yes, uh-huh. Fine.' To a passing sub she said, informatively, 'Can't make omelettes without breaking eggs, Kevvy-poo.'

'So they tell us, chick,' Kevin said.

The Earl, still in his dressing-gown, his jowls quivering, was bellowing down the telephone in his study.

'I give you fair warning, James, I'm going to sue every one of them for their last penny if they dare follow the *World*. Get on to the man *now*. No no no, not Blanchard, the other chap. Blanchard's thick as thieves with half the Press Lords, he'd be useless. Now I want an injunction slapped on every editor's desk by noon, d'you hear? A snowstorm. And, James, get onto the Palace, tell Wickerton what I'm doing, they can't be too pleased either. I've already had a personal word with Carter at the F O. Bent his ear. Look, I said, this is a damned outrage. Clare's a guest in this country, a guest of Her Majesty's among others and I shall not rest until those vultures regret the day they were born. So move, will you, and keep me informed. I'll be right here all day and I want *action*.'

'Geoffrey.' The Countess and several dogs appeared at the door, their thick tails flailing. 'I wish you'd have a word with Florrie.' She looked austere and uplifted, Saint Theresa in wellies. 'Father Garvey phoned. He wants to give a sermon on Sunday, something about Mary Magdalene and the first stone, I really couldn't understand him. But Florrie's being too tiresome. She's threatening to go round to the Priory now and hit him with her parasol. She's already torn up that wretched newspaper and thoroughly blocked one of the loos and then she forgot and used it and the water's all over the floor.'

'It's a Communist plot,' Lord La Fontaine said.

'No dear, it's Florrie, I *saw* her. That loo hasn't been right all this year, it drips underneath and there's a most off-putting smell but I don't think the Communists ...' She advanced into the room. '*Down*, Beulah.'

At his desk, the Earl put a fist to his forehead and screwed up his eyes. 'What's the name of that fellow at MI5, Mamie? The one who was my fag? Tottenham? Tooting? Beck, that's it. Gerald Beck. Hopeless at toast but a good man on Reds. I'll give him a call.'

Lady La Fontaine collapsed on a sofa among the dogs who scrambled up beside her and lay there panting. 'I can't do anything with Clare, either. She's lying up there, Geoffrey, looking quite dreadful. She's not going to wear well, that girl. There's something about her that reminds me of your mother.'

The Earl was prowling, his hands stuck in the pockets of his dressing-gown. 'Mark my words, Mamie, the Communists are behind this. I should have realized it immediately.'

'You'll tear those pockets,' Mamaine said. 'I must take the dogs out.'

'What better way,' the Earl demanded, 'to get at Raul, bring down his government? He's in trouble already, got terrorists skulking about in his woods, blowing up innocent women and children and every last one a Communist. Raul told me himself, at Christmas. His men had found stockpiles of Russian arms in some village. They're Cubans, half of them, or trained in Cuba. Men like that will stick at nothing to bring Raul down and, by God, I believe they've used my daughter to do it.'

Mamaine stood up, brushing hopelessly at the hairs on her skirt. 'Clare's never been to Cuba, dear, as far as I know. Perhaps her maid is Cuban. She hasn't stirred yet, either. Really, it's too bad.'

'I don't know how they organized it,' said the Earl, 'but I know in my bones the Commies are the niggers in the woodpile. You hold up the First Lady of Ventura as a laughing stock and a loose woman to boot and bingo ...' he snapped his fingers, '... the Americans cut off aid and you're halfway to the Kremlin. Those peasants of Clare's adore her, don't they? Think the sun shines out of her elbow. What are they going to think when they see that picture? They're going to lose faith in her, turn to the Commies.'

'But Geoffrey.' She fought off one of the dogs. 'The peasants won't see that picture. They don't see English papers, Raul wouldn't permit it.'

'They'll hear all about it, you wait and see. And that'll put paid to all Clare's work, whatever it was she was doing.' He picked up the telephone again. 'It makes my blood boil, Mamie. We'll have to use the big guns this time. This is war.'

As the Earl issued his battlecry, another higher cry sounded somewhere above them and continued, spiralling downwards, becoming louder. The Countess turned towards the door, fingers on the gold cross at her throat. Voices rose in a babble outside and screaming and footsteps, running. The door opened and Clare burst in, turning her white face blindly from side to side. For a moment she clung, swayed, to the edge of the door and then put her hands to her head and shrieked at her parents.

'She's dead,' she cried, 'Concha's dead. Oh God oh God oh God.' She crumpled to her knees, put her forehead on the carpet and broke into wild crying. The dogs bounded over and flopped down beside her, their tails wagging happily.

On the narrow bed in the small square room adjoining Clare's bedroom, the body of Concepción lay across the rumpled sheets, one arm flung out, the other folded on her breast. A tiny wooden cross was lodged within her fingers. The dark hair sprang from that still head but the face it surrounded was as blue as ice, glacial in death. Above the wide cheekbones, the slanted eyes were closed. On the table beside the bed, its lace cloth askew, a glass lay on its side and, beside it stood a little plastic phial, empty. At the foot of the bed, on another table, roots and stalks and some faded flowers were spread out. They were dry and brittle and rustled faintly in the breeze from a half-open window. Propped up against them was a piece of thick white card and a crumpled roll of paper. On the card, drawn heavily in wavering capital letters, was the name CONCEPCIÓN. It was the only word the dead woman had known how to write.

In the hot little room that housed *Smash Patriarchy* Ruth Maryschild argued heatedly with Bess and Helen, two of SP's regular contributors, over what the broadsheet should run as its lead story. Neither woman had been paid for their last three pieces, the coffers being at their usual low ebb, and this combined with the constraints of feminist democracy forced Ruth to control her words if not the pitch of her voice.

'But the Clare thing is an opportunity we mustn't miss,' she said, inhaling curry – the Bel Puri below was in full swing. 'We should defend her and the time is *now*.'

Bess swung her rucksack off her back and plonked it on Ruth's desk. Her freckled arms were red and her nose was peeling. 'Nukes are now, too, and tomorrow and next year. If there *is* a next year.' She frowned gloomily at Ruth. 'They're being arrested at

Greenham Common, you know, and not for indecent exposure. The nuclear issue is the ultimate patriarchal crime and if SP doesn't recognize that, then ...' She stuck two fingers at the room in general.

'Don't you see? They're one and the same thing. The Clare business, nukes ... they're both a result of patriarchy. They're linked.' Ruth permitted herself to sound fractious.

'Yeah?' Bess said. 'You won't think so when the nuclear shit hits the fan. We'll all survive Clare's little bombshell.' She pulled out a tobacco tin. 'Ever heard of cunts going critical?'

Helen flicked a matchbox into Bess's lap. She was small and plump and wore neon-red overalls that made her look like a radish. 'No,' she said earnestly, 'I see what Ruth means. I see what you mean, Ruth. And I see what *you* mean, Bess.'

'Look,' said Ruth, 'I've got a paper to get out. If you see what I mean.'

Helen scratched her forehead. 'No, listen. What I want to say is about this raid we did last week. That's what I think we should lead with. Those animals ...'

'Animals?' Ruth sighed loudly and glanced at the ceiling. 'Helen. This is the SP. Not the RSPCA.'

'You didn't *see* them, Ruth,' Helen's face scrunched up piteously. 'There were baby monkeys in the cages. Tied down. With things in their poor little heads, sticking out. And their faces. I shan't ever forget their faces. They haunt me.'

'Bastards,' Bess said, snorting out smoke like a dragon.

'I've got photos, everything.' She knelt and began to scrabble in a shopping bag. 'You're right, Ruth, it all links up. Men making bombs, men humiliating that woman and ...' triumphantly she held up a sheaf of photographs, 'men experimenting on poor little monkeys for nerve gas and radiation and goodness knows what else. Look. Just look.' She passed one to Bess.

'Shit,' Bess said. 'Oh shit.'

From below came the sound of scuffles and men's voices

shouting. Ruth shot to the window, heaved it up and screamed down. 'Shurrup, you. Belt up.' She slammed the window down again and the glass cracked in a fork up the pane. 'Bloody hell,' she shouted, her arms spread towards the women. 'I've got six pages. I can't smash patriarchy in six pages.'

'Get smashed yourself, then,' said Bess and passed her a joint.

Judith, who had spent most of the morning struggling for something original to say about Clare in her column, decided at lunch-time to run up and see her mother. She often did this when she had some particularly difficult piece to write. She needed to keep her finger on the pulse of the ordinary woman and who more ordinary than Mum? To Judith, she was an easily available one-woman Gallup Poll who had popped up over the years in her articles under an amazing variety of hats. In the last three months alone, she had starred as a miner's wife bewailing the hardship of managing on strike pay, an NHS patient bewildered by the secretiveness of doctors, the woman-in-the-street analysing the attractions of romantic novels and a British mother confiding her reactions to breastfeeding. This last had been a little naughty, perhaps – it was all of twenty-four years since Judith had suckled at those long milkfree glands – but, she consoled herself, what did time matter? The essential experience remained the same and the intricacies of breastfeeding were not matters she fancied discussing with strangers. Other ordinary women did not figure on the list of Judith's contacts and she was not about to start knocking on strange doors.

The jumble of Hackney roads were choked with traffic and the debris of morning markets and it was past one o'clock when Judith drew up in the parking lot at the back of the council flats where her mother had lived since her father's death from long overdue cirrhosis three years ago.

'You're too thin,' Brenda said, greeting her daughter on the graffiti-scrawled walkway to her front door. 'A good tonic is what you need.'

Brenda didn't look in need of a tonic. Widowhood had put inches on her hips and henna on her once dark brown hair. The gaunt face and suffering eyes of Judith's childhood had been replaced by plump cheeks and upturned sequin-studded glasses. Looking at her, Judith had to suppress a familiar resentment, douse the memory of a little girl desperately pulling at her mother's hand, yelling 'We'll manage, Mum, come *on*'. Mum had come on, all right, but not in time to save her child from misery. She had not made a move for Judith's sake. Judith had been dispensable, a sacrifice at the altar of female masochism. Betrayed.

'You know that Mrs Charlton?' They were sitting in the tiny kitchen, at what Brenda called her 'banquette'. The tea was too strong. Judith winced as it dragged at her throat and nodded. Mrs Charlton was one of two women for whom her mother cleaned, unknown to social security and, for that matter, to any friend of Judith's. Among her feminist acquaintances, cleaning ladies were heroic symbols, the archetypal oppressed women who serviced society, and it would have done Judith's status no good at all for it to become known that her mother was just such an archetype. It was perfectly acceptable, indeed points were scored, for a feminist to be raised by a charwoman mother but once the feminist was a Fleet Street star, an immediate change in the mother's situation was regarded as that daughter's duty. What none of them would have understood — and Judith had no desire to explain — was that her mother enjoyed every moment of her new role and would not have given it up for the world. She gossiped about her employers, well-off women in the Georgian terraces of Islington, with a cheerful fervour, causing pangs of jealousy to her daughter who frequently felt ignored in comparison.

'... bent down and couldn't get herself straight. Slipped disc.'

said Brenda, pouring out more black liquid from the teapot, her eyes twinkling behind the sequin studs. 'So she's going in for an operation and Cynthia's coming to look after her Dad. Giving up her holidays from that job, she is. I call that lovely.'

Cynthia, as Judith knew only too well, was Mrs Charlton's daughter who ran a highly successful catering firm cooking lunches for City businessmen. Whenever Brenda wished to reproach her own daughter with negligence of any sort, she cited Cynthia Charlton, who apparently managed by a kind of magic to combine a well-paid career with all the sacrificial devotion to her parents required of a caring daughter. Judith put her cup down in its saucer with an unnecessarily loud rattle.

'What d'you think of this Clare business, Mum?' she asked. It was already nearly two and she had to get back.

'Her?' said Brenda, drawing her breath through her gleaming false front teeth – teeth, Judith knew, that had been knocked out by her father on one terrible and endless night when she had cowered in her bed, shivering at the screams. 'I got no sympathy. She asked for it. As a matter of fact, I know a thing or two about that Clare, I don't mind telling you.'

'So tell,' said Judith.

Her mother leaned over the teacup, shunting it forward with her overall'd bosom.

'It so happens,' she said, peering at Judith over her glasses, 'Mrs Charlton's Cynthia was at university with that little madam.'

'Oh?' Judith said. 'I didn't know Lady Clare went to university.'

'Anyway,' said Brenda, drawling the word. 'They was both at a dance together, at Cambridge, it was. I think Prince Charles was there and all. So when her picture got in the papers at the airport, Cynthia said to her Mum she said Mum, that Clare was always stripping off. She stripped off at that dance too. Cynthia remembered. She's got a marvellous mind, has Cynthia.' Brenda sat back, well pleased with her nugget.

'Clare stripped off?' Judith jerked upright, staring at her mother.

'That's what Cynthia said. Mind, it wasn't in the papers that time, Cynthia said. Or maybe it was but they didn't know it was her. Something like that. So the point is, you don't want to waste your sympathy on her. She's an old hand at taking off her knickers in public.' Brenda sniffed her disapproval. 'Like another cup?'

Judith had two near-crashes before she got back to the *Chronicle* offices. She parked her CV on the double yellow line right outside the main doors and went straight to the third floor where the *Chronicle* library had its offices. She had Cynthia's telephone number in her pocket but the first place to check was the *Chronicle* files. Fingers quite painfully crossed, she asked the librarian for the 'May Ball' file.

'We've got two,' said the librarian. 'Pre-war, post-war.'

'Post,' Judith said.

Holding her breath, she riffled through the thick wadge of articles and photographs. And there it was, uncaptioned but unmistakable, once you knew. A grainy grey crowd of dancers and, in their midst, an unerotic figure with a cap of blonde hair, gyrating clumsily, the thin limbs clownish, a wide white brassiere and schoolgirlish knickers bound around her, the face turned into concealing shadow. But Clare, indisputably Clare.

Cynthia Charlton, called upon to witness the indisputability of Clare, was not pleased.

'Your mother had no right to pass on that information,' she said crossly.

'But it's true?' Judith said, holding the photograph across Cynthia's desk. 'That's her?'

'Well, yes. It's a mystery why the media didn't know in the first place, what with Clare being Charles's girlfriend at the time. The Queen found out quickly enough.'

'Thanks,' said Judith. 'Thanks a lot.'

Querulously Cynthia said, 'I'll have to tell my mother you know. It's not good enough, Brenda spilling the beans like this.'

But Judith had gone.

Her article next day, complete with a blown-up pic of Clare's so long anonymous girl's body, caused a minor sensation that frothed at the top of the continuing Clare saga.

'Clever girl,' said Andy, patting her back. 'A.K.'s eyes stood out on stalks when he saw it. I wouldn't be surprised if there's a raise for you in the air, you lucky lady.'

'Luck?' Judith said. 'Luck doesn't come into it, Andy. Hard work. Investigative journalism at its best.'

'Yeah,' said Andy.

Ruth's voice on the telephone crackled with disgust. 'How could you?' she said and boringly said it again. 'How *could* you, Judith? She was so young, it was just a bit of fun. You've deliberately reinforced every reader's prejudice against her. Don't ever say you're a feminist again in *my* presence.'

'Piss off.' Judith slammed down the phone, her fingers leaving damp marks on the receiver. Facts were facts and just because Ruth didn't want to face them was no reason for her to let off her disillusion on Judith. An acid wave of disgust with women in general rose from her guts and she snapped her purse open. Two Rennies would settle that. Sod women.

Mrs Charlton gave her cleaning lady notice on the grounds of breach of confidence. 'I'll see you're all right, Mum,' Judith said on the telephone, her voice raised against her mother's sobs. Serve the old bag right. At least she might take more of an interest in her daughter's job now, instead of rabbiting eternally on about the Cynthias of this world.

*

In Minnie's carpeted office the leaves that crowded the window boxes and sprayed from tasselled hammocks on the ceiling were so thick and glossy they seemed to have been cut from new green wellies. Knick-knacks cluttered every surface, a china menagerie of doggies and horsies and bunnies and moggies. A colour television chatted to itself in a corner. Judith, waiting for Min's arrival, scraped three nails clear of perfectly good varnish. As always, the place made her nervous, like a nomad who had wandered out of the desert into the front parlour of a Surbiton semi. Everything was neat and coyly merry, like the padded cocktail bar in a young executive's rumpus room that promised the hard stuff and delivered only Babycham and maraschino cherries. If Min worked for the *Chronicle* she'd be lucky to have a desk of her own, never mind a whole office complete with Ercol furniture, lined curtains, a wood-panelled fridge, a coffee machine, a personal secretary and a back-drop of London that looked like a panoramic scene shot from a helicopter. But then, Minnie wasn't really a journalist. She was a committee creature with committee ideas, a bit of this, a touch of that and a jolly spangled bow to hold it all together so that viewers at home could go on feeling at home. Like so many of her breed she couldn't stick her legs in a pair of knickers without looking over her shoulder for someone else's approval or for someone else to blame if she got in a twist. Compromise was what normal people did when they couldn't do anything else. Min compromised for a living.

'Duckie. *Ages*.' Jingling her bracelets, Minnie came through the door and offered her cheek for Judith to peck. The sickly odour of lilies of the valley came with her — my signature tune, she often said. 'Got any brilliant ideas for guests?' Into the intercom on her desk she murmured 'Moira? A moment of your time lovie please.'

'How about Diana Dors?' said Judith. 'We could pass her off as Clare on a binge after her trauma.'

'Very droll,' Minnie said. 'Clever piece you did this morning with that pic and all. Women must take responsibility for what they do, can't keep playing maidens all forlorn, blaming men for their misfortunes. I like it. Let's take that as the theme of the prog.'

'Could do,' said Judith, her eyes unfocusing. She disliked recalling articles she had written and never read them in the paper or kept copies. For some reason thoughts of them made her acutely uncomfortable and her mind skimmed away. Possibly she was too modest. Judith considered this interesting proposition as Minnie's secretary in trendy guerrilla gear came in and sat down, flicking the pages of her notebook.

'We've never said it out loud on the programme before, though we've dropped hints here and there. I've always thought it was for men to say but they don't much, nowadays.' Minnie shook her head, pondering this weakness in the male sex. Judith, twiddling a curl round her finger, wondered why she always got so angry with Ruth's militancy and so angry with Min's finking-out. It couldn't be because she was a moderate, a piggy in the middle. You didn't earn her sort of money being a moderate. It was because she had an open mind. That was it, an open mind.

'... so I thought,' Minnie was saying, '... that we could use the Clare affair as a peg and talk to women who do the sort of thing that libbers hate. Using their sex, you know? Moira, are you getting this down?'

Moira wrote busily. Judith said, 'Sex?' and raised her eyebrows.

'If Clare is the peg, sex must come into it,' said Minnie patiently, as to a backward child. 'She wasn't splashed across every newspaper because she was a well-dressed First Lady, was she?'

'No,' said Judith, picking at a thread in her coveralls. 'Can't you open a window?'

Moira got up and slid back a sheet of glass, revealing another one directly behind. 'Right,' said Minnie, 'we must get on. Theme: women are their own worst enemies. They pose for sexist ads, they flaunt themselves on cars and calendars, they strip off for pin-up mags, they appear in pornographic films. They do everything the libbers are against.'

'Don't say "libbers",' said Judith.

Minnie took no notice. 'We'll get one of these women on the programme, to tell us why she does what she does and what she feels about it. Okay?'

'I don't know that kind of woman,' said Judith.

'You see? You say that as if you thought they were contemptible.'

'I do,' said Judith. She didn't know yet if she did or not. It depended.

'Well, in a way, so do I,' Minnie said quickly. 'But we should give them their say . . .'

'. . . and it'll make good television,' Judith interrupted. 'Why, our Min, you're as good as any man when it comes to using women's sexuality for selling purposes, by gum you are.'

'Please,' Minnie said. 'Don't pull your more-feminist-than-thou act on me, Jude. We've got to book guests now.'

'I still don't know that kind of woman,' said Judith but she smiled at Moira as she said it, to signal a basically co-operative attitude.

Minnie opened a large address book on her desk. 'I do. There's a photographer . . . the one we used for the holiday programme, remember, Moira? Look him up, love, would you? He does beaver shots. We could talk to one of his ladies.'

'Beaver shots?' said Judith, warming to the project. 'I've always wondered what that must be like. Lying about with your cunt on show and a zoom lens an inch from your clit.'

Moira blinked sandy lashes at Judith, Minnie coughed and glanced around as if, thought Judith, the office was bugged.

'Pardon,' said Judith, clapping one hand theatrically to her mouth. 'Mustn't say rude words in front of china bunnies.'

'Since they slip so easily off your tongue, love,' purred Minnie, 'why don't you do the telephoning?' and she took the ivory receiver out of its cradle and held it up invitingly to Judith.

[17]

The local GP had been and gone. The cause of Concepción's death was obvious enough – a massive overdose of Nembutol. The phial belonged to Clare, it had been taken from her room. There would have to be an inquest but only as a formality. The Earl had departed with the doctor, heading for Lincoln where the Coroner, a personal friend, had his private residence. The first priority on the Earl's mind was the avoidance of further damaging publicity at all costs. Influence must be brought to bear and here in Lincolnshire, unlike the stinking ratholes of Fleet Street, Lord Geoffrey La Fontaine carried weight.

Concepción's body lay under a linen sheet in the upstairs maid's room she had so briefly occupied. Tall white candles flickered, the only light in the quiet room. Worn velvet curtains discarded last winter by Lady Florence – 'There's not a whole thread left in them, Mamie, what do you *do* with Raul's money?' – were drawn against an unmoved outside world. Lady Mamaine had retired to her own bedroom to placate an inexplicably vengeful God and the maids (the La Fontaines had maids again) had gone whispering excitedly to their own quarters, pledged to keep the news to themselves on pain of instant dismissal and worse. Clare was alone in the shadows, a ghost in a chair beside a ghost on a bed. She held Concepción's cold stiff hand in both of hers and stroked the rough skin as if it could be warmed to life again and move and stroke Clare back. Nothing was certain any more but that she must be with Concha every minute until the burial. She should not be left alone in a strange land until that land covered her. In the candlelight Clare's face was puffy with a grief that had caught her unawares. She had been wretched before but the wretchedness had begun to edge slowly into rage until this crippling blow. She was frightened now as well as miserable, afraid to move, afraid to act, afraid even to think. Fate had picked up her scent and was prowling even now outside, sniffing at cracks and keyholes, hungry to rake her again with its claws. Better lie low, frozen in her tracks, until danger passed, if it ever did.

Clare sat. Concepción lay. The candles fluttered and dripped, forming stalactites of wax on their silver columns. From the house around came muffled sounds of life: pipes rumbled, walls creaked, there were distant footsteps, a raised voice, three rings of a telephone. Behind the folds of the curtains birds sang in a blue sky, someone crunched along the gravel drive and far away an engine droned, a harvester perhaps or a tractor in a field. Once the door of the room opened a few inches and was silently closed again. Once Clare lifted the crucifix that lay on Concepción's sheeted breast and stared at the anguished mannikin there, wooden son of that worm-eaten wooden mother hanging on a stone in a ruin down a track in a rainforest half across the world. What connection had they with each other except in men's minds? Carefully she put it back, though what its purpose served she no longer knew. An amulet against evil, perhaps, but the evil had been done. 'And evil shall have no dominion,' Clare said aloud and thought of the dream she had had last night while Concha had been swallowing and swallowing the contents of her phial. She had been sitting at dinner in the Palace, surrounded by the blue-jowled faces of men who talked of incomprehensible things and filled her with foreboding. Concha had been in her dream, standing at the end of the table behind the men. She was all in black, only her face showed pale as a blossom. The men's voices rose, their eyes grew wide and white with anger, they shouted and cursed each other, thumping their fists, under Clare's hands the table shook with their thunder. Only Raul sat

[314]

still and silent but in her dream he was carved out of gold, not a human being at all. Then Concha was beside him, her white lips opening and closing. She was calling to Clare but her voice was drowned by the raging men, her mouth worked painfully but Clare could not hear, could make no meaning of those soundless cries. She had wakened with a thudding heart and her ears full of the cawing of rooks in the nearby churchyard.

Remembering the dream she remembered for the first time since Concha's death the things that had been on the table beside the bed, before she had screamed and run out. Where were they now? The table was bare, the cloth that covered it clean and creaseless. Clare looked swiftly round. Away from the amber pools of the candles there were only dim shapes. She got up stiffly and moved to the switch beside the door. Electric light flooded the room, eclipsing the candles. A mahogany chest stood at the far wall and leaning against it was Concha's battered suitcase, closed and strapped. Clare went down on her knees beside it, unbuckling the strap and clicking up the cheap tin clasps. It held Concha's few clothes, crushed in hastily by one of the maids. She felt around them, running her fingers between the layers. Nothing. Then she found a fabric compartment clipped against the suitcase lid. She slipped her hand in and touched a ball of crumpled paper, something scratchy and dry and the flat edge of a card. Still kneeling, she smoothed out the paper on the floor. A large typewritten label. Puzzled for a moment she stared at it and then understood. It was the label she had torn from the crate, the day she had found the women drunk. She had stuck it in her pocket and forgotten all about it. What had possessed Concha to rescue it, pack it, bring it to England and place it on her bedside table as she set about killing herself?

There were printed capitals on the top of the label that said FRAGILE – GLASS. Below was an address. 'Attencion Señor

K. J. Bogardus Jr, Research Development Corporation (US), Calle de la Virgen 34, Nombre Dios, Ventura.' Bogardus. The name was vaguely familiar. Was this Bogardus one of Raul's Americans, one of those men with close-cropped heads and square jaws who were always in and out of his offices on mysterious errands? Apparently, this American's errand was to receive crates of bourbon from the States and deliver them to a clearing in the jungle so that Indian women could drink themselves into a stupor on the stuff. It didn't make sense.

Clare drew the flat card from the suitcase compartment. Concha had written her name on it in huge wavering capitals – CONCEPCIÓN. Turning the card over, Clare saw that it was the frame for a photo. It was a Polaroid, already darkening, but it showed enough to drive the blood from Clare's face. Plane steps and a girl on them, her skirt blowing up and a light blue triangle beneath. Carrington, grinning amiably. Deborah-Jane Carrington in a replica of the photo that was now notorious, only that one was of Clare and the triangle beneath the skirt was not of fabric but of hair.

She laid the card down on the floor and crouched on all fours staring at it. After a while, the ache made her unclench her teeth. She was shivering in the close air of the room and her eyes stung. She closed them briefly and under her hands, flat on the floor, she felt something crumble. Sitting back on her knees she plucked a dead leaf from the carpet. Bits of it were stuck to her palm. Again she pushed up the lid of the suitcase and this time brought out, bit by bit, pressed flowers, the withered remnants of stalks, a fibrous clump of root, a thick node with stringy tendrils and, wedged in a corner, the tiny crisp corpse of a lizard. Clare's head was completely empty, devoid of thought, only her body was able to move. Over Concepción's clothes was a sheet of newspaper. Clare unfolded it and placed upon it the lizard and the dried plants from Manuel's bouquet, abandoned in her bedroom in the Palace. Carefully she rolled the newspaper over the plants, gathered up the label and the photograph and got to her feet. Dizziness made her stand still for a moment before she walked across to where Concepción lay and folded back the linen on the dear dead face. Her lips touched the cold brow and Concha's wiry hair brushed her forehead. Plunging the room into darkness, she went out and to her own room and put the rolled newspaper and the photograph and the label in a drawer. Then she returned.

The big basement room was warmer this morning. Two fan heaters, one on each side of the raised dais, gushed out dry air that blew balls of dust across the floorboards. Ronnie Garston, in one of the waistcoated business suits he favoured, was pushing a barn door flood across the room with his shoulder, a mug of tea in his outstretched hand slopping brown gouts across the floor behind him. Alice at the door, the baby on her back, flushed at the sight of him, took a nervous breath and coughed. Ronnie looked round.

'Hullo, here comes trouble,' he said jovially and raised the mug at her. He did not look jovial.

'No,' Alice said, ducking her head. 'No trouble.' She needed him on her side. 'I just wanted a word.'

'Oh yes?' He hadn't expected to see the silly cow again, after she'd gone all hysterical on him, pretending she hadn't liked what she obviously had. Was she here for more? She was acting coy again too, looking at him sideways, twitching away. That mark on her face looked bad in the morning light.

'Come on then, come in,' he said, jabbing his chin. 'I've got a model coming in a minute, you'll have to make it quick.'

His brusqueness unnerved her. She swallowed and sidled towards the table, keeping well away from him.

'I won't eat you,' he said and laughed abruptly.

'It's about ...' she started to stammer and paused, clearing her throat. 'It's my boyfriend, Charlie. He said he's going to get in touch with you. He mustn't see the photos.' Her hands were clenched in front of her. 'I don't want him to know that I've been here. Or what I did. Please don't tell him.' For the first time, she looked straight at Ronnie, panic in her eyes.

With pleasure, Ronnie realized she was going to cause him no aggro. Rather the other way round, perhaps. Play it cool, sunshine. There might be something worth having, here. His brain raced, trying to work out possibilities.

'What's he want, this Charlie of yours?'

'He promised me he wouldn't, he promised. But I couldn't bear it if he did, and saw . . .' she looked furtively round the room.

'You're not making sense,' Ronnie said, purposely cold.

Alice made an effort to pull herself together. She straightened up. Those boobs, Ronnie thought, those boobs.

'He's got a photograph to sell. He thinks it will make a lot of money. He wants you to tell him where to take it. He knows you from the pub, knows what you do. I don't think he'll come, I asked him not to but just in case . . . could you please make sure he doesn't see anything I did. He doesn't know, you see. He'd be terribly upset. You wouldn't tell him, would you?'

'That depends,' said Ronnie slowly. Christ, the girl was green. 'What's the merchandise on offer? Charlie's photograph?'

'Oh,' Alice said, 'it's that Lady Clare. Her on the steps. You know, on television.'

What a couple of babes in the wood they were, this Angela and her Charlie. The place was knee-deep in copies of that photo, it wouldn't fetch tuppence. Well, a tenner, say. A sex-aid for some punter to wank to.

'Very interesting,' he said, putting on a thoughtful expression. 'That was quite a picture, that was. What's he look like, this Charlie?'

'Tall, thin. Dark short hair. Grey eyes, sort of heavy-lidded . . .'

'Yeah yeah.' Ronnie cut her short, pursing his mouth, putting his fingers together in a steeple. Deliberately, he let his eyes trail over her. She flinched and hunched her shoulders. What was the best way in, what would the market stand? There had to be something in this for little Ron. There always was, if you knew where to look.

'What's it worth to you, Angela?' he said.

'Pardon?' Alice said woefully.

'Keeping my mouth shut,' he said with patience. 'What's it worth?'

'He probably won't come.' She said it to herself, murmuring.

'If he uses the pub, I can find him myself. Tall, thin, dark hair? Easy.'

'I haven't got any money.' Her voice was so low he had to lean forward to hear. She wore a thin blue blouse with bits of embroidery on it, lifted in the front by those amazing boobs. He remembered the nipples, huge and brown and soft and his mouth grew dry. Okay. Decision time. He wasn't going to be difficult. He could get more beaver shots out of her, use her for a bit of soft porn. Hard porn, for that matter. But he was too professional for that, her reluctance would show and, besides, there was that bloody mark, he couldn't forever be shooting around it. Anyway, she was pretty pathetic. He'd let her off lightly. He leaned back, hands behind his head.

'Tell you what,' he said. 'Let's take it from where we left off, eh?'

Alice shook her head, bewildered.

'You and me'll have a quick screw and, after that, mum's the word. On my mother's grave, right?'

'No.' Her voice broke. She shook her head again violently.

'All right, Charlie, here I come.' He shrugged. He wasn't going to bother, either way, if she did or didn't. Much too busy, was little Ron, to go looking for boyfriends in pubs and run off at the mouth about their tarts; asking for a bunch of fives, that was. Ronnie was all for a quiet life. He was only pushing it now because he couldn't believe she could be that dumb. Dumb enough for him to add more cheap bait. 'I could get good money for the stuff I took of you but I'll tear up the negatives, how's that? You won't have another thing to worry about, I swear. And don't think your Charlie won't come. There might be up to £5,000 in it for him, world rights.'

That did it, she sagged in front of his eyes. She was going to take the hook, the stupid cow. Could you credit it? Ronnie stood up and whipped off his jacket.

'That model . . .' she whispered.

He walked over and turned the key in the door. 'We've got a good half-hour' he said. 'I was having you on.'

'The baby . . .'

'Here.' He picked up a carton from under the table and stuffed a cushion in it. He still couldn't believe it. What kind of True Confessions had she been reading? But there she was, anyway, unstrapping the baby, carting him over to the bloody broom cupboard and sticking him inside. Ronnie couldn't resist it. 'Won't be long, mate,' he called as he closed the door, 'no peeking. It was all he could do not to burst out laughing.

He wasn't laughing when she stood in front of him, naked, her face bent. He was going to take his time, starting with those gorgeous tits. He couldn't remember when he'd had such an easy lay.

All the colours had drained from the streets, everything looked thick and flat, cut out of colourless cardboard. A flat grey bus moved past her and grey dirty cars, concrete piled up on every side and blocked out the sky, robots walked stiffly about quacking at each other. The air was foul with oily fumes, it hurt her lungs. Faces swam up and swam away, gaping fish in a rubber river guttered with filth. Under her feet the city pavements shuddered, stone crusts over the abyss. She went home because there was nowhere else to go. In her absence the stairs had grown steeper and higher and the front door moved towards her, implacable.

In the flat the baby cried as if his heart was breaking. Despair had found its way within the walls, they sweated with it, the windows wept between the thin grey curtains and russet drops stained the sills. Alice nursed the baby, looking at him in her arms, seeing that he was frail and ugly, his small face rashed with tiny pustules, his scalp under the downy hair scaley and yellow. She kissed his nose and held him against her, cupping his eggshell head, and he screamed and jerked convulsively away, kicking at her sore breasts. It was then she realized that because she was unclean her milk was infected. Those cloudy drops that oozed from her nipples contained a cancer that was taking root, beginning stealthily to suck at her child's tissues. The crab would break surface soon and sidle from its infant shell through one orifice or another, its pincers cutting into the jelly of the eyes, protruding from the tiny ears. He would arch his small body in agony but the creature lodged in his throat would choke off his cries.

She looked up and Charlie was in the room. There was something askew about him, out of joint, his eyes were flat in his head and his rubber mouth gaped.

'What's the matter, love?' he said. 'Are you all right?'

'All right,' Alice said. 'All right.'

He put his arms around her and she stood still inside them, sweating. He kissed her face with little kisses and she kept quiet.

'How's my boy then?' Charlie took the baby from her and held him up. The baby gurgled and Charlie laughed. Alice thought he mustn't find out what I have done to him, I must pretend.

'There's spaghetti cooked,' she said.

'Great,' Charlie said, 'I could eat a horse.' Whores. Alice looked quickly at him and saw that he had not noticed what he'd said. She went into the kitchen.

As he ate she watched the long white worms spotting with

blood the napkin tucked under his chin. In the other room the telephone began to ring. Charlie got up.

'It's a Miss something from RTV,' he called. 'For you, Ally. She got your name wrong.'

Alice put out her hand for the receiver. 'Yes,' she said. Charlie was listening.

'Is that Angela?' Judith said in her bright reporter's voice, doodling on a pad in Minnie's office. There was an odd sound at the other end but she ploughed on. 'I was given your number by Ronnie Garston. The photographer. You know?'

'Yes.' Alice tried to think but her brain was packed with wool.

'Look Angela — you don't mind if I call you Angela? — we're doing a programme on Tuesday about this business of Lady Clare. I'm sure you know all about *that*.' Judith gave her special sisterly laugh. 'The exploitation of women's bodies, that sort of thing.' She waited a moment and, lacking response, went on. 'Obviously, doing the work you do, you'll have a different approach. A professional view, d'you see what I mean?'

'Mmm.' What was this woman saying? She could not understand the words.

'*Good*,' said Judith chummily. 'The thing is, we'd love you to come on the programme, you could make a tremendously important contribution. I mean, people are so prejudiced about what you do. About beaver shots, that is. Aren't they?'

'What?' There was so much noise in Alice's ears that she couldn't hear properly. But if she put the receiver down, what would she say to Charlie?

'Beaver shots,' Judith said. The words sounded crude to her but this Angela would be used to the jargon.

'Beaver,' Alice repeated. She had never heard the term.

'Right,' said Judith with relief. Minnie's eyes were registering a certain admiration. Now that the thing was out in the open, Judith felt almost jaunty. 'Well, we've all got them, haven't we?' she said, her voice amused and worldly-wise.

'What?' said Alice again. Charlie was looking puzzled. The mouthpiece of the telephone smelt sour. She must think of something.

'Cunts,' said Judith on a gust of laughter. She had had three Scotches in the studio bar to give her dutch courage for the call. People always thought this sort of thing was easy for journalists. She had never found it easy, persuading strangers to say on television what they wouldn't tell their best friends. God alone knew why they ever did it. 'Listen,' she said to the phone, 'I'll send a researcher over, if that's okay with you. Just to ask a few questions, put you in the picture, so you'll know what's expected.' Judith put her head on the receiver and shook her head at Minnie. No good, this one, very uptight. A bum steer from that Ronnie Garston, no wonder he'd laughed when he passed on her number. Cunt.

Alice made a great effort. 'No thank you,' she said, 'I don't want any insurance.' She put the phone back in its cradle, her hand shaking. Charlie's voice came from a distance.

'Insurance?' he said. 'What was that all about?'

She stood where she was. It would all come out now. Any minute Charlie would know how she'd poisoned their child. The sins of the mother.

'Alice. Baby.' Charlie lifted her limp hand, jouncing it.

Alice shivered. So he saw the connection already. There was not much time left.

'She hung up,' said Judith. 'Never mind. She was no use, I can tell you.'

Minnie patted her back. 'You're very gutsy, Jude. I've got another number, a girl called Shirleen. Try, try and try again.'

'Anything you say, boss,' Judith said and hit the phone.

Smoke shrouded the white sky, flames rolled and cracked along the flat fields and the men on either side of the fire trudged through the lines of plants that should have been green and were grey, the leaves drooping and blistered with mould. They were burning the blighted potato crop, three hundred acres and thousands of pounds of it in a swathe that ran from the La Fontaine land to the smaller fields that were farmed by the Earl's tenants. Alice's father was there with the other men beating to keep the flames in check, his eyes rheumy and bloodshot from the smoke. Ringed by flames the Tucolston graveyard was an emerald square set with grey stones. Where the grass grew long beside a laurel hedge a neat oblong had been cut out of the ground and piled with raw red earth. On the earth lay a single wreath of lilies with a card that flapped in the smut-filled wind. The card, hand-written in ink that had run, said:

FOR CONCHA, MY BELOVED SISTER

REST IN PEACE

CLARE

Despite Earl La Fontaine's best efforts, his wife and his sister had refused to be baulked of Concepción's funeral, though they had taken the precaution of wearing gaudy head-scarves borrowed from the maids to avoid recognition. But the place was deserted.

'My beloved sister,' said Lady Florence to Lady Mamaine. They had retreated indoors, driven from the garden by smoke. 'Rather tasteless, I call that, the woman was only a maid. And she committed a mortal sin. In my day, she wouldn't have got into our graveyard. Concha. Odd name. Reminds me of a shell.'

'Clare was very fond of her,' said Mamaine. She was trying to read.

'Clare was always given to exaggeration. Overboard on everything. When is she going back?'

Lady Mamaine did not lift her eyes from her book. 'I don't know, dear. It's awkward. She says she can't go back.'

'Can't?' Florence pulled herself up on her stick and dumped herself heavily beside her sister-in-law. 'What's this?'

Mamaine looked at her and sighed. 'Florrie, Raul is very upset by what happened.'

'That is hardly to be wondered at.' One of the buttons on the sofa was loose and she picked at it. It came off in her hand. 'You realize, Mamie,' she said, showing Mamie the button, 'we shall all suffer if Clare does not go back. You recall what this place was like. It is her duty to return to her husband. She took her vows before God.'

There were times when Mamaine felt she only retained her patience with Florence through the good offices of Our Lady, with whom she was still on the most cordial of terms. Since the scandal and the lack of response to her prayers to her Father for an immediate and long-lasting strike that would grind the whole of Fleet Street to a halt – a man was surely better at arranging industrial action? – she had gone off the holy males of her Church for the time being.

'You don't understand anything about marriage, Florrie,' she said, keeping her voice triumphantly pleasant.

'I should hope not,' said Lady Florence. 'I made my bed a long time ago and I thank my guardian angel that I sleep on it alone. Nevertheless ...' she frowned sternly at Mamaine, '... marriage is a sacred bond, that I do know. Indissoluble, Mamie. Let no man put asunder.'

An inexplicable bitterness seized Mamaine. 'It's men who put asunder,' she said. 'Men put everything asunder.'

Lady Florence leaned back on the sofa and stroked the small diamond in her left ear-lobe. 'I *know* that,' she said. 'Why do you think I am still Florence La Fontaine? My niece, however, was not as wise.' Kindly, she forebore to include her sister-in-law.

'How can you say that, Florrie?' Our Lady temporarily lost control of Mamaine's voice. 'It was you who pushed her into marrying that man. You.'

'I am not yet deaf, dear.'

'The whole thing is a tragedy. A *tragedy*.' To Mamaine's astonishment, she felt she could actually cry.

'Not entirely, Mamie dear,' said Lady Florence, smiling forgiveness. 'You have gained another hundred years of life for Tucolston. In this vale of tears one must count one's blessings, must one not?' Outside the windows someone was crunching along the gravel. Florence raised herself up as far as she could. 'Speak of the devil,' she said, 'there's Clare going out. Mamaine, is that wise?'

Tucolston Old Hall was still under siege or so it seemed to its inhabitants. Lord La Fontaine had given the servants strict orders that no stranger was to be admitted within the gates on any pretext whatsoever until he, personally, had given permission. In his view, the hyenas of the Press were capable of donning a thousand disguises to attain their nefarious ends and he eyed every bush in the gardens with the deepest misgivings. Those he suspected of harbouring a member of the Fourth Estate he hit with his stick until they surrendered in a welter of lopped foliage, decapitated flowers and badly injured branches. It took a lot out of him – he was not getting any younger – but he spared himself nothing in his defence of home and family and had soon managed to reduce several copses to a shambles resembling the first day on the Somme. The old gardener Fox, seeing his life's work being destroyed in front of his eyes, took the Earl on in a spirited joust over three rare and particularly bushy *Morus alba*. The Earl won. Fox gave in his notice on the spot and limped away muttering imprecations against the La Fontaines and all their works.

'I always had my suspicions about that man,' the Earl told his wife the same evening, defending himself from her protests. 'Give you an example. How long has he had a limp?'

'For forty years,' said Mamaine.

Of them all, Clare was the real prisoner, confined to the house, in limbo. Newspapers had been cancelled and the television set stood blank and glassy-eyed in the drawing-room, its intestines trailing, degutted by her father. Since Concepción's funeral – which Pa had refused to let her attend – she had thought of little else than the plants and the photograph in her bedroom drawer but misery had taken its toll and her exhausted mind skittered aimlessly about and refused to attempt any serious analysis of what they could mean. Overwhelmed by nervousness she had grabbed the phone one evening and telephoned Louise Lawson, Mrs George B. Yarwell, mother of three.

'Who?' said Louise's voice, flat as skimmed milk. 'Oh, *Clare*. as I live and breathe. Good heavens. It's past midnight.' A certain jocularity crept in. 'You *have* got yourself in a pickle.'

Under the faint crackle, Clare could hear her whispering, 'It's Clare. You know. Yes, *that* Clare.'

'Louise,' she said, still too eager for talk to care that an unknown George had his ears flapping. 'It's been so awful. You can't imagine.'

'Yes,' said Louise, 'well, George and I read about it. We couldn't help it. The newspapers in this country are simply dire. We get *The Times*, of course, but even there. As George said, a few years ago they wouldn't have touched such a thing with a barge-pole. I mean ... I don't mean ...'

'It's all right,' Clare said. She tried to think what she had wanted to say. In the pause, Louise began again.

'My dear, our hearts went out to you, truly they did. What an ordeal. How *are* you? *Where* are you?'

'At home. I can't go out.'

'No. Too dreadful. What beasts people are. Do tell. Has it been frightful?'

Clare swallowed painfully.

'Clare? Why don't I nip in the Merc and drive over? I could be with you in an hour at this time of night. It would be *heaven* to see you.'

Once, Clare thought, Louise's voice, acid and permanently

disapproving, would have been so welcome. In the old days she would have lost no time in telling Clare how silly she had been and peppering her with bossy advice. Now her voice carried a whiff of fruit, heavy as a rotting plum. She was avid for gossip. All to be passed on to ghastly George and anyone else within hissing distance. My friend Lady Clare. Yes, *that* Lady Clare. She rang me up especially to tell me ... my dear, do you know, she told me that ...

'Clare, darling. Speak to me.'

'It's no good, Louise. Pa's gone bananas. He'd shoot you at the gates.'

Over the wire, Louise brayed, 'You're teasing. Not really.'

'Really,' said Clare. Louise was still chattering, persuading, as Clare put the phone down.

The next morning she became convinced that unless she could get out immediately into the fresh air her brain, starved of oxygen, would shortly cease to function altogether. She crept down the stairs, across the hall and through the front door but the gravel gave her away.

Mamaine and the dogs came running, Mamaine wailing, the dogs barking joyously.

'Child? Stop it, Beulah. Child, you shouldn't be out, you know how angry your father would be. Bonnie, don't *do* that.'

'Ma.' Pleading, Clare took her mother's soft ringed hands. 'I can't be indoors for the rest of my life. I'll walk straight up the avenue and back.'

'There might be helicopters,' Mamaine said, waving her hand above her head in a helpless way, 'with photographers and long-distance cameras and things. I shall never forget the day the Queen and I — the Queen Mum, that is — were picnicking in the grounds of Balmoral and ...'

'I'm not going to Balmoral, Ma. Just up the avenue and back. I must have some fresh air.'

Eagerly, Mamaine seized her opportunity. 'There's no fresh air out here. Can't you smell? A disastrous year altogether and the crops ruined.'

Clare looked across the trees and saw the smoke like a pall on the sky. It was true, there was a smell of burning. 'What are they doing?' she asked.

'Burning the potatoes. They're blighted, all of them. It's a curse.'

'But what sort of blight? Couldn't any be saved?' She didn't give tuppence for the potatoes but a show of concern would smooth her path. Up the avenue.

'Nobody knows. Pa had a man down from Kew just before you came. Professor Barnaby, or was it Barnabus? Apparently it's a new disease and they've got it in Europe and America, too. Like the Irish famine. Some of the farmers are nearly bankrupt or so Pa says. We've lost a lot ourselves.'

'Awful,' Clare said falsely.

'It is. Very worrying. Bonnie, get off. Poor Beulah. They're both bitches, why do they *do* that?'

'El sexo,' said Clare. It had always sounded ridiculous, that word in Spanish. She walked quickly across the circle of grass and, besieged by dogs, her mother let her go.

The wide grass avenue lined on either side with cypress trees tapered ahead of her to the stone fountain at its far end where mermaids crouched holding up a shell that opened on its pearl, a fat male infant with a peculiarly disagreeable expression. Clare stood for a moment looking towards it and began to walk. She thought better when she was moving, particularly if her thoughts were disturbing. So what had she got? A label, a photograph and some dried plants in a bedroom drawer, pieces of a puzzle that she had to solve. Whatever else they might have in common, one thing they shared was obvious – a person or persons considered all three important enough to send them three thousand miles across the sea to England though whether they were meant for her or that was Concha's decision alone she couldn't guess.

One by one, then, beginning with the photo because that was what she least wanted to think about. Its implications filled her with a stomach-turning brew of anger, hurt and fright and she had to force herself to concentrate. Obviously it proved that her humiliation at the airport was no accident, no random coincidence of inefficient women, a gauzy skirt and an errant breeze. It had been meticulously planned and rehearsed with Carrington as her stand-in. They had organized the plane that had taxied past her as she stood on the plane steps, they had made sure its slipstream would catch her skirts. Then they must also have made sure that she was suitably naked and that was a bad one. She had been drugged; Carrington again. And Concha? Her job was to see that her mistress was properly dressed and she had failed abysmally. Oh Concha.

Clare broke into a jog and its rhythm soothed her. Concha wouldn't knowingly do anything to hurt her, of that much she was sure. So either she was so terrified by her first flight that her wits had gone or she had been forced in some way to co-operate with Carrington. And Raul? Clare found it hard to believe that he hated her so and even if he did, who but a madman would choose such a complicated way of seeking revenge? Yet someone had.

She reached the fountain, panting a little. Out of condition. The constipated face of the toddler leered down at her. She knelt and scooped up water to wet her hot face. From where she was the avenue ran straight back again to the main door of the house where someone — was it Nellie? — was halfway up a ladder doing something to the bracket of the lamp above. Clare circled the fountain and started back between the cypress trees again.

That bourbon label, retrieved from a forgotten pocket for her to read. It might mean very little in itself. The bourbon had made the women drunk and someone — this Bogardus? — may have given it to them but Clare knew well that all sorts of strange things found their way up and down the river and were left high and dry on its banks. Once, she had come across an Indian child in a riverside village playing with an electric toothbrush. She dismissed the label for the time being and went on to the plants and felt again the cool tiles at her back and the bronze face of Manuel over her. Perhaps bringing dead plants to a lady was an ancient Indian courting ritual. No. To be fair, she herself had initiated that little episode – Manuel had only wanted to give her the bouquet to take to England. Her women collected plants, of course. Was there a connection?

Halfway to the house, under the trees, two crouched lions with a stone slab between them made a bench. Clare sat down. It was from here that she had mounted on the stilts Fox had carved for her and wobbled across the grass, his leathery hands supporting her. If only she were eight years old again with no more to worry her then falling from those wooden pedestals such a short way to the ground, with only a scraped knee to show for it. Pedestal. Fall. Clare blinked rapidly, as if clearing her eyes would clear her mind. She had been on a pedestal; she had been La Dorada, loved and trusted by Venturan peasant women, their friend, their hope. And she had not fallen from that pedestal. She had been pushed. Now those women would hear or be told what had happened to her and lose hope and trust in her, believe that she was not their friend but a crazy slut whose shameless-ness shamed them. Who wanted to break their faith in her, to destroy the women's project by destroying her? Had whoever it was heard of her plans to bring contraception back to the women?

Her head ached. So many different threads, so hard to make a web. And what hideous fly was she after? The Women's Co-operative was Raul's idea, why should he want to sabotage it? The FLV guerrillas hated her and they hated her contra-ceptive plans too, they had made that very clear. Were they involved? At Ventura's airport she had hinted to Raul that she knew who was behind the bourbon incident and she'd half meant the CIA, partly because Ventura was crawling with Americans and partly because everybody blamed the CIA for everything that happened in South America. But the CIA backed Raul – or the American Government did – he got massive aid, it was no secret. Though she hadn't known it at the time. ignoramus that she was then, American money had funded Clare's doomed buildings; the hotel, the hospital, the casino. Even Raul's Gulfstream-2. the very jet that had flown her here, though lent to him by the publicity-hungry manufacturers, had its running costs footed by the United States. Carrington had told her that boasted of it. So what reason would the CIA have to ruin her project and humiliate her? None, that she could see. It was all a pointless jumble of names and letters: CIA, KGB, FLV, Raul. Carrington, labels, photos, bits of dead flowers.

Dead flowers. What had Ma said just now? A blight on the potatoes and a Professor visiting from Kew. An expert on plants. Clare got up and started towards the house, walking quickly. There was nothing else to go on and she had to start somewhere and there was the plants. That was it. She would go and see this Professor because plants were the only tangible lead she had and certainly the only one she could discuss with an outsider. He'd think she was mad, of course, some dotty eccentric from haunts of coot and tern with a bunch of old twigs up her jumper but perhaps he was used to that and would be patient. He might even be able to shed some light, however dim – it could happen. As long as he didn't recognize her as the notorious Lady Clare because then he would know she was mad.

Electric with relief at the mere thought of some action, she reached the door. Nellie looked down at her from the ladder propped against the wall.

'What's up with you, Missie?' she called as Clare whisked by.

'I'm going to dye my hair.' Clare called back and ran for the stairs. Nellie shook her head. Poor pet. All the fuss had addled her brains and no wonder.

Wrapped in an old towel, Clare bent over the basin in the bathroom along the corridor from her bedroom. Her hands, clumsy in rubber gloves, kneaded the dark ointment into her scalp and then into a lather that charred every bright strand. After the shampoo she rubbed her head vigorously so that the hair sprang round her face in a black halo. Then she bent the mirror to see her new self and saw, instead, dark behind the glass, the living dead Concepción. For a long second, shock made her stupid. She reached towards the face of her friend and touched the image of her own wide cheekbones, her own blunt nose, the same hollow in the upper lip and, now, the same dark hair. Her friend was crying. Tears came from the once brown eyes and washed them blue. 'Oh Concha,' Clare whispered at the mirror, 'I never saw you were beautiful too.'

She sat down on the lid of the lavatory and pulled some paper from the wall to wipe her eyes. That made one more of a hundred things she didn't know about Concha. Unforgivable, that ignorance. The tears started again and she rubbed them away, disgusted with her own self-indulgence. Grief was a luxury she could no longer afford. Concepción had killed herself and she had done that dreadful thing soon after Raul had said whatever he had said to her on the telephone from Ventura. It could not be that he'd simply fired her. However important her job might have been to her, however financially disastrous its loss, Concha was familiar with poverty, she was raised in a poor country and, besides, she was a strong woman and a devout Catholic. Of all resorts in hardship, suicide was the last a Catholic of Concha's kind would take, Clare was sure of that at least. But without more evidence, she could only guess at other reasons and the guesses made her sick, shot through as they were with rifle fire and images of blood trickling across stones.

[333]

Whatever the reason, Concha had sent her messages before she had arranged herself for death and for Concha's sake she must decipher them. They were objects because Concepción could not write. Probably she had planned to tell Clare about them but had held off because of what had happened at the airport and then Raul's call had killed her before she could explain.

'I promise you,' Clare whispered to the mirror, 'I won't stop until I know what you wanted to say. I promise.'

[18]

In the hushed precinct of the *Chronicle* library Judith was flipping through the day's newspapers and the adrenalin that would fuel her next column was building up nicely. Everything she read seemed to her either disgustingly inaccurate, unforgivably biased, appallingly trivial, revoltingly written or disgracefully stale, all of which did her no end of good. The fact was that almost anything, looked at the right way, could make her boil over; there was in her that temperamental asset of all successful columnists – an apparently inexhaustible vat of simmering anger. How people managed who did not have her weekly steam vent she could not imagine – she would have had to be out most nights vandalizing telephone boxes, chucking bricks through windows and possibly inflicting actual bodily harm. She often got letters from readers accusing her of being deliberately controversial and was outraged each time, calling on the entire Features Department for sympathy in this dastardly impugning of the depths of her feelings. Such attacks gave her violent indigestion – as clear a proof as she could wish of her responsive nature. Judith had once confided to Ruth that she thought she was the exact opposite of a psychopath. 'Psychopaths,' she told her friend, 'don't understand that others feel the same as they do, which is why they murder people.' 'I see what you mean,' Ruth had replied. 'You *do* understand, which is why *you* murder people.' Sad, really, that Ruth had no real talent for friendship. Envy was her fatal flaw as it was, to be absolutely honest, in so many so-called feminists.

As she went through the columns of print she noted that the

Clare business was fading fast though it was still being milked by cartoonists and circulation managers. The *Sun* had a middle-page spread of ten famous women including Princess Anne, Princess Margaret and of course Marilyn Monroe, with their skirts up and the parts below obscured by comic bloomers – readers were asked to send in equally hilarious shots of their own, and the winner got a dirty weekend for two to gay Paree. One cartoon had the wife of the Egyptian President, due to arrive that day, standing at the entrance to a plane swaddled from head to foot like a mummy. 'Better safe than Clare' said the caption. Another, in *The Times*, had no caption, merely a flag-pole with its flag a pair of women's panties flying at half-mast.

Otherwise, nothing much but a few readers' letters dotted here and there complaining about media beastliness to poor Señora de Toro. Didn't stop them buying papers though, Judith thought, and the beastlier the paper the more of it they bought. Most people were very callous, they didn't give a toss what happened to others as long as it didn't happen to them.

She went on reading mechanically. MOTHER AND BABY IN CANAL SUICIDE LEAP said one small headline. Judith glanced at the story below. 'Canal bargee Denis Cooke was steering his boat under teh bridge at Maida Avenue early yesterday when a girl with a baby strapped toh er back jumped from the bridge into the water and ...'

Good grief, she thought, turning the page in disgust, the printers must have packed away a record amount of booze on *that* shift. There were more mistakes than there were words. Standards were falling all over.

Beside her on the desk, the librarian dumped another pile of newspapers and said, 'Saw you on the telly last night. Good racy stuff.'

'Thanks,' said Judith, 'we aim to please.' The programme had gone well and Minnie had said 'Duckie you were wonderful' six times, which meant she was reasonably satisfied. Shirleen Maddox, the beaver-shot girl, all blonde curls and cleavage (she had had the make-up girl deepen the shadow there) had turned up trumps, hammering the obligatory Bishop, the token feminist and the tame psychiatrist into the ground with her jaunty cockney humour. 'If there wasn't no call, there'd be no call-girls,' she said at one point and at another, 'They say I'm sitting on a gold-mine but the gold's no use without the miners, is it?' Her defence of her work was simple: if men didn't want it, she wouldn't do it and it wasn't her fault men were funny that way, couldn't stand that kind herself, creepy lot, but that's life, in'it? And she shrugged her pretty shoulders, winning all hearts.

'A bit gamey,' Head of Programmes had said in Hospitality afterwards but the callers were for Shirleen eight to ten and before Judith left Min had taken the girl aside to book her for another chat show. It looked, Judith thought, rubbing off the make-up in her car, as if our Shirl would be closing her legs and opening her mouth for a living from now on. Foxy lady.

Charlie had filled the little room with flowers, every sterile surface bloomed, the air was sweet with them.

'You'd think she was the Queen,' the nurse said to him, yanking so energetically at the dividing curtains that a pleat tore from its plastic moorings. Some people had to wait six months for these beds while other people with nothing better to do jumped off bridges and jumped the queue.

'She's my Queen,' Charlie said. The nurse gave a smile of glacial intensity and clattered off and he went on stroking Alice's hand, lightly pressing down the length of each finger as if to make sure no tiny bone of hers was missing. The purple drops on the pale face made the only touch of colour in the whiteness of the bed.

Alice opened her sore lips to speak and coughed instead, wheezing and spluttering helplessly. Charlie raised her up and patted her back.

'There,' he said, 'there, my darling.'

Presently she asked, 'He is all right, is he?'

'The baby? He's fine. Your Mum was on the blower this morning. Says the country air's doing him a power of good. He's got the roses back in his cheeks.'

Alice said quietly, 'He never had roses,' while Charlie smoothed the hair from her face and tucked it carefully against the pillow.

'It's you we got to worry about now. You're never going to do nothing like that again, are you? Eh, Ally?'

'I was ... it was ... it doesn't matter,' she said. 'No.'

'Promise? Else we won't be able to leave you alone.'

'I've been alone,' said Alice.

Later, after they had drunk cups of tea and another nurse had changed the dressings on the wounds caused when they dragged Alice onto the boat, Charlie came back between the curtains. 'I been thinking,' he said, sitting down beside her. 'I don't want my kid away. He belongs with us, you and me. So I reckon we should pack up and go to the farm, stay with your Mum and your Dad. I could help him out, he's got no one and he's getting on. Your Mum said so, when she was here. I think she took quite a shine to me, after all that, eh, Ally? Anyway, she was on about these potatoes he's got to get in, some sort of new ones that won't get the blight and I said I'd give him a hand.' Charlie put a bent arm up. 'Here, Ally, look at this. That's good muscle there. And I'm a genius with an engine. I'll have that old tractor your Mum was moaning about. I'll have it doing a ton before you can say Jack the Ripper. What do you say, Ally? How would you like that? Here, Ally, are you listening?'

'Yes,' said Alice.

'So what do you think?'

'They haven't got pretty girls in the country. Not like London, Charlie.'

'What's that to me?' he said and laughed, watching her. 'You're all the pretty girl I need. And there's that Lady Clare of yours, she'll do for afters. No, I'm joking.' He laughed again, holding her hand. 'Ally, all I want is you.'

'Is it?' Alice said.

'And all you want is me.'

'Do I?' Alice said.

'We're going to live happily ever after, that's what we're going to do.'

'Are we?' Alice said.

Charlie took her two wrists and touched her hands together. 'Course we are,' he said. 'Clap hands for your Uncle Charlie.'

Smiling, he clapped her hands.

'Had your eyeful?'

The passenger opposite Clare on the bus was a human pear, the fat rolled down around her in ever-widening waves and spread out in the pool of her lap. But her stare was bone-thin.

'I said seen enough, have you?'

Clare's eyes jumped into focus. She had been thousands of miles away in a sun-baked village hearing again a woman's screams and the truculent voice coming at her, cutting harshly through her thoughts, was a shock. She ducked her head, muttering an apology, struggling to suppress the nervous twitch of a smile. Here she was, star of the Clare Affair, travelling incognito on a London bus in an anonymous plastic raincoat, her silver hair dyed a mousy brown, terrified that at any moment someone would point and gasp, 'It's her,' and flash-bulbs would flare and, instead, a fat woman was angrily defending herself against what she saw as Clare's unwelcome attention. The episode quite cheered her — nice to know there was a world out there unconcerned with the blight that had fallen on her life.

Perhaps, after all, she might soon be able to pick up the bits blown apart by the media and start again. Perhaps.

A bell clanged. 'Kew,' shouted the conductor. Clutching her basket she slipped off the bus and it trundled on, leaving behind the wide expanse of Kew Green. The air here smelled sweetly of the many immigrant flowers and fragrant leaves of the gardens, overwhelming the urban stink of London, offering a promise of beauty and peace. Clare walked across the grass to the lane that meandered along the garden boundaries. On the door of an ivy-covered cottage hard by the great black wrought-iron gates of Kew a brass plaque confirmed that here were the offices of Dr E. Barnabus, PH.D. Birds sang as loudly as they had in Tucolston, bees whizzed between the flowers and grasshoppers leapt away from her feet with indignant chirrups. Except for the highway that bisected the green, the place looked and smelled and sounded like a village. Clasping the handles of her basket, hope running high, Clare knocked at the cottage door.

Timothy Barnabus was unexpectedly young, a heron of a man with tufts of feathery hair erupting from his scalp and an enthusiastic manner. His office was small, partitioned off from another, and the sun poured dustily upon banks of metal filing cabinets and walls that were covered with illustrated maps and pastel drawings of plants. In one corner a peculiarly elongated rubber plant stuck two glossy leaves against the low ceiling and on every surface there were papers and pamphlets anchored at intervals by mugs half-filled with scummy liquid. Barnabus ushered Clare to a chair beside his desk, offered her coffee and picked his way back across the book-covered floor to the door.

'Genus *Coffea*,' he said as he edged out into the narrow corridor, 'Third-World rip-off par excellence. Cash crop, no use to them, we make it soluble, give 'em fifteen per cent. Ha!' He grinned, shook his head in wonder at the predatory human species and vanished.

Clare smiled in confusion at the closed door. The archetypal mad professor, this Blunderbuss. What was he talking about? She looked through the glass partition at a woman gulping soundlessly into a telephone and futility enveloped her. All very well, in the fastness of Lincolnshire, to think that somehow she could sort things out and find answers to questions she did not want even to formulate. But who was she? Not much more than a laughing stock with the laugh nearly over, already jettisoned by time: a poor crazed bag lady mumbling of conspiracies and plots against her person. No one in their right minds would accept what she said and, after all, she had so little to say that made sense even to herself. For a bad moment in that quiet room Clare was stabbed by fright, felt her mind scrabbling against the wall of her skull. Mad people did not know they were mad. They thought the outside world was crazy and they sat inside, sole inheritors of sanity and logic. Just as she did.

Barnabus came in again, holding aloft two mugs that dripped across the sisal carpeting. He set one in front of her and sat down. 'Lovely day,' he said, swivelling his neck on its jutting Adam's apple to the window. 'Come far, have you?'

'Very far,' Clare said and expelled her breath in an explosive sigh. That was unfortunate, the doctor's eyebrows were rising. Hastily she added, 'Shropshire,' the first lie that came to her lips. Shropshire from where Freddie came, the long-forgotten Shropshire Lad himself. An image of Freddie's ungainly presence, his foolish laugh, came up and a weight of loss sank into her for her past self; silly, thoughtless and blissfully carefree, with no more to perplex her than how to evade Freddie's whisky'd embrace at the end of a night's dancing. The sombre substitute with which she was now encumbered filled her with distress. And, she admonished herself, self-pity.

'You don't look ...' The Adam's apple jerked in embarrassment, 'that is to say, I thought perhaps ... Mediterranean. Must be the tan. Sorry. None of my business.' He lit a cigarette and pulled it sharply from his lips as if the tip burned him.

As the moment of fear that she had been recognized died down, Clare was seized by an urgent desire to tell this nice young Englishman everything. She wanted to pour it all out, explain who she was, what she knew about the events here and in Ventura, about Raul, the women, the suicide, the photographs, everything. She was briefly stifled by this need, she could feel his hand already on her shoulders, patting her for comfort, saying 'don't you worry your pretty head, leave it to me, together we'll sort those bounders out' and other perfectly idiotic John Buchan remarks that were not going to be said and wouldn't mean a thing if they were.

'Bit stuffy in here. I'll open a window.' Barnabus bounded from his desk and began banging at the sash like a man fleeing for his life. Clare realized that her face was overly expressive and she bent to hide it, fumbling in the basket at her feet, rapidly gulping back childish tears. As she sat up again with the plants cradled in her hands, he leapt back to clear a space among his papers and she laid her pathetic collection down piece by piece, the brittle curling foliage, the dry stems, the chunky dirt-caked roots.

'These,' she said. 'I'm sure you're very busy but I wondered if you knew what these could be. I tried to look them up in a plant book at home but I couldn't find . . . of course, they're dried and very battered . . .' Her voice trailed off. The plants were certainly battered. They were also ridiculous. Lying there on Barnabus's desk they looked like a voodoo sacrifice or something foetal that had been left out in the sun. She remembered with a slight jolt the dried posy stuffed in a rusty Nestlé tin that had stood – was doubtless still standing – below the wooden Virgin whose protruding navel Raul had made her kiss in the forest.

Barnabus stuck his neck out and peered. The plants rustled where they lay in the breeze from the open window. 'Yes,' he said and clicked his tongue several times. 'You wouldn't find them in an English book. Where did you get them?'

'A friend,' she said, 'a friend brought them back from South America.'

Barnabus clasped his hands and shot them out in front of him, palms forward, cracking the knuckles abstractedly. Then he fingered a bulbous root. 'No mystery about this one,' he said. 'Grows like a weed in that part of the world. *Dioscorea*.'

'*Dioscorea*,' Clare said.

'About five hundred species of it, same genus as yams, the cultivated kind. The sort we eat or, rather, the Americans eat.'

'Oh,' said Clare. She closed her eyes with disappointment. Sweet bloody potatoes, available at high-class fruiterers everywhere. A real breakthrough, that.

'This one,' he said, tapping another of the fibrous clumps, 'this is a *Solanum*. What we scientists call a wild spud.'

Potatoes again, your friendly neighbourhood potato. Boring, useless, without a smidgen of interest. Clare gave a small snuffle of frustration.

'And that is *Lupinus mutabilis*, the one with the pods and this chappie ...' he poked at it, '... I don't know offhand.'

Clare looked up at him, surprised.

'There are a quarter of a million different plants in the world,' Barnabus said defensively. 'No one botanist can know more than ten thousand. Leave it with me.'

'How long will it take you to find out?' Clare asked quickly hopefully.

'Oh, I don't know. A month, two months. Depends.'

'Please,' she said, 'please. It's important. Isn't there anyone who would know now? Someone here, today?'

'You're in a hurry?' he said curiously. She looked down at her lap and then looked at Barnabus, smiling.

'It's a bet. My father bet me twenty pounds I couldn't phone him tonight with the answer. Silly, I know, and I've no right ...' she caught her underlip between her teeth, coy

[343]

and girlish, '... but couldn't you help?' He had to, he had to, she willed him to say yes, she batted her lashes and simpered frantically.

Timothy Barnabus said, 'Well,' and then, 'There are five million pressed specimens at Kew you know, Miss ...?'

'Chedleigh.' Clare put her head to one side. 'Nellie.'

'We don't usually do this.' He coughed discreetly and his Adam's apple bobbed. 'Well, we can try.'

Once he had decided to move, he moved fast. In two seconds they were out of the door and crossing the green, Barnabus striding, Clare hurrying to keep beside him, stuttering her thanks. The mysterious plant swung in the basket in her hand. They rushed up the steps of a pillared Queen Anne house, past grey-uniformed porters, past banks of pigeon-holes and offices where girls' heads turned as they went by and came into a great high hall. Barnabus walked rapidly to its furthest reaches and began climbing a raspberry red iron staircase that spiralled upwards. Clare followed breathlessly, hanging on to the curving banister, grateful for her sensible flat shoes borrowed from Ma. They emerged upon the top tier of the hall, where Barnabus ducked into an aisle of panelled cupboards, ran his fingers along the labels on the cupboard doors, stopped and opened one. Inside, files were stacked to its top in musty profusion. He flipped through them and pulled one out.

'*Dioscorea*,' he said. 'You see? Lots of them. Hastate leaves, a climber. There's the fruit, these are the flowers.'

Clare looked at the dry plant banded to the yellowing page with strips of sellotape. It smelt of stale pot pourri, it curled on its paper backing, the leaves dark and arrowed, the tiny fruit heart-shaped like the Shepherd's Purse of her childhood. 'Is this the yam?' she said. He nodded.

'The root isn't here but you know what that looks like. An elongated potato.'

'And you eat it?'

Ah no. Not this type. You wouldn't enjoy it. This is the wild strain.'

'So it's good for nothing,' Clare said tiredly. Beside her, the doctor coughed indignantly.

'No no, not at all. Very useful, *Dioscorea*. Or can be.' He moved along the wall of cupboards and reached up to point out another label. 'Here. Here's your second plant.'

The label said *Index Generis Solani* and underneath *Solanaceae*. Clare watched as Barnabus pulled out a folder and gazed obediently at the bedraggled twigs pressed between the pages with their long dead clusters of papery flowers. 'Oh,' she said, trying for animation. 'Very ... very interesting.' She listened passively as he described the structure of the plant, nodding her head again and again, yearning to be done. A young woman with a shock of frizzy ginger hair crossed at the head of the aisle.

'Janet,' Barnabus called. The woman paused. 'Are you busy? Would you have a look at this?' He gestured at Clare's basket. The woman came up and Clare picked out the mystery plant. 'Janet's an expert on South American flora,' Barnabus explained and Janet, peering at the plant, shook her head and smiled.

'No one's an expert on South America,' she said. 'The forests there are crammed with unknown species, four or five million perhaps. We know about fifteen per cent. I don't know this. There you are. If you like, I could try and track it down ... ?' she glanced enquiringly at Barnabus who looked at Clare.

'Thank you. It's of no consequence.' The formal phrase concealed a disappointment that made Clare feel exhausted. Her hope disintegrated – it had always been as fragile as the plants themselves and what, after all, were they? Objects of fetish collected by peasants like Concha and Manuel, ignorant and superstitious natives who believed every tree had a soul and there were magic powers contained in old roots. They had risked a lot – Concha had died – to give her the message they imagined the plants carried but the message was meaningless except to themselves and so all their efforts were a bitter waste. Manuel had tried to give her flowers that day they had visited the wooden stump of the Virgin. Some Indian cure for infertility that had no sort of basis in fact. Psychic voodoo. The women who had cared for her in her illness had practised a kind of psychic voodoo too. Perhaps they had cured her with kindness but not with their brews that smelt of the forest. Sadly she thought 'my own strength pulled me through', and she went with Barnabus down the winding stairs and past the piles of plants awaiting classification and out of the Herbarium into the desolate sun. She wanted to leave immediately, now that her hope was gone, but the doctor evidently expected her to collect the plants she had left with him and so she walked back to his cottage, making conversation. At his desk again she said, 'I mustn't keep you,' and held the basket against the table, sweeping the gnarled stems in.

Timothy Barnabus watched her and frowned. She puzzled him. Something about her face was familiar, perhaps because even in that dowdy sack of a dress she was beautiful with the kind of beauty – wide-eyed, blunt-featured – that you saw in glossy magazines and on advertising posters, familiar because it was used so often as a selling aid. 'Buy me,' said her admirable nose, 'and this car'. 'Buy me,' said the soft curve of her lips, 'and this cigar'. Fly me. Still, she was spectacular in the flesh, a real head-turner, he had to admit that. As exotic in her way as any of the exotica of Kew. Yet she seemed unhappy under the superficial vivacity, her neck drooped like a wilting flower, something was wrong.

'I could send the *Solanus* to Birmingham if you'd like to know more,' he said, hesitating.

'Birmingham?' Her voice was dispirited. She pulled on a plastic raincoat.

'The University. They have the world expert there on *Solanus*. *Dioscorea* I can tell you about myself.'

'What more is there to tell?' she said.

Barnabus said, 'The pubs are open. You look as if you could do with a drink. Or are you going somewhere?'

'Me?' Clare gave a rueful laugh. 'No, I'm going nowhere.'

He stood at the bar paying for her Scotch and she sat on a bench by an open window that gave on to Kew Green, gulping at the golden liquid. A long journey and a last hope had ended here in this everyday lunch-time bustle. The good doctor will now tell me the story of his life, she thought, and then ask me out to dinner tomorrow evening. But the good doctor did not. Plants were his first and only love. He was vaguely curious about this pretty stranger but mostly he was piqued by her sudden indifference to the wizened flora that lay in the basket by her side. Her interest had flagged with her lost bet. He challenged himself to revive it.

'Did you know,' he said, 'that more than forty per cent of all the prescriptions issued in America in one year contain a drug of natural origin?'

'No,' Clare said. Her old dislike of being force-fed unwanted facts asserted itself. She watched a sparrow pecking at crumbs on the window ledge, tapping her foot.

'Liana *Chondrodendron tomentosum*, for instance. That's used as a muscle relaxant in surgery. Some lichens act as antibiotics, some of them are sensitive to environmental change – you can use them to monitor pollution in the atmosphere. There are chemicals in the rosy periwinkle that are very successful in treating Hodgkin's disease and lymphocytic leukaemia.'

'I've got Hodgkin's disease and he's got mine,' said Clare. 'Would you like another drink?' It seemed as good an idea as any to sit here until closing time and get smashed.

'No thanks.' He watched her pushing her way to the bar, bewildered. She seemed to have changed in some way, the air of unhappiness had hardened into truculence. He had lost her

[347]

somehow. But Timothy Barnabus was an evangelist when it came to his profession. He had spent ten years fighting on behalf of his precious plants and given hundreds of lectures pleading their preservation to a largely indifferent public and the greedy commercial world and he was not about to be defeated by a fidgety brunette, no matter how attractive

'The tubers of *Dioscorea deltoidea*,' he said precisely as she sat down again, 'are the finest source of diosgenin we have.'

'Really?' She sipped her whisky, hardly listening. Where was she going to go from here? Back to Tucolston, she supposed, but then what? There had been no word from Raul since his last dreadful phone call but her parents showed no signs of taking in the probability that she might never be able to return to Ventura. Only this morning Pa had muttered something about arranging a flight from Northolt. What were they going to do – launch her into space?

Barnabus leaned towards her raising his voice. '*Dioscorea*,' he said loudly. 'Your wild yam. Produces diosgenin. For contraceptives.'

Two men squeezed their bulk around the small table and Clare took her basket off the bench to give them space. 'Contraceptives,' she repeated distractedly and again, 'Contraceptives?'

'The Pill,' Barnabus said. It was getting even noisier around them. 'They make it from ingredients in the wild yam.'

Clare looked dazed for a moment as if – thought Barnabus – she had received a light blow between the eyes. He felt mildly triumphant. Her evident surprise was a vindication of his view that no intelligent person, given any real information about plants, could fail to be amazed and fascinated by their properties.

'Do you mean,' Clare said slowly, 'that this plant in my basket could be made into the Pill?'

'In a manner of speaking, yes. It's the seeds that are valuable.' He'd caught her.

'Valuable? Who to?'

'Drug companies. Your *Dioscorea* is a wild strain, a genetic resource. If a drug company hasn't got it they could be interested in acquiring it. The Mexicans have found that out, they're hanging on to theirs. It's the germ plasm, you see.'

Clare was looking down at her basket. Barnabus pushed his advantage. 'Like the *Solanus*,' he said. 'Your wild potato.'

'Potato?' said Clare. 'But potatoes are everywhere. Everyone's got potatoes.'

'You know,' he said, warming to his theme, 'that ninety per cent of all our food comes from about twenty plants? More than half the wheat grown in the Canadian prairies comes from one single variety. Almost all the coffee in Brazil descends from one plant. The genetic base is dangerously narrow and ...'

'Potatoes,' Clare said, recalling him.

'Potatoes too. Seventy-two per cent of the whole American potato crop depends on four varieties.'

'Yes, yes,' Clare said impatiently, 'but what does all that *mean?*'

There was no doubting her interest now, her face was tense with it, she had quite forgotten her drink. 'Look,' he said, 'in the 1860s almost every vine in Europe was destroyed by *Phylloxera*. An insect. Luckily, American vines weren't affected by the insect, they had a genetic resistance. So they grafted American rootstocks on to the European plant and saved the day. This year half the potato crop in the West has failed. That's very serious. Echoes of the Irish famine.'

'So it has,' Clare said. She heard again the crackle of burning fields, saw the smoke in a grey shroud over Concha's grave. Leaning her elbows on the stained table, she stared at Barnabus. 'Can my plant cure this blight?'

He was pleased, almost smug. He'd managed to communicate his own enthusiasm to her. Now he could afford to go into details. He did so happily. At the end of his dissertation Clare's heart was thudding against her ribs. Somewhere in all this information, if she collected her thoughts and concentrated, she felt certain something could be extracted that would make sense of all her travails. She knew it. 'So,' she said carefully, 'what you're saying is that the wild strains of the plants we cultivate are important. Valuable. Worth money.'

'I'm saying,' Barnabus said, 'that they're absolutely vital. In America the value of medicines made just from the higher plants is already about three thousand million dollars a year and it's rising. If I were to take a guess about your friend, the one who sent you these plants ...'

'Three thousand million dollars,' Clare said in a dream.

'... I'd say he had an economic interest in them.' Barnabus peered at Clare over the top of his empty tankard. 'They're all potentially valuable plants, you see.' He dived for the basket and brought out the podded stem. 'This *Lupinus*, for example. Tarwi, they call it. Very rich in protein, more nutritious than peas or beans or even soyabeans or peanuts and very hardy. It'd make a useful food crop except the seeds taste bitter. Now suppose ...' and he rattled the dried pods at Clare, '... suppose this particular wild strain *didn't* have bitter seeds. Then plant breeders could really get to work on it, with nice profits ahead.'

The man beside Barnabus at the table was staring at Clare as he talked, his brows drawn together. Clare ignored him.

'What about the others?' She pointed below her, to the basket. 'Do they have a value?'

'Well,' said Barnabus, 'the *Dioscorea*, that's steroids and the Pill. As for the *Solanus*, well, the domestic potato is in bad trouble. Unknown disease, crops blighted, experts baffled. Plant the same tubers next year and the same thing will happen because they all come from the same source. What people don't realize is that the loss of genetic diversity in plants ...' he slapped his hand on the table to emphasize his words, '... could be as disastrous to mankind as a nuclear holocaust. But your little fellow might have an in-built resistance. We already know that *Solanum berthaultii* – that's another strain of wild potato – repels aphids where

[350]

cultivated potatoes don't. If your potato repelled whatever caused this blight, then bob's your uncle, money in the till. They're *patenting* seeds these days. you know. We have to pay royalties to the multi-nationals to *eat*. As for that mystery plant of yours, who knows? Could be a cure for cancer. They say there might be five thousand unknown plants that are anti-carcinogenic. Get hold of those and you could be on to a fortune.'

Clare touched her hands to her temples. She felt as if she were undergoing some delicate operation to restore her sight. Blurred outlines were already perceptible in the darkness out there, though she could not yet define them. She shut her eyes briefly and opened them again. 'But how could you find plants like that? You can't just go around picking them at random and testing every one, can you? It'd take years and years.'

'Ethno-botany,' said Barnabus, nodding at her as at a bright pupil. 'That's the key. You tap the traditional knowledge of aboriginal societies.'

'Excuse me,' said the man opposite Clare.

She blinkered her face from him with one hand. 'You mean,' she said slowly to Barnabus, 'you get the people of a country to show you what they've always used for food or medicine and then you check those plants?'

'Exactly,' Barnabus said. 'The obvious short cut.'

'And if they're any good?'

'You take them.' He rocked his hands on the edge of the table.

'Excuse me,' said the man, pushing his face at Clare, 'but haven't we met somewhere? At the Barton shindig, was it? I know your face.'

'No,' Clare said. Two hours ago his interruption would have sent her into a panic. Now, absorbed, she wanted only for him to stop talking. She brushed him away as if he were a cloud of mosquitoes.

'I'm afraid,' Barnabus said, 'that I ought to be going.' He

looked at his watch. Clare caught at his arm as the man relapsed back in his chair, looking baffled.

'Go on,' she urged Barnabus. 'You take them and . . .?'

'Well.' He chose his words. 'The unscrupulous take them. They can process them and sell them back to the Third World at huge profits. The scrupulous experiment with them so that the people who collect them, the natives, benefit later with improved crops or better medicine or whatever.'

'Ah,' said Clare, letting her breath out. 'And aren't there any controls?'

'There are some now, though they're not terribly effective,' said Barnabus. 'In the old days even the most respected botanists were guilty of what we'd call exploitation today. You'll remember it was an expert from Kew in the nineteenth century who took rubber seedlings from the Amazon and set up a rival rubber industry in Malaysia. That was when the bottom fell out of the South American rubber boom. Not . . .' he added hastily, '. . . that anyone ever quite proved whether or not he had permission or simply bribed officials. The fact is, Kew was practically founded for economic botany. For the good of the British Empire and all that.'

'Uh huh,' Clare said, feeling her way. This ancient theft of seedlings was news to her but it seemed to fit. Where, she wasn't sure, but somewhere.

'Nowadays,' Barnabus went on, 'that sort of exploitation tends to be deliberately under the counter, if only because of bad publicity.'

'Under the counter?' prompted Clare.

'Really, I must be going.' He'd done his job too well. She was never going to let him get back and that paper for the conference next day wouldn't write itself.

'*Please.*' She put her hand on his. 'Just one example.'

He thought quickly. 'Like the pharmaceutical company that sent their men into an Indian village . . .'

'Indian?' Clare stared at him, biting hard on her thumb.

'In India.'

'Oh, *India*,' she said and relaxed momentarily.

'I heard of an incident just the other day. Par for the course. The men go in and offer money to the villagers – usually the women – to bring them the plants they use. Food, spices, herbs, medicines, that sort of thing. The biggest and the best specimens, of course. So the women scour the place, uproot everything and the men hand out a few rupees and go off with the booty. Leaving the villagers with a few genetically degraded plants that are quite useless to them. The poor old villagers sell for nearly nothing and are left with less than nothing for themselves. For that matter, nothing for their children or their children's children either. In fact ...' he leaned at Clare confidentially, '... in this particular instance the company men took every green thing they could lay their hands on and didn't pay the women with money at all. Paid them with alcohol.'

In a sudden sharp movement Clare knocked the remains of her whisky across the table. The man opposite staggered awkwardly to his feet, his trousers wet. Barnabus stood up too, mopping clumsily about him with a paper napkin. The whisky glass rolled to the edge of the table and burst in a small explosion of splinters on the floor. The barman started towards them, cloth in hand. Clare rose unsteadily to her feet as the barman's cloth enveloped the table. The men looked down, brushing at their sodden trousers. When they looked up again, Clare had gone.

Dishevelled, dragging her raincoat after her, she pushed out of the pub door and began running along the pavement, stumbling now and again on the uneven slabs. There was a weight pressing down on her skull and the bones around her eyes felt tender. The high red bulk of a bus groaned to a halt at the traffic lights behind her and she back-tracked, jumped on and hoisted herself up the stairs to sit alone at its front in the afternoon haze. She would go with it as far as it went wherever it went because it was moving and she could not move forward or backward or in any direction for the time being. London exposed its shabby streets ahead of her: scabrous buildings, grey hedges, the lines of decaying molars that were houses pitted with shops, rubbish piled up everywhere in bags that, torn, set their debris adrift in the faded sun.

Under that same sun, burnished to a red-hot ball, Ventura burned with a green flame and the people there, axed by the heat, hung motionless in hammocks or toiled while the sweat seeped from their brown trunks as the resin seeped from the trees. The women would be at work in the village, bent over their stony patches, squatting to blow at the flames of their fires, grinding maize between heavy stones, perched by the river to wash clothes and pots, peeling and skinning, chopping and cooking what little they had to nourish chickens and donkeys and pigs and children and men. Thick blue veins crawled up their legs, the leathery feet were flattened with toil, their bellies swollen with more children to be born and fed or to bury. Clare felt their dark eyes on her, willing her as they willed the chipped statuettes of the Madonna to end their travails and bring them hope and food for their children and medicine for fevers and a monthly supply of little yellow pills, the sources of which they had already uprooted from their forest and brought, upon Clare's instructions, to Clare.

For several seconds then, Clare was hit by such a blast of fury as she had never experienced before. Her whole body shook and trembled, sweat burst out from under her arms and her hands, gripped on the bar of the window, were slippery ridged fists. She unhooked them and pressed them to her mouth, to stop the shaking of her jaw. A red-hot skewer pierced her shoulder blades and she bent double, trying to control waves of nausea. London moved by below her and in a while the conductor swung along the seats towards her and fumbling, unseeing, she passed him some coins.

[354]

'Piccadilly?' he asked.

She nodded. He left her alone again.

The telephone kiosk at Piccadilly stank of urine and didn't work. Clare came out and walked stiffly past groups of sunburnt youths and news-vendors and couples peering at maps to the Piccadilly Hotel. A man interposed himself between her and the glass doors, mumbling something. She stared down at his black shoes, at the dark grey edges of his trousers. The bulk removed itself and she went on. Beside the bank of perspex hoods in the hotel foyer she waited and then dialled, cupping her ears from the chatter around.

'Miss Carrington please,' she said in a minute, her voice low. 'Miss Deborah-Jane Carrington.' There was a pause and then she said, 'But I must talk to her. Yes. Yes, especially if she is leaving for Ventura tomorrow.' The receiver shook in her hand. Another pause came and this time she said, very clearly, 'This is Mrs Carrington. *Mrs* Carrington, tell her.' She held grimly on to the receiver. No use to risk giving her own name. After all that had happened, after all that Deborah had made happen, it was more than likely that the last person on earth she wished to talk to was Señora de Toro y Plata. Clare silently prayed that the girl had a mother, a sister-in-law, a grandmother, any living female relative at all who answered to the name of Mrs Carrington.

'Mom?' The familiar nasal voice was miraculously there at the other end of the line, breathy with astonishment. 'What in the world are you doing in London, Mom?'

'Deborah, I have to see you. This is Clare.'

Carrington's voice said 'Oh' and sank away.

Clare raised hers, forcing into it every shred of past authority that she could muster. 'They tell me you are flying back to Ventura tomorrow morning. I must talk to you this evening. I have a message that must be passed on to the President. It is most urgent. It is a matter that affects his security. Do you understand?'

'Er. Oh, very well,' Deborah's voice said. 'Where do you want me to come?'

Clare told her. She added 'At six o'clock, please. And, Carrington, tell no one, do you hear? No one.'

She put down the receiver and dialled again, her heart beating slowly and thunderously inside her, making her feel sick. If he wasn't there, her plan would fail. Please God, let him be there. The distant buzz of the bell rang emptily in her ear, four peals, five peals, please God oh God, and the ringing stopped.

'Freddie,' Clare said. 'Freddie.'

He came to the door to greet her, more substantial, better clad than she remembered, altogether nattier. She was damp inside her clothes and a shower had made her damp outside as well, her hair was matted and straggled in her collar, the old mac – Ma's mac – flapped wetly at her knees. The welcome on his face turned into a furtive unease. He thinks I am crazy, thought Clare. he is embarrassed by me.

'Good Lord,' Freddie said. 'I hardly recognize you. What have you done with your hair?'

She had forgotten about her hair. She put up a hand to its tangled mass and tried to make her smile convincing. 'My disguise. I'm rather well-known about town these days, Freddie. As you are probably aware.' She essayed a wobbly giggle.

It worked and Freddie's face cleared. All that sobbing down the phone had thoroughly upset him, he couldn't stand weepy women at the best of times and to get Clare La Fontaine on the line having hysterics out of the blue had unnerved him. Particularly after all that kerfuffle in the papers. The poor girl had obviously flipped her lid, he had thought, but noblesse oblige and all that and thank God she had pulled herself together now. 'Yah,' he said, 'you can say that again, old girl. What on earth were you up to, eh? Tanked to the gills, were you? That was my guess. Like a snort now?' He hung up her mac in the narrow hall and Clare walked ahead of him into the pale green sitting-room. Everything looked much the same as it always had, but distinctly cleaner and tidier. The carpets were new, thick and spotless, there were even flowers in a vase. She flopped down on a sofa, relieved beyond measure that Freddie had remained in the flat whose address she knew so well.

'It looks nice,' she said. 'Nicer than it did. Got a new cleaning lady?'

Freddie, pouring out drinks, chortled. 'You could say so,' he said. 'I'm married. Jennie Bellingham as was. You wouldn't know her, she's from Cape Town. Met her over there. Lots of lovely lolly. She's in the country. This place is up for sale, we've bought a bolt-hole in Eaton Square. I hear your people sold Flood Street?' He gave her a glass.

'Yes,' Clare said, 'otherwise I wouldn't have bothered you.' She looked round the room quickly. A small carriage clock on the mantelpiece said five o'clock. 'Freddie, look. I didn't make much sense on the phone. I've got a big favour to ask you.'

'Fire away,' said Freddie, looking uneasy again. 'Chin chin.'

'Cheers.' She swallowed and sat up, edging her legs sideways along the sofa in the classic model's pose. 'I'll tell you about it later, the yummy details and all, but Freddie, would you be an angel and lend me the flat for an hour or so at six?' She fluttered her eyelashes at him. It wasn't easy, with swollen lids and cheeks still stiff with tears, but it had the desired effect.

'Ah ha,' Freddie said, 'you haven't changed, you naughty thing. Well, I don't know that the missus would approve. Very strict on these matters, she is.' He looked smug. 'But, yes, why not? Must be rather a problem, having a jolly under the gaucho's beady eyes. Consider yourself off the lead here, my dear. I'll take myself off, don't you worry. I have a dinner, anyway, so the place is yours for the evening. Absolutely.'

Clare had been terrified that he might have people coming and so refuse. Now she was terrified at the thought of what lay ahead. The drink made her feel queasy and she laid it aside. It was vital that she kept a clear head. She thanked Freddie effusively, trying hard to act like a woman with nothing but a lover's tryst on her mind. It was heavy going and the next half-hour seemed to crawl past but her years in Ventura had taught the skills of diplomacy, the ability to chatter amusingly while her real self was far away. Freddie's frequent laughter attested to her training. He was relaxed, enjoying himself and it was twenty-five to six.

She stood up and held out a hand to him, smiling like a hostess. He took it and heaved himself out of his chair. 'I need time to primp,' she said. 'I look a sight.'

'Sure, sure.' Freddie waved about him. 'You know where everything is. Bathroom and so on. Haven't forgotten my little nest, have you?' He put a clumsy arm round her shoulders and squeezed her to his chest. 'Jennie's a marvellous girl, of course, wouldn't change her for the world, but ...'

Clare ducked from under his arm. Her stomach was churning with apprehension. She walked to the door, swaying her hips, saying with a comic pout, 'Freddie, you're incorrigible, you rogue, you. Now run along and we'll see each other soon. Alone.' She winked. 'I promise.'

Freddie broke off the head of a flower, stuck it in his buttonhole, gave her cheek a wet kiss and ran along.

In the silence that followed his departure Clare concentrated hard to control the thudding inside her that made it difficult to think. A quisling rose up, smiling with her face, it wanted nothing more than to wrench itself away from here and run for dear life towards laughter and the crowded streets and blessed normality. Come, it said, beckoning. This is pointless, ridiculous, a joke. This is none of your business. Resolutely, Clare walked to the bathroom and there washed her stained cheeks and brushed at her brown mop of hair. The quisling looked out of the mirror. You're only a woman, it coaxed. You weren't meant for this sort of thing, all this plotting, this melodramatic nonsense. Silly bitch. Clare traced lipstick carefully onto her dry lips and stood a moment with both hands pressed against her rebellious stomach. The quisling jeered. Who do you think you are? A female James Bond, licensed to kill? Please. Don't make me laugh. Clare went back into the sitting-room and looked at the clock. A quarter to six. The voice in her head became honeyed. Take a valium, it said, rich with sympathy. Calm yourself. You need so badly to be calm. Well half a valium then, go on, go *on*. Clare sat down on the sofa and clicked her handbag shut. The quisling lost its cool. What are you going to say to this Carrington? What idiot scheme have you dreamed up? You haven't an idea, have you? Fool, poor fool.

Clare sat upright, took a deep breath and yelled at the top of her lungs 'Fuck off'. The noise cracked her ears but when the echo had died her body was no longer trembling and the quisling had gone. A cold energy replaced it. 'I want the truth,' she said aloud, 'I only want the truth.' When the fury she had felt in the bus had drained there was only one name in her mind – Carrington, Deborah-Jane. She it was who had impersonated Clare so she it was who knew what was going on, who knew what caused the filthy stink of treachery and greed. The humiliation at the airport was no longer central but only a vengeful part of a far larger whole, a whole that somewhere paralleled that other Indian village in Barnabus' story, denuded of its heritage. She had been set up as the front for the Women's Co-operative and the women had been bribed with money and then with drink to bring in the loot from the forest. Then they had ditched her and, through her, the women, making them ashamed with her shame. Those men around Raul in their creased suits, carrying their bulging briefcases in and out of his offices

[359]

eating at her table, they must be involved. But behind Raul's back or with his connivance? Had he used her or were there so many others happy to see her brought down? Whoever they were, they had not believed they could rely on her complicity.

That thought, at least, made her glad, it put the seal on her own knowledge that she had greatly changed. The Clare that Raul had met and bribed with his emeralds five years ago no longer existed. That frivolous money-hungry girl who could have been relied on to countenance or wilfully ignore any injustice for the sake of her comfort had withered and died under the implacable eyes of the poor. At least that. God knows, she had done her best to avoid that confrontation but when it had finally come in the forest villages she had responded. Too well, indeed, for some people's peace of mind. They'd had to discredit her. And the odd thing was that her moment of utter humiliation was the proof that she had chosen the right, the good.

From a great distance she heard her father's words as she knelt in her nightgown by the fire at Tucolston. The dragon is evil, you can always tell and you have to fight it. But Pa's dragon was Communism and he'd got that wrong. Communism, like all the other 'isms', was no more than paper, paper held up to make a dragon's mask. If you tore off that mask, tore off all the dragons' masks, you saw the real face beneath and the face was the face of a man. Men were the dragons, the heart of darkness was male. A deformed thing, stunted, shrunken and arid and fearsome in its own fear, a dwarf in jackboots that roamed the earth raping and pillaging, torturing and slaying, blind and cruel and sick with greed so that nothing would do in the end but to threaten the whole world with destruction and then, because that would not be enough either, then destroy it.

Clare sighed with the tension of waiting. Her thoughts slipped, shuffled into each other, a disordered pack of cards. There were good men too, men of peace and courage who knew and feared the dwarf, who battled with it in themselves and chased its dwarfish shape across the world. And whose were the faces behind the faces behind the masks? Veiled women, phantom women with bloodless hands and the dwarf like a leech at their breasts as they smiled and crooned. Not me, thought Clare, my face is not among them, any longer.

[19]

The doorbell rang.

Clare opened the door. Carrington stood in the dim well of the stairs smiling her amiable smile, pushing her glasses up on her nose. She looked large and rather cheerful and very ordinary in her tight jeans and sneakers and cotton vest with writing over her small breasts that said she loved New York. Clare was taken aback by the sheer ordinariness of Carrington, she had a grubby plaster round one finger and a button dangled on a thread at her neck and her smile bared a row of well-brushed teeth so that there was no evil but only a human being to whom Clare smiled back. She had no wish to smile but she could not control that movement of her lips that was an instinctive, reflex action, its roots reaching down into fear, a polite grimace of fear.

'Come in,' Clare said and Carrington walked past her and the air that she moved carried the faintest trace of the sweet smell of menstrual blood. Carrington was a woman like herself and, like herself, she menstruated. Naturally she did. It was all quite natural and a waste of time and inane and it would soon be over.

Clare went to the table where the bottles stood and said, 'Would you like a sherry? There's some nice dry sherry.'

'That would be fine, thank you,' Carrington said. Clare poured the pale liquid and had a sudden image of her own fingers sprinkling powder – a truth drug perhaps – into the drink like a Victorian poisoner or a secret agent and almost laughed at her fevered imaginings. Melodramatic nonsense. Nevertheless, she could feel Carrington's eyes on her back and she turned and met them. Carrington groped at her glasses and began to talk fast.

'Señora, I haven't been in touch, I wanted to phone you but I thought ... everything happened so fast ... it was really so awful ... I didn't know what to say. I am sorry. It must have been terrible for you. I am really so sorry.'

She looked sorry. Was she, too, taken aback by Clare's actual presence or was she acting? Or maybe, after all, she had nothing to do with it all, perhaps the whole thing was a figment of Clare's imagination, a paranoid fantasy to explain her own foolishness and shift her own guilt. She could feel the vital fuel of anger draining away out of her body, leaving her limbs heavy and her mind inert. Before it left her altogether, she heard her voice saying without rancour, offering the sherry, 'Why did you do it, Debbie-Jay? Why did you do it?'

'Do what, Señora?' Carrington took the little crystal glass. Her voice was light and mild but one amber drop of sherry spilt down the glass's stem. She wiped at it quickly and looked round the room.

'I didn't know you had a place in London,' she said. 'My, it's pretty and what about that *view*.' The long windows overlooked a green square where small children played under the benevolent eyes of au pairs and nannies and well-dressed women walked their tiny shaggy dogs. 'I just love London, Señora. I've been working, of course, but I've managed to see a lot of the sights. The Tower. The Palace. The wonderful pictures in your National Gallery. I even got to see ...'

'Carrington.' Clare's voice was sharp and loud in the small room. If she didn't get it out now she would shortly stifle in banalities and Carrington would walk from the flat quite undisturbed and off down the shaded pavements, as from a pleasant social visit with her boss's wife, humming. 'Please sit down.'

Deborah-Jane sat. She sipped at her sherry and raised her eyebrows slightly, looking a little to the left of Clare's eyes.

'Carrington, don't pretend. It's no use. I know, you see. I know that you were responsible for that incident at the airport, you made sure that it happened. I know it because I have a photograph of you in my clothes and you are standing in the door of a plane and your skirts, my skirts, are blowing up exactly as mine did. It was planned and I want you to tell me why.'

'*Señora*.' Deborah-Jane spread her hands in amazement, shaking her head so that the tousled hair flapped from side to side. 'No. *No*. It was a horrible accident. I feel very guilty about it. I was inefficient, I blame myself very much. I should have checked and double-checked that you ... that you were correctly dressed but how can you think it was on *purpose*? We were all tired, we were nervous, the bathroom in the plane was so cramped, I had a hangover. I admit it. And I understand ... oh I *do* ... how distressed you must still be but, Señora, to imagine it was *planned* ...'

'The photograph, Carrington.' Clare's voice was icy. 'The photograph.'

Deborah blinked rapidly several times and put her glass carefully down. Then she took her spectacles off. Her eyes underneath were soft, unfocused, vulnerable, they sought Clare's, pleading gently. 'I know nothing about a photograph, Señora. Of course I went to the airport in Ventura, to rehearse for you, in your clothes. Concepción came with me, your own maid. I don't remember that there was any breeze. Breeze, in Ventura?' she gave a soundless laugh, 'but if there was, if my skirts blew up, I don't remember. And if they did, it was a coincidence. Not so strange, either, when you think. You stand up there, the dress is flimsy ... I should have noticed but I didn't. Señora, I swear. It was all a dreadful mistake. Concepción ...'

'Concepción is dead,' Clare said. 'She killed herself.'

'Yes.' Deborah looked down at her feet. 'I heard. Poor Concepción.'

'Who told you?'

'I just heard.' She gestured vaguely. 'Someone at the Embassy ...' She examined one of her sneakers, moving it slowly from side to side. In the street, a car began to hoot peremptorily. A man shouted. 'You fucking bastard. Bloody savage. Get out of it, you fucker.'

The women's eyes met as they listened. Deborah stood up. She went over to where Clare stood and took her hand. 'Please, Señora,' she said. Their eyes were level. 'Forgive me.' Her hand was cold. 'I may have been stupid. I was stupid. But what happened was an accident, a tragic accident. You must see that. You can't organize a breeze, can you? You're upset, Señora. Of course you are. You must be tired out with the whole horrible business and then you imagine things. I understand, believe me.'

Clare let her hand lie in Carrington's cold palm. It was true that she felt tired. She felt washed up, washed out, dragged to and fro by a tide of exhaustion, her eyes were heavy, a wave of sleep flowed into her, rocking her thoughts, lapping into them like the sea moving between a shoal of minnows, separating them one from another with fingers of foam. The tug was strong, it was pulling her inexorably into acquiescence. Let go, let it all go, let it drift away and say goodbye now and think again tomorrow.

Loudly the voice from the street came again. 'I'll fucking *kill* you. Cunt. You fucking *cunt*.' A clamour broke out, a woman screamed, there were running footsteps, the car hooted rhythmically, over and over again, blasting against the window panes.

'I'll kill you,' Clare said under her breath.

She took three steps over to Deborah and gripped her arms. 'I'll kill you,' she repeated, tasting the words. She shook Deborah, her hands hard. The other woman gazed at her confusedly, her head jerking backwards and forwards. Then she pulled her arms away and they stood breathing heavily, staring at each other.

'I'm going,' Deborah said and darted for the door. Clare reached it before her, slammed it shut and turned the key in the lock. Her heart pumped hard, shooting the blood through her veins, driving energy into her limbs. She was engorged, every cell alerted, alive again. Triumph at this unexpected marshalling of forces flooded through her. She smiled, held up the key to Deborah and dropped it in her pocket.

'Not until you tell me the truth,' she said. 'So help you God.'

'Stop it,' Deborah said, 'there's nothing to tell. *Nothing.*' This was a shout. Then softly, 'Let me go, please. I want to go.'

'You're going nowhere,' Clare said.

Carrington jumped back. 'You're crazy,' she said. 'You're a crazy woman.'

'I am,' said Clare, 'and you better watch out. Go on, sit down.' She pushed Carrington down into a chair and pinioned her with an arm across her throat. Carrington looked dazed, she didn't struggle. Then, talking fast, Clare told her. The plants, the bourbon bribes, the way her own humiliation fitted in, her suspicions about Concepción's suicide. Deborah sat, her neck stiff behind Clare's arm, her eyes fixed ahead, unmoving. 'So,' Clare finished, 'you tie up the ends, Carrington. You tell me the rest. Who's behind it, what it's all for. Go on.'

Deborah sat rigid, her mouth shut.

'Go *on*,' Clare said loudly. Carrington's face was shuttered, one tiny vein throbbed in her neck. Silence. The little clock on the mantel ticked, the street sounds had subsided. Unnerved by frustration, Clare jerked her arm, hitting Carrington's throat with a sharp blow and the girl jackknifed forward, gulping and choking. Clare whipped her arm away and got up, staring at the spluttering red-faced figure. Then she leaned to pat the heaving back.

Carrington lunged forward and grabbed at the patch pocket on Clare's skirt. The material ripped and the key fell to the floor. Instantly, both women were on their knees, clawing for it. Head down, Carrington butted Clare away. Gasping at each blow. Clare laced her fingers through the mane on the butting head and pulled. Carrington reared up, and Clare dived for the key that lay beneath her, her nails gouging along the other woman's bare arm. Deborah panting stuck her arm out and, on all fours now, Clare with the key in her fist, they both stared at the long graze. Blood.

'I'm sorry,' Clare said breathlessly, 'I didn't mean to hurt you. I don't want to.'

'Let me go, then,' Deborah said, looking at her arm. Then she looked straight at Clare. 'Let. Me. Go.' The end of her nose was white.

'Look,' Clare said. It was almost a moan. 'It's not for myself. I have to know what you know for other people's sake. You must understand, Deborah.'

Carrington got up and stood patting her arm with the hem of her T-shirt. Clare got up, Carrington turned from her and walked to the window.

Clare followed. 'I *love* those women in Ventura, Deborah.' She still found it difficult to catch her breath. 'They're poor, they have no one to help them, they rely on me and someone's robbing them. *Robbing* them. Taking away the little they have. Food. Medicine. Giving them drink in return. I don't care what happens to me now, I only care about them. Please.' She tried to catch Carrington's attention. 'Please tell me who it is.'

Very loudly Carrington shouted 'Help'. The sound boxed Clare's ears and she smacked her hand over Carrington's mouth, holding it there. A woman walking in the street outside glanced sideways and walked on. Clare stared into the eyes above her hand. Carrington took her wrist delicately and picked it off. 'It's okay,' she said, her voice curiously brisk. 'I don't actually want publicity. Just thought I'd try it on.' She stretched her lips soundlessly — like a snake, Clare thought — and sat down in a chair. Clare sat opposite her. A silence ensued.

'All the same,' Carrington said. 'You didn't care about those women for a long time, right? Funny you should get so sentimental just about the time when ...' She paused, examining her nails.

[367]

'When what?' said Clare.

Carrington slumped in her seat and her voice took on a whining note. 'You had all the luxuries you wanted, didn't you? You were rich. You travelled. You had beautiful clothes. a beautiful home. You hadn't a thing to worry about in the world. But look at me. My Daddy's a drunk, an alky. He was fired from his last posting in São Paulo and he vanished. Woof. Mom was left flat broke and broke in São Paulo is no fun at all, believe me. Raul, the President, he took me out of that. Ever since, I've worked hard for him and I've kept Mom, too. Isn't it about time I had my turn? You won't starve.'

'I don't understand,' Clare said. She was bewildered by this sudden intrusion of Carrington's private life. 'I won't excuse myself to you. That's got nothing to do with it. The point is, there's a terrible injustice going on in Ventura and I must know ...'

Carrington sat forward, staring at her. 'You married Raul for his money.'

'That's none of your ...

'It is.' Carrington's voice was loud. 'You only started working against him when you found out about ...

Clare's groan cut through. '*God.*' She leaned back and looked up at the ceiling. 'You're having an affair with him.'

Carrington said nothing.

'As it happens, I didn't know,' she said. 'It is of no interest to me. None.' Nevertheless, the revelation muddled her, she was unsure how to proceed. Her thoughts kept making odd genuflexions, dipping into blankness. Deborah imagined she knew about Deborah and Raul and so ... so what? Did it make any difference to what she needed Deborah to tell her? No. Nervously she smoothed the cretonne arm of the chair, tweaking at a loose thread, feeling baffled and dismayingly incompetent. What could she do? In films, men threatened other men with guns to make them talk or tied them up and pulled out their fingernails. She didn't have a gun, she didn't have the strength or the rope for that matter to tie Deborah up and the very idea of fingernails made her feel sick. There was nothing, at this moment, that she wanted more to do than to get up, put the key in the door, open it and let Carrington go. Well, what else was there to do? Sit here guarding the woman until her scratch became gangrenous and in agony she sobbed her story out? Clare gave a small moan of contempt for herself. Anger leaked out of her so quickly, like air from a punctured tyre, and she must repair that treacherous gash. Concepción was dead, the women betrayed and her own life in shreds, yet here she was yearning, yes, actually yearning to see the back of the only person who might possibly shed some light on the whole horrible mess so that she, Clare, could take some salvaging action. Concepción had killed herself. Concha, her friend, that poor peasant woman who had worked hard all her life for very little reward, had been driven to a lonely death in a strange country and, even so, had spent her last hour comforting Clare and her last minutes trying desperately to make her understand something ... something ...

'You can't keep me here for ever.' Deborah was truculent now. 'I've got to pack. If I'm not on that plane tomorrow, the President will want to know why. And he isn't going to like what I tell him.'

That did it. Incensed, she stepped in front of Deborah and slapped her hard. Adrenalin shot through her with the sting of her palm and she slapped again jerking that face from side to side, grunting and slapping. Carrington brought up her knees and kicked out wildly. Clare reeled back and Carrington was on her and they fell together, clutched together, flailing out, gasping and panting. Carrington's nose began to bleed, blood ran from her nostrils on to Clare's shoulder and down her neck, they writhed and struggled and the small table with the glasses on it teetered and crashed. Carrington rolled sideways on to a jagged stem of crystal and screamed. She threw herself back on to

her stomach and lay there making barking sounds. Clare, straddled over her, saw the rent in the white cotton and, underneath,
a spongy pink fissure from which bright scarlet blood welled up
and spilled, turning the cotton in a second to a damp dark cloth.
Dizzily, Clare staggered to her feet.

'Stay there,' she said raggedly, 'don't move.' She got to the
bathroom, snatched towels off a rail and laid them on Deborah's
soaked red back. The blood was still splashing out, it was not
believable that so much blood could pour from so short a slit
in flesh. Clare raced back to the bathroom and fumbled frantically
in the medicine cupboard over the basin. She found a spool of
adhesive tape, scissors and gauze – oh thank you, Freddie – and
ran back.

'Lie still, Deborah, it's all right, it's okay. I'm going to pull up
your shirt and close the cut with tape. It won't hurt, I promise.'
Quickly she worked, making comforting noises as Carrington
winced, placing the long strips across the wound, slowly closing
the cruel little mouth, stitching its gaping maw with plaster. The
gauze pad grew a soggy pink but the tape held and as Carrington
lay and Clare watched, the blood slowed and ceased to run. Clare
collapsed back on her haunches, Carrington turned her face
sideways on the carpet and they looked at each other in a kind
of awe.

'You'll be all right,' Clare said and Carrington nodded.

'I'd better tell you,' she said.

'No,' Clare said, 'don't think about it.' She scrabbled on the
floor and held the broken glass where Deborah could see it. 'It
was that. You rolled over on it.' She needed to make it clear.

'Raul is leaving Ventura,' Carrington said. She wrenched her
neck round and Clare, to help her, lay down beside her.

'Leaving? What, to come here?'

'No,' said Carrington. 'Miami. Land's sakes, Clare, you're
covered in blood.'

'So are you. So is everything. The place looks like a slaughterhouse. I borrowed it from a friend of mine. He thinks I've got a lover. Oh Lord . . .' she started to shake with laughter.

'Some lover,' said Carrington, snorting. 'Count Dracula, I presume.' Then she winced again.

'I'll call a taxi,' said Clare, 'that cut must be stitched.'

Carrington turned her cheek to rest on the carpet spattered with blood. 'You'll have to come with me,' she said.

'Of course,' Clare said.

There were clean towels in the linen cupboard, there was soap, hot water and, in the bedroom, a selection of Freddie's new wife's clothes. Jennie, it seemed, was a larger woman than either Clare or Carrington and obviously undaunted by her size, the dresses were flamboyant shifts that engulfed them, giving them the air of weary participants in some Caribbean carnival that had gone on far too long. Nevertheless, by the time Clare had finished, both women looked acceptable enough not unduly to alarm the taxi driver, who gave them only a brief glance before he drove them to the Casualty Department of St Stephen's Hospital. There, an incurious doctor put eight neat clamps in Carrington's back while Clare held her twisting hand. Another taxi took them to the small service flat nearby that the Venturan Embassy rented for its visiting personnel. In the neat anonymous room, Carrington lay on her side on the narrow bed and watched Clare removing clothes from the drawers and packing them in her suitcase.

'You don't have to do that,' she said. 'There's some bourbon in the cupboard.'

Clare found the bottle, held it up and saw the label: Jack Daniel. For the first time, her mind ran back to Carrington's words in the flat.

'Miami,' she said. 'Deborah, why is Raul going to Miami?'

Carrington frowned. 'Listen. You *really* didn't know about me and Raul? Swear?'

'No,' Clare said, 'I had no idea.'

'So that year you spent with the women, that wasn't because ...?'

'No.' Her voice was sharp now, the numbness of the past hour was lifting.

Carrington said in a low whisper, 'Anyway, it makes no difference now.' She pulled herself up to look at Clare, her face intent. 'If I tell you, I'll have to tell Raul you know. I'm going away with him, Clare. I won't give that up. But I don't want ...'

'Oh come on,' Clare said impatiently. 'Just *tell* me.'

So Deborah told her and Clare stopped packing and stood motionless, her arms hanging limply at her sides, listening. When the voice had stopped, she groped for her handbag and felt her way to the door as if she had lost the sight of her eyes.

'You can't do anything, it's too late,' Carrington said. Clare opened the door and started down the stairs.

Holding her back rigid, Carrington twisted herself out of the bed and stumbled across the room. 'What does it matter?' she called into the dark well of the stairs. 'They're all Commies, Clare. They'd kill us all if they could.' She gave one last cry into the darkness. 'It's too late.'

Beneath her, the swing doors thumped and Clare walked out into the sulphurous night.

Carrington, treading slowly and softly so as not to jar her wound, went to the telephone by her bed and picked up the receiver.

Sir Robin Day heaved his body towards the bald Professor of Political Science to his right in a movement less indicative of matiness than of a need to relieve intolerable pressure upon his left buttock. A post mortem was being held on a by-election that had taken place the night before. The atmosphere, Judith thought disgustedly, was inexorably clubby, with the assortment of guest MPs and pundits behaving like dusted-off pillars of the

Athenaeum discussing a blackballed cad over a snort or five of the best port.

'... important to take into account,' said an MP in a dark blue shirt, 'that the electorate of this country is extremely volatile and ...'

'Volatile', in this context, meant pig-ignorant, that was obvious. The electorate of this country is pig-ignorant. But no point at all in being honest. Much more rewarding to talk admiringly of British democracy and the unfailing perspicacity of the voter and brand anyone who attempted political teaching as a malcontent of the Marxist persuasion. Things being what they were, this accusation was often correct. Look at Ruth.

'With all due respect, may I put it to you ...' said Sir Robin, tenderly clutching a floating kidney and easing over to his right buttock, an expression of deep haemorrhoidal concern on his face, 'that ...'

'No you may not,' Judith said aloud and, rising, clicked off the box. On the whole, she tried not to watch television unless she was on it herself. Other people on the screen either irritated her or reminded her that she had not yet progressed beyond an afternoon slot watched by waiters on shifts, the devout, the disabled, the unemployed and housewives, a public that was not best fitted either to savour her words of wisdom or sufficiently pad out her bank account. Which reminded her of the subject of her next programme, out of which she could squeeze a column too, with luck. Female circumcision. An appalling affair, of course, but also high profile, likely to grab the attention of reviewers who, in their chauvinist way, frequently ignored the female ghetto of afternoon telly.

She crossed the untidy room to her desk, a table that contained a lamp, a grimy typewriter, an overflowing ashtray and the telephone, and began reading through a pile of pamphlets.

'Dr Abu Hassan Abu, a gynaecologist, presented some slides showing one of the dangerous side effects of female circumcision, which is urinary fistula. He told his audience that this occurs when women who have been pharaonically circumcized give birth. The baby then presses on the vagina which leads to the stoppage of . . .'

The telephone bleated and Judith reached quickly for it. Charlie, perhaps. He hadn't been around for days. Not that she cared, she was far too busy to care about things, but usually it was her that did the dropping. 'Yes?' she said.

It was the paper, the wheezy voice of one of the unknown men on the night desk. 'Got a call for you,' he said. 'A woman. Sounded rattled. Wanted to get in touch with you immediately, said it was very urgent. I told her we didn't give out home numbers but she seemed in a right old state so I said I'd ask you if it was okay. She's ringing back.'

'A nut,' said Judith, 'it's half eleven. Last time one of our beloved readers got through, she said she'd been locked in a bin by her wicked hubby and would I visit her and bring Maggie Thatcher, Bjorn Borg and Princess Di.'

'Yeah. Well, I'll fob her off.'

'No, wait,' Judith said. It was a dodgy business, giving out a number, it could mean being driven crazy for the next three months by someone who thought they were Mary Queen of Scots. On the other hand, though rarely, good stories came that way. She couldn't afford to miss out. 'Let her phone. But soon, please. I'm filling my hot water bottle now.'

'Will do. Cheers.'

Judith went back to her pamphlet.

'. . . the blood that feeds the vagina. After labour, the woman can no longer control her urine which is passed all the time, stated Doctor Abu.'

'Christ,' said Judith aloud, 'is there anything they won't do to women?'

The telephone rang. The voice at the other end was slurred

and peremptory. 'This is Clare de Toro y Plata. You know who I am.'

Uh huh, a nutter it is, Judith thought. Aloud she said neutrally, 'Yes?'

'I have to see you now. I want something written in the *Chronicle*. You were the woman at the airport. I must talk to you. I won't ... I can't trust a man.'

Have, want, must, won't. Autocratic lady. 'Won't tomorrow do?' Judith asked.

'No, no. *Now*.'

Judith grimaced at the phone. 'Well how do I know you are who you say you are?'

'Oh,' said the voice again. 'You have to believe me.'

Brightly, Judith said, 'Say something in Spanish, then.'

'La vieja selva llora tanto que ya está podrida la tierra. Yo lloro tanto, yo lloro ...' Unaccountably, there followed a sob that sounded like a hiccup.

'Thank you,' said Judith, aching to add 'don't call us'. The poor creature was certainly in a state though whether all that was Spanish or rubbish she wouldn't know. But she gave her address and the line went dead and she put down the receiver, slicing one hand ruefully across her throat.

[20]

The woman came out of the rain dripping like a mermaid, her face livid in the lamplight at the door, her dark hair soaked and the rain running down her cheeks. Judith recognized her immediately in spite of the hair and felt pity before pity was swept away in a wave of excitement. This would be some story. No one had talked to Lady Clare since the airport, no one but lucky old Jude. She led the way down the stairs and the woman stumbled after her as if she were being pursued. Helping her off with her wet mac, Judith felt a stirring of doubt. It was Clare all right, no doubt about that, but there were many other things wrong, very wrong. She was a mess. Her face was drawn and the flesh almost green or perhaps that was the fault of the vile green dress that hung from her thin shoulders and bagged around her knees in uneven scallops. One stocking torn, dirty nails, a thin tang of whisky in a nimbus around her. Trouble.

'Sit down, do.'

Clare backed into the chair shivering and Judith saw that even in her distress her beauty was astonishing, far more so than in the photographs, with those ice-maiden bones and the eyes almost violet under lids that were puffy now and that marvellous mother-of-pearl skin. And that with dyed hair – what must she be like with her own famous crowning glory? Judith hardly cared to think.

'I'll get you a coffee. Won't be a moment.'

But her visitor wouldn't stay put. In the kitchen, waiting for the kettle to boil, Judith could hear her pacing about, talking to herself. 'Hold on, I'll be with you in a minute,' Judith called once but she didn't stop. She went on and on about something – 'terrible', Judith heard twice, 'terrible'. Then she started to cry, sobbing out loud like a child, her mouth open, not even trying to be quiet, her nose running, making awful sounds right down in her chest. Judith grabbed a box of Kleenex and pushed it at Clare but she took no notice at all and Judith had to push her back in the chair and put a piece of tissue to her nose and say 'blow' and she blew.

There were great heaves still coming from her chest and Judith made her drink some brandy, a few sips, and she sank back. Judith thought she had never seen any human being so utterly exhausted, she was too tired even to close her mouth, she let it hang open and mucus ran from her nose and Judith wiped it again. She drank the coffee in gulps, slopping it down her front and patting at herself in an aimless way while Judith watched her as an adult watches a clumsy child.

Then she stuck the mug out and said in a gasping voice but crossly, 'I don't *take* sugar.'

'Beg pardon, Your Highness, I should have known,' Judith said, trying to nudge the woman into some ordinary reaction but the huge unfocused washed-out eyes registered nothing, they stared distractedly about the room and then at Judith or through her to some image of horror beyond. Judith put a spoonful of sugar in the mug and stirred it and handed it back but Clare wouldn't have it, she waved it away and leant forward to grip Judith's arm, quite hurting her.

'Can't you understand?' Her voice was harsh and loud in the quiet room. 'When it happened to me, the airport thing, I thought he ... they ... wanted my disgrace. His revenge I thought, in just that way, because I wasn't a virgin. But I found out about the plants, how they bribed the women to get the plants ...'

'The *plants*?'

'... they trusted me, they wanted money to feed their children, they brought the plants to me and the men took them and I didn't know. I didn't *know*.' Clare gave a dry sobbing cough and shook Judith's arm. 'They were stealing everything from the women, they were hungry and ill and they couldn't stop having babies and the plants could have helped them but they took them away.'

'Look,' Judith said, 'I don't know what you're talking about. What women? What plants? Who was taking what?'

Clare was up on her feet, pacing about, haranguing some invisible audience, or an unknown person. 'How could you, how *could* you? Swine, greedy swine. There's nothing left there, they'll have to buy it back, everything that was theirs by right, from their own earth. *We'll* get the benefit, we'll be even healthier and better fed and we'll take the Pill that comes from their plants and have one point four children and they'll go on and on and on and nobody cares. Who cares?' She turned on Judith furiously. 'D'you think they care, any of them? Him? The others? Their own husbands? The FLV, los chicos?'

'I don't ...'

'They don't give a fuck.' Clare snapped her fingers. 'All that bombing and killing, his men, their men. Maybe they'll get their land in the end but there'll be nothing left in it. Nothing at all.'

'Clare,' Judith said, trying for some authority over this hysterical rambling creature. 'Let's get back to what you said about your disgrace, at the airport.'

Clare gazed at her with empty eyes.

'The photographs,' Judith said earnestly. 'It must have been terrible for you. How did you feel?'

'It doesn't *matter* any more.' Clare was shouting now. 'Don't you see? None of that matters now.'

'But surely,' Judith said, doggedly searching for a way in, 'surely you must have felt ...'

Clare breathed heavily in and looked up at the ceiling. Then she dropped on her knees beside Judith and hit both her fists on

Judith's knees. The smell of whisky was strong. 'Listen,' she said, 'listen. When he told me about the plants at Kew, I thought that was it, I thought that was all.' She moaned a moment to herself. 'That was dreadful enough, taking the seeds, leaving only the weakest, the degenerate ones, robbing the people. But then Carrington said ... Carrington said ...' She tried to get more words out but the sobs took her breath away. She put her head on Judith's knees and wailed in anguish.

Judith patted the matted hair uneasily, turning her nose from the whisky fumes. There was a thin crust of blood, she could see it in the hollow of Clare's collar bone. And more blood, scales of it, rusty on her hands. Oh shit, Judith thought, what have I got into? She's gone mad. The poor girl has flipped her lid and there's no copy in a madwoman. 'Please,' she coaxed, trying to move the head on her lap, 'tell me what you're going to do now. Your plans. Are you going back soon to Ventura?'

The head lifted and Judith found herself staring at a death's head, the skin pinched and tight so that the bones showed through. 'There is no Ventura,' the skull said and the voice was almost light now, almost merry. Judith folded her arms across her chest. It was cold in the flat. A warm evening but it was cold here and she shivered. The merry voice went on.

'You see, it's been sold, Ventura. He put it up for sale. He played king, he played with his soldiers and now he's playing shops because he's cross. Because he thinks they're going to take his toys away. So he's selling them first. Good morning, sir, what can I sell you? Monkeys to torture? Certainly, sir, I'll wrap them up. Your lady wife would like a fur? The ladies do, don't they, sir? Lots of pretty skins I've got, beautifully marked. Some of them very rare. Almost unobtainable these days, buy now is my advice. Last chance, going, going ...'

'Please, Clare,' Judith said and tried to get up but Clare's hands restrained her, hooking into her skirt. Clare's face smiled gaily up.

'No, no,' she said, 'don't go away. Satisfaction guaranteed or your money refunded. Would you like some timber? Very useful, timber. We've got a lot of it here, whole forests. Just wait a moment and we'll cut it down for you. These are our last stocks, of course, nothing will grow afterwards but all the better for you, eh? Strike while the iron's hot, I say, and the devil take the hindmost.' She laughed aloud, a laughter as bright as bells.

Judith tried to rise again but Clare's hands pressed hard.

'We aim to please,' she said. 'Can I interest you in frogs? We have innumerable species of frogs and they're not easy to get these days, no sir. Ours are excellent for dissection and cheap at the price. I can't quite recall the going rate, but I'm sure we can undercut whatever it is, for a quick sale. And here . . .' Clare's voice grew warm, '. . . how would your kiddies like a pretty Polly, sir? Yes, of course they would. Hullo Polly, pretty Polly. Look at them, aren't they lovely? That beautiful green, those pink tail feathers, there's nothing like a bird, a feathered friend, and only a thousand pounds each. A bargain, sir, that's what they are. A bargain.'

Judith prised the clinging fingers off her. 'I have to go to the bathroom,' she said, 'excuse me.' She went out of the room and Clare followed. 'If you don't mind,' she said rather desperately and bolted the door. Outside, Clare talked on, her voice rising and falling, punctuated by little laughs, carrying on a macabre conversation with herself. What now, Judith thought, frozen on the lavatory seat, what now? The poor thing is mad or drunk or both, she looks as if she were going to die and there's blood on her shoulder. *The dictator's wife came to see me last night*, she wrote in her head, *Señora de Toro y Plata the beautiful Lady Clare who is beautiful no longer because.* Because? *she has been driven out of her mind by the tragic humiliation of her arrival. On the steps of her own private jet she was attacked in full view of a hundred waiting journalists by a horde of wild plants who surged around her sticking their green fingers up her skirts, causing her hair to turn black over-*

night ... oh God. She rearranged her clothing and stepped out into the storm again and was half-dragged by Clare back into the sitting-room.

'Write it. Write it down.' Clare ran over to Judith's desk, found some paper and a pencil and pushed them at her. 'Put down what I'm saying, it's their only chance.'

Judith wrote, filling pages with meaningless scribble as Clare hung over her, pouncing every time she stopped, stabbing at the paper with her finger. 'Write.' Her hand ached, her ears rang with the clamour of that monotonous voice. Clare flailed about the dingy room and drank her way slowly through Judith's Scotch, upending the bottle, slopping it everywhere, grimacing and coughing and drinking more. Her voice grew thick, she stuttered and mumbled and nothing she said made sense to Judith, scratching with her pencil under Clare's brilliant eyes.

As the church clock over the road chimed three o'clock Clare went to the window and drew back the curtains and yelled to the street. 'Every stick,' she yelled, 'every stone, every tree, anything anyone will pay for he's selling and going while the going's good with their blood in his pocket, in *cash*.' She slammed at the window again and again with the flat of her hands. 'Nothing left for the people, nothing at all for ever and ever.' She howled '*Amen*'.

Judith, her hand numb, her whole body stiff, closed her heavy stinging eyes. Sleep surged at her and she went under and still heard Clare's voice crying out. *The earth, he's selling the earth.*

Some time in the night Clare fell asleep, sprawled on a sofa, twitching and moaning, the tears flaking on her cheeks. Judith, waking with a pain in her shoulder, pulled herself out of the chair and staggered to the bathroom, where she washed her face, took off her clothes and put on her nightdress. Then she tiptoed into the room where Clare lay twisted in her awful green dress, a battered little heap. Looking down at her Judith felt a spasm of genuine pity followed by a growing pleasure that even at this dreadful time of the night after so many gruelling hours she could feel such real pity. Some people thought journalists were hard. Not she, not Judith. We have done this to her, she told her compassionate self. The media. Clare was put on trial without benefit of jury and sentenced and left to go out of her mind. And she is innocent, poor woman, so the shock destroyed her. The sleeping Clare was so pathetic and really — Judith looked more closely — no longer even pretty, the face was somehow submerged, coarsened by unhappiness and the crude black of the dyed hair.

Quite suddenly Judith was amazingly cheerful, her heart lifted in kindness, she felt drunk with the sweet wine of sacrifice. I will not write about this, she thought. Not a word will I write. I could have a great story and I would be praised and perhaps they would put my salary up and even make me Columnist of the Year but I will not write it. I am a caring human being and a woman and I am not prepared to use another woman's weakness and distress against her, for my own ends. At that, a glow of respect for herself lit her up, she smiled in the wan lamplight. I will protect Clare from herself.

An image of Ruth, dear plain Ruth, came into her mind. There, Ruth, she said to the image of her friend, you think I would sell out women for money, for my own ambition, but you see, you are so very wrong. This is a golden opportunity and I will not take it. I pass. Fondly now, she gazed down at the crumpled woman she had saved. Gently, she patted one grimy hand. 'You're all right with me,' she said softly into the silence. 'I won't betray you.' Then she went into her bedroom and fell immediately asleep.

In the grey light of morning Clare peeled back the skin from the grapes of her eyes and moved involuntarily. Every cell and sinew in her body screeched. Shock, drink, the fight with Carrington had taken a heavy toll, she was no more than stretched flesh over loose and jangling bones that might never make a whole again. Gingerly she slid her legs to the floor and gathered herself precariously up upon them, a bag on stilts. Peering through the pulpy grapes she could dimly discern furniture, glasses, bottles and butt-filled ashtrays. There was also a notebook. It was spread on the carpet, its open pages black with the watery lines of shorthand. Slowly she bent, picked it up and held it to her chest, a magical poultice that warmed her through and through, curing all that ailed her. She looked up at the ceiling and smiled for joy. Aloud, very quietly, she said, 'I've done it,' and had to breathe deeply to stop the victorious tears. 'Concha, I've done it.'

Carrying the notebook flat on her hands like a gift for a god, she moved stealthily into the darker recess of Judith's bedroom. The sleeping mound on the bed did not stir. Delicately, Clare laid the notebook across the mound and crept out. In the hall, she clasped her hands together and shook them over her head, her mouth open on a silent shout of triumph. Then God, thank God. She was in time. The bastards would be stopped. Her women would be spared. At the edge of her eye a figure moved and she whirled round, her heart leaping. Only a mirror, only herself but, Jesus, what a self. A nightmare, a witch, a corpse thrown up in a storm. She crossed the chest of the corpse, forehead, heart, left shoulder, right, and turned away to unhook her raincoat from where it hung, diving into its clammy folds with a shiver. The basket full of broken plants leant against the wall. No need for them now, their job was done. Message over, DV. Nevertheless her hand reached out and took the basket up in case, in case.

Then Clare was on the stairs, heading up and out. She would go to Freddie's flat again to clean herself up and make her explanations and work out what came next. Thinking of that she pushed open the heavy front door and filled her lungs with the fresh morning air. The weight that had lain on her so long shifted and lifted, the tentacles of misery loosened and euphoria flooded in. Nothing much had changed yet and she had no future that she could see but at this moment on this London street, to her own amazement, she was happy. Swinging her basket, she set off lightly across the deserted road. Behind her a car roared into life and swerved, tyres shrieking, from the kerb. Judith, floating up from a dream, heard it in her basement bed and sank again, the feathery duvet closing round her ears, closing out the dull thump of metal and the one high scream.

The car door swung open and a man scrambled out. Head down, ducking from the lines of curtained windows, he crouched among the broken stems and twigs and dragged a handbag from white fingers laced with red. In again, door slammed shut, the car lurched back, arced in a howling curve and shot away.

Judith, a hundred yards away, gave a small contented snore.

It was bedlam on the river, the uproar could be heard two miles away. A mushroom cloud of dust hung below the sun, choking the lungs, gritting machinery. Chainsaws screamed at the far green wall of a canyon as wide as two motorways gouged straight ahead into the forest from the river bank opposite the Nombre Dios wharf, its floor pitted with stumps, its high sides fenced by flayed tree-trunks. Barges lay low in the muddied waters of the river, anchored end to end and creaking under their loads of crates and timber. Ropes snaked everywhere across the cemented slope of the wharf, toiling men bellowed over the screech of winches and the heaving and rumbling of trucks backing in, backing away. The pandemonium was made worse this day by the frantic shrieks of the monkeys in the crates that swung and banged along the ropes overhead, gibbering and grinning with terror at the bars of their prisons. This lot were squirrel monkeys, jammed in five or more to a crate, with females clutching jug-eared infants to their woolly yellow breasts. Already a number of babies had lost hold of their mothers' fur and dropped to the floors where they lay still, curled up and frying in the heat.

President de Toro y Plata sat in a canvas chair in the doorway of a portakabin near the river at the bottom of the wharf. He had been there, morning or afternoon, for ten days, watching through sepia-tinted glasses the men labouring in the blistering sun, their backs oiled with sweat. The President's face was dry, his glossy white suit immaculate, its perfection marred only by a black band that circled the sleeve of his upper right arm. He talked rapidly in Spanish to the man who stood in front of him.

'According to my calculations this is the last consignment of the 35,000 squirrels. Is that correct?'

Lopez riffled through the documents on his clipboard. There were cloudy rings round the black irises of his eyes. 'Sí, Señor,' he said. '35,000. Also ...' he consulted his clipboard, '... 31,000 ocelots, 30,000 margay, 15,000 jaguars and roughly 20,000 assorted spotteds as of the end of last week. The otters are due in any moment, they should be off down the river this evening.'

The President nodded. 'Good,' he said, 'we're keeping on schedule. Good.'

Lopez backed into the sun, circled the hunched vulture that was tethered by the cabin door and began to pick his way over the rubble towards the quay.

'That bird gives me a pain,' Carrington said. She sat below Raul on the concrete steps, her hair drawn off her damp neck with a piece of cord, her eyes hidden behind black shields. The vulture, its thick neck sunk between its shoulders, waddled gloomily to the end of its tether and Carrington tucked her knees away from it in disgust. 'What's it doing there?'

'Sentry,' Raul said shortly. Shading his eyes, he watched

another crate swing along the rope. The monkeys with their black skull caps looked like Jews, he thought.

The steaming air stank of urine, the floors of the monkeys' cages were soaked with it and crawling with flies. Pale mosquitoes drifted over and settled in a whirring cloud round Carrington's head. She shot to her feet and batted furiously around her.

'Jesus,' she exclaimed, 'I just hope all this is worth it.'

Raul smiled without amusement. That nasal drone lacked all femininity. Clare's voice ... Quickly, he guillotined the thought. 'That lot,' he pointed to the crate, now suspended between wharf and barge, 'is worth one million dollars, even allowing for thirty-five per cent wastage. I would say that cancels out a few mosquitoes.'

'So much?' Carrington sat down abruptly.

'The parrots will fetch more. What was it? Three hundred and fifty macaws, that's approximately another million and we have a dozen Amazonians as well. They pay five thousand dollars apiece in the States. A profitable plaything, that bird.'

A loud splash and an outburst of curses interrupted him. One of the crates had crashed off its rope, hit the deck of the barge and bobbed, half-submerged, in the water. Raul swore and picked up a megaphone that lay on the ground beside him, shouting angrily through it. The water churned with men and slowly they hauled the dripping crate ashore. The bars were yanked up and bedraggled monkeys fell into the mud. A man picked one up. It hung limply from his hand, one thin leg twitching. 'They do it on purpose, those bastards,' Raul snapped. 'They'll make a meal of them tonight.' He scowled, his eyes fixed on the knot of men and the monkeys that littered the ground. Dust was in his throat.

'Yuk.' Carrington turned her face away, fanning herself with one hand. 'Clare's plants must have been a lot less trouble.'

The megaphone dropped from Raul's hand with a clatter. '*My* plants,' he said and gave a hard cough. 'Please do not forget that

I own every square millimetre of this land. Everything in it is mine. Owned by my family for five hundred years.'

Startled, Carrington touched his knee. 'Sure. I know. It's yours.'

Raul moved his knee. His hands meshed and the fingers writhed. 'They thought they could take it away from me with their guns and their bombs and their Communism but they were wrong. I am taking Ventura away from them. From under their feet, from over their heads, from the waters they fish for their food. Twenty thousand caimans I sent down the river last week. Snakes, too, and reptiles. Two thousand boas, one thousand and fifty iguanas. One orchid, Deborah ...' he held up a long finger at Carrington, '... one. Four thousand dollars. You think I should leave all that to traitors and terrorists and savages? No. Ha! I loved my country but it is no longer mine and they will be made to regret it, as my late wife was made to regret her betrayal of me.' He unclasped his hands and slapped viciously at his neck. 'You don't understand, no one understands, how dear Ventura was to me. It was everything to me. My home, my inheritance, my family. Clare hated it, always. Despised it.' His voice shook and he pressed two fingers hard between his eyebrows.

Carrington got up and, putting her hands on his shoulders, massaged the sinews that ran from his neck. 'I understand. I do,' she said. He stared ahead. A yard away the vulture gave a strident cry and spread its great grey wings, shadowing the dust. It looked, thought Carrington, like a crippled eagle, once a king but now reduced to scavenging for a living.

Raul turned his head to look at the bird and looked back again, over the river to the long burnt highway where the chainsaws howled. 'King Lear,' he said. 'Blow blow thou winter wind, thou art not so unkind as man's ingratitude.'

Carrington stood still, amazed. 'Hey – that's really weird,' she said, 'how did you ... ?'

'Shakespeare?' Raul said, frowning. 'How does an ignorant

Creole who lives in a backwater swamp know Shakespeare? Know Kipling? Know anything, *feel* anything?' He snatched off his dark glasses and rubbed his eyes. 'Money, that's all I was good for. She had contempt for me but she liked my money and her family liked my money. Well ...' He stretched his neck and smoothed his hands down his lapels, '... I have more now than she ever dreamed of and she lies dead in a churchyard in England.' He cupped his hands, blinkering his face.

Stroking his neck, Carrington leaned close to him. 'Raul,' she said, her voice low. 'About Clare. I understand your feelings but her death ... you didn't ...?'

A metallic clang cut off her words. A truck grated to a halt nearby, its drop-side banging, and men jumped out. They began to heave at the boxes loaded on the back. Raul stood up and shouted for Lopez through the megaphone. Then he walked over to the truck. The men stopped what they were doing, nodding at him, and Lopez jogged up, his pale blue shirt soaked with sweat. Briefly, the two men conferred. A box was prised open. Raul walked back to Carrington. 'Otter,' he said, 'for loading tonight.'

Carrington eyed the stiff cardboard cut-out in his hand. She touched the velvety fur. 'It smells,' she said, wrinkling her nose.

'Of money.' Raul gave a bark of laughter. 'There are thirty of these. Giant otters. Almost as rare as the Amazonian parrots. A thousand, each pelt. The rest ...' he gestured at the truck, 'are ocelots. Ten to a coat. In Munich, they tell me, the women are very fond of ocelot coats.' The pelt creaked in his hands.

'How much?' asked Carrington.

'A coat? Maybe forty thousand dollars.'

Flies began to gather on the skin and Raul took it back to Lopez.

'I thought there were laws,' Carrington said when he was in the canvas chair again. She had got the message. No more talk of Clare.

'Nombre Dios is a free port,' Raul said. 'Here, there is no control on transit goods. And we have our contacts at the other end.' He rubbed his thumb against bent fingers and smiled sourly. 'A little of this and the world asks no questions. Zoos, dealers, fur-traders, pet shops, multi-nationals, laboratories, tourists — none of them ask questions. And pretty women, eh?' He flipped a finger at Carrington's chin. 'Pretty women like pretty things. Pretty coats to keep them warm, furry gloves and furry hats. Elegant handbags made of skins. Cute birds to keep them company while their husbands work, tortoises for their children. Scientists are the same. They buy thousands of pretty monkeys so they can test their vaccines and their nerve gases and their germs for war. And lipsticks for pretty girls, of course. I'm doing them all a favour. Isn't that what you Americans say?'

The heat was terrific. Carrington scratched at a red bump on her leg, leaving white lines on the brown skin. 'And Cla ... the plants?' she said. She wanted badly to leave this stinking place and stand under a cold shower at the Palace, sluicing off the sweat and filth.

'That was the deal.' Raul moved back his cuff and glanced at the gold watch on his wrist. 'Lutz, O'Reilly, they get the plants, I get the rest to ship out. We should go now. There's going to be a storm.'

He pulled himself up. Carrington moved close to him. 'I can't wait to be in Miami,' she said, pushing her glasses up her nose and wiping her cheeks under the rims. 'It'll be heaven after this.'

Raul looked at her damp face. There was a bite at the corner of her mouth, swelling towards her small swollen lips. Dirt and lipstick were flaked in the furrows. There were tiny blackheads on her chin. He would pay her off along with Lopez and the rest, once they got to Miami. She knew little enough and would not dare talk of her own involvement. Lutz, O'Reilly, the Organization would see to that. She imagined she was going to be with him in America. The thought brought bile into his throat.

They began to walk towards the waiting car on the road above the wharf. Lopez came running behind them, his shirt flapping. A gold crucifix bounced against the dark hairs on his chest. 'Señor. If you could sign before you go.' He held out the clipboard to Raul.

Carrington read out the Spanish words on the document. 'Esta permiso es emitido por la autoridad siguiente. This permit is given by the following authority.' She watched as Raul scrawled his signature illegibly across the seal of Ventura. At that moment, a plate of thunder cracked across the sky and the first raindrops splashed on the paper. Lopez stuck the clipboard under his shirt. 'Gracias, Señor Presidente,' he said. Raul and Carrington ran for the car.

A couple of printers in jeans and T-shirts sat in one corner drinking bottled lager, otherwise the canteen was empty. Judith dumped a plate of salad on to a table, stuck the tray by her chair and sat down, wrinkling her nose. 'This place smells like a clean lavatory,' she said. 'A nasty smell covered up by cheap perfume. Yuk.'

'Better than plain old shit,' Andy said, sitting opposite.

'You think so?' said Judith. 'Personally, I prefer my shit unadulterated, you know where you are.' She began to fork up coleslaw. 'That's what gets me about the Clare thing. It stinks of cover-up.'

Andy poured wine into plastic cups and pushed one across to Judith. 'So you keep saying.'

'I can't help it,' Judith said. 'It gets up my nose.'

'Look.' Andy set down his cup rather hard and wine spilt on to the white formica. 'You told me yourself that she was drunk. The police report said she was drunk. Two hundred and fifty milligrams of alcohol to every hundred millilitres of blood. So she crossed the road without looking, probably staggering. The car came at her and *whup.*' He smacked a fist into his hand.

Judith winced. 'Why didn't they stop?'

'It's called hit and run, my darling,' Andy said, mopping at the spilt wine with a paper napkin. 'Happens a lot. Early morning, empty streets, no one around. The driver took a chance and zoomed off. That's life.'

'Or, in Clare's case, death,' said Judith. She put her fork down and stared at the crumpled napkin, soggy and red.

'Very sad,' Andy said. Judith looked up at him. 'No, Jude, I mean it. It *is* sad. A sad end for a sad lady. You feel it more this time because you'd just been with her. You're identifying.'

'Oh,' said Judith, 'spare me the shrink talk. It's simply, I know there's more to it.'

'Want a pud?'

'No.'

She watched Andy at the counter. Ten days had passed since the accident. Clare was in her grave. The newspapers with their shrieking headlines were wrapping fish and chips and still she felt almost as shaken as she had when the news had come through to the paper. It had taken nearly a week before someone in the morgue had had a closer look at the mangled face with its aureole of dark hair and passed on his hunch. It was difficult even now to believe that Clare had been mown down only a hundred yards from her flat. She'd slept so late that day that it was afternoon before she'd emerged on to the street and by that time – Judith closed her eyes briefly – nothing remained. The old lady from the flat above her had been gossiping on the steps with a next-door neighbour but, as always, she'd been in a rush, horribly late. Anyway, she didn't know the neighbours except to nod now and then as she charged by. That was London for you.

'There's more to it, she said as Andy sat down with a large jam roll. 'Why didn't she have any identification on her? No handbag. No cheque book, no driving licence, no letters, nothing. Now that's weird, you have to admit.'

'She was pretty weird,' said Andy, through sugary crumbs. 'She'd dyed her hair. She was incognito. Maybe she left anything that could identify her at home, in Lincolnshire. Or . . .' he paused, wiping his mouth, '. . . the driver went through her stuff. I mean, the longer it took to identify her, the better for him.'

'D'you think he knew, then? Who she was?'

Patiently, Andy said, 'No. Not if it was an accident. He might do it anyway, whoever it was.'

'That's it. I don't believe it was an accident, Andy. I never have. Clare was too upset. Okay, I thought she was drunk. Upset in general, because of . . . all the fuss. But maybe she was frightened. Maybe she thought someone was after her.'

Andy flipped open a pack of cigarettes. 'Jude, I already asked you that. Did she say anything about being frightened?'

'No.' Judith pushed two hands through her hair leaving it standing on end. 'Not in so many words. No.'

Blowing smoke at her, Andy said, 'Pity you didn't take proper notes, isn't it? You might have a nice little story.'

'I told you.' She gave an infuriated groan. 'You know why I didn't. I wanted to spare her. Fool that I am.'

'If you're not careful,' Andy said, 'you'll get into *The Guinness Book of Records* as the journalist who's missed the most scoops.'

The chair screeched as Judith pushed it back and stood up. 'Oh, piss off,' she said, her face flushing with anger.

Andy smiled. 'I'll finish my smoke first, if you've no objection.'

'I hope it chokes you,' Judith said. She banged through the swing doors and walked heavily down the corridor to the Features Room. At her desk, she rifled through her notebook for the hundredth time. Page after page of meaningless scrawls. Here and there, in the margins, her own doodles stood out, scratchy little drawings – thin stems with loopy petals, the skeletons of leaves, a stick woman with circles for breasts, more leaves sprouting from her stick legs. Exasperated, she slapped the notebook shut and saw. in elaborate dawdling script, one word on its cover.

'Kew,' she said, lifting her head, saying it aloud. Wasn't that where Clare had been, before coming to her flat? Hadn't she said so, once, before she started raving? Through the window ahead the sky was bright grey. Rain, rain, go away. Kew. From the four directories piled at the back of her desk she pulled the A to K volume. No entry under K. There wouldn't be, nothing was ever that simple. She heaved out a second book, L to R. If in doubt, in a monarchy, look under R for Royal and there it was. Kew, however, wasn't. It wasn't under B for Botanical or G for Gardens, either. 'Oh balls,' she said.

Lorna, typing at the desk opposite, raised an eyebrow. 'Kew Gardens,' Judith said. 'It is in London, isn't it?'

'It is,' said Lorna. 'In Kew, actually. Surprise, surprise. Go down to Kew in lilac-time.'

'What?' said Judith.

'Poem,' said Lorna.

Judith squinted past her head and saw that it was raining now, with a vengeance. No point in getting soaked, might as well hang about.

Into the telephone she said, 'Directory Enquiries, please.' It was still raining when she got through to Kew Gardens and finally, after a confusion of explanations, heard a man's voice.

'Barnabus,' it said.

Once again, she began her questions.

'Ah, yes,' said the voice at last, when all hope had really gone, 'I remember her well.'

One hour later, soaked, Judith was sitting in the office of Professor Barnabus. This time she took careful and copious notes.

As the last barge, loaded to below the plimsoll line, edged slowly from the harbour to start its long journey down the river,

Gary Lutz and Gerard O'Reilly walked through the double doors of the Presidential suite in the Palace in Nombre Dios. A woman rose startled, from her typewriter and ran towards them.

'You have no appointment, Señor Lutz,' she said. 'The President is very busy. Mañana, please.'

Lutz smiled pleasantly at her as he moved her aside. 'No more mañanas,' he said. O'Reilly opened the door of the President's office, embossed with the Venturan seal.

Raul, at his desk, looked up and frowned. 'I have no time now,' he said coldly. 'There is much to do before I leave.'

O'Reilly and Lutz entered. O'Reilly closed the door and walked over to stand behind Raul. Lutz sat down in a chair by the desk and mopped his damp forehead with a large blue handkerchief. The rims of his spectacles glinted.

'You did not hear me.' Raul stood up, his long fingers sloping from the desk. 'I said I have no time now.'

The fan on the ornate ceiling whirred steadily, stirring the air, rustling the papers on the cluttered desk. O'Reilly put both hands on Raul's shoulders and pressed him back into his chair. 'Relax, Mr President, take it easy. You've got all the time in the world.' His voice was patient, soothing.

Raul said, 'What is this, Lutz?'

Gary Lutz got to his feet, eased his thumbs along the belt at his belly and ambled over to the window. He yawned, screwing up his eyes against the glare outside. Then he turned to face Raul.

'You have to see it our way, Mr President. We've put in a lot of work, here in Ventura. A lot of work and a whole lot of money, over the years. I'd say we pretty well owned the place now. I'd say it was pretty well ours. What would you say, O'Reilly?'

'Yep,' said O'Reilly. His hands were deep in his jacket pockets, his eyes on Raul's back.

'So.' Lutz sucked at his teeth, considering Raul. 'We're gonna stay here, sir, and you're gonna stay here with us. You've got your money, you can spend it in little old Ventura, Mr President, sir. We'll get you the latest Sears Roebuck and you can send off for whatever you want. Sir. Isn't that right, O'Reilly?'

'Right,' said O'Reilly.

Lutz sat down again. 'You see, Mr President, you're no use to us in Miami. No use at all. We need you here, sir. A de Toro in Miami won't keep the Commies from Ventura's door and you're the only de Toro we've got. Right, O'Reilly?'

'Right.'

'So we'll just sit here, the three of us, and wait for Bogardus. He'll explain everything, Mr President, sir.'

The fan whirred. After a while, Lutz said, 'What does cura ... curupira mean, sir? Someone's painted it on the Palace wall, noticed it coming in.'

Raul stared ahead.

'D'you know, O'Reilly?'

'No.'

Lutz sighed and stretched out in the chair. 'Well,' he said, 'who gives a shit?'

In the outer office, a telephone rang. A minute later the President's personal assistant, Señora Mendoza, knocked at the President's door and went in. She glanced quickly at the two Americans and then at Don Raul.

'Please excuse me,' she said in fast Spanish. 'Señor Presidente, an urgent call from England. A woman wishes to speak to you. She says, Señor ...' and here her eyelids fluttered and she swallowed, '... she says she speaks on behalf of our poor Señora Clare.'

The telephone whirred emptily, cut off. The trick had failed, he hadn't taken the call. Judith sat still, the dead receiver at her ear. She thought of her mother, first love, first traitor. She thought of indomitable Ruth and her prophecy: 'one of these days you'll sell out women ...' and she thought of Clare, sold out. She heard herself persuading the reluctant Angela, a Madam breaking in the new girl for the brothel. She saw Charlie beside her in her bed and Clare's naked image, used for their game. She looked at the woman who was Judith and disgust choked her. Betrayal, that was the name of the game and she had played it well. Now Clare was in her grave and Clare's beloved women, their country, abandoned to the vultures.

Judith crashed the phone down and pushed back her chair. 'Lorna,' she said. 'Book me on the next flight to Ventura.'

A CHOICE OF PENGUINS

☐ *The Englishman's Daughter* **Peter Evans**   £1.95

From London and Venice to Moscow, Peter Evans's brilliant, surprising thriller traces a grey landscape of treason and sexual duplicity. 'Stunningly plotted' – *Guardian*. 'As fast-moving as *Gorky Park*' – Len Deighton

☐ *A Dark and Distant Shore* **Reay Tannahill**   £3.50

Vilia is the unforgettable heroine, Kinveil Castle is her destiny, in this full-blooded saga spanning a century of Victoriana, empire, hatreds and love affairs. 'A marvellous blend of *Gone with the Wind* and *The Thorn Birds*. You will enjoy every page' – *Daily Mirror*

☐ *Death in Zanzibar* **M. M. Kaye**   £1.95

Holidaying on the beautiful 'Isle of Cloves', Dany Ashton is caught up in a plot whirling round buried gold, blossoming romance, and murder ... 'I recommend it wholeheartedly to those who fancy the idea of Agatha Christie with a touch of romantic suspense' – *Standard*

☐ *Running Time* **Gavin Lambert**   £1.95

From child starlet to screen goddess, this is the story of the meteoric rise of Baby Jewel, propelled through the star system by her glamorous, calculating mother. A Hollywood bestseller and 'a funny, dazzling showstopper' – *Good Housekeeping*

☐ *The Best of Roald Dahl*   £4.95

Twenty ingenious and blood-curdling tales chosen from Dahl's bestselling volumes – *Over to You, Someone Like You, Kiss Kiss* and *Switch Bitch*.

A CHOICE OF PENGUINS

☐ *The Far Pavilions* **M. M. Kaye**   £4.95

Exotic with all the romance and high adventure of nineteenth-century India, M. M. Kaye's magnificent – now famous – story holds at its heart the passionate love of an Englishman for Juli, his Indian princess. 'Wildly exciting' – *Daily Telegraph*

☐ *Rumpole and the Golden Thread* **John Mortimer**   £1.95

Here Horace Rumpole continues to deftly juggle the vagaries of law, taking on the con-o-sewers of the art world, dabbling in some female politics and, unfortunately, incurring the wrath of Hilda . . . 'A fruity, foxy masterpiece' – *Sunday Times*

☐ *The Sunne in Splendour* **Sharon Penman**   £3.95

A soaring historical novel that re-creates the passions, the treacheries and the rich Gothic tapestry of medieval England during the Wars of the Roses. 'A very fine book' – Rosemary Sutcliff

☐ *The Watcher* **Charles Maclean**   £1.95

The compulsive thriller about Martin Gregory, who used to regard himself as a fairly ordinary man . . . '*Not* a book for bedtime' – Piers Paul Read. 'I'm something of an insomniac. I read *The Watcher* and stopped sleeping altogether' – Paul Newman

☐ *19 Purchase Street* **Gerald A. Browne**   £1.95

By the author of *11 Harrowhouse*; the international bestseller about 'a dazzling billion-dollar heist so daring and elaborate that it makes most episodes in *Mission Impossible* seem like fraternity pranks' – *The New York Times Book Review*

A CHOICE OF PENGUINS